THE PENGUIN NOVELS

Andrey Kurkov was born in St Petersburg and now lives in Kiev. Having graduated from the Kiev Foreign Language Institute, he worked for some time as a journalist, did his military service as a prison warder at Odessa, then became a film cameraman, writer of screenplays and author of critically acclaimed and popular novels including *Death and the Penguin* and *Penguin Lost*.

George Bird has translated extensively from Russian and German, including three previous novels by Andrey Kurkov. In 1986 he won the Pluto Crime Prize for his novel *Death in Leningrad*.

ALSO BY ANDREY KURKOV

A Matter of Death and Life
The Case of the General's Thumb

ANDREY KURKOV

The Penguin Novels

Death and the Penguin
and *Penguin Lost*

TRANSLATED FROM THE RUSSIAN BY
George Bird

VINTAGE BOOKS
London

Published by Vintage 2006

2 4 6 8 10 9 7 5 3 1

Death and the Penguin first published in 1996 with the title
Smert'postoronnego by the Alterpress, Kiev and first published
in Great Britain in 2001 by The Harvill Press

Penguin Lost first published in Great Britain in 2004 by
The Harvill Press

Vintage
Random House, 20 Vauxhall Bridge Road,
London SW1V 2SA

Random House Australia (Pty) Limited
20 Alfred Street, Milsons Point, Sydney,
New South Wales 2061, Australia

Random House New Zealand Limited
18 Poland Road, Glenfield, Auckland 10, New Zealand

Random House (Pty) Limited
Isle of Houghton, Corner of Boundary Road & Carse O'Gowrie,
Houghton, 2198, South Africa

Random House Publishers India Private Limited
301 World Trade Tower, Hotel Intercontinental Grand Complex,
Barakhamba Lane, New Delhi 110 001, India

The Random House Group Limited Reg. No. 954009
www.randomhouse.co.uk/vintage

A CIP catalogue record for this book
is available from the British Library

ISBN 9780099507062 (from Jan 2007)
ISBN 0099507064

Papers used by Random House are natural,
recyclable products made from wood grown in sustainable
forests. The manufacturing processes conform to the
environmental regulations of the country of origin

Printed and bound in Great Britain by
Mackays of Chatham plc, Chatham, Kent

Death and the Penguin

For the Sharps,
in gratitude

A Militia major is driving along when he sees a militiaman standing with a penguin.

"Take him to the zoo," he orders.

Some time later the same major is driving along when he sees the militiaman still with the penguin.

"What have you been doing?" he asks. "I said take him to the zoo."

"We've been to the zoo, Comrade Major," says the militiaman, "and the circus. And now we're going to the pictures."

CHARACTERS IN THE STORY

Viktor Alekseyevich Zolotaryov	a writer
Misha	his penguin
Igor Lvovich, the Chief	an editor
Sergey Fischbein-Stepanenko	militiaman
Nina	his niece
Misha-non-penguin	an associate of the Chief
Sonya	his daughter
Sergey Chekalin	"friend" of Misha-non-penguin
Stepan Yakovlevich Pidpaly	a penguinologist
Lyosha	a guard
Ilya Semyonovich	a vet
Valentin Ivanovich	Chairman, Antarctic Committee
Fat Man	

1

First, a stone landed a metre from Viktor's foot. He glanced back. Two louts stood grinning, one of whom stooped, picked up another from a section of broken cobble, and bowled it at him skittler-fashion. Viktor made off at something approaching a racing walk and rounded the corner, telling himself the main thing was not to run. He paused outside his block, glancing up at the hanging clock: 9.00. Not a sound. No one about. He went in, now no longer afraid. They found life dull, ordinary people, now that entertainment was beyond their means. So they bowled cobbles.

As he turned on the kitchen light, it went off again. They had cut the power, just like that. And in the darkness he became aware of the unhurried footfalls of Misha the penguin.

Misha had appeared *chez* Viktor a year before, when the zoo was giving hungry animals away to anyone able to feed them. Viktor had gone along and returned with a king penguin. Abandoned by his girlfriend the week before, he had been feeling lonely. But Misha had brought his own kind of loneliness, and the result was now two complementary lonelinesses, creating an impression more of interdependence than of amity.

Unearthing a candle, he lit it and stood it on the table in an empty mayonnaise pot. The poetic insouciance of the tiny light sent him to look, in the semi-darkness, for pen and paper. He sat down at the table with the paper between him and the candle; paper asking to be written on. Had he been a poet, rhyme would have raced across the white. But he wasn't. He was trapped in a rut between journalism and meagre scraps of prose. Short stories were the best he could do. Very short, too short to make a living from, even if he got paid for them.

A shot rang out.

Darting to the window, Viktor pressed his face to the glass. Nothing. He returned to his sheet of paper. Already he had thought up a story around that shot. A single side was all it took; no more, no less. And as his latest short short story drew to its tragic close, the power came back on and the ceiling bulb blazed. Blowing out the candle, he fetched coley from the freezer for Misha's bowl.

2

Next morning, when he had typed his latest short short story and taken leave of Misha, Viktor set off for the offices of a new fat newspaper that generously published anything, from a cooking recipe to a review of post-Soviet theatre. He knew the Editor, having occasionally drunk with him, and been driven home by his driver afterwards.

The Editor received him with a smile and a slap on the shoulder, told his secretary to make coffee, and there and then gave Viktor's offering a professional read.

"No, old friend," he said eventually. "Don't take it amiss, but it's no go. Needs a spot more gore, or a kinky love angle. Get it into your head that *sensation's* the essence of a newspaper short story."

Viktor left, without waiting for coffee.

A short step away were the offices of *Capital News*, where, lacking editorial access, he looked in on the Arts section.

"Literature's not actually what we publish," the elderly Assistant Editor informed him amiably. "But leave it with me. Anything's possible. It might get in on a Friday. You know – for balance. If there's a glut of bad news, readers look for something neutral. I'll read it."

Ridding himself of Viktor by handing him his card, the little old man returned to his paper-piled desk. At which point it dawned on Viktor that he had not actually been asked in. The whole exchange had been conducted in the doorway.

3

Two days later the phone rang.

"*Capital News*. Sorry to trouble you," said a crisp, clear female voice. "I have the Editor-in-Chief on the line."

The receiver changed hands.

"Viktor Alekseyevich?" a man's voice enquired. "Couldn't pop in today, could you? Or are you busy?"

"No," said Viktor.

"I'll send a car. Blue *Zhiguli*. Just let me have your address."

Viktor did, and with a "Bye, then," the Editor-in-Chief rang off without giving his name.

Selecting a shirt from the wardrobe, Viktor wondered if it

was to do with his story. Hardly . . . What was his story to them? Still, what the hell!

The driver of the blue *Zhiguli* parked at the entrance was deferential. He it was who conducted Viktor to the Editor-in-Chief.

"I'm Igor Lvovich," he said, extending a hand. "Glad to meet you."

He looked more like an aged athlete than a man of the Press. And maybe that's how it was, except that his eyes betrayed a hint of irony born more of intellect and education than lengthy sessions in a gym.

"Have a seat. Spot of cognac?" He accompanied these words with a lordly wave of the hand.

"I'd prefer coffee, if I may," said Viktor, settling into a leather armchair facing the vast executive desk.

"Two coffees," the Editor-in-Chief said, picking up the phone. "Do you know," he resumed amiably, "we'd only recently been talking about you, and yesterday in came our Assistant Arts Editor, Boris Leonardovich, with your little story. 'Get an eyeful of this,' said he. I did, and it's good. And then it came to me *why* we'd been talking about you, and I thought we should meet."

Viktor nodded politely. Igor Lvovich paused and smiled.

"Viktor Alekseyevich," he resumed, "how about working for us?"

"Writing what?" asked Viktor, secretly alarmed at the prospect of a fresh spell of journalistic hard labour.

Igor Lvovich was on the point of explaining when the secretary came in with their coffee and a bowl of sugar on a tray, and he held his breath until she had gone.

"This is highly confidential," he said. "What we're after is a gifted obituarist, master of the succinct. Snappy, pithy, way-out stuff's the idea. You with me?" He looked hopefully at Viktor.

"Sit in an office, you mean, and wait for deaths?" Viktor asked warily, as if fearing to hear as much confirmed.

"No, of course not! Far more interesting and responsible than that! What you'd have to do is create, from scratch, an index of *obelisk jobs* – as we call obituaries – to include deputies and gangsters, down to the cultural scene – that sort of person – while they're still alive. But what I want is the dead written about as they've never been written about before. And your story tells me you're the man."

"What about payment?"

"You'd start at $300. Hours up to you. But keeping me informed, of course, who we've got carded. So we don't get caught on the hop by some car crash out of the blue! Oh, and one other condition: you'll need a pseudonym. In your own interest as much as anything."

"But what?" said Viktor, half to himself.

"Think of one. But if you can't, make it *A Group of Friends* for the time being."

Viktor nodded.

4

Before bed, he drank tea, and gave not over-serious thought to the subject of death. His mood was of the best, a mood more for vodka than tea. Except that there wasn't any vodka.

What an offer! And though still in the dark concerning his new duties, he had a foretaste of something new and unusual. But roaming the dark corridor, banging every so often against the closed kitchen door, was Misha the penguin. Overcome at last with a feeling of guilt, Viktor let him in. Misha paused at the table, using his almost one metre of height to see what was on it. He looked at the cup of tea, then shifting his gaze to Viktor, considered him with the heartfelt sincerity of a worldly-wise Party functionary. Thinking he would like to give Misha a treat, Viktor went and turned on the cold tap in the bathroom. At the sound of running water Misha came plip-plopping and, without waiting for the bath to fill, leaned over and tumbled in.

The next morning, Viktor looked in at *Capital News* for some practical tips from the Editor-in-Chief.

"How," he asked, "do we select our notables?"

"Nothing easier! See who the papers write about and take your pick. Not all our country's notables are known to it, you see. Many prefer it like that . . ."

That evening Viktor bought all the papers, went home and settled down at the kitchen table.

The very first he looked at gave him food for thought, and the VIP names he underlined he then copied into a notebook *for action*. He would not be short of work – there were 60 or so names from the first few papers alone!

Then tea, and fresh thought, this time concerning the *obelisk* proper. Already he thought he saw how it might be *vitalized*, and at the same time, *sentimentalized*, so that even the simple collective farmer, never having known the late whoever-it-was he was reading about, would brush away a tear. By next morning Viktor had earmarked a possible first *obelisk*. It only remained to get the Chief's blessing.

5

At 9.30 next morning, having got the Chief's blessing, drunk coffee, and been solemnly presented with his Press card, Viktor bought a bottle of *Finlandia* at a kiosk, and set off for the office of sometime author, now State Duma Deputy, Aleksandr Yakornitsky.

Hearing that a correspondent of *Capital News* wished to see him, the State Deputy was delighted, and immediately told his secretary to cancel all his remaining appointments and admit no one else.

Comfortably ensconced, Viktor put on the table the bottle of Finnish vodka and a dictaphone. Equally promptly, the State Deputy produced two small crystal glasses, placing one either side of the bottle.

He talked freely, without waiting for questions – of his work, his childhood, his time as Komsomol organizer of his university year. As they finished the bottle, he was boasting of his trips to Chernobyl. These, it appeared, had the added bonus of enhancing his potency – as, in case of any doubt, his private-school teacher wife and National Opera diva mistress would testify.

Taking leave of each other, they embraced. Viktor was left with the impression of an author-State-Deputy of great and, for obituary purposes, perhaps undue, vitality. But that was it! Inasmuch as the departed had lately been alive, an obituary should retain their passing warmth – not be all hopeless gloom!

Back at his flat, Viktor wrote the obituary, swiftly *obelisking* the State Deputy in a warm, two-page account of the vital and the sinful, and without recourse to the dictaphone, so fresh was his memory.

"Wonderful job!" Igor Lvovich enthused the next morning.

7

"Provided singer's hubby keeps his mouth shut . . . *Many women may be mourning him today, but with them in mind, it is to his wife that we shall extend our sympathy; and to one other lady, whose voice, heard by all soaring to the dome of the National Opera, was for him.* Beautiful! Keep it up! On with the good work!"

"Igor Lvovich," began Viktor, growing bolder, "I'm a bit short on facts, and to go interviewing everyone will take time. Have we no carded information?"

The Chief smiled.

"Of course, I was going to suggest it – in *Crime*. I'll tell Fyodor to give you access."

6

As he attuned himself to the task, Viktor's life regulated itself accordingly. He applied himself with a vengeance . . . Fyodor from *Crime* proved a godsend, sharing all that he had, which was plenty – from VIPs' lovers, male and female, to VIPs' lapses from virtue and other life events. In short, from him Viktor gleaned precisely those extra-CV details which, like fine Indian spices, transform an *obelisk* of sad, established fact into a gourmet dish. And each new batch he put regularly before the Chief.

Everything in the garden was lovely. He had money in his pocket – not a lot, but more than enough for his modest requirements. His one occasional anxiety was his lack of recognition, even under a pseudonym, so tenacious of life were his *obelisked* notables. Out of more than 100 written-up VIPs, not only had none of them died, but not one had so much as fallen ill. Such reflections, however, did not affect the rhythm of his work. Assiduously he leafed through the papers, noting names, worming his way into lives. *Our country must know who its notables are,* he kept telling himself.

One rainy November evening, when Misha the penguin was taking a cold bath and Viktor was pondering his subjects' tenacity of life, the phone rang.

"I was put on to you by Igor Lvovich," wheezed a man's voice. "Something I'd like a word about."

At the name of the Editor-in-Chief, Viktor said he would be glad to see him, and half an hour later was welcoming a smartly dressed man of about 45. He had brought a bottle of whisky, and they sat down straight away at the kitchen table.

"I'm Misha," he said, to the amused embarrassment of Viktor.

"Sorry," he explained, "but so's my penguin."

"I've got an old friend who's seriously ill," began the visitor. "Same age as me. Known each other since we were kids. Sergey Chekalin. I'd like to order an obituary . . . Will you do it?"

"Of course," said Viktor. "But I'll need some facts, preferably personal ones."

"No problem," said Misha. "I know all there is to know and can tell you."

"Go ahead."

"Son of a fitter and a nursery governess. His dream, as a child, was to have a motorbike, and when he left school, he bought himself a *Minsk*, though it meant a bit of thieving to do so . . . Deeply ashamed now of his past. Not that his present's any better. We're colleagues, he and I. We set up and we wind up trusts. I'm good at it, he isn't. Wife left him recently. Been alone since. Not even had a lover."

"Wife's name?"

"Lena . . . All in all, he's had a rough time of it. Healthwise, too."

"In what way?"

"Suspected stomach cancer, chronic prostate."

"What did he most want out of life?"

"What he'll never have, now: a silver *Lincoln*."

The effect of their cocktail of words and whisky was to render Sergey Chekalin – failure, deserted by wife, ailing, alone and in poor health, dreaming the unrealizable dream of a silver *Lincoln* – a real presence at the table with them.

"When do I come for it?" asked Misha finally.

"Tomorrow, if you like."

He left, and hearing a car start, Viktor looked out and saw a long, pretentious silver *Lincoln* draw away.

He fed Misha freshly frozen plaice, topped up his bath, then returned to the kitchen and set to work on the obituary order. Through the tiny window between bathroom and kitchen he could hear splashing, and as he drafted the *obelisk*, he smiled, thinking of his penguin's love of clean, cold water.

7

Autumn, season of dying nature, of melancholy, of seeking the past, was best for writing obituaries. Winter, joyous in itself – bracing frost, snow sparkling in the sun – was good for living. But till winter came, there were still a few weeks in which to accumulate an *obelisk* surplus for the coming year. There was a lot to do.

When Misha-non-penguin came it was raining again. He read his order, was delighted, and producing his wallet, asked "How much?"

Accustomed so far to monthly payment, Viktor shrugged.

"Look," said Misha, "work well done should be work well paid."

Unable to disagree, Viktor nodded.

Misha thought for a bit.

"Double at least what the priciest whore charges . . . $500 do you?"

Liking the amount, if not the basis of calculation, Viktor nodded, and was handed five $100 bills.

"Can send more clients, if you like," said Misha.

Viktor was all for it.

Misha-non-penguin left. The grey, rainy morning dragged on. The door opened, and there stood Penguin Misha. After a moment he came over and snuggled against his master's knee. Dear creature, thought Viktor, stroking him.

8

Sleeping lightly that night, Viktor heard an insomniac Misha roaming the flat, leaving doors open, occasionally stopping and heaving a deep sigh, like an old man weary of both life and himself.

Next morning Igor Lvovich rang asking him to call in.

Over coffee they discussed the *obelisk* index. On the whole, the Chief was happy.

"One drawback," he said, "is that our future departed all come from Kiev. Being the capital, it does, of course, vacuum up all the more or less notable, but other cities have their quota too."

Viktor listened attentively, now and then nodding.

"We have our own correspondents everywhere, collecting the necessary info," the Chief went on. "It's merely a question of gathering it in. The post's dodgy. Even fax isn't entirely reliable. So what I'd like is for you to come in on it."

"Doing what?"

"Visiting a city or two and collecting. Kharkov, for a start, then, if you wouldn't mind, Odessa. At our expense, naturally . . ."

"I'd be glad to."

Again it was drizzling. On his way home, he dropped into a café, and to get warm, ordered cognac and a large coffee.

The café was empty and quiet – an ambience suitable for dreaming or, conversely, for recalling the past.

He sipped his cognac, his nose prickled by the familiar bouquet, happy in the enjoyment of a drop of the real stuff.

This agreeable café interlude, this stop-off between past and future, over cognac and coffee, induced a mood of romance. No longer did he feel lonely or unhappy. He was a valued customer, satisfying a modest demand for inner warmth. A glass of good cognac and already a flow of warmth in contrary directions: up into his head, down into his legs, and a slowing of thought processes.

He had dreamt once of writing novels, but had not achieved so much as a novella, in spite of all the unfinished manuscripts lying around in folders. But unfinished they were fated to remain, he having been unlucky with his muses, they, for some reason, having never tarried long enough in his two-room flat to see him through a short story. Hence his literary failure. They had been amazingly fickle, his muses. Or he had been at fault for picking such unreliable ones. But now, alone with his penguin, here he was, churning out little pieces regardless, and getting well paid.

Warm at last, he left the café. It was still drizzling. Still a grey, wet day.

Before returning to his flat, he dropped into a shop and bought a kilo of frozen salmon – for Misha.

9

A problem to solve before Kharkov was who to leave Misha with. The odds were that he would happily put up with three days alone, but Viktor was uneasy. Having no friends, he ran through everyone he knew, but they were all people he had little in common with and wasn't keen to approach. Scratching his head, he went over to the window.

It was drizzling. By the entrance, a militiaman was chatting with an old lady from the block. Remembering the joke about the militiaman and the penguin, he smiled, then went over to the phone on the bedside table and looked up the number of the district militiaman.

"Junior Lieutenant Fischbein," came a clipped male voice at the other end of the line.

"Sorry to trouble you," said Viktor hesitantly, searching for words. "There's something I'd like to ask . . . Being resident in your district . . ."

"Trouble?" interrupted the officer.

"No. And don't, please, think I'm trying to be funny. The fact is, I'm going away for three days in connection with work, and I've no one to leave my penguin with."

"Look, I'm sorry," replied the officer in a calm, steady voice, "but living with Mother in a hostel, I've nowhere to keep him . . ."

"You've got me wrong," said Viktor, growing flustered. "What I wondered was whether you could just pop in a couple of times and feed him . . . I'd leave you the keys."

"I could. Name and address, and I'll come round. Will you be in about three?"

"Yes."

He sank into his armchair.

Here, on the broad arm beside him, was where, just over a year ago, petite blonde Olya, of attractive little snub nose and perpetually reproachful expression, was wont to perch. Sometimes she would rest her head on his shoulder and fall asleep, plunging into dreams in which he, very likely, had no place. Only in reality was he allowed to be present. Though even there, he rarely felt needed. Silent and thoughtful – that was her. What, since her pushing off without a word, had altered? Standing beside him now was Misha the penguin. He was silent, but was he thoughtful too? What did being thoughtful amount to? Just a word describing the way one looked, perhaps?

He leant forward, searching the penguin's tiny eyes for signs of thoughtfulness, but saw only sadness.

At 2.45 the district militiaman arrived, taking off his boots inside the door. His appearance belied his surname. He was a broad-shouldered, fair-haired, blue-eyed chap, almost a head taller than Viktor. If he had not been a militiaman, he would have been an asset to any volleyball team.

"Well, where is he?" he asked.

"Misha!" Viktor called, and emerging from his hidey-hole behind the dark-green settee, the penguin came and looked the militiaman up and down.

"This, Misha –" began Viktor, and turning to the officer, said, "Sorry, would you tell me your name?"

"Sergey."

"Strange. You don't look at all Jewish."

"Nor am I," smiled the militiaman. "Stepanenko's my real name."

With a shrug Viktor turned to the penguin again.

"Misha, this is Sergey. Sergey's going to feed you while I'm away."

He then showed Sergey what was where, and gave him the spare keys to the flat.

"All will be well," said the militiaman as he left. "Don't you worry."

10

Kharkov was freezing, and the moment Viktor stepped from the train, he realized he wasn't dressed warmly enough for strolling round the city.

From his hotel, The Kharkov, he rang the *Capital News* correspondent and they agreed to meet that evening in a café beneath the Opera.

When evening came, he set off on foot along Sumy Street to the Opera, face rimed with frost, hands numb in the pockets of his short sheepskin coat.

The buildings loomed grey over the pavement. Everyone was

in a hurry, as if afraid of finding their block on the verge of collapsing or shedding its balconies – both occurrences being no longer uncommon.

It was another five minutes to the sub-Opera labyrinth of bars, shops and cafés. There he had to locate a café with a stage and seating on two levels, and sit at the front of the upper level, looking towards the stage. And yes, order orange juice and a can of beer, the latter to be left unopened.

Although they had allowed half an hour – from 6.30 till 7.00 – for making contact, he hurried along, spurred on by the cold.

He would get something to eat there, he decided, something hot and meaty . . .

At the Opera he spotted the way down to civilization *sub terra*, away from darkness feebly illuminated by the windows of a nocturnal city, to a blaze of window displays.

On the upper steps two old women and a blurry-faced young drunk stood begging.

Through well-lit corridors he made his way to the café. Inside the glass door sat a man in the uniform of the Special Task Militia, who looked up from his book as Viktor entered.

"And where are *you* going?" he demanded, with only a trace of military insistence.

"To eat."

Special Task Militia waved him on.

He walked the length of a bar at which customers of criminal aspect were drinking beer. The bald-headed barman smiled wryly, catching his eye, as if to say, *Just keep going, don't look back!*

Drawn by bright lights ahead, Viktor quickened his step, and came upon a small stage in a semi-circle of little tables on two levels, one half a metre higher than the other.

He ordered orange juice and a can of beer at the bar.

"That all?" asked the plump, peroxide-blonde barmaid.

"Anything with meat?"

"Cured fish fillet, fried eggs . . ." came the monotone reply.

"All for the moment, then," he said softly.

He paid and took himself to a table on the upper level, facing the stage. One sip of the orange juice made him hungrier than ever. Right, he decided, they would eat at the hotel where there was a restaurant. He consulted his watch: 6.20.

It was quiet. At the next table two Azerbaijanis were drinking beer in silence. Turning to take in the rest of the café, Viktor was momentarily blinded by a flash of light, and when he regained his sight, saw a man with a camera heading for the corridor. He turned to see who had been photographed, but apart from him and the Azerbaijanis, there was no one.

So it was them, he decided, sipping his watery orange.

Time passed. No more than a sip remained in his tall glass. He eyed the unopened can, toying with the idea of getting another, which he would open.

A girl appeared at his table wearing jeans and a leather jacket. Wound tightly about her head was a Rocker scarf, a chestnut ponytail trailing from the knot.

Sitting beside him, she quizzed him through her mascara.

"Waiting for me?" she smiled.

He struggled with embarrassment.

No, the correspondent was a man, was his first fevered thought. Though he might have sent her in his stead . . .

He looked to see if she had a carrier or briefcase such as might have contained the necessary papers, but she had nothing but a vanity bag, too small for even a bottle of beer.

"Well, love, how about it? Or haven't you got time?" she asked, reasserting her presence, and the obvious dawned.

"Sorry," said Viktor, "but you're mistaken."

"I'm not often," she said sweetly, rising from the table. "But there's always a first time."

Relieved to be alone again, he took another look at the unopened can, then consulted his watch: 7.15. He should have appeared by now.

But the correspondent did not appear. At 7.30 Viktor drank the beer and left. He ate in the hotel, and returning to his room, again rang the correspondent, but got only long beeps, until he replaced the receiver.

The warmth of the room was relaxing and conducive to sleep. His eyes refused to stay open. He would try again in the morning. That decided, he lay on his bed and slept.

11

In Kiev it was drizzling again. District Militiaman Sergey Fischbein-Stepanenko let himself into Viktor's flat. Removing his boots, he proceeded in knitted green socks to the kitchen, took a large piece of salmon from the freezer, and breaking it across his knee, put half in Misha's bowl on the low, nursery bedside table.

"Misha!" he called, and listened.

Without waiting for a response, he looked into the living room, then into the bedroom, and there found Misha standing, sleepy or sad, between the settee and the wall.

"Grub up!" he cajoled. "Come on!"

Misha stared.

"Come on!" he pleaded. "Master back soon! Of course, you miss him! But come on."

Slowly, followed attentively by Sergey, the penguin dragged himself to the kitchen. Sergey watched him to his bowl, saw him start eating, and returning, conscience clear, to the corridor, put boots and coat back on, and went forth into the Kiev drizzle.

Heaven send a day without call-outs, he thought, seeing the low, louring sky.

12

Woken next morning by a confusion of shots, Viktor yawned, got out of bed and looked at his watch: 8.00. He went over to the window. Parked below, were a militia jeep and an ambulance.

The sky, when he looked up, was blue, and from behind grey Stalin baroque a pale yellow sun had appeared, promising fine weather.

Seated at the telephone table, he dialled the correspondent.

"Who do you want?" a female voice enquired.

"Is Nikolay Aleksandrovich there?"

"Who's calling?"

He sensed tension in the woman's voice. "His paper . . . *Capital News* . . ."

"You are?"

It wasn't right. With a trembling hand he replaced the receiver.

Coffee, must have coffee, he thought, dressing, splashing his face with handfuls of cold water, and going down to the hotel bar where he ordered a large one.

"You sit. I'll bring it," said the barman.

Sitting on a broad soft velour pouffe at a glass-topped table in a corner of the bar, he reached for the heavy glass ashtray, also of cast glass, and twisted it thoughtfully this way and that. The bar was quiet. The barman came with his coffee.

"Anything else?"

He shook his head, then looking squarely at the barman asked, "What was that shooting this morning?"

The barman shrugged.

"Some foreign-currency whore got murdered . . . Must have got up someone's nose."

The coffee, though bitter, proved immediately restorative. His fingers stopped trembling, the throbbing in his head eased. Calm once more, he took stock.

It wasn't the end of the world, he found himself thinking, and with an assurance dismissive of any doubt. That was life. As per usual. Just a question of calling the Chief and asking what to do.

When he had finished his coffee and paid, he went to his room and rang Kiev.

"You've got your return ticket for today," the Chief said calmly. "So back you come. Carry on with Kiev. The provinces can hang fire for a bit."

Taking his seat on the night train, Viktor opened the *Evening Kharkov* he had bought at the station. As he turned the pages, he came to a *Criminal Chronicle* setting forth, in small print, all the most recent crimes, and under *Murders*, read:

> *Capital News* correspondent Nikolay Agnivtsev was shot
> dead at his flat yesterday afternoon by persons unknown.

With a sick feeling, he lowered the paper to his knees. The train gave a sudden jolt and the paper slid to the floor.

13

On the way up to his flat the next morning, Viktor met the district militiaman.

"Good day to you!" said Sergey Fischbein-Stepanenko gaily. "You're looking a bit pale, though."

"How is he?" asked Viktor anxiously.

"In fine shape!" said the militiaman with a smile. "Missing his master, of course. And your freezer's out of fish."

"I can't thank you enough." His attempt at a grateful smile produced a sickly sour grimace. "I'm in your debt. How about raising a glass together some time?"

"Wouldn't say no," confirmed the militiaman. "Just ring – you've got my number. And if you need me again, don't hesitate! I love animals. Real ones, I mean, not the sort I deal with every day . . ."

Misha, standing in the corridor, was delighted to see Viktor come in and turn on the light.

"Hello, old fellow." Viktor squatted and looked at him.

He seemed to be smiling.

And as he took a lumbering step towards his master, he had a happy twinkle in his eye.

At least someone in this world's glad to see me, thought Viktor.

Straightening up, he removed his jacket and went through to the living room, Misha plip-plopping behind him.

14

Next morning Viktor lay in bed with a headache and no inclination to get up.

The alarm clock showed 9.30.

Heaving himself over onto his other side, he became aware of Misha standing by his bed.

"Oh God!" he muttered, swinging his feet to the floor, "I've not fed him since yesterday!"

And in spite of his splitting head and buzzing temples, he washed and dressed.

The frosty air perked him up a little. Winter seemed to have followed him from Kharkov.

Must phone the Chief, he decided as he walked, say I'm unwell . . . Get the papers, and maybe do a bit of work . . .

At the fish counter of the food store he purchased two kilos of frozen plaice; then, after a moment's hesitation, a kilo of live fish.

Back at his flat he ran a bath of cold water, released the three silver carp, and called Misha. Misha took one look at the fish swimming in the bath, turned away, and plip-plopped back to his room. Viktor shrugged. He was at a loss.

The doorbell rang.

Espying Misha-non-penguin through the peephole, he let him in.

"Hi," said Misha. "Got a couple of obituary orders for you. You all right?"

Viktor gestured vaguely.

They went through to the kitchen, just as the penguin came plip-plopping that way.

"Hi, namesake!" grinned the visitor, then, looking at Viktor, asked, "Why so gloomy? You off colour or something?"

"Yes. Everything's bloody . . ."

He felt like having a moan, although something inside him protested that he shouldn't.

"Here I am, writing and writing, but nobody sees what I write," he declared, more in anger than in a bid for sympathy. "Two hundred pages to date. And all for nothing."

"What do you mean *for nothing?*" interrupted Misha-non-penguin. "You – like so many in the good old Soviet days – are writing *for the drawer.* With the difference that you, sooner or later, *are* going to be published . . . *That* I guarantee."

Unsmiling and unrelenting, Viktor acknowledged as much with a nod.

"Who do you reckon you've done best by?" Misha-non-penguin asked amiably.

"Yakornitsky," said Viktor, recalling their lengthy, Finnish-vodka-assisted table talk.

"The author-State-Deputy?"

"That's him."

"Right," said Misha. "And here's something of interest for you. Have a look at that lot."

Viktor glanced at the several pages: names he was unfamiliar with, biographical details, dates. Not what he felt like immersing himself in just then. With a nod of thanks he laid them aside.

"Ring when you're ready," Misha-non-penguin said, handing him his card.

The first snow was falling. Viktor was reading, over coffee, what Misha-non-penguin had brought a couple of days before: files on the Deputy Head of the Taxation Service and the Manageress of *The Carpathians*. The lives of this pair were garish enough to make quite exceptional *obelisks*. With characters like them – anti-heroes of the first water – a thriller would write itself! Except that novel-writing called for unlimited free time, which Viktor didn't have. True, what he did have now was money, Penguin Misha, and three silver carp in the bathroom. But was he to regard all that as compensation for an unwritten novel?

Reminded of the carp, he fetched a piece of bread and went to the bathroom to feed them.

He had just crumbled the bread, when he heard breathing beside him. He turned and saw Misha gazing dolefully at the fish in the bath.

"Don't care for freshwater fish, is that it?" he asked. "But of course!" he continued, supplying his own answer. "We creatures of Antarctic and of ocean . . ."

Going to the phone, he rang the militiaman and invited him to a fish supper.

It was still snowing.

He put his typewriter on the kitchen table, and word by word, set about painting vital images of the future departed.

Slowly but surely the work advanced, every word as rock solid as the base of an Egyptian pyramid.

> Much against his will, the departed acquiesced in the mur-
> der of his younger brother, the latter having chanced upon

a list of shareholders of an as yet unprivatized washing-machine factory. However, the monument erected by the deceased in memory of his brother has become a veritable adornment of the cemetery. Often life makes it necessary to kill, while the death of someone close makes it necessary to live on regardless . . . Everything in this world is united by virtue of blood. The life of all is a single whole, and for that reason the death of one small part of the whole still leaves life behind it, since the number of living parts always exceeds the number of deceased . . .

District Militiaman Fischbein-Stepanenko came to supper wearing jeans and a black sweater over a striped flannel shirt, carrying a bottle of cognac and a bag of frozen fish for the penguin.

Supper being still in the making, they together set about frying the former occupants of the bath. Misha, meanwhile, was in the bathroom, splashing about in fresh cold water. Viktor and Sergey could hear him above the sizzling of the fish in the frying pan, and exchanged smiles.

At last the meal was ready.

Host and guest downed a cognac before addressing themselves to the fish.

"Bony," said Viktor, as if apologizing on the fishes' behalf.

"Not to worry," said the militiaman shaking his head. "Everything has its price . . . The bonier the fish, the better the flavour. I remember I once tried whale. That's fish too, of course! No bones, but no flavour either . . ."

They helped the fish down with cognac, watching whirling snowflakes lit by the dim light of other people's windows.

Their supper had a touch of New Year about it.

"Why do you live alone?" asked Sergey, in the new intimacy of having drunk to their friendship.

Viktor shrugged. "It's the way it's been. No luck with women. They've always been the otherworldly sort. Quiet. Mousy. Here today, gone tomorrow . . . Got me down. I took on Misha, and somehow things improved. Except that he's always down in the dumps for some reason . . . Better perhaps to have got a dog . . . They're more emotional: bark when they see you, lick you, wag their tails . . ."

"Think so?" Sergey waved dismissively. "Two walks a day . . . Stinking the flat out . . . Better off with a penguin. But you, what do you do?"

"I write."

"For children?"

"Why *for children*?" asked Viktor in surprise. "No, for a newspaper."

"Ah," Sergey shook his head. "Don't care for newspapers. They always upset you."

"I don't care for them either. – But where, if you don't mind my asking, did the *Fischbein* come from?"

Sergey gave a deep sigh.

"From being bored and having an aunt in *Documents*. I thought one day I'd turn Jew, and get the hell out of it. So I just wrote, like Auntie said, *reporting loss of identity card*, and she made me out a new one in a new name. Seeing later how unenviably émigrés from here lived abroad, I thought I'd stay, and to get myself a weapon, went into the militia. It's a safe job, basically: sorting out domestic brawls and every sort of bloody fool complaint. Not quite what I dreamt of, of course."

"And what was that?"

At this point the door opened, and Misha the penguin appeared, dripping water. He stood for a moment, then, marching past the table to his bowl, looked quizzically at his master. The bowl was empty.

Viktor went to the freezer, and breaking three plaice from the frozen mass, cut them up and put them in the bowl.

Misha rested his head against the frozen fish.

"He's thawing it!" cried Sergey, watching with interest. "He really is!"

Returning to his chair, Viktor watched, too.

"Well, that's it," said Sergey, reaching for his glass. "We all of us deserve better fish, but eat what we've got . . . So, here's to friendship!"

Clinking glasses, they drank. And Viktor felt a sudden sense of relief. Past dissatisfaction with himself and others was wholly forgotten, and with it, his *obelisks*. It was as though he had never worked anywhere, but just lived, planning a novel which some day he would write. Looking at Sergey, he was moved to smile. Friendship. Something he had never had. Any more than a three-piece suit, or real passion. Life had been pale, sickly and joyless. Even Misha was down in the dumps, as if he, too, knew only a pallid life devoid of colours, emotions, delight, and joyous splashings of the soul.

"Look, let's have another," Sergey suggested suddenly, "then go for a walk, all three of us."

It was late and quiet. All children were long since in bed, the street lamps were off, only the odd light and the occasional lighted window lit the newly fallen first snow.

They slowly made their way to the waste area where there

were three dovecotes, cheeks stung by the frosty air, snow crunching underfoot.

"Behold!" cried Sergey, striding towards a figure in a shabby overcoat recumbent in the snow beneath one of the dovecotes. "Your neighbour Polikarpov from Flat 30, who, if he's not to freeze to death, must be lugged into the nearest block and parked against a radiator."

Grasping him by his coat collar, they dragged the drunken Polikarpov through the snow to the nearest five-storey block, Misha waddling behind.

When they came out, they found Misha and a massive mongrel standing nose to nose, each, apparently, sniffing the other. Seeing them, the dog ran off.

16

The next morning Viktor was woken by the phone.

"Hello?" he answered in a husky, half-awake voice.

"Congratulations, Viktor Alekseyevich! You're off the mark! Didn't wake you, did I?"

"Time I was up anyway," said Viktor, recognizing the Chief's voice. "What's the trouble?"

"You're in print! And how are you feeling, by the way?"

"Better already."

"Call in, then. We'll talk."

Viktor washed, breakfasted, drank tea, looked in on Misha and found him standing asleep in his favourite hidey-hole behind the dark-green settee.

Returning to the kitchen he put a large piece of frozen cod in Misha's bowl, dressed and went out.

Outside lay a fresh fall of snow. A blue-grey sky was pressing down almost to the rooftops of the five-storey blocks. There was no wind and it was not very cold.

Before boarding the bus, he had bought the latest *Capital News*, and having secured a comfortable seat, he opened it out and scanned the headlines, coming at last to a rectangle of text set high on the page and framed heavily in black.

> Writer and State Deputy Aleksandr Yakornitsky is no longer with us. In the third row of the Chamber, a leather seat stands empty. To be occupied, before long, by another. But in the hearts of the many who knew Aleksandr Yakornitsky there will be a sense of emptiness, of profound loss . . .

So there it was, his first publication.

But he did not feel particularly happy, despite the long-forgotten sense of personal satisfaction that stirred deep down. He read through to the end. Every word in place, no sign of a cut.

His eye rested on the signature – *A Group of Friends* – more like a phrase than a pseudonym, the four words serving as an umbrella for any number. The funny thing was that this was exactly how he had typed it, both nouns with a capital. And even this the Editor had left, treating Viktor more like a respected writer than a journalist.

Lowering the paper, he looked out at the approaching city.

"Look, a little bird!" said a mother sitting in front of him with her child, and pointing. Glancing automatically in the direction indicated, he saw a sparrow fluttering inside the bus.

The Editor-in-Chief greeted Viktor cordially, as if he had not seen him for a year. Coffee, cognac and $100 in a long elegant envelope made their appearance. It was quite a celebration.

"Well," said Igor Lvovich, raising his glass of cognac, "a start's been made. Let's hope our remaining *obelisks* don't hang around for long either."

"How did he die?" Viktor asked.

"Fell from a sixth-floor window – was cleaning it for some reason, apparently, though it wasn't his. And at night."

Clinking glasses, they drank.

"Do you know," the Chief confided further, "I've had colleagues from other papers ringing. Green with envy, the parasites! I, they say, have invented a new kind of obituary!" He smiled smugly. "The credit's all yours, of course. But you being *under wraps*, I take the compliments, and the kicks! OK?"

Viktor nodded, though he was secretly pained at being kept out of the limelight, fame still being fame, albeit journalistic. Something of which became apparent to the Chief from Viktor's expression.

"Don't take it to heart. Everyone will know your real name some day – if you want . . . But for the moment, best keep to the *Group of Friends* that no one knows. You'll see why in a day or two. And incidentally, don't forget: everything underlined in the files from Fyodor, *you're to use*. I don't cut your philosophizings, do I? Even though they have, quite frankly, damn all to do with the late lamented."

Viktor nodded his agreement. He sipped his coffee, and was

reminded suddenly, by the bitterish flavour, of the hotel bar in Kharkov and the morning he had been woken by shooting.

"What *did* happen in Kharkov, Igor?" he asked.

Sighing, the Chief poured cognac and gave Viktor an inhibited, arrested sort of look.

"Bowed his head did our brave young Red,"

he crooned softly:

"Cruelly shot through his Komsomol heart . . .

"As a newspaper, we've had our losses. This one's our seventh. Before long we'll be unveiling a pantheon . . . Still, no skin off your nose! The less you know, the longer you live!" said the Chief. Then, in quite a different, somehow weary voice, and looking hard at him, he added "And it's not your business any longer. Just that you know a bit more than others do . . . OK . . ."

Viktor regretted his curiosity. The whole ambience of their little *tête à tête* celebration had been lost.

18

The end of November saw the transition from deep autumn to deep winter. Children threw snowballs. An icy chill crept under coat collars. Cars drove slowly, as if frightened of each other, the roads being now much narrower. The cold diminished, shortened, shrivelled everything. The kerbside mounds of snow were the only things to grow, and these only by virtue of the hard work and broad shovels of the clearers of courtyards and pavements.

Having completed the second of Misha-non-penguin's *obelisks*,

Viktor looked out of the window. Today had been a day when he had neither wanted nor needed to go out. To break the silence, he switched on the set-programme speaker standing on the fridge. The carefree hubbub of parliament (plus hiss) burst forth. He turned down the volume, put the kettle on for tea, and glanced at his watch: 5.30. A bit early to be finishing for the day.

He rang Misha-non-penguin.

"All ready," he reported. "Come and collect."

Misha came, but not alone. With him was a little girl with round inquisitive eyes.

"My daughter," he said. "No one to leave her with . . . Tell Uncle Vik your name." He stooped to unbutton her little coat of reddish fur.

"Sonya," she said gazing up at him. "And I'm four. – Have you really got a penguin living here?"

"You see? And she's hardly been here a minute . . ." He removed her coat and helped her off with her little boots.

They went through to the living room.

"Where is he?" she asked, looking round.

"I'll go and see," said Viktor, but first he fetched Misha-non-penguin the two new *obelisks* from the kitchen.

"Misha," he called, looking behind the dark-green settee.

Misha, standing in his hidey-hole on a treble thickness of camel-hair blanket, was staring at the wall.

"All right?" Viktor asked, stooping down to him.

The penguin stood staring wide-eyed.

Viktor wondered if he was ill.

"What's wrong with him?" asked Sonya, having crept to join them.

"Misha! We've got visitors!"

Sonya went over and stroked the penguin.

"Are you feeling bad?" she asked.

Misha jerked round and looked at her.

"Daddy!" she cried, "He moved!"

Leaving them together, Viktor retired to the living room. Misha-non-penguin, deep in an armchair, was getting to the end of the second obituary. From the look on his face he seemed pleased.

"Good stuff!" he said. "Touching. Absolute shits, that's clear, but reading this, one feels sorry for them . . . Any tea going?"

They moved to the kitchen, and while waiting for the kettle, sat at the table talking of the weather and other trivial matters. Tea made and poured, Misha-non-penguin handed Viktor an envelope.

"Your honorarium," he said. "And there's another client coming. – Oh, and you remember the one you did for Sergey Chekalin?"

Viktor nodded.

"He's recovered . . . I faxed him your effort. I think he liked it . . . Anyway, he was impressed!"

"Daddy, Daddy," came the little girl's voice, "he's hungry!"

"So he can talk, can he?" grinned Misha-non-penguin.

Viktor took cod from the freezer and put it in the bowl.

"Sonya, tell him food's on the table," he called.

"Hear that?" They could faintly heard her telling him. "You're to come to table."

The penguin arrived first, trailed by Sonya. Following him to his bowl, she watched with interest as he ate.

"Why's he on his own?" she asked suddenly, looking up.

"Oh, I don't know," said Viktor. "Actually he isn't. We live here together."

"Like me and Daddy," said Sonya.

"What a chatterbox!" sighed Misha-non-penguin, gulping tea and contemplating his daughter. "Come on, time to go home."

Thoroughly dejected, she left the kitchen.

"Have to get her a puppy or a cat," said Misha-non-penguin, watching her go.

"Bring her again, to play," Viktor suggested.

Outside, the inky blackness of a winter evening. Barely audibly, the set-programme speaker was reporting events in Chechnya. Viktor sat at the typewriter at the kitchen table, feeling lonely. He would have liked to write a short story – or a fairy story – even if just for Sonya. But filling his head was the mournful, heartfelt melody of an as yet unwritten *obelisk*.

"Am I ill?" he wondered, staring at the blank paper protruding from the typewriter. "No, I must, must, sometimes at least, make myself write short stories, or else I'll go mad."

He fell to thinking of Sonya's funny little freckled face, her red ponytail with its elastic band.

Odd times to be a child in. An odd country, an odd life which he had no desire to make sense of. To endure, full stop, that was all he wanted.

19

A few days later the Chief rang, telling him to be more on his guard, and not to come to the office or go out for the time being, unless he had to.

Puzzled, Viktor kept the receiver to his ear for a minute's

worth of short beeps. What had happened, he wondered, still hearing the calm, self-assured, professorial voice of the Chief. He shrugged. He couldn't take it seriously, that call. But his morning acquired, unaided, two profitless hours. He spent a long time shaving, and ironing, for no good reason, a shirt he had no intention of wearing.

Towards midday he sallied forth, bought papers, popped into the food store for fish for Misha and for himself, together with a kilo of bananas.

Back at the flat he scanned the papers, but they provided no answer to the Chief's call. However, new names caught his eye, and fetching his notebook, he duly entered them, to work on in the future, only not now. He was in a state of complete enervation. Sitting at the kitchen table on which reposed his bag of shopping, he extracted a banana.

The kitchen door creaked open. Misha the penguin came in and stood in front of his master, looking pleadingly at him.

Viktor held out the banana he was eating.

Misha leant forward and bit a piece off.

"Think you're a monkey, do you?" exclaimed Viktor. "But you watch it! If you go poisoning yourself, where do we find a doctor? We haven't enough to cope with us humans! I'd better give you some fish."

The silence of the kitchen was broken by the sound of Misha tackling his cod, and the breathing of a profoundly pensive Viktor. At last, with a sigh, he got up and turned on the speaker. Militia siren. It must be a radio play. But no. It was a report *from the scene of battle,* this time at the intersection of Red Army and Saksagansky Streets, practically in the city centre. He turned up the volume. An agitated account of pools of blood on the road, three ambulances taking 30 minutes to arrive, seven bodies, five wounded. First indications were that among the dead was the Deputy Sports Minister, State Deputy Stoyanov. Turning automatically to his notebook, Viktor checked: the newly departed Stoyanov was there. With a nod of satisfaction he resumed listening, leaving his notebook open. But the reporter proceeded to repeat the facts already given, these, apparently, being all he knew. He would, he promised, be back in half an hour with further details, and a pleasantly spoken woman took over with a weather forecast for the weekend.

Saturday tomorrow, thought Viktor, and turned to look at Misha.

Working from home, he had lost any sense of distinction between working and non-working days: working if he felt like it, or not, if he didn't. Mostly though, he did feel like it. It was just that he had nothing further to work on. As to writing stories, starting a novella or even a novel, that had not come off. It was as if he had found his *genre* and was so constrained by its limits that even when not writing *obelisks*, he was thinking *obelisks*, or thoughts so elegant and attuned to mourning that they could be slotted, by way of a philosophical digression, into any obituary – and sometimes were.

He rang the District Militiaman.

"Lieutenant Fischbein," came the clear, familiar voice.

"Hi, Sergey. Vik."

"Vik?"

"Master of Misha."

"Why didn't you say? What's new? How is he?" was the cheery response.

"He's OK. Look, are you off-duty tomorrow?"

"Yes."

"Got a bright idea, and wonder if you're game," said Viktor hopefully. "All we need is a vehicle. A militia jeep would do . . ."

"If it's not in furtherance of a punishable offence, no problem . . ." laughed Sergey. "But why a jeep, when I've got my own *Zaporozhets*?"

20

In the icy cold of Saturday morning, Viktor, Sergey and Penguin Misha emerged from a red *Zaporozhets* parked on the Dnieper Embankment near the Monastery Gardens. Sergey collected a bulging rucksack from the boot, shouldered it, and they descended the stone steps to the frozen river.

The Dnieper was under a thick layer of ice, on which, at polite distances from one another, the winter anglers sat like fat, motionless crows, each by his own hole.

Steering clear of them, Viktor, Sergey and Misha headed deep into the Dnieper ice fields.

They paused at every free hole, but they were all either frozen over or too small.

"Let's try the bay," said Sergey. "Where winter swimmers go."

They made towards a narrow spit, the tail of an island, which they crossed.

"There, look!" said Sergey pointing. "See that patch of blue?"

The hole, when they reached it, was vast, with many naked heel-prints at its edge. Without waiting for the go-ahead, Misha lunged forward and dived smoothly in without so much as a splash.

Viktor and Sergey stared at the heaving mash of ice and water, hardly daring to breathe.

"Can they see under water?" Sergey asked.

"I daresay," said Viktor. "If there's anything to see."

Taking off his rucksack, Sergey pulled out an old quilt, which he spread on the ice a metre or two from the hole.

"Come and sit down," he called. "Each to his own holiday amusement."

Viktor came and sat, Sergey having meanwhile produced a thermos and two plastic cups.

"We'll start with coffee."

It was sweet, and made a pleasant drink against the cold.

"And I never thought to bring anything," Viktor confessed sadly, warming his hands around his cup.

"Never mind, there'll be another time. Spot of cognac?"

Sergey poured some into each cup, then slipped the flat bottle into a jacket pocket.

"To all that's good!" he proposed.

They drank, warmth pervading their bodies and minds.

"He won't drown, will he?" Sergey asked, looking towards the ice-hole.

"He shouldn't," shrugged Viktor. "But I'm in the dark really about penguins. I've looked for books on them, but haven't found any."

"If I come across anything, you shall have it," Sergey promised.

Viktor looked around anxiously. The nearest angler and hole were a good 30 metres away. The angler was sitting on his tackle box and every now and then could be seen raising a litre-sized water bottle to his lips.

"Think I'll take a stroll," said Viktor, still watching the angler.

"I shouldn't. Let's sit for a bit and have some more cognac. He'll be back. He won't drown, that's for sure!"

A sudden gurgling came from the ice-hole. Viktor looked at once, but it was only the mash of ice and water slopping to and fro.

Sergey raised his cup of cognac. "Come, let's drink to him. People are legion, penguins are not – and ought to be cherished!"

As they drank, a cry rent the frosty silence. Swinging round, they saw an angler some 50 metres away leap back from his hole, pointing at it with both hands. Two other anglers were heading his way, abandoning their rods in their holes.

"What's up with him?" Sergey asked, speaking to himself.

Oblivious to events 50 metres away, Viktor was sipping his cognac and considering how each new day brought to one's life something new, totally unplanned for. A time would come when it would be trouble of some sort, perhaps even death.

"Look!" shouted Sergey, clapping him on the shoulder.

Returning to the here and now, Viktor looked first at Sergey, then, following his gaze, saw Misha approaching from the direction of the island.

"Where's he popped up from?" asked Sergey in amazement.

Misha came to a halt at the edge of their quilt.

"Perhaps he'd like a cognac," quipped Sergey.

"Come on, Misha," called Viktor, patting the quilt.

Misha stepped awkwardly onto it and looked from one to the other of them.

Reaching once more into his rucksack, Sergey produced a towel and wrapped it around him.

"So he doesn't catch cold," he explained.

Misha stood in his towel for five minutes or so, then threw it off.

Hearing footsteps, Viktor turned.

It was the owner of the nearest hole.

"Fish biting?" asked Sergey.

Eyes fixed on the penguin, the fisherman shook his head.

"Look," he said at last, "is that a penguin you've got there, or am I seeing things?"

"You're seeing things," Sergey assured him firmly.

"Christ!" he whispered, aghast.

With an ungainly wave of his arms, he turned and set off back to his hole.

"Now, perhaps he'll ease off the drink a bit," said Sergey hopefully, as they watched him go.

"You're not on duty now," Viktor reproached him. "Why go scaring drunks to death?"

"Professional instinct," said Sergey with a smile. "Like something to eat? Or shall we have another first?"

"We'll have another first."

Suddenly Misha began marking time impatiently, flapping his flippers.

"Think he needs a bog?" Sergey grinned, unscrewing the cognac.

Misha, having meanwhile abandoned quilt for ice, set off at a comical waddling run and dived once more into the ice-hole.

21

In the small hours of Monday morning, Viktor was roused by the insistent ringing of the phone. When finally awake, he didn't feel like getting up, but lay waiting for the caller to lose patience.

But the caller didn't lose patience, and even the penguin woke and gabbled.

Viktor got out of bed and made his way unsteadily to the phone.

Some idiot's idea of a joke! he thought, lifting the receiver.

"Vik?" It was the Chief and he sounded impatient. "Sorry to wake you. Urgent job! Are you listening?"

"Yes."

"A courier's on his way with an envelope. He'll wait in his car while you get cracking on the *obelisk*. It's for the morning edition."

Viktor glanced at the alarm clock on the bedside table. It was 1.30.

"All right."

He put on his blue towelling dressing-gown, washed in cold water, then proceeded to the kitchen. Here he put the kettle on the stove, his typewriter on the table, and listened to the silence of the night. He looked out at the block opposite. Only two lighted windows in the whole building.

Not his problem, other people's insomnia. He was his waking self again, except for a heavy head. He fetched paper, inserted it in the typewriter, and again listened to the silence of the night.

A car drew up outside. A door banged.

He waited patiently for the doorbell. A short while later, instead of a ring, there was a guarded knock.

A red-eyed, sleepy-looking man of about 50 handed him a large brown envelope.

"I'm down in the car. Hammer on the door if I'm asleep," he said, without coming in.

Sitting at his typewriter, Viktor drew from the envelope a sheet of paper and a theatre programme.

Parkhomenko, Yuliya Andreyevna, *b.* 1955. Since 1988, singer Nat. Opera. Married, two children.

he read.

1991, mastectomy. 1993, summoned as witness re disappearance of Nat. Opera diva Sanuchenko, Irina Fyodorovna, who she was at daggers drawn with. 1995 opted out of planned Italian tour, nearly aborting it.

Followed by the handwritten addendum:

Severely affected by death of Nikolay Aleksandrovich Yakornitsky, author, State Deputy, and (since 1994 and her appearance at a private celebration of Ukrainian Independence at the Mariynsky Palace) her most intimate friend.

This underlined in red pencil, at once recalled his last conversation with Igor Lvovich.

He read it a number of times. Not much to go on, but already his thoughts were attuned to the requisite degree of pathos.

On page two of the programme he discovered a colour photograph of the singer: a comely, shapely lady, with flushed, undoubtedly rouged cheeks; almond eyes; chestnut hair cascading over shoulders; revealing costume.

Back to blank sheet in typewriter.

For Arabs, white was the colour of mourning, he reflected, fingers poised above the keys.

All that is possessed of life in this world has a voice of its own. The voice is a sign of life. It may grow in strength, break off, be lost, sink to a barely audible whisper. In the chorus of our lives the individual voice is not easily distinguished, but where, suddenly, it falls silent, there comes an awareness of the finitude of any sound, of any life. One voice that we are given to hear no more is a voice that has been loved by many . . . Suddenly, prematurely, it has been lost. To which extent the world has become more silent, though not as sought by lovers of tranquillity. The silence now fallen serves, like a black hole in the universe, only to emphasize the finitude of any sound and the infinity of past and future losses . . .

Getting up, Viktor went and made tea, returning with a large cup.

. . . The voice of Yuliya Parkhomenko is now silent. But so long as the walls of the Mariynsky Palace endure, and the splendour of the National Opera is reflected in the gold of its inner cupola, she will abide as a golden haze dissolved upon the air we breathe. Her voice will be the gilding of the silence she has left behind.

A bit too much gold, he thought, pausing. Again he picked up the sheet of notes, and for the umpteenth time perused the underlinings. How was he to bring in Yakornitsky? Love? Love . . .

Gulping tea, he pondered the point. He read what he had written, before continuing:

She suffered, not long ago, the grievous loss of the voice of one dear to her. Silenced abruptly it was, that voice, lost as a dying fall into that abyss, whither, by Death's Laws of Gravity descends all that, having fought the good fight, or simply lost out, has had its day.

Here, breaking off again to look more closely at the programme, he permitted himself the ghost of a smile.

Only recently, as *Tosca* in Puccini's opera, she acted out her own tragedy to the full in her final leap from the battlements. The manner of her death is not of importance. Had it been of a different order, we who have given ear to her life would still face the difficult task of now accustoming ourselves to silence, and seeking therein golden traces of her late presence. Let us, therefore, all fall silent, the better to distinguish her voice – distinguish, recall and cherish in memory until our own voices are mingled with silence and eternity . . .

He straightened up, breathing hard, as if having completed a 100-metre sprint, not sat tapping away at a typewriter. To relieve the strain imposed by this urgent nocturnal commission, he massaged his temples. Still, the job was done.

He reached for what he had written and read it through, feeling suddenly sorry for the opera singer who had died, or met death, he knew not how.

He looked out of the window. The car was down below, waiting.

Getting to his feet, he turned, and was startled to see Misha looking on thoughtfully from the doorway, standing immobile, tiny eyes alone burning with vital fire, but quite inscrutable, simply observing his master dispassionately, and for no particular reason.

Taking a deep breath, Viktor squeezed between penguin and door and out into the corridor, threw his sheepskin jacket over his dressing-gown, and made for the landing and stairs, clutching his text.

The courier was asleep, head sunk forward onto the wheel. Viktor tapped the window. The man rubbed his eyes. Without a word, he opened the door, relieved Viktor of the page of text, started the engine and drove off.

Viktor returned to his flat. The night was all in pieces. He didn't feel like sleep, he was brimming with superfluous energy.

Discovering some sleeping tablets in the medicine cabinet, he washed down two with water still warm from the kettle, and retired to his room.

22

Next morning at ten, the Chief rang again. He was happy with the *obelisk* and apologized once more for disturbing Viktor's sleep. A couple more days, he said, and Viktor would be able to come to the office, the main thing being to remember his Press card, as the Special Task Militia was now on duty at the entrance and on every floor.

Outside, winter continued crisp with frost. It was fairly quiet.

Standing over his Turkish coffee-maker at the stove, Viktor was wondering how to fill his day. One possibility, in view of his night's work, was take the day off. But a day off involved an even greater need for interesting content than a normal day. He therefore decided to go, after coffee, to the kiosk for the papers, and then make up his mind what to do.

His second cup he drank over the papers. First, he read his night's work, now in half a million copies, on the last page but one. It was all there, untouched by the Editor-in-Chief. *He* would have been enjoying his night's sleep while the text was being set ready for the press. Going back to page one, he read the lengthy, full-page leader: NOT AN END TO WAR BUT A TRUCE. Pictures reminiscent of the assault on Grozny broke up the soldierly columns of print. He ploughed on. The more he read, the more absorbed he became. What emerged was that while he had been leading a normal life in Kiev, near-battles had been fought by two warring Mafia clans. At least, so the article claimed. Seventeen dead, nine wounded, five bomb blasts. Among the dead were the Editor-in-Chief's driver, three militiamen, an Arab businessman, persons as yet unidentified, and a singer from the National Opera.

The other papers, he noticed, devoted far less space to the *war* than *Capital News*. Against that, there was a little more about the death of the singer, whose body had been discovered in the early hours at the lower funicular station. She had been strangled with a leather belt. Furthermore, her architect husband had vanished and their flat was in disorder, having evidently been ransacked in search of something.

Viktor pondered. The singer's death had, on the face of it, nothing to do with clan warfare. A completely *extraneous* crime, in fact. The missing husband might have had a hand in it. And – the thought horrified him – so might *he*, having referred to her in his Yakornitsky obituary. He had not named her, of course, but for many a nod was as good as a wink, and that might have been the last straw for hubby . . .

He sighed, and for a moment felt appallingly wearied by his own assumptions.

"What rubbish!" he said under his breath. "Why would hubby ransack his own flat?"

23

The day ended, oddly enough, on a fairly productive note. Three *obelisks* lay ready on the table. Through the window the light of the winter evening was fading. Steam was rising from a freshly made cup of tea.

He skimmed his latest efforts. A bit on the short side, but all because he had not been to the office for some time for additional information on his notables from Fyodor. But that was no problem. Pending printing he could still work on them, still revise them.

He drank his tea, turned off the kitchen light, and was on his way to bed, when there was a knock at the door.

Taken aback, Viktor stood in the corridor listening to the silence. Then, discarding his slippers, he went barefoot to the door and peeped through the spyhole. It was Misha-non-penguin. Viktor let him in.

Misha had Sonya in his arms, asleep. He came in without a word, merely nodding hello.

"Where can I put her?"

"In there," whispered Viktor indicating the living room door.

Misha laid Sonya on the settee, then tiptoed back to the corridor.

"Let's go to the kitchen," he suggested.

On again went the kitchen light.

"Put the kettle on."

"It's only just boiled."

"I'll stay till morning," Misha said dully. "And Sonya can live here for a bit . . . OK? Till things settle down."

"What things?" asked Viktor.

But he received no answer. They were sitting opposite each other at the kitchen table, except that Misha was now where Viktor usually sat, and Viktor had his back to the stove. For just an instant he seemed to detect a flash of hostility in Misha's eyes.

"Cognac?" he asked, in an effort to lift the black cloud of tension hanging over them.

"All right," said his visitor.

Viktor poured. They drank in silence.

Lost in thought, Misha drummed the table with his fingers. Looking around and spotting the pile of newspapers on the window sill, he drew it towards him. Picking up the topmost, he pulled a wry face and thrust the papers back again.

"Life's funny," he sighed. "You try to give pleasure and end up crash-diving like a submarine . . ."

Viktor heard what he was saying, but the meaning eluded him, like gossamer in the wind.

"Pour me another," said Misha.

Downing his second glass, he went and looked at Sonya still peacefully asleep in the living room, then came back.

"I daresay you'd like to know what's happened," he said slowly in a weaker voice, looking hard at Viktor.

Viktor said nothing. He no longer wanted to know anything. Sleep was what he wanted, and Misha-non-penguin's odd behaviour was beginning to get him down.

"The shootings, the bombs, you know about, don't you." Misha gestured towards the papers.

"Well?" asked Viktor.

"Know who's to blame for that lot?"

"Who?"

Misha combined a longish pause with a smile that was weary and unfriendly.

"You."

"*Me?* How – how could I?"

"Not entirely you, of course . . . Though without you, none of this would have happened." He stared unblinkingly, seeming to gaze through and beyond Viktor. "Just that you were feeling bloody – I could see you were. I asked you why. You told me. We were open about it. That child-like openness was what I liked about you. You wanted to see your little bits in print, edged round with black. And why not? So then I asked you who your best future lamented was . . . Simply out of a wish to give you pleasure . . . Give me another."

Viktor got up and poured them both cognac, hands trembling visibly.

"You mean, *you* killed Yakornitsky?" He was aghast.

"Not me, *we*," corrected Misha. "But don't you worry, he more than had it coming . . . Another thing is that his death leaves out in the cold the privatization fanatics he milked of funds *on account*. Apart from that he retained certain documents touching on parliamentary colleagues by virtue of which he prolonged his own existence and security. It's a tough life they lead at the top . . . A kind of war."

A lengthy pause followed. Misha-non-penguin looked out of the window, leaving Viktor grappling with what he had been told.

"Listen," he said at last, "am I involved in the death of his mistress, too?"

"You haven't grasped it," said Misha in a calm, schoolteacher-like voice. "What you and I have done is pull out the bottommost card of the card house. Result: total collapse. Now we just wait for the dust to settle . . ."

"Me too?" Viktor asked, sounding alarmed.

Misha shrugged. "Individual matter," he said, replenishing his glass. "But you'll be all right. You, it seems, enjoy good protection . . . Which is why I've come to you."

"Whose?"

Misha gestured vaguely.

"I don't claim to know. Just a feeling. You wouldn't still be with us if you didn't." He became lost in thought. "Can I ask you to do me a favour?" he enquired after a while.

Viktor nodded.

"Go off to bed, and I'll sit on for a bit and have a think."

Viktor went to his room, lay down, but didn't feel like sleeping. He listened, but the silence of the flat was absolute. Everyone, it seemed, was sound asleep. Faintly from the living room came a child's voice. It was Sonya muttering *Mummy, Mummy*.

Who, he wondered, was where?

Eventually he dozed off.

A little later, the penguin emerged from behind the dark-green settee, and sauntered towards the half-open living-room door. En route he paused by the sleeping girl, gazed thoughtfully at her, then continued on into the corridor. Pushing the next door open, he proceeded to the kitchen.

Sitting asleep in his master's place, head resting on the table, was a strange man.

For several minutes the penguin considered him, standing motionless by the door, then turned about and retraced his steps.

24

The clock on the bedside table showed 7.00. Outside it was still dark and quiet. Having woken with a headache, Viktor lay on his back contemplating the ceiling and thinking about his conversation with Misha-non-penguin. Headache or no headache, he now had some questions for his caller of the night before.

Slowly, trying to make no sound, he got up, put on his dressing-gown, and went to the living room.

Sonya was still asleep, thoughtfully covered with Viktor's grey autumn overcoat from its hook in the hall.

Steeling himself, he went out into the corridor, only to be brought up short by the doors left open on the way to the kitchen.

The kitchen was empty. On the table was a note.

> Time to be off. Leaving Sonya with you. She's your responsibility – you answer for her with your life. Back when the dust settles. – Misha.

Caught unawares, Viktor sat at the table staring at the handwritten note, trying to put from his mind the questions he had intended to ask Misha-non-penguin, and hadn't.

Through the window, the grey of a wan winter dawn was contending with night.

His thoughts were interrupted by the creak of the living-room settee. Getting to his feet, he went and looked into the living room.

Sonya was sitting up, rubbing her eyes.

"Where's Daddy?" she asked, becoming aware of Viktor's presence.

"He's gone," he replied. "You're to live here for a bit."

"With Misha the penguin?" she asked brightly.

"Yes," he answered dryly.

"Yesterday we had our windows broken," she said. "And it was very cold."

"Your windows at home?"

"Yes," she confided. "Crash! Bang! they went. It was awful!"

"Like something to eat?"

"So long as it's not porridge."

"Haven't any," Viktor confessed. "I'm not a great eater."

"Me neither," said Sonya with a smile. "Where are we going today?"

"Where?" he repeated, trying to think. "I don't know . . . Where do you want to go?"

"The zoo."

"Right," he said, "but first I must do a couple of hours' work."

25

For lunch Viktor gave Misha fish, while he and Sonya had fried potatoes.

"I'll buy a bit more food tomorrow," he promised.

"This'll do me," she said, taking the larger plate.

Viktor smiled. Faced for the first time with another's childhood, he observed, cautiously, curiously, as though still a child himself. Sonya's spontaneity, her replies – not so much inopportune as somehow off at a tangent – brought a smile to his face. He ate with half an eye on her sitting opposite, eating more with interest than appetite, narrowly inspecting every forkful, while between her and the stove, Misha was busy at his bowl.

Once, she twisted round and transferred a fried potato to Misha's bowl on her fork. Head cocked comically to one side, Misha looked at her in surprise. Sonya burst out laughing. Misha stood for a while, then returned to his bowl and ate the fried potato.

"He likes it!" she reported, well pleased.

Viktor drank his tea, put Sonya into her coat, and they set off for the zoo.

It was snowing lightly, the wind in their faces, and coming out of the Metro he wrapped her up to the eyes in her scarf.

Beyond the gates there was a notice stating that owing to winter conditions only a small section of the zoo was open to visitors.

Not many people were about. Following a sign saying TIGERS, he led Sonya along a snow-covered path past an enclosure with a large drawing of a zebra and a stencilled description of its life and habits.

"Where," asked Sonya, looking around, "are the animals?"

"Further on," he said encouragingly.

They passed more empty enclosures with boards descriptive of recent inmates, and came to a roofed-in area.

Here, behind thick iron bars, sat two tigers, a lion, a wolf, and other predators. At the entrance there was a notice:

FEED ONLY WITH FRESH MEAT AND BREAD

Neither of which they had.

They walked along the cages, stopping briefly at each.

"Where," asked Sonya, "are the penguins?"

"Probably not in this part . . . Still, we'll come to them, if we keep looking."

He tried to remember exactly where he had first seen Misha. It had been just beyond reptiles and amphibians and the concrete den for brown bears.

Walking on, they came to an empty sunken enclosure with railings around it and a frozen lake in the middle. A board depicting penguins hung above the railings.

"Well, as you can see, there aren't any here," said Viktor.

"A pity," sighed Sonya. "We could have brought Misha to make friends with the others."

"Except, as you can see, there aren't any others," he repeated, stooping down to her.

"What does still live here?" she asked.

For a whole hour more they wandered, seeing fish, snakes, two bald kites and a solitary long-necked llama. As they headed for the exit, Viktor spotted a sign:

SCIENTIFIC INFORMATION CENTRE

"Let's pop in," he suggested. "Maybe they can tell us about penguins."

"Yes, let's," Sonya agreed.

He knocked at the one door of the little single-storey building and went in.

"Excuse me," he said addressing a prematurely grey-haired woman sitting at a desk reading a periodical.

"Yes?" she said, looking up. "What can I do for you?"

"Just over a year ago," he said, "I took on one of your penguins. You don't happen to have anything about penguins, do you?"

"No. Pidpaly was penguins. Got fired when we gave them up. Took the literature with him. Noxious old man."

"Pidpaly, you say? Where can I find him?"

"Try Personnel," she shrugged, and looking with interest at

54

Sonya, asked, "You couldn't, I suppose, do with the odd snake? Reptiles and amphibians go from January."

"Thank you, no. Where is Personnel?"

"Back of toilets, left of main entrance."

Leaving Sonya to wait at the entrance, Viktor went and obtained Pidpaly's address. Folding the piece of paper, he put it into his wallet, took her hand, and they set off for the Metro.

26

Next morning he decided to go and see the Chief. Firstly, because he had a backlog of copy to deliver, and secondly, out of a desire to confess – or rather explain – what had happened to Yakornitsky – and why.

"Could you stay here alone?" he asked Sonya after breakfast.

"Daddy told me," she said. "*Let no one in. Don't answer the phone. Keep away from windows.* That right?"

"Yes," sighed Viktor. "But today you can go to the windows."

"Can I?" she said happily, running to the balcony door and pressing her nose to the pane.

"And what can you see?"

"Winter."

"Back soon," promised Viktor.

He had to show his Press card three times before arriving at the Chief's office.

"How are we?" enquired Igor Lvovich.

"Fine," said Viktor without conviction. "I've brought you these new *obelisks*."

The Chief reached out a hand. "And this," he passed over a fat folder, "is from Fyodor."

"Igor," Viktor began, plucking up courage. "It seems it's me who's actually to blame for Yakornitsky's death."

"You don't say!" grinned the Chief. "See yourself as a heavy, do you?"

Viktor looked bewildered.

"No need to fret," said the Chief in a more amicable tone. "I know everything."

"Everything?"

"Considerably more than everything. Yakornitsky had the skids under him anyway . . . So don't worry! Though you would do better to stick to what concerns you, of course."

Viktor stared aghast, unable to take it all in.

"So it's not the end of the world," he said at last.

"Why should it be? Just because we're one little group with government connections the fewer? Relax. You're out of it, and if you're not, you're only very indirectly in. Let's have some coffee."

The Chief phoned the order to his secretary, then looked hard at Viktor, thoughtfully biting his lip.

"No wife? No girlfriend?"

"Not at the moment."

"Bad," said the Chief with a half-humorous shake of the head. "Women are the strength of the male nervous system. Time you took your nerves in hand . . . Still, just my little joke."

The secretary brought coffee.

Viktor took half a spoonful of sugar, but the overstrong coffee was still bitter, making him think of his recent trip to Kharkov.

"Do I have to go to Odessa?" he asked suddenly, remembering their pre-Kharkov conversation.

"No," replied the Chief. "Someone's very much anti our getting involved in the provinces . . . Still, we've enough to be getting on with here. So no need to worry. Look at me, serene as a tank, even though they've just murdered my driver! Believe me, life's not something to be concerned about."

Seeing the Chief in his expensive suit, French tie, solid gold tie-pin, and director's chair, Viktor doubted whether he did, in fact, set so little store by life.

"Before New Year we must split a bottle together, you and I, eh? Unless you'd rather not?"

"All for it," answered Viktor.

"Good." The Chief got to his feet. "I'll be in touch."

27

Stepan Yakovlevich Pidpaly lived on the ground floor of a grey Stalin-baroque block near Svyatoshino Metro station. Stamping the snow off his feet, Viktor rang the bell.

Lengthy spyhole scrutiny followed, then a trembly old man's voice asked, "Who do you want?"

"Stepan Yakovlevich," said Viktor.

"Who are you?"

"I got your address at the zoo," explained Viktor. "I've come about penguins."

The apparent idiocy of this explanation notwithstanding, the door opened, and an unshaven, not so very old-looking man in a blue woollen tracksuit invited him in.

He went through into a spacious living room in the middle

of which was an old-fashioned round table with chairs.

"Sit down," said his host, looking elsewhere.

"Interested in penguins, are you?" he went on, now looking squarely at Viktor, at the same time feeling for and retrieving an old dog-end from the grubby table cloth. The hand descended below the table then came up without the dog-end, and rested on the cloth.

"I'm sorry to trouble you," began Viktor, "but I wanted to ask if maybe you had any books on penguins."

"Books?" Pidpaly countered, looking pained. "Why should I? I've got my own unpublished works . . . I've studied penguins for more than 20 years."

"So you're a zoologist?" said Viktor as deferentially as he knew how.

"*Penguinologist*, more like, though it's not a speciality you'll find listed, of course." His tone softened. "Still, what's your interest in penguins exactly?"

"I have one, but know nothing about them. I'm worried in case I'm doing something wrong."

"You have, have you? Splendid! Where did you get him?"

"From the zoo, a year ago. When smaller animals were being given away."

Pidpaly frowned. "What species?"

"King, I think. Called Misha. Fully grown, about as tall as this table."

"*Misha!*" Pidpaly pursed his lips, scratched his stubble. "From our zoo?"

"Yes."

"Well I never! But why take on a sick one? There were seven of them, I remember. Adèle, Zaychik — they were the younger, fit ones."

"What's wrong with him?"

"Depressive syndrome. Bad heart. I'd say congenital. So *that's* where he got to," he said sadly with a sigh.

"What can be done about it? Can he be treated?"

"That's a good one!" Pidpaly laughed. "They don't treat people nowadays, let alone penguins! What you must realize is that our climate's fatal to creatures from the Antarctic. The best thing for him, of course, would be to be living where he belongs. You mustn't take it amiss, and I'm clearly talking rubbish, but if I were a penguin and found myself in these latitudes, I'd do myself in. Imagine the torment of living where it's up to 40°+ in summer and *occasionally* down to -10° in winter, when you've got two layers of fat protecting you against intense cold, to say nothing of hundreds of blood vessels doing the same. Just imagine: you get superheated internally. You burn up . . . Practically all penguins living in zoos exhibit depressive syndrome . . . And they tried to tell me penguins had no psychology. I proved it! And I'll prove it to you! And as to his heart: what heart *would* tolerate superheating to that extent?"

As Viktor listened, Pidpaly became more and more worked up, and waved his arms about ever more wildly. From time to time he switched to rhetorical questions, pausing briefly to catch breath before continuing. Never had Viktor received such an earful: period of incubation . . . physiology . . . mating peculiarities . . . Eventually, with a headache coming on, he knew he must somehow arrest the flow.

"Excuse me, but may I read what you've written?" he interposed, exploiting one of Pidpaly's periodic rhetorical questions. "On penguins, I mean."

"Of course," said Pidpaly slowly. "As long as I get it back."

Going into the next room – which, seen through the open door, was clearly a study – he bent over a great writing desk and rummaged in one of the drawers. At long last he straightened up and came back with a fat loose-leaf file.

"Here we are," he said, putting it down on the table. "It won't all be of interest, of course, but if some of it is, I'll be happy."

"May I perhaps do something in return?" asked Viktor, anxious to show appreciation, but uncertain how.

"Yes," confided the penguinologist quietly, "what you could do, when you return my manuscript, is bring a couple of kilograms of potatoes."

28

Two weeks passed. Sonya grew accustomed to the new flat and asked less often about Daddy. Viktor became accustomed to Sonya, as he had earlier to Misha. But he often thought of her father, having no idea what was happening to him, or even if he was still alive.

The window looked out on winter. Some evenings, when it was dark and not many people were about, he took Sonya and Misha for a walk. They strolled the waste area by the three dovecotes, snow crunching beneath their feet. Sometimes stray mongrels came running up to Misha, and instead of barking, sniffed this strange, unresponsive creature in silence. Waving her arms and puffing out her cheeks, Sonya would rush at them and off they would run, leaving her happy.

Viktor had read the whole of Pidpaly's manuscript. A lot of

it was beyond him, but he had still discovered useful things. He made a note of the most important pages and had them photocopied at the nearest bookshop, after which he put the manuscript in a prominent place in the kitchen, to be returned in the near future.

Work was also advancing. The folder he had received from the Chief had been duly processed, and twelve new *obelisks* lay on the window ledge awaiting their appointed hour. They had given him trouble, the Chief's underlinings having proved too extensive for the *obelisk* as elaborated and perfected by Viktor. It had meant altering the rhythm, adding pace, and presenting the underlinings as brief biographical inserts, which made them look more like quotes from an indictment.

With this batch completed, he was struck for the first time by the thought that only one of his obituaries – an unplanned one – had had as subject an unsullied victim, with no fact or hint suggestive of a dubious past. Yuliya Parkhomenko, the singer, was who he had in mind. But now he had his doubts. He recalled the allusion to involvement in the disappearance of another artiste . . . And her love for the late Yakornitsky . . . No. The pure and sinless did not exist, or else died unnoticed and with no obituary. The idea seemed persuasive. Those who merited obituaries had usually achieved things, fought for their ideals, and when locked in battle, it wasn't easy to remain entirely honest and upright. Today's battles were all for material gain, anyway. The crazy idealist was extinct – survived by the crazy pragmatist . . .

District Militiaman Sergey had phoned a number of times, and the previous Sunday they had been for another picnic on the Dnieper ice, only now with Sonya. A pleasant time had been had by all. Misha swam to his heart's content in the broad ice-hole. Viktor and Sergey drank cognac-laced coffee, lying on the same quilted blanket. Sonya had the Pepsi Cola and sweets that had been bought for her. And all three watched the ice-hole from which Misha would leap as if bitten, becoming airborne for a metre or so before landing, comically, on the ice, and hurrying back to the blanket. Sonya would towel him solicitously, and he would then comically pick his way back to the hole.

They sat there almost till dusk, then had to hurry across the grey-blue ice of the frozen Dnieper to the *Zaporozhets*, parked as before, by the lower Monastery Gardens.

After which the week began again as usual, except that Viktor was conscious of additional concerns now that he was responsible for Sonya, and they began to eat better as a consequence. He took to buying German fruit yogurts and fresh vegetables, and the penguin's fare included frozen shrimps, which he relished.

"Why haven't you got a telly?" Sonya asked one day. "Don't you like cartoons?"

"No, I don't," said Viktor.

"I do," the little girl answered gravely.

New Year approached. Trees decorated with toys appeared in the shops. In Kreshchatik Street they were assembling the National Tree from smaller firs. People were looking more relaxed, and the papers contained hardly anything about shootings or bomb blasts. It was as if the whole of Kiev, regardless of profession, was on holiday.

Viktor had already bought Sonya's New Year present and hidden it in a cupboard. It was a Barbie doll. Together they selected a little fir tree with a base, took it back to the flat and decorated it with ribbons and old toys found in the attic.

"Do you believe in Grandfather Frost?" he asked once.

"Yes," she said in surprise, "don't you?"

"Yes," said Viktor.

"Wait for New Year – he's bound to bring you something," she promised.

29

Leaving Sonya at the flat, Viktor shopped at the food store, and travelled out to Pidpaly's.

Again it was a blue-tracksuited Pidpaly who came to the door, and he was barefoot.

"All for me?" he asked, delightedly examining Viktor's edible gifts. "You really shouldn't have."

At the bottom of the bag, under all the purchases, was the penguinologist's file, which Viktor handed back with thanks.

"Any use to you?"

"A great help."

"Sit down. I'll make some tea," said Pidpaly, bustling about.

It turned out to be green. Pidpaly passed it to him in a bowl, setting down a little box of chipped sugar of heaven alone knew what provenance, such as Viktor had seen only in old films.

Snapping off a piece, he washed it down with the tea, and took a sly look at the little box.

"Doesn't spoil, you see," said Pidpaly, following the direction of his gaze. "Ages back I bought three loaves, and I've still got some . . . Time was, there was more shape, more taste to things. Remember Capital Meat Loaf?"

Viktor shook his head.

"Missed out on the time of abundance, you have," said the old man regretfully. "Every century there's five years of abundance, after which everything goes to pot . . . You won't see the next five, I'm afraid – I certainly won't. But I did at least come in for one lot. How's the penguin?"

"Fine," said Viktor. "You remember you mentioned penguin psychology."

"I do indeed."

"Just how much do they understand?"

"They're quick to distinguish mood – in people and other animals, of course. Apart from that, they're very unforgiving. They've also a good memory for anything good. But their psychology, you understand, is far more complex than, say, a dog or a cat's. They're more intelligent, more secretive; capable of concealing feelings and affections."

Having drunk his tea, Viktor jotted down his telephone number on a piece of paper.

"If you want anything, ring," he said, handing it to the penguinologist.

"Thank you, thank you. And you ring, too, and come and see me."

As the old man got up, Viktor again noticed that his feet were bare.

"Won't you catch cold?" he asked.

"No," Pidpaly assured him. "I do yoga. I've a book with photographs – all Indian yogis go barefoot."

"Only because India has no winter, and shoes are expensive," Viktor said, letting himself out. "Goodbye."

"Happy New Year!" called Pidpaly after his departing visitor.

30

Waking very early a few days before New Year, Viktor noticed three large brightly wrapped parcels under the tree in the living room. He looked in at Sonya. She was still asleep.

Who had put them there? Sonya or Grandfather Frost?

He washed, went to the kitchen, and there on the table was an envelope.

This, on top of an uneasy night's sleep, was the limit.

He remembered dreaming he had been hiding from someone at dead of night in a strange flat, listening tensely to a silence occasionally broken by faint footsteps and the squeaking of doors. The envelope was sealed. He cut off one end with scissors, and clearly written in block-capitals, read:

HAPPY NEW YEAR! MY THANKS FOR SONYA. HER PRESENTS

AND YOURS ARE UNDER THE TREE. NAMESAKE'S PRESENT

IS IN THE FREEZER. HOPING NEW YEAR WILL BRING YOU

SOME RELIEF. SORRY I CAN'T POP IN . . .

TILL THEN — MISHA.

Viktor looked around, bewildered, as if expecting to see who had brought it.

He went and tried the door. It was, as usual, double-locked on the inside.

Shrugging, he returned to the kitchen. What had occurred was as inexplicable as it was blatant, and left him totally perplexed. His locks no longer protected him, whether sleeping or awake, and in case of danger would be useless.

He was not so much alarmed as amazed.

Outside, cottony snow was gliding down at an angle to the wind.

31

When Sonya woke, she was delighted to find presents under the tree.

"You see!" she said. "Grandfather Frost! He could come again."

Viktor gave a knowing smile.

After breakfast Sonya wanted to open her presents, but he stopped her.

"Mine's there too," he said, squatting down in front of her, "but it's only the 29th! Two more days to go!"

Reluctantly she agreed to wait.

While Sonya busied herself telling Misha a fairy story in the bedroom, Viktor made coffee, then sat, cup in hand, at the table facing the window.

The year that was ending had brought much that was strange into his life. And it was ending strangely, engendering mixed feelings and thoughts. Loneliness had given way to a kind of semi-loneliness, a kind of semi-dependence. His own sluggish life force had borne him as on a wave to a strange island, where suddenly he had acquired responsibilities and money to discharge them. Remaining, in the process, remote from events and even from life itself, he had made no effort to grasp what was taking place around him. Until recently, with the arrival of Sonya. And even now, life around him was still dangerously unfathomable, as if he had missed the actual moment when the nature of events might have been fathomed.

His world was now him, Penguin Misha and Sonya, but so vulnerable did it seem, this little world, that should anything happen, it would be beyond his power to protect it. Not for lack of a weapon or karate skills, but simply because, containing no genuine attachment, no sense of unity, no woman, it was too ready to crumble. Sonya was someone else's little girl temporarily in his care, his penguin was sickly and sad, and under no obligation to show gratitude doggy-fashion, wagging his tail after fresh-frozen fish.

His reflections interrupted by the phone, he went back to the living room to answer it.

It was the Chief.

"Coming round for half an hour. All right?"

"Fine," said Viktor.

He peeped into the bedroom. Sonya and the penguin were standing facing each other.

"Have you understood what I've said?" she was asking, and her tone was insistent.

They were, he now saw, much the same height.

"Very well," said Sonya, "and then I'll make you a new suit in quite a different colour . . ."

Smiling, he tiptoed away. An hour later the Chief arrived, and spent a long time shaking snow from his long overcoat before finally coming in.

"Happy New Year!" he said, putting down a heavy carrier bag.

They went through into the kitchen, where Igor Lvovich pulled from his bag a bottle of champagne, a lemon, a couple of tins and several packages.

He called for a cutting board and knives, and together they sliced sausage, cheese and baguette. After which Viktor fetched glasses.

"Got a cat, have you?" the Chief asked, noting the fish head in the bowl on the little bedside table by the stove.

"No, a penguin."

He laughed. "You're joking!"

"I'm not. Come and see."

Viktor took him to the bedroom.

"And who's this then?" asked the Chief, seeing the little girl. "Didn't you say you weren't married?"

"It's Sonya!" she said, eyeing the strange uncle. "And this," she said, pointing at the penguin, "is Misha."

"Daughter of a friend," murmured Viktor so that Sonya shouldn't hear.

The Chief inclined his head.

"Pity I didn't know about the penguin," he said, back in the kitchen. "My youngest has only seen them in books."

"Bring him another time."

"Another time?" the Chief repeated thoughtfully. "Yes, of course. This year he's been with my wife in Italy. It's quieter there."

Head back, gaze directed at the ceiling, the Chief restrained the cork from flying there, and poured champagne.

"Happy New Year!" he said.

Viktor raised his glass. "Happy New Year!"

"Where are you seeing it in?" the Chief asked after a gulp of champagne.

"Here."

Prodding his fork into the salami, the Chief nodded, shooting Viktor another of his looks, this time one of concern.

"You see," he said, "I've got some rather unseasonable news for you . . . But it's the way it's turned out."

Viktor looked at him intently.

"They're on to you. They're pumping people in my office as

to who our *obelisk* writer is. It's good that no one knows, apart from Fyodor and me."

"What are they on to me for?" Viktor asked, putting down his champagne half drunk.

"The fact is," the Chief said hesitantly, carefully choosing his words, "that you, Viktor, have done us proud . . . Getting in all my underlinings, I mean. In actual fact, each obituary, apart from mentioning the late lamented's sins, has hinted where those advantaged by his death are to be looked for. Evidently someone's guessed what the game is – that they're simply being set on collision courses. Still, we've achieved quite a lot. And we'll do better. We'll just have to change tactics."

"*We?* The paper, you mean?" asked Viktor, utterly dismayed, trying to remember where he had heard about *collision courses* before.

"Not just us," the Chief said gently. "And not so much us as a paper even, but as a body of people endeavouring to clean this country up a bit . . . Don't worry, though – our security's on to whoever's on to you. But to give time for our boys to cope, you'll need to lie low for a while."

"When?" Viktor asked, flabbergasted.

"The sooner the better," came the calm reply.

Viktor sat at the table, a picture of dejection.

"Nothing to be afraid of. Fear's dangerous," said Igor Lvovich. "Best be thinking where to lie low . . . And don't tell me. Just give the odd ring. OK?"

Viktor nodded mechanically.

"And now let's drink to all going well at my end," said the Chief topping up their glasses. "If it does, *you* won't be the loser, I promise."

Reluctantly Viktor raised his glass.

"Drink up!" urged the Chief. "There's no escaping fate. Drink while the champagne lasts!"

Viktor took a gulp, and almost choked as bubbles of gas prickled his nose.

"I wouldn't be here now, if I didn't value you highly," Igor Lvovich said, preparing to leave and donning his long dark-green overcoat. "Ring in a week or so. No work for the time being, so you find some nice secluded spot and lie doggo."

The door banged. The Chief's footsteps died away, leaving Viktor to an uneasy silence and musings much inhibited by the champagne he had drunk. He stood staring at the closed door, trying again to solve the riddle of the nocturnal Grandfather Frost who had brought news and presents from Misha-non-penguin.

"Uncle Vik!" called Sonya from the living room. "Uncle Vik! He knocked me over!"

Returning to the present, he quickly went to her.

"What happened?" he asked, looking down at her lying on the floor.

"Nothing," she said, with a guilty smile.

Beside her stood Misha, *regardant*.

"I was trying to see what your present was, and he knocked me over," she confessed at last. "I wasn't looking at mine. Just taking a peep at yours."

"Up you get," said Viktor, giving her his hand.

Sonya got to her feet.

"Can I go for a walk?"

"No," he snapped.

"Just a teeny-weeny one."

But why not? There were plenty of children around.

"All right, but not for long, and don't go away from the block."

Having put her into her fur coat and muffled her up to her eyes in her scarf, he let Sonya go, settled himself at the kitchen table, and became lost in thought. With every day bringing far from pleasant surprises, he had plenty to ponder.

32

He was seized with sudden panic. He was still sitting at the table, the champagne finished, the sausage eaten, the slight feeling of intoxication gone. His head was clear, his legs steady.

He looked out of the window. The snow had eased enough for him to see, down below, several children from the block busy building a snow castle.

Standing on the little bedside table, he stuck his head out of the small vent and shouted, "Sonya! Home! Quick!"

The children looked up from building their castle, but they all stayed standing where they were.

Hard as he stared, he couldn't see Sonya among them. Quickly putting on his sheepskin coat and fur hat, he dashed from the flat. Spotting some other children a short distance from the block, he ran towards them, but there was no Sonya.

Hearing an engine start up behind him, he swung round. An old Mercedes was moving off from the block opposite. Something prompted him to give chase. Managing by some miracle not to fall, he caught it up at the turning before the exit to the road, but here, feet skidding beneath him, he fell forward onto the boot, to the consternation of the driver, the sole occupant of the car. Picking himself up, Viktor walked back to the block.

He had been foolish to let her go out, after what the Chief had said.

At the top of the stairs, he found her leaning against the door of the flat.

"Where have you been?" he shouted.

"At Anya's, on the ground floor," she said guiltily. "She was showing me her Sindy doll."

He ought to punish her in some way, he thought, but gradually he grew calmer.

"Like something to eat?" he asked.

"Has Misha eaten?"

"No."

"Then we can eat together," she said happily.

33

After supper Viktor rang Sergey Fischbein-Stepanenko, asking him to come as soon as he could. He did, and they shut themselves in the kitchen, leaving Sonya and Misha in the living room.

Viktor thought first of inventing some cover story for Sergey's benefit, but in the end saw the stupidity of doing so. Why, when needing help, bring in deceit? The account he gave, if lacking in coherence, found Sergey quick on the uptake.

"I've got a dacha," he said. "One of an MVD group. There's a public phone, a fireplace and a TV, and food in the cellar . . . Why not celebrate New Year there?"

"But where were you planning to celebrate it?" Viktor asked cautiously.

Sergey shrugged. "Nowhere," he said. "You know the extent of my intimate circle."

"And your mother?"

"Won't have anything to do with New Year. Doesn't like festive occasions. When would you like to go?"

"The sooner the better. Today?"

Sergey looked out of the window. It was getting dark.

"Right, but I must pop home first as I haven't got the keys with me." He rose from the table. "Back in an hour. You get your things together."

After seeing him out, Viktor looked into the living room.

"Sonya," he said, squatting down in front of her, "we're going away."

"When do we come back?"

"In a few days."

"What if Grandfather Frost comes and we're not here?"

"He's got keys," said Viktor. "He'll leave his presents under the tree."

"Will there be a tree where we're going?"

Viktor shook his head.

"Then I shan't go," she declared firmly.

He sighed a deep sigh.

"Listen," he said sternly. "When Daddy comes back, I shall tell him how naughty you've been."

"And I shall tell him you don't read to me, or buy me ice-creams," vowed Sonya.

Finding the reproach justified, Viktor fell silent.

"OK," he said after a while. "You're absolutely right. But

we're expected. We can take our tree with us, if you like."

"Is Misha coming?"

"Of course."

"OK."

Together they removed the decorations and toys from the tree, and wrapped them in paper.

"We'll take the presents, too," Sonya insisted, and obediently Viktor put them into a shopping bag.

"Wait," she said, suddenly stopping. "What if Grandfather Frost comes and there's no tree, where will he put his presents?"

He was at a loss. No sensible answer suggested itself. He felt infinitely weary.

"Perhaps we should paint a fir tree on the wall to tell him where," said Sonya, pondering the matter aloud. "Got any green paint?"

"No," said Viktor. "I know what – we'll leave a note in the kitchen saying put them on the table."

Sonya thought.

"*Under* is better."

"Why?"

"So nobody sees."

That settled, Viktor wrote the note. Sonya read it syllable by syllable, and gave it back with a nod of approval.

Down below a car hooted. Viktor looked out, and in the late afternoon gloom, was just able to make out the familiar *Zaporozhets*.

First he carried down the tree, trussed in washing-line, together with a shopping bag of toys and presents, and a carrier bag of food from the freezer; then he and Sonya went down, he with Misha in his arms.

"I've brought a couple more blankets," said Sergey in the car. "Until the place heats up, it'll be cold."

Misha and Sonya sat at the back, Viktor in front. Misha edged closer to Sonya when the engine started, as if scared by the noise. Seeing them in the mirror snuggled up together, Viktor nudged Sergey and pointed. Adjusting the mirror to this amusing rear-seat idyll, Sergey gave a weary smile and accelerated away.

34

At the entrance to the dacha plots was a hut from which two men in camouflaged combat gear emerged, walked around the *Zaporozhets*, and took a good look inside. Sergey wound down the window.

"Dacha 7."

"Carry on," said one of the guards.

They stopped outside a little brick-built house with a steeply angled roof. Sergey got out. Looking into the back before following, Viktor saw that Sonya was asleep.

"Just a mo while I unset the trap," said Sergey.

"What trap?"

"Anti-burglar."

Stooping, and with a creaking of boards, he shifted something in front of the door.

"All's well," he beckoned. "We can enter."

Opening the door to a glassed-in veranda, Sergey switched on the light, throwing a yellow pool onto the snow in front of the house and the car. Sonya woke, rubbed her eyes, and turned to Misha, around whom she had had her arm for the whole of the journey. Sensing she was awake, he turned towards her and they looked hard at one another.

In no time they were all sitting in a cold room before a dead hearth, with a single bulb dispensing light and an illusion of warmth from the ceiling.

Sergey brought wood, built it into a wigwam in the hearth, and inserted a lighted newspaper.

The flames took hold, and slowly began to radiate heat.

Misha, who had tucked himself away in a far corner, suddenly livened up and came and stood in front of the fire.

"Uncle Vik," yawned Sonya, "when are we going to see to the tree?"

"Tomorrow morning," said Viktor.

The small room contained a settee and an armchair facing the fire, and against the left-hand wall, a bed.

They put Sonya on the settee close to the fire with the two blankets over her, and she soon fell asleep, leaving Viktor, Sergey and Misha to keep vigil by the blazing hearth. Sergey added more wood. Apart from the occasional hiss of moisture issuing from the logs, there wasn't a sound.

Viktor perched on the edge of the settee, Sergey sat in the armchair, and Misha, not taught by nature how to sit, stood.

"I'm off to work tomorrow," said Sergey. "I'll get champagne and some meat afterwards and come back."

Viktor nodded.

"It's so quiet here," he said dreamily. "A silence to sit and write in."

"No one's stopping you," Sergey said amiably.

"Life is," said Viktor, after a silence.

"It is you who's made it complicated . . . Let's have a smoke on the veranda."

Viktor went, though he didn't smoke. After the slightly warmed air of the living room, the veranda was like a refrigerator, but invigorating.

Sergey exhaled a stream of smoke towards the low ceiling. "Look," he said, "if you're in that sort of a mess, why drag a small girl around with you?"

"Her father seems to be in the same boat. I've no idea where he is. So what can I do?"

Sergey shrugged. "Ah, we're not alone," he said a minute later, looking out of the window.

Two windows were shining bright in the darkness.

"Like some cherry brandy?" Sergey asked suddenly.

"Rather!"

"They went through to the tiny ice-cold kitchen, where there was just a stand with an electric hotplate and a small table with two stools. Sergey raised a rectangle of wooden floor and thrust a torch at Viktor.

"Light me down," he told him, and Viktor obeyed.

Lowering himself into the cellar, Sergey passed up two old champagne bottles corked with babies' dummies, then climbed back up.

They sat straight down in the kitchen, filled cut-glass tumblers with cherry brandy, and drank in leisurely fashion, listening to the silence. Sergey went to put more wood on the fire.

"Is she asleep?" Viktor asked when he returned.

"Yes."

"And Misha?

"Keeping an eye on the fire," Sergey grinned. "Well, shall we drink to the New Year?"

With a sigh Viktor grasped his glass. That, too, was cold.

"As a butcher friend of mine was wont to say," continued Sergey, "*Let's drink to not being worse off. We have known better days.*"

35

Next morning Sergey left for Kiev, and Viktor filled a bucket from the water pipe running overground through the plots. After putting the kettle on the electric hotplate, he looked into the living room. The fire had burnt itself out in the night, but warmth and a scent of pine remained. Sonya was asleep and smiling. Misha stood brooding over the heap of black ash in the hearth.

Viktor slapped his thigh, and as Misha turned, half opened the door and beckoned.

"Come," he whispered.

With a backward look at the dead hearth, Misha came waddling.

"Hungry? Of course you are. Come on, let's go out."

From the shopping bag he took a couple of plaice, which he laid on the top step.

"Tuck in!"

Misha came out onto the step, and swivelled his head left and right, taking in his surroundings. Descending to the snow, he marched around in a circle and headed towards the trees, but coming up against the water pipe, turned back, his tracks not unlike those of crooked skis, describing irregular geometric figures on the clean page of snow. Returning, he edged round the steps, and treating the topmost as a table, addressed himself to the fish.

Well pleased at such a display of animation, Viktor proceeded to the kitchen and made tea. He looked into the living room. Sonya was still sleeping and he didn't want to wake her.

He sat with his cup of tea at the kitchen table. On the window ledge beside him stood the two bottles of cherry brandy, one half empty, the other full. Romantic thoughts stirred in the silence, touching again on unwritten novels and the past. He suddenly had the sensation of being abroad, out of reach of yesterday's existence. This abroad was a place of tranquillity, a Switzerland of the soul blanketed in snows of peace, permeated with a dread of causing disturbance; where no bird sang or called, as if out of no desire to.

At a sound from the veranda door, he went to investigate, and came face to face with Misha, who, seeing Viktor, comically bowed his head, giving him to understand that he liked it here. Ample food and suitably cold, Viktor decided, pleased at his friend's good spirits.

Soon after, Sonya woke, putting an end to silence and reflection. First he must give her breakfast, then get to work on the tree.

The tree took more than an hour, but finally there it stood, decked with ribbons and toys, in trampled snow and less than lofty splendour, with Misha beside it, keeping an eye on events.

Sonya walked back to see how it looked from the dacha.

"Like it?"

"Yes!" she said, delighted.

They made a tour of the little garden, then went back in. Viktor re-lit the fire, and Sonya settled down in the armchair with a pencil and an exercise book she had found.

Towards five, when it was dark and the room was warm, suffused with the yellow light of the single ceiling bulb, Sergey returned. He dumped two shopping bags on the veranda, then parked his car behind the dacha.

"Brought you the latest," he said, handing Viktor a bundle of newspapers. "I've got a couple of bottles of champagne and one of pepper vodka – in case of colds. Will that be enough?"

"Ample," said Viktor, opening out the first of the papers.

BANKER MURDERED

ATTEMPTED ASSASSINATION OF STATE DEPUTY

The headlines jolted him back to reality. Skimming both articles, he tried to think. The banker's name rang no bell. He was not *obelisk*-carded. The State Deputy – *only wounded*, albeit in the head – was.

"Look, old friend," said Sergey, "I didn't bring these to furrow your brow!"

Viktor let the papers slide to the floor by the hearth. "They'll do for fire-lighting," he said.

"Quite right! News you can't read calmly, don't read at all!" said Sergey. Then, turning to Sonya in her armchair, he asked, "And what are you up to?"

"Drawing a stove."

"Show me."

He studied the drawing in the exercise book, and turned to her with a puzzled expression.

"Why's the fire black?"

"It's not, it's grey," she corrected. "Because I only found one pencil."

80

"Didn't look hard enough," said Sergey. "OK, tomorrow we'll both look. There must be others – my niece brought some."

They fried potatoes, made a good supper, then settled Sonya for the night.

"I shan't sleep," she warned. "I shall watch the fire, and if it goes out, I'll call."

Leaving it at that, they sat at the kitchen table and retrieved yesterday's cut-glass tumblers from the window ledge. Sergey filled them, and dropped the empty bottle on the floor.

"One more day, and that's it," said Sergey. "Then back to the same old thing, except that the year will be new."

At two in the morning they were still sitting, hotplate glowing red for warmth. Though the second bottle was empty, they felt unjustifiably sober. Only indolence kept Sergey from the second visit to the cellar that seemed highly desirable.

Suddenly an explosion set the windows rattling and made them start up in alarm.

"Shall we go and see?" Viktor asked uncertainly.

Sergey looked into the living room. Sonya was muttering in her sleep. The fire was burning low.

"Yes," he said, returning to the kitchen. Standing on the top step they found Misha.

"Seems to be asleep," whispered Viktor, after bending to look.

Voices broke the silence. Words couldn't be distinguished, but the intonation was one of alarm. Snow crunched beneath the feet of people invisible in the darkness. The cones of light shed by solitary lamps at 100-metre intervals along the main avenue had merely the effect of provoking the darkness into closing in more impenetrably.

"Come on," called Sergey, now more decisive.

"But where?"

"Not far."

Coming to one of the footpaths that served to delimit the plots, they followed it for 100 metres or so, before stopping and listening.

"Over there!" Sergey pointed in the direction of voices made louder by the silence of the night.

As they made their way towards the voices, they saw the beam of a powerful torch moving slowly over the snow.

"Local man," they heard a wheezy voice declare.

"That's Grandpa Vanya, dacha caretaker," Sergey whispered. Advancing, they made themselves known.

"What's up, Vanya?" Sergey enquired.

"The old story," said the caretaker, directing the beam of his massive accumulator-powered torch at a body lying on the snow. The snow, Viktor saw, was red, and the body minus a leg and an arm. The latter, torn off at the elbow, lay some distance away, still in its padded sleeve.

Two men, one tall and wearing a tracksuit, the other slightly shorter, bearded and wearing a down jacket, were standing there saying nothing.

Someone could be heard running, stamping down the snow as he came, and a man dressed in camouflage combat gear and holding an automatic pistol came over to them and halted, breathing hard.

"What's up?" he panted.

"This," said the caretaker, directing the beam of his torch at the body lying face down in the snow. "Local man. Out stealing. Trod on a mine."

"Ah," said Camouflage Suit, putting away his weapon. "Killed in furtherance of attempted burglary."

A dog burst suddenly out of the darkness, darted, tail wagging, around the caretaker's legs, went and sniffed the corpse, then, snatching up the arm in its jaws, raced away into the darkness.

"Druzhok! Stop, damn you!" shouted the caretaker, but as the echo played back his hoarseness, he fell silent.

"Do we report it?" asked Camouflage Suit.

"What the hell for?" asked Down Jacket with Beard. "We didn't come to have our holiday messed up giving evidence!"

"So what do we do?" the caretaker asked of no one in particular.

"Cover him with snow, tramp it down, and leave him till after the holiday," Camouflage Suit suggested, after a moment's thought.

As his leg was jabbed suddenly from behind, Viktor started forward, thinking it to be Druzhok returned from burying tomorrow's breakfast, but it was Misha.

Viktor squatted down in front of him. "How did you get here?" he asked. "I thought you were asleep."

"Whatever have you got there?" Camouflage Suit asked coming over. "Not a penguin? Hell's bells! So you have!"

"Ruddy marvel!" laughed the man in the tracksuit. "Ruddy marvel!"

In next to no time, all were crowded round Misha, the corpse in the snow forgotten.

"Is he tame?" asked Down Jacket with Beard.

"Not very," said Viktor.

"What do you call him?" asked the caretaker.

"Misha."

"Ah, Misha, little Misha," coaxed the caretaker hoarsely. Then, turning to those assembled, said, "All right, off you go.

And if there's a bottle in it, I'll cover him over."

"There will be," Down Jacket with Beard promised. "Pop in first thing tomorrow."

Viktor, Sergey and Misha followed the boundary footpath back.

"Are all the dachas here mined?" Viktor asked.

"Not all," replied Sergey. "I've got a different, more humane sort of trap."

"What sort?"

"Ship's siren. Wake every village around, that would!"

The snow crunched under their feet. Cold stars pierced the clear, immeasurably deep sky. There was no moon and the night seemed the darker for it.

"Here we are then." Sergey stopped at the steps and looked round at Viktor and the penguin who were following. "Ah, you've decorated the tree!" he said in surprise. "I missed that when I drove in. Well done!"

The veranda door creaked, after which silence fell once more over the dacha plots.

The room was warm. Ash glowed in the hearth. Sonya was sleeping and smiling.

Not feeling sleepy, Viktor and Sergey shut themselves in the kitchen again.

36

Next morning Sergey and Viktor devoted themselves to preparations for New Year. The first thing was to bring the ancient television down from its hiding place in the loft. They put it in the warm living room, plugged it in and got it working. As good luck would have it, cartoons were showing, and Sonya settled herself in the armchair to watch.

From the cellar they brought up a three-litre jar of cucumbers, tomatoes and peppers, jointly pickled, two more bottles of cherry brandy and a couple of kilos of potatoes.

"What we have to do now," said Sergey, rubbing his palms together with satisfaction, "is see to the meat and get wood for the bonfire."

Time dragged, as if the year was no longer in a hurry to depart.

When the meat had been cut up and left to marinate, wood chopped and built into a nice little stack near the tree, and other minor tasks completed, it was still only midday by the clock.

It was sunny and frosty. Misha stood on the top step watching a tiny flock of bullfinches wandering over the snow.

"How about a glass?" Sergey suggested, and sitting down at the kitchen table, they poured themselves cherry brandy.

"To time – and may it fly," proposed Sergey, clinking glasses with Viktor.

The toast did the trick, and time did go a little faster. After lunch all save the penguin lay down for a rest, and even Sonya made no objection to Sergey's switching off the TV and declaring a quiet hour.

When they woke, it was dark and the clock said 5.30.

"That was a good sleep!" said Sergey, stepping outside and rubbing his somewhat puffy face with snow to freshen up, as a result of which it turned lobster-red.

Viktor, in similar need, did the same.

Sonya came out, looked on in amazement at the two grown-up uncles braving the cold, then retreated into the dacha.

Until nine she watched TV, while Sergey and Viktor played cards. Then they broke off and got the bonfire ready for the New Year kebabs.

"What," asked Sonya, coming out for another look, "have a penguin and the telly got in common?"

Sergey and Viktor exchanged glances.

"Both sleep standing?" Viktor suggested.

"Both black and white," she said, closing the veranda door behind her.

As the fire blazed, Sergey threaded the pieces of meat onto skewers. Viktor stood and watched.

"Do we eat them this year, or next?" he asked jokingly.

"Start them this year, and finish them next," said Sergey. "We've got two kilos of meat!"

When all was prepared, they sat and watched the old favourite *Diamond Arm* on TV. Sonya dropped off before the end, and the friends decided not to wake her until New Year. They moved the kitchen table to the veranda, also the hotplate, and while it warmed the air, spread an old cloth and laid the table. They made a centre piece of the two bottles of champagne and a two-litre bottle of Pepsi, opened the tinned fish, and sliced the cheese and sausage, giving the table a genuinely festive look.

"And one for Misha," declared Sergey, carrying in the low magazine table.

He put it beside their table, and fetched a large dish.

"Poor Misha," he sighed. "Never known a hot meal, or strong drink. Perhaps we should pour him a glass, for the hell of it."

Viktor objected vehemently.

"Sorry, I wasn't serious. What's the time?"

"Nearly eleven."

"In Moscow they'll be clinking glasses already. We can take our seats," said Sergey. "Do we wake Sonya? Or limber up first?"

"Limber up first," said Viktor fetching the already opened bottle of cherry brandy from the kitchen.

Limbering-up completed, Viktor woke Sonya, who at once asked for the TV to be switched on. The voice of the announcer, though unintelligible out on the veranda, seemed, in a strange way, to brighten the proceedings.

"Why hasn't *he* got anything?" she asked, looking at Misha standing beside them.

Dipping into his shopping bag, Viktor brought out a bulging, brightly coloured paper carrier.

"This is his New Year present really," he said, feeling inside, "but we'll take it that it's already New Year in the Antarctic!"

What then emerged was a trade pack, which had to be slit open with a knife, after which Viktor emptied the contents into a large dish on the occasional table.

For a moment all stood in silence, staring – as well they might – at a small octopus, a starfish, king prawns, a lobster and other denizens of the deep now in process of defrosting. Misha, coming to the table to see what his present was, seemed equally amazed.

"You've been lashing out!" said Sergey under his breath. "More than I've ever eaten the like of !"

"Not me, her father – it's from him," whispered Viktor, turning to see if Sonya was listening.

She wasn't. She was leaning forward, pointing at the starfish.

"That's a star," she told Misha, then, pointing to the lobster, "I don't know what that is."

They sat down at the table. The penguin started on the king

prawns without waiting for any special signal. As the television chimes rang out in the living room, Sergey seized a bottle, unwired the cork and gave the bottle a shake. The cork shot out with a pop, and champagne flowed into the cut-glass tumblers. Viktor poured Sonya's Pepsi.

Coloured rockets crackled into the sky from other dacha plots and descended, bathing the winter scene now in green light, now in red. Mingled with the noise of rockets was the sound of actual shots.

"Tokarev semi-automatic," Sergey observed knowledgeably.

The New Year had arrived. The bonfire blazed, lighting up tree and decorations. Rockets shot up from various points around. And in the glassed-in veranda celebrations proceeded apace, with Sergey and Viktor doing justice to the champagne, and Sonya – the Pepsi. Misha, temporarily forgotten, was still standing at his little table. Having finished the prawns, he was sizing up the small octopus.

Once the bonfire had burnt down, they transferred the embers to an iron brazier over which they laid the first three kebabs.

"But the presents – where are my presents?" asked Sonya, coming back to earth.

Viktor reached again into the shopping bag, and brought out two wrapped presents from Misha-non-penguin, and his own, unwrapped, Barbie doll.

"No, not like that!" said Sonya. "Put them all under the tree!"

Dutifully he carried them out.

"There was one for you, too!" she reminded him.

After laying her presents on the snow under the tree, he went back to the veranda. Feeling in the shopping bag for his own present, he was aghast at its shape and weight. Still holding it in the bag, he stripped the coloured paper off, and came to cold metal. There was no doubt about it. Misha-non-penguin's present was a gun. His hands trembled. Without giving it a look, he rewrapped it and zipped up the bag.

"Well, where is it?" shouted Sonya. "We've got to open them together!"

"Forgot it. Left it at home," he shouted back.

Sonya gestured despairingly and gave him a look such as grown-ups reserve for offending children.

"Really! A great big man like you, and you forget!"

But Viktor had gone to join Sergey, who was squatting by the brazier turning the kebabs.

"Come on, show us your presents, Sonya," Sergey called.

She crawled under the tree and sat on the snow. A tearing of paper followed. Viktor went over and bent down to look.

"What is it?" he asked, calmer now, doing his best to feign curiosity.

"A toy," said Sonya.

"What sort? Show me."

"A speaking clock. Like I've seen. Here, listen."

"*0100 hours precisely,*" said a metallic female voice.

"And what this is, I've no idea," she muttered, feeling the second present.

Coming from under the tree, she held it out to Viktor.

"What is it?" she asked.

He took it from her. It was a very fat bundle of dollars, held together by elastic bands.

"What is it?" she repeated.

"Money," Viktor said quietly, staring dumbfounded.

"Money?" asked Sergey, joining them.

Bending to look, he started back, thunderstruck.

"It's all hundreds!" he whispered.

"Can I buy things now?" Sonya asked.

"You can," said Viktor.

"A telly?"

"Yes."

"A little house for Barbie?"

"That, too."

"OK, give it to me," she said, taking the bundle of dollars from Viktor. "I'll put it in the dacha."

She climbed the veranda steps.

Sergey gave Viktor quite a look.

"From her father," Viktor said, answering his unspoken question.

Biting his bottom lip, Sergey went and squatted down by the brazier.

"Shame I never had a kind Daddy like that," he whispered.

Viktor wasn't listening. He had a new load on his mind. Presents from Misha-non-penguin entailed obligations, or so it seemed. He remembered his *you answer for her with your life* . . . Rubbish, he thought. Some sort of New Year insanity. Why do I need a gun? Why does she need all that money?

Sergey touched him on the shoulder. "Listen," he said, "I reckon you've been engaged as tutor . . . And she'll be doing the paying!" He gave a smile. "Our kebabs are ready. We can continue to eat . . ."

Viktor welcomed the diversion. He went up the steps to the veranda. Sergey had already taken in the kebabs.

Viktor looked into the main room to call Sonya, but she was already asleep, one hand resting on the bundle of dollars.

Viktor went out as quietly as he could, shutting doors behind him. He took his place at the veranda table and looked round for the penguin. Misha was standing a little way off.

"Well, how about some vodka with our kebabs?" asked Sergey, opening the bottle.

"Good idea!" Viktor held out his empty glass.

After a kebab each and a fair amount of vodka, they retired to bed, overwhelmed with fatigue.

"*0300 hours precisely*," said the female speaking clock.

37

At getting on for 11.00 the next morning, Viktor was woken by a tapping at the window.

"Your neighbours are here," called a hoarse but cheerful voice. "Happy New Year!"

Going to the window, Viktor saw two young men with girls standing there. The men's faces seemed familiar. He had seen them by the body of the burglar blown up by the mine. Both looked the worse for wear, the girls – not their best.

The one with the beard banged on the window, holding up a bottle of champagne. "Hi! How about a dekko at the penguin?"

Viktor shook the sleeping Sergey.

"We've got visitors!"

"Visitors?" muttered Sergey, but in two minutes he was wide awake.

Soon all were sitting at the table on the veranda. There was plenty of food left and outside, on the extinguished brazier, were the not yet grilled, now refrozen kebabs from the night before.

Having seen their fill of the penguin, the visitors ate, drank and told jokes. Viktor began to find these festivities wearisome and to look forward to their termination. It was not slow in coming. One of the girls suddenly started wailing drunkenly to the effect that she wanted to go to bed, and the visitors very soon left.

Sergey massaged his temples, looking darkly at Viktor. "Work tomorrow," he said sadly.

This set Viktor thinking. He couldn't go back to town yet, and it was too soon to call the Chief.

"Could I stay on a few days more?" he asked.

"Stay forever!" gestured Sergey. "I'm easy. All the better for me – no idiot'll try breaking in."

That evening, in spite of a thumping headache, Sergey set off for Kiev.

"If you need to, ring – there's a public phone, end of main avenue, by the caretaker's place," he said as he left. "I'll tell Security you're here. But I'd be a bit more careful with that wad of hundreds . . . Hide it away somewhere."

Viktor nodded.

The *Zaporozhets* sprang into life and departed. Silence returned. Except for faint sounds from the living room where Sonya was watching a film on TV.

"Shouldn't I look after that money for you?" asked Viktor, perching beside her on the settee.

"Here," she said, handing him the bundle. "Only don't lose it."

Putting the dollars with the gift gun into the shopping bag, he dropped both into the cellar.

38

The next few days passed quietly and uneventfully, apart from the arrival of the local militia to collect the body of the hapless burglar, when, at the request of the caretaker, Vanya, everyone kept indoors. "Not keen to appear as witnesses, are we?" he had asked, and Viktor agreed that he wasn't.

When the militia had gone, Vanya came around with the all-clear.

"It's OK," he said.

"Won't the owner of the dacha be in trouble?" Viktor enquired.

Grandpa Vanya grinned.

"The Colonel? He's just been. Reckoned they'd put the mine there for him, not the thief. *Obvious, he said, wasn't it? Lots of that sort of thing about nowadays.*"

Sonya spent most of her time in front of the TV, and only when something really boring was on did she go outside or potter with the penguin on the veranda.

Viktor found idleness difficult to bear. He wanted to do something, *anything*, however useless. But at the dacha there was nothing to do, and he was miserable, first joining Sonya in front of the TV for a bit, then sitting in the kitchen, to where he had moved back the table and hotplate from the veranda.

Unable, finally, to endure it any more, and telling Sonya not to go out, he went and rang the Chief from the public phone.

It was the secretary who answered.

"Can I speak to Igor Lvovich?"

"I'll take it, Tanya," intervened the familiar voice. "Yes?"

"It's me, Viktor. Can I come back yet?"

"Didn't know you'd gone away," said the Chief, feigning surprise. "Of course. Everything's fine. Come and see me as soon as you can. Got something to show you."

Viktor then rang Sergey asking him to pick them up as soon as possible.

Walking back to the dacha, he was in a happier frame of mind. At last New Year had an aura of holiday about it, albeit of a holiday now past. Again, the crunch of snow, but now it was a cheerful sound. Looking about him, he took in what so far he had not noticed: the sculptural beauty of winter trees, of bullfinches wandering over snow covered with tracks of cat, or dog. And from forgotten depths surfaced a memory of natural history lessons at which, long, long ago, they had learnt to identify animal prints; and of text-book illustrations – *Tracks of the hare* . . . *Hopping* . . . *Bounding* . . . And out of the past, the voice of his first lady teacher: "The hare, when fleeing pursuit, *bounds!*"

39

Leaving the shopping bag with gun and bundle of dollars on top of the wardrobe, and Sonya at home with Misha, Viktor set off for the editorial office.

Smiling smugly, the Chief sat him in an armchair, produced coffee, asked about the New Year festivities, blatantly putting off any mention of business. When, after coffee, a pause ensued which it would clearly have been foolish to fill with idle conversation, he produced a large envelope from his desk drawer.

Keeping his eyes fixed on Viktor, he drew out several photographs and passed them over.

"Take a look. You may know them."

The photos showed two well-dressed corpses. Young men of 25 or so lying on the floor of someone's flat, tidily and obediently supine – no outflung arms, splayed legs or faces distorted by fear or agony. Their faces were calm, indifferent.

"Don't recognize them?"

"No," said Viktor.

"You were their target . . . Here's a memento!" He passed over two more photos.

Viktor saw himself at the little table in the café beneath the Kharkov Opera House; and in the street, also in Kharkov.

"Modest lads," said the Chief, "only one silencer between them . . . Anyway, they didn't get to you. But the negatives are still somewhere in Kharkov . . . I don't think they'll send anyone else, but watch it."

Finally, he handed Viktor a batch of fresh *obelisk* material.

"So, quietly back to work," he said, patting Viktor on the shoulder and seeing him out.

40

In January winter was lazy to the extent of making do with December's snow which, thanks to continuing frost, still blanketed the earth. Shop windows still had their New Year decorations, but the festive spirit had waned, leaving folk alone with the old routine and the future. Viktor was processing his next batch of files. He now received all documents direct from the Chief, Fyodor having retired before the New Year break.

The *obelisk* index was growing steadily. These latest files were on directors of major factories and chairmen of joint-stock companies. Almost all were charged with the theft of funds and their transfer to Western banks. Some were dealing in banned raw materials, others contriving to barter off plant abroad. Facts were legion, but mercifully not all were underlined in the Chief's red pencil. Viktor's task was not easy. He either ran short of philosophy, or lacked inspiration, as each *obelisk* now involved tense hours at the typewriter. And though, in the end, he was pleased with the result, fatigue weighed heavily upon him, leaving little energy to spare for Sonya or the penguin. So it was as well that he had, at Sonya's insistence, bought a colour television on their return from the dacha. And now they came together in front of it, but always with Sonya in charge of the remote control.

"It's my telly!" she said, which Viktor, having in fact bought it with her money, had to concede.

Misha also took an interest in the television, sometimes going right up to the screen and blocking Viktor and Sonya's view. Sonya would then gently lead him off to the bedroom, where he liked to stand in front of the mirror studying his reflection. Viktor was surprised how easily she managed him. Although that was not surprising perhaps, seeing that she spent far more time with him than he did. Several times she even took him for a walk on the waste area by the dovecotes.

One evening the doorbell rang, and seeing a complete stranger through the spyhole, he was filled with alarm. He at once thought back to the photos of the two dead young men who had been after him. Sighing audibly, the stranger, a man of about 40, gave the button another press, jangling the bell right above where Viktor stood with bated breath.

Behind him the living-room door creaked and Sonya called: "Do go to the door. Someone's ringing!"

"Open up. Nothing to be afraid of," came a voice from the other side of the door.

"Who do you want?"

"You! Who else! What are you afraid of? I've come about Misha."

Viktor reached for the lock, wondering which Misha, and finally opened the door.

A thin, unshaven, sharp-nosed man in a Chinese down jacket and a black knitted hat came in. From his pocket, he pulled out a sheet of paper folded in two or three, and passed it to Viktor.

"My calling card," he said with a grin.

An icy shiver ran down Viktor's spine as he unfolded it and held it up to read. It was his *obelisk* on Misha-non-penguin's friend-cum-enemy, Sergey Chekalin.

"Know me now?" asked the visitor coldly.

"Sergey Chekalin," said Viktor, and seeing Sonya still standing in the open door, told her sternly to go back in, before turning again to his visitor.

"Could we sit down somewhere? We need to talk."

Viktor took him into the kitchen, where he sat straight down in Viktor's chair, leaving him to sit opposite.

"Got some bad news," said the visitor. "Misha, I'm sorry to say, is dead. And I've come for his daughter. There's no longer any sense in keeping her hidden. OK?"

Very slowly, bit by bit, what had been said got through to Viktor. But the two basic facts: that Misha was dead and that this man had come for Sonya, somehow refused to connect. He put his hand to his forehead, as if at a sudden stab of pain, and it was as cold as ice.

"How did he die?" Viktor asked suddenly, looking down at the table top, his expression one of dismay.

"How?" Sergey responded. "As they all do, tragically."

"And why does she have to go with you?" Viktor asked after a short pause to collect his thoughts.

"I was his friend. It's my duty to look after her."

Viktor shook his head. The visitor stared, astonished.

"No," said Viktor, his voice suddenly firmer. "Misha wanted *me* to look after her."

"Listen," said his visitor wearily, "with all due respect to your *protection*, you've got it wrong. And can you prove he wanted you to?"

"I have a note from him," Viktor said calmly. "I'll show you."

"Do that."

Viktor went into the living room and searched through a sheaf of papers on the window ledge for Misha's note promising to be back when the dust settled. As he turned to where Sonya and the penguin were absorbed watching figure skating on the TV, he heard the front door bang. He went and poked his head into the kitchen. His visitor had beaten an unceremonious retreat, leaving his obituary on the kitchen table.

A few minutes later an engine started up. Viktor looked out, and in the light of a street lamp, saw a long car just like Misha-non-penguin's moving off.

"What did that man come for?" Sonya asked, looking into the kitchen.

"For you," he said under his breath, without turning to her.

"What did he come for?" she repeated, not having heard.

"Just for a talk."

She went back to the TV, and Viktor sat down at the kitchen table to think – about his life, and Sonya's part in it. An inconspicuous one, it might seem, but one that still bound him to look after her and think about her. Except that *looking after* amounted to no more than food and the odd conversation. Sonya's presence in his life was much like that of Misha the penguin in his flat. Still, when someone had turned up to take her away, alarm had given rise to sudden determination. Again there had been talk of *protection*, of *security*, of which he knew nothing. His life was split in two halves, one known, one unknown. And what was in the other half? What did it consist of? He bit his lip. Riddles were the last thing he wanted to contend with. The Chief's red pencil had trained him in the use of basic facts as starting points for any text or idea. That evening he was hard put to it to determine which of the ideas dancing around inside his head would, when committed to paper, merit red pencil.

41

It was strange, but in a couple of days Viktor had forgotten Sergey Chekalin's visit, being, after a polite telephonic hastener from the Chief, completely absorbed in his work. In brief breaks between *obelisks* he drank tea and thought that he ought to devote more attention to Sonya, take her to the puppet theatre and that sort of thing. But all that would have to be deferred pending more free time. One way he did manage to make the little girl happy was with the ice-cream and other sweets he now purchased in large quantities. Shopping excursions provided his only opportunities for a breath of fresh, frosty air. The more frequently he sallied forth, the happier Sonya and Misha were. Sonya's happiness, unlike Misha's, took vocal expression. More often than not she called him *Uncle Vik*, and that pleased him. But the main thing was that she didn't object to spending most of her time in the flat. And in the evening, when they sat in front of the TV watching the latest episode of a Mexican serial, Viktor had a calm, comfortable feeling, while giving no thought to what he was watching. He was enjoying this winter. Anything bad was quickly forgotten over work, or in front of the TV.

"Uncle Vik," began Sonya, pointing at the screen, "why does Alejandra have a nanny?"

"I expect she's got rich parents."

"Are you rich?"

Viktor shrugged. "Not very . . ."

"Am I?"

He turned and looked at her.

"Me, am I rich?" she asked again.

"Yes," he nodded. "Richer than me."

It was a conversation he recalled the next day during one of his tea breaks. How much a nanny cost he had no idea, but the notion of engaging one for Sonya came that day as a revelation.

That evening his district militiaman friend looked in with a bottle of red wine. They sat in the kitchen. Wet snow was falling and flakes were sticking to the window pane.

Sergey was a bit on edge.

"Do you know, I've been offered a district militia job in Moscow. Ten times what I'm paid here . . . Free flat."

Viktor shrugged. "But you know what it's like there," he said. "Shooting, explosions . . ."

"Got that here, too," said Sergey. "But it's not Special Task I'm joining . . . I'll be what I am now . . . I don't know – maybe I'll go for a year, earn a bit of money."

"Up to you."

"Yes." Sergey sighed. "How about your troubles? Over and done with?"

"Looks like it."

"Let's hope so."

"Don't happen to know of some normal young woman, do you?" Viktor enquired earnestly. "I'm looking for a nanny for Sonya . . . Reliable and not too expensive?"

Sergey thought. "I've got a niece. Twenty. Unemployed. Like me to ask?"

Viktor nodded.

"How much a month would you offer?"

"$50?"

"Right," said Sergey.

42

Next day, out of the blue, the old penguinologist phoned.

"It's me, Pidpaly," he said weakly. "That you, Viktor?"

"Yes."

"Could you come? I'm feeling ill."

Putting his work aside, Viktor set off for Svyatoshino.

The old man was pale. His hands were shaking. The skin

below his sunken eyes was yellow.

"Come in," he said, visibly cheered.

The room was warm and stuffy.

"What's the matter?"

"I don't know . . . Stomach pains. Three days I haven't slept," the old man complained, sitting down at the table.

"Have you called a doctor?"

Pidpaly waved an arm dismissively. "What for? What am I to them? No money to be got out of me."

Viktor went to the phone and called an ambulance.

"No point!" Another dismissive wave. "They'll come, and go away. I know them."

"Sit where you are," Viktor ordered. "I'll make tea."

The kitchen table was a heap of dirty crockery and leftovers. The cups had soggy cigarette ends in them. He washed out two of the cups in the sink and put the kettle on.

Time passed. The tea was ready and they sat at the table in silence and a state of expectancy. The ghost of an ironic smile played over the old man's features. From time to time he shot Viktor a glance.

"I told you, I *did once* come in for the better things of this life," he said didactically, his voice hoarse and feeble.

Viktor said nothing.

At last, the doorbell rang. A paramedic and an orderly entered.

"Who's the patient?" asked the paramedic, teasing burnt tobacco from a just-extinguished cigarette with the fingers of his right hand.

Viktor nodded at the old man. "He is."

"What's the trouble?" The paramedic scanned Pidpaly's face.

"My stomach . . . Here."

"Give him Papaverine?" queried the paramedic turning to the orderly, who was gazing sourly around at the walls.

"No need. Won't do any good," said Pidpaly. "I've had some."

"Well, that's all we've got," said the paramedic helplessly. "So we'll be on our way." Beckoning to the orderly, he turned to go.

"Hang on!" said Viktor.

The paramedic looked back.

"What?"

"Could you get him to a hospital?"

"We could, but who'd take him in?" he asked, heaving an almost genuine sigh.

Viktor produced $50.

"Isn't there somewhere?" he asked.

The paramedic dithered, looked again at the old man, as if gaugeing his value.

"The October might," he shrugged, sidling up, awkwardly taking the proffered note and thrusting it into the pocket of his grubby smock.

Leaning over the table and locating a pencil and piece of paper, Viktor jotted down his telephone number.

"Ring and let me know how he is and where he is," he said, handing it over.

The paramedic nodded.

"Come on then," he flung at the old man.

Pidpaly flapped around, went unsteadily to the kitchen, and came back jingling something in his shaky hand.

"Have these keys, Vik," he said, "and lock up when you go."

The paramedic and the orderly waited patiently while the old man dressed, then led him away, more like a prisoner than a patient.

Alone in the strange flat, Viktor sat for a while at the table, breathing stuffy, dusty air overlaid with an irritant odour of humid warmth. He didn't feel right. Eventually he got to his feet, but was reluctant to go. It was a home in ruins, this flat, and it moved him to genuine pity. The very walls bore the stamp of their owner's helplessness, as did everything within them, together with an air of total isolation.

He washed up and tidied things a bit before leaving. Let Pidpaly at least come back to comparative comfort for a day or two, he thought, locking up behind him.

That evening the nameless paramedic phoned.

"Not long for this world, that old man – it's cancer," he said.

"Where is he?"

"October Hospital, Oncology, Ward 5."

"Thanks." Viktor replaced the receiver.

Saddened, he looked round at Sonya.

"Are we going to the waste area today?" she asked, catching his eye.

"Supper first," he said, making for the kitchen.

43

A couple of days later, the Chief's courier arrived with a fresh batch of files. Glancing over them, Viktor saw he was now dealing with senior ranks of the military. About 20 were due for *obelisks*, all featuring nostalgia for the past seamlessly combined with arms dealing. Beyond that, it was every man for himself – even to the extent of ferrying illegal emigrants over the Ukrainian–Polish frontier in military helicopters, and the permanent renting out of transport aircraft. The further he read, the grimmer it got. But this bunch had something about them that marked them out from previous notables. Putting the papers aside, he thought about it, looking out at on-going winter. He gathered up the papers again. They had all been good husbands and fathers, these generals, colonels and majors, morally sound to a man.

Another read through, and he was in the mood for work. He put the kettle on and fetched out the typewriter from under the table.

He worked away for two hours, until distracted by the phone. It was district militiaman Sergey.

"I've had a word with my niece," he said, "and she's happy to come. I'll bring her along in half an hour, if that's all right."

"Good."

The darkness of a winter evening was descending early over the city. Putting work aside, Viktor went and sat in the living room. Sonya was playing with her Barbie doll.

"Where's Misha?" he asked.

"In there."

"Sonya, we've got an auntie coming," he said, "a young auntie who's going to be your nanny."

Feeling he had put it clumsily, he paused.

"Will she play with me, Uncle Vik?" Sonya asked.

"Of course."

"What's she called?"

"I don't know," he admitted. "She's a niece of Uncle Sergey, whose dacha we went to for New Year."

The doorbell rang. Getting to his feet, Viktor looked at his watch. A bit early, he thought, for Sergey. But Sergey it was.

"This is Nina," said Sergey, as they removed their jackets in the corridor.

Viktor shook hands, took Nina's jacket, and hung it on a peg.

"This is Sonya," he told Nina as they gathered in the living room.

Nina gave her a smile.

"And this," he told Sonya, "is Nina."

Again he was tongue-tied by the awkwardness of the situation, half expecting the little girl and the young lady to talk away, making him superfluous. Instead, they looked at one another and said nothing. Viktor, meanwhile, took in Nina: small, round-faced, short chestnut hair, looking about 17, in close-fitting jeans emphasizing a certain plumpness, and a blue sweater gently outlining small breasts. There was something of the teenager about her – the smile, perhaps, though that was visibly restrained. The reason, he soon saw, being to hide yellow-stained teeth. Probably a smoker, he thought.

"I can begin tomorrow," she said suddenly.

"And what shall we do?" Sonya asked.

Nina smiled her half-smile. "What do you want to do?"

"Go tobogganing."

"Have you got a toboggan?"

"Have I?" asked Sonya with a wide-eyed, skittish glance at Viktor.

"No," he confessed.

"Don't worry, I'll bring one," Nina said quickly, as if to forestall anything Viktor might say. "Transport's good from Podol where I live."

Viktor nodded.

It was agreed that Nina would come at ten and take care of Sonya until five.

Having seen Sergey and his niece out, Viktor sighed with twofold relief. To his delight, the business side of their conversation had proved less than mercenary, and more to the point, Sonya now had a nanny. He felt more comfortable, more relaxed for the future.

"Well, what do you think?" he asked, returning to the living room.

"She's all right." Sonya said cheerfully. "We'll see what Misha thinks of her!"

<h1 style="text-align:center">44</h1>

For Viktor, the arrival of Nina was a kind of liberation. Not because he had previously given a lot of time to Sonya – he was giving just as much now – breakfast, supper, the same evening television sessions together. But he was still left with the feeling of having considerably more time, not necessarily free time, but just time – simply by virtue of reproaching himself less, thinking less often of Sonya and no longer accusing himself of not doing anything with her. Now Nina came for her in the morning, and they set off together he knew not where, and in the evening a weary Sonya would boast, *We walked around Hydropark* or *We've been to Pushcha-Voditsa!*

Viktor was happy. Work was making quiet progress. Winter was relenting. Misha was again roaming the flat at night, and once scared Sonya into screaming. She had been sleeping with her arm hanging over the side of the settee, when Misha bumped, then nestled against it.

She had probably been dreaming, and the sudden physical warmth of Misha had produced a nightmare effect.

Having finished the military, Viktor decided not to ring the Chief for further files, but take a day off. It was sunny, and a pre-spring thaw was in progress.

Sonya and Nina had gone for a walk again. Misha, after a solid breakfast, had returned to the living room, and was standing by the balcony door, where the cold was to his liking.

Viktor decided to pay old Pidpaly a visit.

The thaw had made the pavements treacherous, and on his way to the October Hospital he had several falls, the last of them on the steps of Oncology.

Ward 5, which he located unaided, was huge, like a school gymnasium. To some extent, and probably by reason of the strict alternation of beds and bedside tables, it was like a barracks. Not a nurse was to be seen. A sour medicinal odour pervaded the place. Some beds were screened off.

After a good look round he spotted Pidpaly, lying staring at the ceiling, on a bed by a window. His head seemed to have shrunk.

Picking up a heavy stool inside the door, he went and sat by the penguinologist's bed, but went unnoticed.

"Hello," said Viktor.

Pidpaly turned, and his thin pale lips extended into a smile. "Greetings."

"How are we? Are you getting treatment?"

A smile was the old man's response.

"I didn't bring anything," Viktor said guiltily, noticing two oranges on a neighbouring bedside table. "Somehow I didn't think."

"No matter . . . the good thing is you've come." The old man extricated an arm from under the blanket of grey greatcoat material, raised it to his face and fingered the stubble on his flabby cheeks. "The barber comes once a week, on Friday. Gets paid only for two hours, so he'll never get to me."

"And you want your hair cut?" Seeing how little hair he had, Viktor was surprised.

"A shave is what I want," said the old man again, fingering his stubble. "My previous neighbour," he nodded at the bed on the right, "gave me his shaving kit. The whole works. Brush and all. But I can't shave myself . . ."

"Like me to?" ventured Viktor.

"If you would."

Taking the razor, brush and squat plastic beaker, also part of the kit, from Pidpaly's bedside table, Viktor got to his feet.

"I'll just fetch some water."

He walked the whole length of the corridor twice in search of a nurse or doctor, without finding either. He did find a toilet, but the water from the tap was cold. In the end he enquired of a patient, who sent him to the kitchen, one floor down. There an old woman in a blue smock looked out a half-litre jar, and filled it with hot water from a boiler for him.

The actual shave took the best part of an hour, the razor being old and the blade blunt. He could see the cuts left on the old man's cheeks, but no blood came. When at last he had finished, he collected Eau de Cologne from others in the ward, and pouring a little into his palm, rubbed it on the old man's cheeks. Pidpaly groaned.

"Sorry," Viktor said mechanically.

"No matter," said the old man hoarsely. "Means you're still alive if it hurts."

"What does the doctor say?"

"Give my flat over to him and he'll give me another three months." Again he smiled. "But what's three months to me? I've no unfinished business."

Viktor's right hand balled itself into a fist.

"Do they give you no medicines?" he asked.

"There aren't any. Those who bring them, get given them. For the others, it's bed and rest."

Viktor said nothing, waiting for his fury to abate.

"And what did he offer for your flat?" he asked when calmer. "Medicines?"

"Some sort of American injections . . ." The old man put a hand to his shaven cheek. "Look, there's something I want to ask you . . ." He edged towards Viktor, turning with an effort onto his side. "Bend down closer."

Viktor bent down closer.

"You've got the flat keys?" he whispered.

"Yes," Viktor whispered back.

"Listen. Don't let me down. When I die, set fire to my flat," whispered the old man. "I beg you! Don't want anyone sitting in my chair, rummaging in my papers, rubbish-binning the lot. Understand? It's my things . . . What I've lived with, and don't want to leave here . . . Understand?"

Viktor nodded.

"Promise you will when I'm dead," he said, gazing questioningly, beseechingly into Viktor's eyes.

"I promise," Viktor whispered.

"That's good." Again the bloodless lips formed a smile. "I told you, I *did once* come in for the better things of this life, didn't I?"

With a heavy sigh he turned onto his back again.

"So off with you," he said hoarsely. "Thanks for the shave. Otherwise, it's lie unshaven, like a corpse!" He pointed to the nearest screen.

"Is that one?" Viktor whispered uneasily.

"Screen today, morgue tomorrow!" whispered Pidpaly. "Off you go."

Viktor got to his feet, stood for a moment looking down at Pidpaly. But Pidpaly was gazing at the ceiling, thin lips moving as if shaping words audible to no one but himself.

45

The next day began as usual. The sun shone in at the window, and Viktor and Sonya sat at a breakfast of fried eggs and tea in the kitchen. Misha, moody since daybreak, refused, however much cajoled, to come and join them.

Sonya kept casting eager looks at the alarm clock on the window ledge, as if willing the minute hand forward.

At 9.40 the doorbell rang and she darted out, almost knocking her stool over.

Nina had arrived. A happy exchange of greetings ensued, after which Nina, still in her coat, looked in to say hello.

"Where are you off to today?" Viktor asked.

"Syrets. Walk in the woods, then to Podol and to my place for lunch."

She gave a dutiful nod and a teeth-concealing half-smile.

"So where's your little jacket?" he heard her asking Sonya in the corridor. "And now your little boots."

Five minutes later she looked in again.

"Just off," she said, with another half-smile.

The door banged. Silence descended, except for a faint stirring in the living room. The door creaked open, and Misha peeped out. Apparently satisfied that the corridor was empty, he advanced to the kitchen door and pushed it open. He contemplated his master from the doorway, then came over and snuggled up against his knee. Viktor stroked him.

After several minutes of this, Misha went to his bowl, and stood looking back. Viktor took two small plaice out of the freezer, cut them up and gave them to him. He then returned to his seat, having topped up his cup of tea.

The relative silence – apart from the sound of Misha's breakfasting – took Viktor back to when there had been just the two of them living there in peace and quiet, without any sense of strong attachment, but with a feeling of interdependence creating a kind of blood tie between them – as if, in the absence of love, there was concern. After all, even relatives didn't have to be loved – taken care of, worried about, yes, but feelings and emotions were of secondary importance in that, and not, so long as all was well with them, obligatory . . .

Making short work of his breakfast, Misha returned to his master who, struck by this unusually affectionate behaviour, stroked him, at which he pressed more firmly against his knee.

"Not feeling ill, are we?" he asked gently, looking him over.

We seem to have been neglecting you, he thought. First it was the TV with Sonya, now it's Nina. I'm sorry. And there was I thinking you and Sonya were playing as you used to. I'm sorry . . .

Viktor sat on at the kitchen table for a good 20 minutes, not wanting to disturb Misha, considering the recent past and thinking about the future. Life, despite the short-lived dangers he had sat out at the dacha over New Year, seemed on an even course. All was well, or appeared so. To every time, its own *normality*. The once terrible was now commonplace, meaning that people accepted it as the norm and went on living, instead of getting needlessly agitated. For them, as for Viktor, the main thing, after all, was still *to live*, come what might.

The thaw continued.

At about two the doorbell rang. Expecting it to be Nina and Sonya, he went to the door, but it was Igor Lvovich who marched in, banging the door behind him, took off his coat, and went through to the kitchen without removing his footwear.

Pale, baggy-eyed, the Chief was clearly not himself.

"Make some coffee," he said, plumping himself down in Viktor's place.

Seeing to coffee-maker and coffee, Viktor looked back at the Chief. He appeared to be trembling, and for just an instant Viktor felt similarly affected. He lit the burner, poured coffee and water into the coffee-maker, and put it on the flame.

"So what!" the Chief was muttering abstractedly. "So what!"

"Has something happened?"

"It has," said Igor Lvovich, looking away. "Just wait . . . Till I warm up . . ."

Again silence. Viktor stood watching the coffee. As the foam rose, he took the coffee-maker off the heat, fetched cups and poured.

Hands clasped round the cup, the Chief looked across at him.

"Thanks," he said.

Viktor sat down at the table with him.

"Look," the Chief began suddenly, "it's best I tell you nothing.

What's it to you? Remember how *you* had to lie low for a day or two?"

Viktor nodded.

"Well," he smiled wrily, "now it's *my* turn. Just for a day or two. Till the boys clear the way. Then back to the grind."

"I've done all the military," said Viktor. "They're there, on the window ledge."

In no mood for *obelisks*, the Chief dismissed them with a wave.

He drank his coffee, lit a cigarette, and looking in vain for an ashtray, used the table instead, and for some minutes sat lost in thought.

"It's hard, you know, finding you've been put on the spot by your own." He sighed. "Very hard . . . Busy just now?"

"No."

"Well then," said the Chief, looking earnestly at him, "you can go to my office for me – I'll ring my secretary to let you in – and bring back the brown briefcase from the safe. I'll give you the key. If you find you're being followed, ditch the key, and wander round till dark."

Viktor suddenly felt afraid. Gulping his coffee, he looked up and into a steady gaze dismissive of any thoughts or qualms.

"When?" he asked, like a doomed man.

"Now."

The Chief handed over a key from his wallet.

"But wait till I've rung through," he said, as Viktor rose from the table.

The Chief went to the living room.

"Off you go," he said, returning.

Thaw or no thaw, it was freezing, of which none was more aware than Viktor, walking slowly to the trolleybus stop, no longer afraid, but mind and whole body numb with cold.

When, an hour later, he entered the newspaper building, he had to show his Press card to three lots of Special Task Militia before finally arriving at the Editor-in-Chief's reception. The pale secretary nodded recognition, and without a word, unlocked the Chief's sanctum. Having closed the door behind him, Viktor found himself trembling all over, and remembering he hadn't once checked to see if he was being followed, felt suddenly afraid.

To calm himself, he went over to the desk and sat in the Chief's chair. The safe was to his left, on a low table. He got out the key. After a moment or so's hesitation, he opened the safe. The brown briefcase was on the lower shelf. He placed it on the desk before him. Once again trembling precluded thought. He had no inclination to get to his feet and leave the office, as if he were aware of danger lurking beyond its walls. He had another look in the safe, to spin out time. On the upper shelf lay a folder with several typed sheets on top. Without thinking, he reached for the topmost sheet, and recognized it at once as his *obelisk* for the Director of Ferro-Concrete Reinforcements. In the top left-hand corner someone had written

Approved.

For 14.02.99

with a bold, sweeping signature.

His growing astonishment proved a release from fear and trembling. *Today was only February the third!* A glance at the other sheets confirmed that they, too, were recent *obelisks*, each *approved* for some date ahead. Returning to the safe, he took out the folder and untied the ribbons. More *obelisks*, the more or less recent on top, all of them *approved* – one for that very day, the third, and with the same bold, sweeping signature. He extracted some from the middle of the pile. The first of these, as well as *approved* for a date now past had

Processed

written in a different hand.

With his head in a whirl, Viktor sat staring at the brown briefcase, the *obelisks*, the open safe, and suddenly there was a nasty bitter taste in his mouth. He picked up one of the papers lying on the desk. It was a letter to the printers, word-processed except for the signature, and this he studied closely. It wasn't the Chief who had written *approved* on the *obelisks*. His signature, unlike the bold, sweeping one, was straightforward and legible. But something about it still seemed familiar, and looking back at the old obituary from the middle of the pile, he saw that *Processed* had been written in the same unsteady, shivering-with-cold characters.

The phone on the desk rang, and he jumped guiltily. He looked at it, expecting it to stop, but it didn't. And again he was gripped by fear. He looked about him, as if to check whether he was being watched, and suddenly spotted the lens of a video camera mounted on a bracket directly above the door and pointing down at him.

Slipping the *obelisks* back in the folder, he returned it to the safe with the others, and locking the safe, stole a last look at the video camera. The phone had stopped ringing, but the renewed silence was no less intimidating. Fearful of disturbing it, he got gingerly to his feet, picked up the briefcase, and left.

The secretary turned from her computer and the graphic escape-from-pursuit game frozen on its screen. She looked tense.

"Finished already?" she asked.

With difficulty he managed a *Thank you* and a *Goodbye*.

116

46

Oblivious to the city, looking neither to left nor right, he made for home, tightly gripping the handle of the briefcase. His feet knew the way.

Not until he was actually at the door of his flat did it register that, sitting on a bench down at the entrance, there had been a young man in training suit and woolly ski hat watching him closely. Having got the door open, he stopped, listened, and hearing no sound from the entrance below, went on in, carefully shutting it behind him.

"Well?" said the Chief coming out into the corridor to meet him.

Seeing the briefcase, he smiled and bore it off to the kitchen.

By the time Viktor had removed his boots and jacket, Igor Lvovich had the contents of his briefcase – green trident-embossed diplomatic passport, credit cards, notebook and receipts – spread out on the table.

"Down at the entrance," said Viktor, "there's a young chap sitting –"

"I know. One of ours," confirmed the Chief without looking up. "Got anything to eat? I'm peckish."

The Chief was his old self again, calm, confident, steady as a rock, intrepid.

Opening the fridge, Viktor got out polonies, butter and mustard, and proceeded to the stove, now with his back to the Chief, but with the acrid taste of the Chief's tobacco in his mouth.

As he lit the gas, he heard the Chief get up and go through to the living room, and while the water boiled, could just hear him talking to someone on the phone, but had no inclination to turn and listen. His instinct was to keep his back turned on all that was happening, and let it happen unseen, away from him and his life.

Again the door creaked, footsteps sounded, a stool scraped. The Chief was back at the table.

The polonies were already in boiling water.

"Got any dollars handy?" asked the Chief.

"Some," said Viktor without turning.

"You can lend me $800."

After that they ate in silence, Viktor kept an an eye on the old alarm clock on the window ledge. It was getting on for four. Nina would soon be bringing Sonya. And what then? What did the Chief have in mind? To lie low here? For how long? And where would it all end?

Viktor dipped his little circles of sliced polony in the mustard and munched mechanically. Something was missing, he felt suddenly, then saw that it was bread. But across the table the Chief was eating away just as happily without. Instead of dipping each little fork-impaled circle in mustard like Viktor, he doused it in melted butter before conveying it to his mouth.

"Tea," ordered the Chief, pushing away his empty plate.

Viktor made tea. Again they sat opposite each other in silence. The Chief was busy with his own thoughts, and watching him, Viktor thought of the notes adorning his *obelisks*. He would have liked to know who and what lay behind those *approveds*, but was more than certain that the Chief wouldn't say, but would put him off with a *What's that to you?* and that would be that.

He sighed, and the Chief, his train of thought broken, shot him a look.

"Another job for you," he said. "Collect my air ticket, Victory

Square, Window 12, taking the $800 with you. You'll get them back. Flight booking 503."

It was getting dark. Viktor didn't feel like going out again, but knew that he had to, whether he liked it or not.

"All right," he said, but tardily enough to earn a look of surprise, which was replaced by a weary smile.

Viktor put on his jacket and boots. As he left the block, he noted, out of the corner of his eye, the continuing presence of the sportsman in the knitted ski hat.

Apart from a lone Azerbaijani dolefully studying a flight timetable, the airline booking offices were deserted.

At Window 12 was a woman of about 40, with blue-rinsed hair piled high.

"Booking 503," he said.

"Passport," she responded, without looking up, tapping the booking into her computer.

Not having the Chief's passport, Viktor was sunk.

"Ah!" breathed the window lady suddenly. "*No passport required. It's all here. $750 at exchange rate or $800 cash*," she said, pointing to the pay desk, still without looking up.

Viktor handed over eight $100 bills. They were counted by a young lady in a blue uniform who put them through a forgery detector, turned and shouted, "Cash received, Vera."

Window 12 gave him the ticket. For *Kiev–Larnaca–Rome*. He folded it and placed it in an inner pocket of his jacket.

It was about six when he reached the flat. Nina and Sonya were still not back. The Chief was still sitting in the kitchen, having earlier brewed coffee which he was now calmly drinking.

He studied the ticket carefully before concealing it in his wallet.

"Nobody been?" Viktor asked.

"Who are you expecting?"

"Sonya's nanny should be bringing her."

"No, no one's been," said the Chief thoughtfully. "But I'd advise getting her to take the little girl to her place for the night." To add weight to his words, he nodded in the manner of one imparting wisdom.

Nina brought Sonya at 6.30, full of apologies for being so late.

"I hope you weren't worried," she said, while still in the corridor. "I *am* sorry. We got delayed at the station. Seeing Sergey off."

"I wasn't worried," said Viktor. "But Nina, could Sonya possibly stay with you for tonight?"

Nina looked at him in surprise. Sonya, who had already taken her boots off but was still wearing her jacket, was looking too, though more in curiosity than surprise.

"Of course," said the puzzled Nina.

"Hold on." Viktor went to the bedroom and returned with $100.

"That's for this week and for your trouble."

"When do you want her back?"

"Tomorrow . . . Late afternoon."

Alone in the corridor, Viktor sighed. Noticing bootmarks and puddles of melted snow on the linoleum, he fetched a rag from the lavatory and mopped them up before returning to the kitchen.

"Sit with me till half past one," the Chief said quietly. "I've a car coming, and as I'm tired, I might fall asleep . . . Got any cards?"

The time passed surprisingly slowly. It had long been dark, and the city was hushed. They played Preference-with-dummy, keeping a note of their stakes. Viktor kept losing. The Chief smiled as he played, glancing occasionally at the alarm clock. At intervals he lit another cigarette, and as the mound of ash on the left of the table grew, he moulded it into a little pyramid.

At 1.30 exactly the car arrived. The Chief looked out of the window, then totted up his winnings.

"$95 you owe me," he grinned. "You'll win it back!"

He got to his feet and put on his coat.

"Have a holiday," he said, preparing to leave. "When the dust settles, I'll return, and we'll continue the good work."

"But, Igor, what *is* the real point of my work?" Viktor asked, stopping him in his tracks.

The Chief considered him through narrowed eyes.

"Your interest lies in not asking questions," he said quietly. "Think what you like. But bear in mind this: the moment you *are* told what the point of your work is, you're dead. This isn't a film, it's for real. The full story is what you get told only if and when your work, and with it your existence, are no longer required." He smiled a sad smile. "Still, I do, in fact, wish you well. Believe me."

He opened the door, and there was the familiar sportsman. The latter gave a nod and he and the Chief set off down the stairs.

Viktor shut the door. The silence of the flat was unnerving. The tang of tobacco was bitter in his mouth, and he had a sudden urge to spit to rid himself of it.

Back in the kitchen the air was even thicker with tobacco smoke – almost opaque. He opened the window vent. He felt the cold air, but the smoke, illuminated by the bulb, refused to budge, as if the air was still, despite the open vent. Removing his papers from the window ledge, he threw the window open. An icy blast slammed the kitchen door shut. Gradually the haze dispersed. With the cold came fresh air. He was indifferent to the wind, but watched it blow the chief's pyramid of ash across the table, reducing it to tiny specks which it rolled to the edge of the table and over. In the end, no trace of the little pyramid remained.

The door opened and there, attracted by the cold, was Misha. Coming over to his master, he stood gazing up at him.

Viktor gave him a smile. He had another look to make sure the air was clear of smoke. Dazzled suddenly by the kitchen bulb, he switched it off and sat in the dark.

47

Viktor woke at about eleven feeling cold. Jumping out of bed, he ran to the kitchen, closed the window and vent, and went straight back to the bedroom. For a while he lay in bed in his clothes to warm himself, then got up again.

After a hot bath and some strong coffee he felt better, and gradually warmth returned to the flat. He remembered the events of the day before – what had been written on his obituaries in the safe, the airline booking office, cards until 1.30 in the morning. It all seemed to have happened not the day before, but long ago, in the distant past. Then, as he caught a sudden whiff of tobacco smoke, it all came flooding back in vivid detail.

It was a calm, cold day. Thaw had again given way to winter.

Cup of hot coffee clasped in both hands, he wondered what he should do. There was no longer any work, and there probably wouldn't be, the Chief having done a bunk. He had money for the time being, though he was $800 down. So, back to short stories perhaps, or maybe a novel . . .

As he attempted to divert himself with thoughts of future

prose, he had a sudden sense of emptiness. His prose was, in fact, all in a distant past – a past so distant as to raise a doubt as to whether it was *his* past at all. And not perhaps something read and forgotten, that now seemed part of what he had himself experienced.

Gulping his coffee, he remembered that Nina would be bringing Sonya back towards evening. Reality was asserting itself over his thoughts. What lay ahead was simply life as before: his duty to Sonya, care of Misha. Then, in all likelihood, a search for new employment . . . And solitude, as before.

He thought suddenly of Nina and her saying that they had been seeing Sergey off at the station. So he had, after all, gone to Moscow, and without so much as a goodbye. Another brick in Viktor's wall of solitude. And back to Nina. Nina of the half-smile, unsightly teeth and beautiful eyes. What colour they were, he couldn't recall.

But why think of her? He looked out of the window again. Fresh frost patterns were appearing on the glass. He would soon be 40, and the one creature closest to him was Penguin Misha – who had nowhere else to go, and being, moreover, denied the power of thought, was unable to contribute to the matter . . . And there was Sonya, not in the picture at all, with her pile of money and calm *The telly's mine!* Which, indeed, it was. And were they – he, Sonya and Misha, the four of them, including Nina – to go for a walk, someone would say *What a happy family!*

He smiled sadly, toying in imagination with happy illusions, real enough, from one point of view, to justify actually sitting for a family photograph.

48

Nina brought Sonya at six. She wanted to be off immediately, but Viktor asked her to join them for supper, and quickly boiled some potatoes.

Sonya behaved badly, and left the kitchen having eaten hardly anything.

Viktor and Nina ate on in silence, stealing the odd glance at each other.

"Has Sergey gone for long?" he asked.

"For a year, he said, but he's promised to come for a couple of days in the summer. His mother's still here. I'm doing her shopping for her now."

"What's she like? Old?"

"No, but her legs are bad."

They drank tea, and then Nina thanked him for the supper and said goodbye until tomorrow.

After seeing her out, Viktor went into the living room. The television was on and Sonya was asleep on the sofa, still dressed.

Tired out, he thought.

He undressed her and covered her with a blanket. As he went over to switch off the television, he saw penguins jumping comically from an iceberg into the water, all to a quiet commentary concerning Antarctic fauna.

He looked round for Misha, picked him up from where he was standing by the balcony door, and set him down in front of the TV.

Misha muttered.

"Watch," whispered Viktor.

Seeing his fellows, Misha stood gazing raptly at the screen.

124

For some five minutes they watched penguins jumping and diving, and when the programme ended, Misha shot over to the set and banged his chest against it, rocking it on its little table.

"Hey! You mustn't do that," Viktor said quietly, steadying the set.

Next morning the hospital rang.

"Your relative has died," announced a calm female voice.

"When?"

"In the night. Will you be collecting the body?"

Viktor said nothing.

"Will you be burying him?"

"Yes," he sighed.

"We can hold him in the mortuary for up to three days," said the voice, "while you organize the funeral. Don't forget to bring identification when you come to collect."

He replaced the receiver. He looked round at Sonya, no longer asleep but looking drowsily out from under the blanket.

The clock showed 8.30.

"You can sleep on for a bit," he said, leaving the room.

At 10.00 Nina arrived, and as she had a bit of a cold, said they would be staying in for the day.

"Any idea where scientists get buried?"

"The Baykov."

Dressed extra warmly against the cold, Viktor set off for the Baykov.

At the cemetery office, he was received by a fat elderly lady in a red woollen cardigan, sitting at an ancient desk and clasping in both hands a pair of pebble-lensed spectacles. Circumventing the centrally placed heater, he sat down opposite her and she put on her spectacles.

"A relative of mine has died," he began, "a scientist."

"Right," she said calmly. "Academician?"

"No."

"Any relatives buried here?"

"I don't know."

"So you'll need an individual plot," she said, mainly to herself, and opening a fat notebook lying on the desk, wrote something on a page and pushed it over.

Drawing the book towards him, Viktor read $1,000.

"Price of plot," she said, lowering her voice, "inclusive of special bus and gravedigging . . . It is, as you know, winter, and the ground's frozen solid."

"Right," he said.

"Name of deceased?"

"Pidpaly."

"Bring the money tomorrow, and the funeral's the day after, at eleven. Call here first, and I'll tell the driver the number of the plot. You can, incidentally, order a monument here."

49

The next day seemed to Viktor the most difficult of his life, but not from his having spent it organizing the funeral, because he hadn't. Emma Sergeyevna, mistress of obsequies at the Baykov, had produced a sheet clearly detailing the order of events:

11am., meet Special Bus number 66–77, at October
Hospital Mortuary where Deceased, prepared by Funeral

Cosmetician ($100 extra), will await embusment. Deceased to repose in own attire in inexpensive quality pine casket.

Money had relieved Viktor of bother, but not of what weighed on his mind. He was in no mood to return to the flat – Nina and Sonya were there. He had told Nina that morning that a friend of his had died, and she had responded sympathetically, saying she would stay until he returned.

But instead of returning, he went to Podol, and sat at *Bacchus's* until closing time, drinking three glasses of red wine. From the warmth of *Bacchus's* he wandered around Podol until the cold got the better of him.

He reached the flat at about nine.

"I've made some soup – like me to heat it for you?" asked Nina.

After supper he asked her to stay, and she did.

With Sonya asleep in the living room, Viktor held Nina close to him in the bedroom. In spite of the two blankets over them, he still felt cold. Only in pressing close to her was there any warmth, though he was riled by the pitying look in her eyes. He tightened his grip, compressing her ribs, trying to hurt her, but she said nothing, just looked pityingly. She had her arms around him – he could feel her hands on his back – but her hold had something submissive and lacking in strength about it, as if she was simply hanging on to him. And just as submissively, she gave herself to him, saying nothing, uttering no sound. Still he had the urge to hurt, make her cry out and stop him, but soon wearied after achieving none of these things. Relaxing his embrace, he lay, eyes closed but not sleeping, unable to bear her pitying expression. He felt ashamed now – of himself, his fury, his irritation, his grossness. And when at last he fell asleep, she lay for a long while, open-eyed, gazing at him and thinking – perhaps of the ability to endure.

When he woke next morning, she was no longer beside him. Fearing she might have gone, and for good, he got up, put on his dressing-gown and looked into the living room.

Sonya was still asleep. Hearing a sound in the kitchen, he found Nina, dressed and standing at the stove, boiling rice. He felt the need to say something, perhaps apologize. Turning, she nodded a greeting.

"I'm sorry," he whispered, gently embracing her.

Stretching up on tiptoe, she kissed him on the lips.

"When do you have to go?" she asked.

"At ten."

50

The funeral bus jolted mercilessly. The driver tried to drive slowly, but flashy foreign-made cars, in a hurry as always, kept sounding their horns, causing him to keep an anxious eye on his rear-view mirror.

In front sat two intelligent-looking little men, one wearing a short sheepskin coat, the other a black leather jacket, both 50-ish. One was the cosmetician, the other the undertaker, but which was which Viktor didn't know, since they had appeared simultaneously, helping the mortuary orderlies carry out the coffin and shove it through the rear door of the bus.

Viktor sat at the back with an arm around Misha to keep him

in his seat. Beside them, creaking as they rounded corners, was the coffin, nailed shut and covered with red and black material.

From time to time he met the inquisitive gaze of the little men, though it was Misha, not him, who was the object of their curiosity.

Arriving at the Baykov Cemetery, they stopped outside the office. The driver went to ask the plot number, and Viktor used this time to buy a large bunch of flowers from one of the old women standing there.

The way through the cemetery avenues seemed surprisingly long, and Viktor found the endless succession of monuments and railings wearying.

The bus stopped.

Viktor got up, preparing to make for the door.

"Not yet," said the driver, poking his head round the transparent partition.

"Look at that lot! Watch you don't scrape them!" said one of the little men, gazing ahead.

Viktor looked too. The right-hand side of the avenue was lined with flashy foreign-made cars, leaving a tight squeeze for the bus.

"Best make a detour," said the driver. "Out of harm's way."

They reversed and turned off into another avenue. Five minutes or so later they drew up at a newly dug grave. To one side was a heap of brown clayey soil and a couple of muddy spades.

Viktor got out. Surveying the scene, he saw a crowd of people about 50 metres away, and from the opposite direction, two skinny-looking cemetery hands in quilted jackets and trousers, both full of holes, were approaching.

"This the scientist?" asked one.

"Let's have him then," said the other with a jerk of the head.

They lowered the coffin to the ground beside the grave. One fetched a coil of stout rope and arranged it for the lowering of the coffin.

Viktor slipped back to the bus, lifted Misha out, and set him down. The rope-arranger looked askance, but worked on.

"Poor sort of do, this, isn't it?" the other workman asked the driver. "No priest, no palaver."

The driver looked pointedly in Viktor's direction to shut him up.

Having lowered the coffin, the workmen turned expectantly to the man with the penguin.

Going to the graveside, Viktor dropped the flowers onto the coffin lid, followed by a handful of earth.

The workmen plied their spades and in ten minutes the grave was formed. They then went their way, each with a million tip in the inflated currency of the country, saying he should look them up in May, when the grave had settled. Cosmetician and undertaker departed in the bus, and Viktor, who had declined the offer of a lift to the entrance, was left alone with Misha.

Misha was standing stiffly by the grave, as though deep in thought, and looking across at the neighbouring funeral. Viktor found its intrusive noise more than a little irritating.

It was odd to be playing sole mourner. Where were the friends, the relatives? Or had Pidpaly outlived them? More than likely. And, but for Viktor's interest in penguins, who would there have been to bury him, and where?

Cheeks nipped by the cold, gloveless hands freezing, he looked about him. He had no idea how to find his way out, but he wasn't worried.

"Well Misha," he sighed, stooping to the penguin's level, "that's how we humans bury our dead."

Turning at the sound of his master's voice, Misha fixed on him his tiny sad eyes.

"So, shall we look for the exit?" Viktor asked, and taking a more determined look around, saw a man heading towards them from the other funeral.

The man waved, and since there was no one else for him to wave at, Viktor stood and waited.

The man was short, bearded, and had binoculars slung about his *Alaska* anorak. Strange attire for a funeral, but his face seemed vaguely familiar.

"Sorry," he said. "But checking this sector" – he patted his binoculars – "and spying an animal known to me, I thought I'd pop over. New Year. Militia dachas. Remember?"

Viktor nodded.

"Lyosha," the bearded man said, extending his hand.

"Viktor."

They shook hands.

"Friend of yours?" Lyosha asked, indicating the grave.

"Yes."

"We're burying three," he sighed sadly.

Squatting down in front of Misha, he slapped him on the shoulder.

"Hi, Penguin. How are you doing? Afraid I've forgotten his name," he said, looking up.

"Misha."

"Ah, that's it, Misha! Bird in a suit . . . Handsome fellow!"

Straightening up, Lyosha looked back at his funeral.

"Do you know the way out?" Viktor asked.

Lyosha looked around.

"I don't . . . But if you're not in any hurry, hang on and I'll

give you a lift. We've nearly finished over there. The priest's a
bore – half an hour's Bible over each one . . . You wait here – I'll
give a wave when we're through."

Some 20 minutes later, Viktor saw movement in the crowd of
mourners. They were dispersing. The flashy foreign-made cars
were starting up. He looked hard for the bearded Lyosha, but
having no binoculars, found his eyes watering from the icy wind.
At last he saw someone waving.

"Come on, Misha," he said, taking a few steps and looking
back, and slowly Misha followed.

By the time they arrived at the three wreath-heaped graves,
only one car, an elderly Mercedes, was left.

"I'll drive you home if you like," said Lyosha, while still
negotiating the cemetery. "Never does to be first at the wake."

Viktor readily accepted, and half an hour later was outside
his block.

"Take my phone number – maybe we'll meet again," said Lyosha
handing him his card. "And let me have yours, just in case."

Pocketing the card, Viktor wrote his number on the dashboard
notepad.

51

Towards evening Nina made ready to leave.

"Won't you stay?" Viktor asked. "For the funeral supper."

He looked weary, and sounded unsure of himself. She nodded.

"You go and sit with Sonya – I'll think what to eat," she said.

He went into the living room where Sonya had already

switched the television on. Nina headed for the kitchen.

"What's it today?" he asked, sitting beside Sonya.

"*Elvira*, episode five," was the ready reply.

Taking out his handkerchief, he wiped her nose.

A lengthy commercial break was in progress. To spare his eyes the short sharp kaleidoscopic flashes, he looked at the floor, while Sonya feasted on them.

Eventually the frantic succession of commercials finished, to be followed by the serial credits and an enervating torrent of sickly music.

"Wouldn't you like to go to bed?" he asked.

"No," said the little girl, eyes riveted on the screen. "Would you?"

He said nothing. The treacly sweet Latin-Americanness of the characters was beginning to irritate him. He had no wish to enter into what was happening on the screen. He looked around for Misha, but he wasn't there. He was in the bedroom, standing still as a statue in his hidey-hole behind the dark-green settee. Viktor squatted down beside him.

"How are we?" he asked, patting a black shoulder.

Misha gave him a look, then stared at the floor.

Viktor found himself thinking of Pidpaly – how he had shaved him, what the old man had asked him to do, and how he had promised to do it, a memory he at once shelved, though with a shiver running down his spine.

Result of standing about at the cemetery, he thought.

He remembered how lightly, and without posture, the old penguinologist had faced imminent death. *I've no unfinished business* he had said. Viktor shook his head in sheer amazement, at which Misha stepped back and eyed him in alarm.

And nor have I, he thought, though the falsity of this brought a guilty smile to his face.

He *did* in fact have business to finish, and even if he hadn't, was hardly likely to treat the approach of death so lightly. *A hard life is better than an easy death* he had once written in his notebook. It was a phrase he had taken pride in for a time, trotting it out when appropriate and when not, and then forgotten. And here it was years later, floating to the surface of his memory, after Pidpaly's words that had so affected him. Two men, different ages, different attitudes.

Seeing his master squatting motionless, lost in thought, Misha came and nuzzled his neck with his beak, a chilly show of tenderness that broke Viktor's train of thought and roused him from his reverie. He stroked the penguin, sighed, straightened up and went over to the window.

The block opposite presented a crossword pattern of lighted windows. It was a crossword with many spaces. They were testimonies to the sheer ordinariness of life, those windows. There was a sadness about it, but a sadness softened, allayed, by darkness. And by degrees, a strange, slightly unnatural calm, like the lull before a storm, possessed him. Palms resting on the cold window sill, legs against the hot radiator, he stood, aware how temporary it was, that calm, and waiting for it to pass.

A little later, at the sound of gentle breathing, he swung round, and there in the half-darkness was Nina.

"It's ready," she whispered. "Sonya's asleep – dropped off watching the telly."

They went through the living room, now dimly lit by a standard lamp in the corner.

The kitchen smelt of garlic and fried potato, and on a stand in the middle of the table reposed the covered frying pan.

"I saw you had some vodka," Nina ventured, indicating the wall cupboard. "Shall I bring it?"

He nodded. She fetched the bottle and two small glasses, served the meat and fried potatoes, and filled their glasses.

Viktor sat in his place, Nina opposite.

"How was the funeral?" she asked.

"Quiet. No one there, except Misha and me."

"Well, may he rest in peace!" She raised her glass before putting it to her lips.

Viktor drank too. He cut up his meat, and looking across at Nina, saw a round face all the more charming for the flush the vodka had brought to it.

He knew nothing about her, he thought suddenly, who she was, where she was from. Niece of Sergey, yes, but what did he know about *him*, beyond that he had been easy to make friends with. The *origin* of his name had been enough to engender a warm feeling towards him. The story of that seemed to set him on an invisible pedestal, elevate him to a point where delight in the man was sufficient to inspire complete confidence.

Viktor poured refills and raised his glass.

"Did you know him well?" Nina asked.

Viktor drank.

"I think so."

"What was he?"

"A scientist. Worked at the zoo."

She nodded, but with an expression showing plainly that interest in the deceased was now terminated.

They ate, and in deference to the occasion, drank without clinking glasses. Nina then placed their dirty plates in the sink and put the kettle on. Waiting for it to boil, she looked out of the window, face contorted, as if in pain.

"What's wrong?"

"It's this city, I can't stand it . . . The anonymous crowds . . . The distances . . ."

"But why?" He asked in surprise.

Thrusting her hands in the pockets of her jeans, she shrugged.

"My fool of a mother threw everything over, and moved here . . . I wouldn't have! Your own place with your own little garden. All yours. That's what's best."

Viktor sighed. Being city-born, he had no special feeling for the country.

The kettle boiled.

Again they sat opposite each other, separated by silence, thinking their own thoughts.

Feeling sleepy, Viktor got to his feet, surprised at the heaviness of his legs.

"I'm off to bed."

"Off you go. I'll wash up."

Once in bed he fell instantly asleep. Waking in the small hours because he was hot, he became aware of another warmth, that of Nina sleeping with her back to him.

Placing a hand on her shoulder, he fell asleep again, satisfied, as if his doubts were dispelled, and the hand on her shoulder was a channel of vital warmth between them, precious, and no obstacle to slumber.

52

And again it was morning. Viktor woke with a heavy head and no Nina beside him. The clock showed 8.30.

He made his way through the living room, where Sonya was still asleep, to the kitchen. He could hear water splashing in the bathroom.

As he went to the stove to make coffee, he caught sight of an envelope on the table. It was sealed, but bore no name. Tearing it open, he extracted a folded sheet of paper and eight $100 notes.

Debt repaid with thanks. Things
on the mend. Back soon. – Igor.

Viktor dropped the sheet on the table, keeping hold of the dollars.

He looked into the bathroom. Nina was under the shower, the smooth lines of her body emphasized by the flow of water. Seeing him standing stiffly in the doorway, she was more surprised than embarrassed.

"Has anyone been?" he asked.

"No," she said, staring at the dollar bills in his hand.

"How about the letter on the kitchen table?"

"I haven't been in there yet." She said, shrugging so that her tiny apple breasts quivered.

Shutting the bathroom door, he stood in the corridor, trying to concentrate, but distracted by the splashing. He thought back to all that had happened the evening before, to everything Nina had said at table. After which he had gone to bed, and now, next morning, evidence of a visitor. No marks on the floor, but the evidence remained . . .

At this point he switched on the corridor light and examined the floor for traces of the night visitor or visitors, but there were none.

Returning to the kitchen, he made coffee and sat down at the table. He remembered his discovery of Misha-non-penguin's note and presents before New Year. This was an exact repeat – only this time, with delivery of a letter from the Chief in place of presents. *Things on the mend* . . . Did that mean there would soon be work? That he would soon be seeing the Chief and could ask what sort of postal service it was that had keys to his flat?

Keys . . . He got up, went and tried the door. It was tight shut. He returned to the kitchen.

He could, he comforted himself, replace the lock. There had long been plenty to choose from: alarmed, coded, electrically controlled . . . He might even get a couple of combination locks. His flat, personal life and sleep would then be totally secure.

Reassured, he brewed coffee for Nina, and was taking it to her when he met her coming in. She was wearing his dressing-gown.

"Just made you some coffee," he said.

"Thanks," she smiled, took the cup and sat down at the table.

"Vik," her expression now was half-serious, half-entreating. "What I wanted to say . . ." she hesitated, as if choosing her words. "Well, it's about us . . . Now we've somehow become a couple . . ."

She fell silent.

"How do you mean?" he asked, filled with unease at the ensuing pause.

"It's my wages," she said at last. "It means a lot to me . . . The money I get for Sonya."

"Of course, and you'll still get it," he said in surprise. "What made you think you wouldn't?"

She shrugged.

"Don't you see, it's a bit awkward – our being a couple, and me working for you at the same time."

The heavy head he had banished with his first cup of coffee was suddenly back.

"It's all right," he said gravely. "Don't worry – it's not me who's paying. It's Sonya – it's her father's money."

Embarrassed, Nina sat staring at the table and the coffee cup before her.

"Don't worry," he said, getting up and smoothing her wet hair. "It's all right."

She nodded, but did not look up.

"I'll be back late," he said. "Don't open to anyone. And here's something in advance . . ."

He put two green $100 bills on the table, and left.

53

Before taking the Metro to Svyatoshino, Viktor wandered the city for a while. After several clearly fortuitous thaws, February had turned sharp again. The sun shone, the snow sparkled underfoot, and his hands were like ice in the pockets of his short sheepskin coat. Clutched, no less ice-cold, in his right hand, were the keys to Pidpaly's flat.

This time, the cold lending wings to his feet, it took him about ten minutes to walk from the Metro to Pidpaly's flat. Quickly letting himself in, he stamped the snow off his feet and went through to the kitchen. It was tidy, and only the combination of damp and stuffiness recalled the day when the ambulance he had summoned carried Pidpaly off for ever.

Something in the air made him sneeze.

He would have done better to die at home, he thought, gazing round at the ancient kitchen furniture, the stopped clock, the terracotta ashtray on the window ledge, obviously never used, either because the old man had forgotten about it or because he wished to keep it safe.

He entered the living room. Old-fashioned chairs were drawn up to the round table. A chandelier with five frosted-glass shades hung from the centre of the ceiling. Facing the door was a chest of drawers supporting three towering bookshelves. The books were concealed behind photographs and newspaper cuttings. There were also photographs on the walls, framed and redolent of the past. The whole furnishing of the flat was of a past age.

It reminded Viktor of the flat of the grandmother who had brought him up after his parents divorced and went their separate ways. Part of an old house in Tarasov Street, that had been old-fashioned too, in some respects, though he had paid no heed to it at the time. There had been a chest of drawers there, as well, only smaller, and standing on it a glass cabinet displaying Granny's proudest possessions: the china vases presented to her for her achievements at work. There were five or six of them, each bearing her name and initials, the date, and a brief account of the occasion, neatly and painstakingly inscribed in gold ink. And there had been the same framed photographs of the same

140

epoch, that same recent but already so far distant past of a country that no longer existed.

He went over to the chest of drawers. In the bookcase photographs he recognized Pidpaly – with a woman, against a background of palms, and underneath was *Yalta, Summer 1960*. He looked closely – Pidpaly was then 40, 45, and the permed lady evidently of similar age. In another photograph Pidpaly was standing alone beside a swimming pool out of which a dolphin poked its head. *Batumi, Summer 1981* ran the legend.

The past believed in dates. And everyone's life consisted of dates, giving life a rhythm and sense of gradation, as if from the eminence of a date one could look back and down, and see the past itself. A clear, comprehensible past, divided up into squares of events, lines of paths taken.

Here, despite the odour of damp books, and perhaps by virtue of being on the ground floor, he felt at ease and safe. These walls with their faded paper, the dust-laden shades of the chandelier, the rows of photographs, had something of a mesmerizing effect.

He sat down at the table, and again thought of his grandmother, Aleksandra Vasilyevna, who, when she was old, used to take a little stool and sit outside the block. *God grant I'm never paralysed, she would say, it'd ruin your life and lose you a wife!* He had laughed, but Granny, decrepit as she was, had wormed out of her neighbours the phone number of a flat-fixer. Two months later Viktor had a two-room flat, and Granny had moved to a ground-floor one-roomer in a Khrushchev slum, where, quietly, virtually unnoticed, she died. Social Security buried her, and her neighbours gave three roubles each towards a wreath. All of which Viktor had learnt six months later, returning home from the army.

Feeling like a cup of tea, he went to the kitchen. Darkness was falling. As he switched on the light, the ancient refrigerator rumbled into life. Surprised, he took a look inside. Green sausage, and an open tin of condensed milk. He took out the milk, and in the tall, narrow kitchen cupboard found a packet of tea.

His sensation of comfort, albeit someone else's, was mixed with unease. He drank the tea, eating solidified condensed milk with it. The voices of people walking by outside alternated with the noise of a passing car.

Feeling a tickle in his throat, he poured himself a second cup, drank it, and returning to the living room, switched on the light. He looked into the study – all bookshelves and bookcases – went over to the desk, and lighting the table lamp, also ancient and with a marble base, sat down on the black leather chair.

The desk was scattered with notebooks. Noticing a thick diary beside the lamp, he leafed through it – pages of hurried minuscule handwriting interspersed with paper markers. The diary opened by itself at one such marker – a newspaper cutting. He moved closer to the light. It reported Britain's gift to Ukraine of a station in the Antarctic. The report ended with an appeal for sponsors, *without whose financial support it would not be possible to send Ukrainian scientists there.* A telephone number was given for inquiries, and a bank account number for donations.

What, wondered Viktor, had the Antarctic to do with Ukraine?

There was, he saw also, a receipt in respect of a postal draft. Examining it, he almost doubted his sanity. Pidpaly had sent the Antarctic Appeal five million, in the grossly inflated national currency, probably the pathetic total of his savings.

Putting receipt and cutting aside, he studied the old man's notes, but could decipher only a few odd words. Pidpaly's

142

thoughts were encoded and inaccessible to the outsider, by virtue of his writing.

Again he had a sense of unease and an itching in his finger-tips, as though from contact with something incomprehensible, inexplicable.

He had not forgotten his promise to the old man, but preferred for the moment not to think about it. And although he had come not thinking about it, it was after all what had drawn him there, the cold keys in his cold hand guiding him like a compass.

And here he sat amid things and papers that were no longer anybody's – in a whole world left without its creator and master. The old man had wanted no outsiders to have contact with it, or to see the destruction of a cosy little world three or four decades behind the times.

He gave a deep sigh and had a sudden urge to pull out the desk drawers or rummage in the chest of drawers in search of something to salvage as a memento. But the frozen integrity, the immobility of Pidpaly's little world prevented him. He sat contemplating the cutting and receipt, the diary and other notebooks.

The street was silent now, and the combined silence of street and flat stirred him into action. He put the newspaper cutting in his jacket pocket.

He looked round at the study walls, but didn't touch anything else. He fetched matches from the gas stove in the kitchen. In a small wall cupboard in the corridor he found a bottle of acetone, which he took back to the study. Closing his mind to what he was doing, he splashed acetone over the books on the lower shelves and on a pile of old newspapers under the desk. Half the pile of newspapers he took into the living room and put under the dinner table, throwing the tea-stained cloth to join them. He then went around setting light to the papers and anything that would burn. Flames hissed in both rooms, but as yet too feebly to engulf that doomed world. Discovering sheets, pillowcases and towels in the chest of drawers, he added them to the blaze, together with Pidpaly's raincoat from its peg in the corridor.

In a whirl of black smuts, the air grew hotter, filling the room with smoke and sparks and forcing him out into the corridor.

The crackle of burning grew steadily louder. Flames had already penetrated the table top and were now licking at the legs.

Feeling for Pidpaly's keys, he made for the door, but darted back to switch off the living room light. The fire glowed a deeper red in the dark, more beautiful and terrible than before.

He locked the outer door behind him.

He made a circuit of the block, then stopped opposite Pidpaly's windows and watched the flames shooting up to the ceiling. He looked up at the first floor. No lights were showing – the people there were either asleep or not yet back.

He took another look through the window at the dancing flames.

So that was that. He had kept his promise.

But his hands were shaking and cold shivers were running up and down his spine.

Turning away, he spotted a telephone at the corner of the neighbouring block, and from here he called the fire brigade.

Glass shattered, as if the fire were forcing its way out. A woman screamed. Five minutes later he heard the wail of fire-engine sirens. With two appliances on the scene and their crews bustling about, rolling out hoses and shouting. Viktor took a last look at the now doomed flames, and set off at an unhurried pace to the Metro.

He had the taste of smoke in his mouth. Snowflakes fell lightly on his face, but before they could melt, were blown away by an icy wind.

54

"Your hair smells of bonfire," Nina whispered sleepily as Viktor slipped into bed.

He muttered some reply, turned away and fell asleep immediately, totally exhausted.

He woke at about ten, hearing Sonya conversing with Misha beside the bed.

"Sonya, where's Auntie Nina?"

"Gone. We had breakfast and then she went. We've left you something."

On the kitchen table he found two boiled eggs and under the salt cellar, a note:

> Hi! Didn't want to wake you. Going to give Sergey's mother a hand: shop and do the washing. Be back the moment I've finished. Love, Nina.

Screwing up the note, Viktor felt the eggs. They were cold. He made himself some tea and breakfasted.

He went back to the bedroom.

"Fed Misha, Sonya?"

"Yes. He's had two fish today, but he still seems unhappy.

Why, Uncle Vik?"

He perched on the settee.

"I don't know," he said with a shrug. "I think they're only happy in cartoons."

"All animals are, in cartoons," Sonya said with an airy wave of the hand.

He noticed, looking at her, that she was wearing a new emerald-coloured dress.

"That's new, isn't it?"

"Present from Nina. Yesterday on our walk we went into a shop . . . That's where she gave it to me. Pretty, isn't it?"

"Yes."

"The penguin likes it, too."

"You've asked him, have you?"

"Yes. But he's not happy. Maybe it's bad for him here."

"That's probably it," he agreed. "What he likes is cold, and here it's warm."

"Perhaps we could put him in the fridge."

He looked at Misha standing beside her, rocking slightly on his feet, chest rising with each breath.

"We mustn't do that – he'd be too cramped, you see. I expect he wants to go home, but home's a long way away."

"Very, very far?"

"The Antarctic."

"Where's that?"

"Think of the earth as round. Can you do that?"

"Like a ball? Yes, I can."

"Well, we're standing on the top, and penguins live at the bottom, almost underneath us . . ."

"With their feet in the air?"

"In a way, yes. But we seem to them to have our feet in the air when they think of it . . . Do you see?"

"Yes," she declared loudly. "And I can stand with my legs in the air!"

And resting her back against the edge of the settee, she had a go at standing on her head, but couldn't keep it up.

"But I *can* do it," she said, sitting down on the carpet again. "It's just that I'm heavier after breakfast."

He smiled. This was the first time in these several months that he had chatted with Sonya so easily and without secret irritation, and it seemed strange. For he had not lost the feeling of Sonya's being someone else's and accidental to his own life. She had, so to speak, been dumped on him, and he had been too good-natured to take her to wherever dumped children get taken. Of course, it hadn't been quite like that. He had been guided by an odd sense of duty towards her. It was to him that Misha-non-penguin, whom he had hardly known, had entrusted her when danger threatened. Had he lived, he would have come and collected her. But now there was no one to come. Misha-non-penguin had made no mention of Sonya's mother. Friend-enemy Sergey Chekalin's half-hearted, half-cock attempt to take her had ended in his making off without a word. And now, here was Sonya at home in his flat, and not being specially disturbing or tiresome. Thanks, it was true, to Nina, who, but for Sonya, would never have come on the scene. In which case he and Misha would have gone on as before, and life would have been neither bad nor good, just ordinary.

Nina arrived at about three. From Sergey's mother's she had gone back to the shops, and now unpacked curds for Sonya, frankfurters, cottage cheese . . .

"Do you know," she said, as Viktor came into the kitchen, "Sergey rang today from Moscow. He's OK."

She kissed him.

"And you still smell of bonfire!" she added, with a smile.

55

Several days passed. Quiet, monotonous days. Viktor's sole activity during this time was the changing of the two door locks. He did the buying and changing himself. The feeling of satisfaction lasted several hours, but then boredom set in again. He had to do something, but there was nothing to do. And he didn't feel like writing.

"Uncle Vik!" Sonya cried delightedly, standing at the balcony window. "The icicles are crying!"

The thaw was back. And not before time – it was the beginning of March.

He was waiting for spring, as if warmth might prove the solution to all his problems. Although when he actually fell to thinking about his problems, he realized that he had practically none as such. He had money for the moment, especially since the Chief's mysterious night-mail repayment. And up on the wardrobe, in a bag together with the revolver, there was still a good fat bundle of $100 notes, which, though they were Sonya's, he had a moral right to a share of as her unofficial guardian.

As before, Nina kept Sonya amused during the day, sometimes at home, sometimes out and about, leaving Viktor on his own. But at night they were reunited, and knowing that neither love nor passion came into it, he still found arms and body anticipating that time with eagerness. Embracing, caressing Nina, making love, he became oblivious of himself. The warmth of her body seemed to be that very spring he so looked forward to. And then, in the small hours, with Nina asleep and breathing gently, he lay open-eyed, with the curiously comfortable sensation of leading an ordered, normal life – for which the essential requisites: wife, child, pet penguin, were present; and obviously artificial as this foursome was, Viktor shut his eyes to this fact for the sake of his feeling of comfort and a temporary illusion of happiness. But who could say? Maybe his happiness was not as illusory as the sober thoughts of morning suggested. But what, at night, were the thoughts of the morning? The very alternation of nocturnal happiness with morning common sense, and the constancy of it, seemed to prove that he was, at one and the same time, both happy and clear-thinking. So that all was well and life worth living.

Just as he was fetching Misha's breakfast from the freezer, the phone rang. He threw the slices of fish into the bowl and went and picked up the receiver in the living room.

"Greetings!" came a familiar voice. "How's life?"

"Fine."

"I'm back in Kiev," said the voice, now clearly the Chief's. "You can consider your holiday at an end."

"Shall I come and see you?"

"Why waste time? I'll send a courier. Give him the finished work, he'll give you the new. Will you be in?"

"Yes."

"Splendid! Incidentally, it's a paid holiday you've just had, although not a union member. Bye!"

Viktor made coffee, rejoicing in the peace of the flat – Nina and Sonya having gone to Pushcha-Voditsa to look for snowdrops. A peace which enabled him to sit down with a cup of coffee and calmly think it all over. A peace which made it possible to sit without thinking even, just drinking coffee, dwelling on its flavour, keeping at arm's length thoughts capable of disturbing equanimity.

But sitting sipping strong coffee, he felt suddenly on edge, and as Misha dropped a piece of fish, he gave a start and swung round to look.

The flavour of coffee became of secondary importance. His edginess increased. Disquieting thoughts prompted an onslaught of questions.

What now? Back to *obelisks*? Back to red-underlined biographical facts of people unaware that their obituaries were already in hand? Occasional coffee-drinking sessions in the Chief's sanctum? The Chief's kindly attitude, the shaky roundness of his handwriting? His laconic brevity, his attachment to that one word *processed*, entered repeatedly, neatly, painstakingly on the originals of *obelisks* which had already informed readers of the terminated life of whoever was next to merit an extensive obituary?

This new genre, *his* invention, lived. Unlike so many of its subjects. But no longer did he yearn for recognition or feel an urge to shout *I wrote that!* The anonymity of *A Group of Friends* suited him completely. The Group, he sensed, was not just him alone. The Chief was one of the Friends, too. And there was another, the Principal Friend perhaps, that someone whose bold, sweeping signature approved Viktor's *obelisks*. Though whether it was the text he approved or the subject, was now not at all clear. And then there were the dates, obviously determining the day of publication, but clearly predetermined during the subject's lifetime! Death as *planned economy!*

No, it was not the quality of his text, his philosophical digressions, or felicitous presentation of U-turns in the lives of his notables that this someone was approving, but the notables themselves – determining how long they had left to live. And the Chief's role in all this was a surprisingly minor one – a peculiar cross between courier and ticket inspector. And although his duties certainly included publishing *obelisks* on schedule, even that did not now seem particularly significant – any more than his own role, which Viktor still did not completely understand.

Out of the blue, and contrary to this logical line of thought, he remembered something that diverted him from it and made his blood run cold. And just as he seemed about to grasp what was going on, he was back where he started, with his attempt to solve an equation having two knowns and one unknown frustrated. What he had remembered was how the Chief had responded to his probing on the night when the car had been waiting to take him to the airport: *The full story is what you get told only if and when your work, and with it your existence, are no longer required.*

It had seemed then that he and the Chief were parting for ever. And Viktor had naturally thought that his work was now at an end, although the mystery unearthed in the Chief's safe continued to disquiet him. But by the next day it was as if time had relegated that to the distant past. And the time distance created in imagination between past mystery and a Viktor now entering upon a new stage of existence, blunted interest in the former, regardless of his own obvious involvement. Better, he thought, not to know, yet still be alive – especially as it was now all over and done with.

And now it turned out that far from over and done with, it

was still going on, with him still working, still paying especial attention to underlinings in red.

Was it worth trying to discover *what* was going on? Worth risking comfort – curious though it might be – and peace of mind? He would still have to write *obelisks*, still have to be needed in order to stay alive.

Again the Chief's parting shot came to mind.

To hell with it, Viktor decided. Easier all round not to give it a thought.

Picking up the long-completed batch of military *obelisks* from the window ledge, he ran through the names and what he had written.

What difference did it make to him what happened to these generals? Or for what date some unknown person had planned their deaths and subsequent obituaries, the latter suggestive of their richly deserving to die?

If then his life was that dependent on his work, let that work continue. In which case it might be best simply to distance himself from what was going on. Not do anything foolish, like trying to disappear or lose himself in some other city – but, more simply: realize Nina's dream – buy a little house in the country, move and live happily there, all four of them together, he writing his *obelisks* and sending them off to the city, as one might to another land where not all was as it should be.

Out of which thoughts he was jolted by Misha laying his head upon his knee, and looking down at the penguin, he stroked him.

"How about a move to the country?" he asked Misha, smiling wrily at the apparent unreality of his dreams.

56

As if to confirm yesterday as indeed the end of his holiday, Viktor sat now at his typewriter, sipping hot coffee and contemplating the new *obelisk* laboriously taking shape. The other half of the kitchen table was occupied by Sonya with her pencils and felt-tipped pens, Nina having gone somewhere that morning, leaving no note. But he wasn't worried – she wouldn't be long.

In the folder of new material brought by courier the evening before, as well as files on a number of representatives of the Ministry of Health, he had found an envelope of *holiday pay*. At least, those were the words typed on the slip of paper accompanying the $500. Money which gave a little lift to his creative spirit. Even so, progress was terribly slow. Words refused to deploy in battle formation, sentences scattered, only to be slaughtered by irritable x's and reformed.

"Is it like him?" Sonya asked suddenly, showing her drawing.

He looked closely. "What's it supposed to be?"

"Misha!"

He shook his head.

"It looks," he said thoughtfully, "more like a chicken."

Sonya frowned, looked at the drawing, and threw it on the floor.

"No good being cross," he coaxed. "Learn drawing from life is what you've got to do."

"How?"

"Just sit down in front of Misha, look at him, and draw. That'll make it like him."

Pleased with this idea, she gathered up pencils and felt tips, got a few more sheets of paper from Viktor, and set off in search of Misha.

Viktor went back to work. He managed, in the end, to get through the first *obelisk*, and having done so, massaged his temples. Clearly he was rusty.

A door banged.

Nina, he thought. The alarm clock on the window ledge showed just short of noon.

A minute later she looked into the kitchen.

"Hi!" She was all smiles.

His response was on the cold side.

"Notice anything?"

He looked. Same jeans, familiar sweater. No change.

He shrugged, looked at her, puzzled at first, then more closely.

"Well?" she urged, still smiling.

"Your teeth!" he exclaimed, astonished.

And it was – beautifully white, no trace of yellow. Hers was now the smile of the dentifrice advert.

He too smiled.

"At last!" She kissed him resoundingly on the cheek. "I had to wait a whole month. $400, and I could have had it done without waiting. I got it for $80 . . ."

Sonya came running in with a sheet of paper. "Nina, look! I've drawn Misha!"

She showed Nina, who squatted down, studied the drawing, and patted her on the back.

"Well done!" she said. "We'll frame it and hang it on the wall."

"Can we?" Sonya was delighted.

"Of course! So everyone can see it."

Viktor also had a look. Her drawing had caught something of the penguin.

"Right!" said Nina standing up. "I think we all deserve a good lunch today, so clear the kitchen!"

Sonya took her drawing to the living room, and Viktor followed.

Nina was already behaving like the lady of the house, he thought, but he was not the least bit angry. On the contrary, he was even cheered by the thought.

57

The first drizzle of spring was falling. The snow in the courtyard had almost all melted, and only under bushes were doomed remnants of winter still to be seen in the shape of frozen lumps. Another few days and fresh green blades of grass would peep from the warm soil.

Viktor was sitting at the kitchen table, chair turned to the window, a cup of tea forgotten and growing cold beside him, staring down at the courtyard. He was looking forward to the warmth of spring. And although it was hardly likely to change his life, a certain vague, in no way justified feeling of hope brought a smile of pleasure to his face, as he saw the sunlight shafting through a light mix of bright and dark cloud.

The latest batch of *obelisks* lay ready in their folder on the table. He could ring the Chief and say the job was done, or he could wait another day, putting off work on the next batch for a bit.

Shifting his thoughts from the rain, he wondered who the

next lot of *obelisk* notables would be. Cosmonauts? Submariners?

He had become accustomed to the files he received bringing together people already linked by interests or professions – military, health officials, State Deputies – and it no longer struck him as strange. The notebook he had opened when he started had lain forgotten since the Chief had called a halt to personal initiative in the choice of notables. After that, Viktor had given up reading papers in search of VIPs. He now worked exclusively on *semi-finished material*, in the form of detailed files. This was both easier and more suspicious. The more he worked, the more his suspicions grew, until they became the absolute certainty that this whole *obelisk* business was part of a patently criminal operation. The realization of this in no way influenced his daily life and work. And although he could not help thinking about it, he found it easier to do so every day, having recognized the complete impossibility of ever changing his life. Harnessed as he was, it was a question of hauling his load until he dropped. So he hauled.

The sitting-room phone rang, and the next moment Nina poked her head round the kitchen door.

"For you, Vik."

He went and picked up the receiver.

"That you, Vik?" an unknown man's voice enquired.

"Yes."

"It's me, Lyosha, remember? Gave you a lift from the cemetery."

"Ah, hello."

"Something rather important. I'll be outside your place in 20 minutes. Come down when you see me."

"Who was that?" Nina asked, seeing Viktor standing perplexed, still holding the receiver.

"Someone I know."

"Sonya and I are learning to read, aren't we, Sonya?"

"Yes," the little girl confirmed, sitting on the settee with a book.

Hearing a car draw up outside, Viktor put on his jacket and went down.

"Get in," said Lyosha.

The door banged shut. It was cold in the car.

"How's the animal?" Lyosha asked amiably, stroking his beard.

"All right."

"It's like this," his face grew serious. "I'd like to invite you and said animal to a certain occasion . . . Not exactly a jolly one, but there'll be money in it."

"What sort of occasion?" Viktor asked drily, becoming interested.

"The boss of some friends of mine has died. Funeral's tomorrow. A big affair, as you can imagine. Bronze-handled coffin – cost a packet. I'd told them about your penguin, and now they've remembered . . . You and he are invited."

"What for?" Viktor stared amazed.

"How shall I put it . . . " hesitant drawing in of lower lip. "A touch of style's called for . . . And to have a penguin there would supply it, they thought. With a vengeance. Naturally suited, isn't he, being black and white? . . . Get the idea?"

He did, though it all seemed like a stupid joke.

"Are you serious?" he asked, looking sharply at Lyosha and meeting an expression that was gravity itself.

"I'd call $1,000 for hire of a penguin serious," he replied, forcing a smile.

"I'm not too happy about it," Viktor confessed, finally convinced that Lyosha was serious.

"To be frank, you've no option," declared the bearded Lyosha. "It's an offer you can't refuse. The departed's friends could take it amiss . . . Don't make problems for yourself. I'll pick you up tomorrow about ten."

Viktor got out and watched until the car disappeared around the block, heading for the road.

Back in the flat he locked himself into the bathroom. While the water ran, he stood in front of the mirror, staring, as if at a photograph he wanted to remember.

58

Next day they drove to the Baykov Cemetery in Lyosha's ancient foreign-made car, Viktor and Misha in the back. They drove in silence.

At the cemetery entrance they were stopped by a young fellow in camouflage combat gear, who bent down at Lyosha's window, nodded, and waved him on.

Monuments, railings flitted past. Viktor felt fit for nothing.

The avenue ahead was blocked by a cortège of parked foreign-made cars.

"We'll have to walk a bit," said Lyosha, turning to Viktor in the back.

Taking binoculars from the glove compartment and slinging them around his neck, he got out.

The sky was cloudless, the sun shone, and the air was filled with inappropriately cheerful birdsong. Viktor looked about him.

They made their way slowly past the impressive, new, foreign-made cars to where a crowd of people were waiting.

"Why the binoculars?" Viktor asked as they walked.

Lyosha, slightly ahead of him, looked back.

"We all have our job to do. Mine is to provide protection and ensure order, so no one spoils the –" he stopped short – "so that everything's in order."

Viktor nodded.

The crowd of sombrely well-dressed men made way for them.

They stopped at the graveside by the open coffin, in which lay a man in his 40s, grey-haired and wearing gold-rimmed spectacles. His stylish suit was covered up to the chest with sprays of flowers.

A tense look around showed that Lyosha had vanished, and that he and Misha were surrounded by sombre-faced strangers, none of whom seemed to pay him or the penguin any attention whatever.

At the head of the coffin stood the priest, Bible open, muttering into his beard. Standing behind him was a young man in a cassock, who was evidently his curate.

Viktor would have liked to shut his eyes until all was over. But there was a kind of almost electric tension in the air that every now and then produced an unwelcome, yet annoyingly invigorating pricking sensation to face and hands. He stood, like the penguin, motionless. The burial ritual took its course. On the brow of the deceased was a strip of paper bearing a cross and an inscription in Old Church Slavonic. The priest opened his book at the next marker, and in a strained baritone, launched into his gloomy recitative. All bowed their heads, except Misha, who stood as before, head bent, gazing into the grave.

Viktor squinted down at him.

They were part of this ritual, Misha and he.

The coffin having been lowered on ropes by two spotlessly attired gravediggers, the mourners came back to life. Earth drummed down on the coffin lid.

And for the first time, Viktor and Misha seemed to attract interest to the extent of receiving oblique glances, of curiosity, perhaps, or sorrow.

"You're invited by the next of kin to join them at the wake," Lyosha announced, coming over to him. "Just you, not the animal. Six o'clock this evening. *Hotel Moscow* restaurant. And I've been given this for you."

He handed over an envelope which Viktor mechanically pocketed without a word.

"Go to the car. I'll catch you up," Lyosha added, slipping away.

Looking round, Viktor saw there was a little old man videoing the proceedings.

"Well, shall we go home?" he asked, squatting down in front of Misha, saddened by the indifference his eyes reflected.

They drove home. Again in silence.

"Don't forget the wake!" called Lyosha, as they parted.

Viktor nodded. The car drove off.

"To hell with the wake!" he thought, climbing the stairs with Misha in his arms.

59

With Sonya abed, Viktor and Nina sat in the kitchen that evening, drinking wine and talking. He gave her an account of the *funeral with penguin*.

"So what?" she asked skittishly. "For $1,000, why worry?"

For a minute he was silent, then he said, "I don't . . . It's a lot of money . . . Just that it's strange . . ."

"Maybe you'll raise my wages, now Misha's earning," she said, smiling but serious. And then in a gentler tone she added, "I'm always spending on our behalf anyway. I bought some little boots for Sonya . . ."

"For heaven's sake, don't call it wages," he said with a sigh. "I'll let you have some money in the morning. When that's gone just tell me."

He looked at her and shook his head.

"What is it?"

"Just that you're very much the country girl, sometimes."

"I was born in the country," she confirmed, smiling again.

"Right. Let's go to bed," he said, rising from the table.

Next morning he woke to find Nina shaking him.

"What is it?" he asked sleepily, and with no inclination to get up.

"In the kitchen, there's a bag." She was clearly worried. "Come and see."

Getting up, Viktor threw on a dressing-gown, and headed uncertainly for the kitchen.

There was indeed a bag on the table. Back to the old tricks, he thought wearily.

He went and checked the locks. The door was securely shut.

Returning to the kitchen, he gingerly felt the bag, and emboldened by the outline of a bottle, set about unpacking it.

Five minutes later, having examined the contents, he called Nina.

Nina came in, stopped dead, and gazed in amazement at what

was laid out on the table: a plate of fish in aspic, a clingfilm-covered restaurant selection of traditional meats, fresh tomatoes, a chop, a bottle of Smirnoff vodka.

"Where did this come from?"

Pulling a face, Viktor pointed to the blue letters forming the abbreviation of *Ukrainian Restaurants* on the rim of a plate.

"There's a note," Nina said, indicating the bottle.

Scotch-taped to the neck was a folded piece of paper which, detached and unfolded, read:

> Don't do that again, old chap. Respect for the dead! This is from the relatives. It's Aleksandr Safronov's memory you'll be drinking to.
>
> See you! – Lyosha.

"Who's it from?"

He handed her the note. She read it, then looked at him, perplexed.

"What was it you did?"

"I didn't go to the wake."

"You should have gone," she said quietly.

Giving her an irritable look, he went and felt in the pockets of his sheepskin jacket for Lyosha's card, and snatching up the receiver, dialled his number.

For a long time there was no response.

At long last a thick, sleepy voice said, "Hello?"

"Lyosha?" Viktor asked coldly.

Lyosha, clearly the worse for a night's drinking, muttered indistinctly.

"It's me, Vik. Look, about this stunt with the bag –"

"What stunt? Is it really you, Vik? How's the animal?"

"Listen, that bag, how did it get into my kitchen?" Viktor demanded irritably.

"*How?* By request of the next of kin . . . What's bugging you?"

"What's bugging me is how it got through closed doors!" His voice was now almost a shout.

"Take it easy. I hear you. But I've got a headache . . . *Through closed doors* – you ask? But no doors ever are completely closed! Grow up! Drink to Safronov's memory. Me, I've got to sober up, too, but I'd like a bit of sleep first. What the hell did you have to wake me for?"

He hung up.

Viktor shook his head, sick at heart at this evidence of his own impotence and defencelessness.

"Vik!" Nina called from the kitchen.

"Coming."

The table was already laid. Two plates had vodka glasses beside them.

"Why waste good stuff? When it's still fresh . . . Sit down. – Sonya!" she called into the corridor. "Come and eat. We must drink to this person – it's bad not to," she said, turning to Viktor, who was still standing by the table, and following the direction of her eyes, he unscrewed the Smirnoff bottle.

"Look what I've drawn!" said Sonya, coming in with a sheet of paper and holding it out to Nina.

Nina took the drawing and put it on top of the fridge.

"First we'll eat, and then we'll look," she said in a school-mistressy way.

60

A day passed, and with a fresh batch of files from the courier, Viktor sat at his typewriter. A spring sun was shining, and though it was still cold outside, in the kitchen its yellow rays not only flooded the table but even warmed the air. Work and the long-awaited warmth eased the burden of the recent past. And although all that had transpired was still, in a sense, present, the work of interspersing the philosophico-literary with facts underlined in red, provided an escape from affliction and all that served to remind him of his own helplessness.

One of his coffee breaks was enlivened by his suddenly calling to mind having written, some time ago, an *obelisk* on one Safronov. Who he had been and the nature of his attainments underlined in red Viktor had completely forgotten. But he felt sure that it was this Safronov whom he and Misha had buried a few days before. He couldn't, of course, be absolutely sure, but the fact that the funeral had been so patently obituary-worthy seemed to confirm the accuracy of his guess.

The thought that he who had first written the obituary had then attended the funeral, in the role of inspector to check that burial was indeed taking place, even brought a smile to his face.

Nina had taken Sonya to the Dnieper for a walk, so there was nothing to distract him from work. And that day work went smoothly. Reading through what he had written, he was well satisfied, and forged ahead with his improvisations on other people's deaths.

With four *obelisks* completed, he squinted out of the window at the sun, and went over to the stove. He put the kettle on and walked about the flat. Misha was standing by the balcony door, as if in expectation of an icy draught, and Viktor squatted down beside him.

"How are we doing?" he asked, taking a good look at him. "Very nicely, very nicely," he said, answering for his penguin and straightening up.

Noticing two framed drawings on the wall, he went over. One was the familiar portrait of Misha, the other – a threesome and a tiny penguin. *Uncle Vik, me, Nina and Misha* said the wobbly letters, but then, obviously in Nina's hand, *Uncle* had been corrected to *Daddy*, and *Nina* to *Mummy*. Nina's writing was neat and schoolmistressy. The signature at the bottom looked as if it had been improved by Teacher. All that was missing was the mark. Eight out of ten, probably, in view of the two corrections.

That drawing gave him a chilly feeling. He didn't care for Nina's corrections. There was a certain violence about them, to words and to the actual situation. The fact that the drawing was hung rather high up where Sonya could see it only by standing on a chair, meant that Nina had made the corrections for herself and for him.

Nina, too, seemed to be pretending they were a family, nursing, like him perhaps, the illusion of their being a single entity. Only it was an illusion shattered daily, lightly and unintentionally, by Sonya, the words *Daddy* and *Mummy* being either unknown to her, or ones she saw no reason to employ.

She was closer to reality: too young to invent a complicated world for herself, and too straightforward to suspect the thoughts and feelings of two grown-ups.

Would she not like a child of her own? he wondered uneasily, his thoughts returning to Nina. To call her Mummy to the end of her days? There would be no difficulty about that . . .

But was *he*, he fell to thinking, anxious to be called *Daddy*? He had no objection in principle. He had money, work, everything. Even a young, attractive woman capable of motherhood. There was no love in it. Love wasn't the main thing, but something that came with time. Maybe one had only to move to the country and a spacious two-storey house with all conveniences, for it to light up like a candle.

He shook his head as if to rid it of so foolish a notion.

61

March brought warmth. Every morning, like a conscientious caretaker, the sun climbed into the sky and shone its brightest.

Viktor was getting through the latest batch of files, breaking off at intervals to make coffee and take his cup out onto the balcony. Misha joined him occasionally, seeming also to enjoy the sun.

Just another five minutes, and then it was back to the kitchen table, to hammer away at the typewriter.

His sunny mood accorded easily with the poetic gloom of his *obelisks*. Even a recent, second *funeral with penguin* had failed to unsettle him, although it had meant sitting through the wake of the unknown departed. But, strange as it seemed, even that proved not so very terrible. Of the good 200 or so mourners not one paid Viktor any special attention. Apart, of course, from Lyosha, sitting beside him. But he had soon become drunk, and pushing his plate aside, had fallen asleep, head on table cloth, or, more precisely, his table napkin.

There were no speeches. The well-dressed men seated at the two long tables exchanged business-like looks of sorrow, raising glasses of vodka to each other – a form of silent association Viktor had no difficulty in imitating, raising his glass, inclining his head, and looking with genuine grief at those sitting opposite. His sadness was unfeigned, but had nothing to do with the departed. It was just that the ambience of these wakes oppressed him, added to which the company at table was mainly male – Viktor did, looking around, notice some women, but no more than three or four, of mature years and marked by their conspicuous mourning as the original sources of grief.

At the end, he was put into one of the cars waiting outside the restaurant, together with three other men who did not introduce themselves, but simply asked where he lived and told the driver where to go. A night delivery service with a vengeance. Arriving home at about one, he encountered Misha in the corridor.

"Why aren't you asleep?" he asked, happily drunk. "Must get your sleep. What if we have got to shoot off to the cemetery again tomorrow?"

A week had now passed with Viktor hammering away at his typewriter and rejoicing in spring and sunshine. And life seemed easy and carefree, despite painful moments and less frequent scruples over his own part in an ugly business. But what, in an ugly world, was ugly? No more than a tiny part of an unknown evil existing generally, but not personally touching him and his little world. And not to be fully aware of his part in that ugly something was clearly a guarantee of the indestructibility of his world, and of its tranquillity.

Turning again to the window, he let the sun fall on his face.

Maybe he really should buy a little dacha, sit in summer at

a table in the garden, writing in the fresh air. With Sonya, who would like growing things, pottering in flower beds and vegetable plots, and Nina content . . .

He thought back to their New Year dacha, to Sergey, and how they had sat before the fire. How long ago that had been! How long, though not much time had passed since then!

62

On Sunday the sun continued to shine, and although in the morning there had been a thin haze of cloud, by eleven it had dispersed, revealing a sky of springtime blue.

After breakfast Viktor, Nina and Sonya set off for Kreshchatik Street, leaving Misha on the balcony with a bowl of lunch, and the door ajar so that he could, if he wished, go back inside.

He took them first to *Café Passazh*, where they sat on the terrace. For Sonya and Nina he ordered ice-cream, and coffee for himself.

Sonya having chosen to sit facing the sun, now screwed up her eyes, shielding them with the palm of her hand, playing peekaboo, watched by a smiling Nina.

Sipping his coffee, Viktor spotted an open newspaper kiosk, and saying he wouldn't be a minute, left the table.

Returning with *Capital News*, he quickly ran an eye over the headlines and finding, to his joy, neither menace nor a single *obelisk*, went calmly back to page one, taking another sip of coffee.

Remarkable that on so fine a spring day the news should seem so amazingly peaceful. No shooting, no scandals. Quite the reverse, as if the paper was commanding its readers to be happy with life, with headlines inspiring gladness and hope.

"Would you like to go to Italy, Sonya?" he asked jokingly.

Licking the little plastic spoon, she shook her head.

"No – I want to go on a swing," she said.

Nina wiped the ice-cream from Sonya's mouth with a napkin.

As they walked through the park above the Dnieper, they came to a play area, sat Sonya on a swing and swung her, laughing, high above the ground.

"No more! No more!" she cried after a few minutes.

And again they walked through the park, Sonya between them, holding their hands.

"I was thinking, Nina," he said as they walked, "we could buy a dacha."

She smiled and became thoughtful.

"That'd be nice," she said a minute later, having evidently pictured the dacha she would like.

At lunch-time they went back to the flat and ate there.

Sonya joined Misha on the balcony. Nina and Viktor sat in front of the TV.

A Ukrainian version of *Cine-Travelogue Club* was on. A pretty blonde in a bright yellow bathing costume stood on the deck of a motor vessel, telling of exotic islands, then appeared on the beach of just such an island, exchanging smiles with sun-bronzed natives. Every so often captions ran across the bottom of the screen, with the telephone numbers of travel agents.

"Why were you asking Sonya about Italy?" she asked with sudden interest.

"They've done away with the visa requirement."

"Could we go one day?" she asked dreamily.

The pretty blonde was back again, now dressed more warmly in tight knitted skirt and dark-blue jacket.

For the past year, she announced, a Ukrainian scientific research station has been operating in the Antarctic. In an earlier programme we appealed for contributions towards sending our scientists a planeload of supplies. Many of you have responded, but unfortunately more is still needed than the amount so far received. I appeal to private entrepreneurs and others with funds – on you depends whether our scientists will be able to continue their work in the Antarctic. Have pencil and paper ready for the account number to which sponsor donations can be made, and a telephone number on which you can hear details of what your money will be spent on.

Darting to the kitchen, Viktor seized a pen and a sheet of paper, and returned in time to write down the numbers from the screen.

"What's that for?" Nina asked in surprise.

He shrugged. "Thought I might send them $20," he said uncertainly. "In memory of Pidpaly. I told you about him, remember? I've got a cutting about the station somewhere."

Nina shot him a look of disapproval.

"Waste of money," she said. "It'll only get stolen. Remember how they collected for a hospital for the Chernobyl children?"

Viktor said nothing, folded the paper and put it in his pocket. What business was it of hers where he sent his money?

63

Towards the end of March rain set in.

With the disappearance of the sun Viktor's spirits slumped. He worked away at his typewriter as before, but painfully slowly and with little inspiration. Even so, *obelisk* quality remained unimpaired, and reading over what he had written, he was invariably satisfied. No longer was his professionalism dependent on his mood.

Nina and Sonya kept to the flat for days on end.

Sometimes, when Nina went to the shops, Sonya, evidently weary of Misha's company, came into the kitchen to distract Viktor. With great forbearance he answered her questions, breathing a sigh of relief when he heard Nina return. Sonya then ran to her and he got back to work.

When Lyosha rang to say there was a funeral the next day, his spirits hit rock bottom. He spent ten minutes attempting to convey that it was too raw, too wet, that he was feeling low, as well as worried lest Misha catch a chill. Lyosha heard him out, then said that he, Viktor, was not all that essential. The animal was the main requirement. "You stay at home," he said finally, "I'll take Misha and bring him back afterwards. I'll keep an umbrella over him at the cemetery, so he doesn't catch cold."

A solution, a partial victory, Viktor decided, glad to give the funeral a miss.

And while he felt sorry for Misha there was nothing he could do about it. The possible consequences of a sudden refusal to release him for graveside attendance were all too obvious.

Viktor's firmness paid off handsomely. The next time Lyosha

did not expect him to participate. It was agreed that in future Lyosha would collect Misha and bring him back, and surprisingly this change of arrangement was not reflected in the amount of his honorarium. Each time it was the same $1,000, only now more easily come by, without any standing at gravesides or obligatory wakes. Misha was now earning on his own account, and the whole thing savoured of penguin hire.

Viktor was irked, of course, to think what Misha received for a single appearance, against his wage of $300. And though both lots of money came to him, the underlying inequality remained. There was nothing for it but to bow yet again to the inevitable. None of which in any way affected his attachment to Misha.

Ought he, he wondered, to ask the Chief for a rise, but immediately he sensed it wouldn't be worth the effort. He was, after all, fairly relaxed in his work. No one breathed down his neck or chased him for his *obelisks*. He was his own master. Batch completed, he rang up and swapped it with the courier for another. He had money enough, and so no cause for complaint.

No, all was as it should be, and God grant it stayed that way. And when the rainy spell was over, he could start looking for a dacha!

And as he visualized a little house surrounded by a garden, a hammock stretched between two sturdy trees, and himself kindling a fire for kebabs, his mood brightened.

All would be well, said the persuasive voice of his imagination, all beauty and bright sun.

And Viktor believed it.

But the rain and the task of *obelisk*-writing continued. And funerals involving Misha became more frequent, regardless of the rain, as if there had been a rise in the death-rate among those whose friends and relatives could not imagine a funeral without a penguin.

The day after one such funeral, as Viktor was studying a fresh batch of files, Sonya dashed in in great alarm.

"Uncle Vik, Misha's sneezing!"

Viktor went to the bedroom, and for the first time ever saw Misha *lying on his side* on his camel-hair blanket, trembling and wheezing.

Viktor stood paralysed with fear, at a loss what to do.

"Nina!" he shouted.

"She's at Sergey's mum's," said Sonya.

"Hold on, Misha, hold on," he said in a voice charged with emotion, gently stroking him. "We'll think of something."

Going to the living room, he turned, not very hopefully, to V in the telephone book, and to his amazement found no fewer than ten vets listed. But what experience would any of them have of treating penguins? Dogs and cats would be more in their line.

In spite of these doubts, he rang the first number.

"Is Nikolay Ivanovich there?" he asked the woman who answered, having checked he had got his names right.

"Hold on."

"Yes?" came a man's voice almost immediately.

"Sorry, but I've got a problem – my penguin's ill."

"*Penguin?*" the voice repeated, and Viktor knew at once that he had got the wrong man. "Not my province, but I can tell you who to ring."

"You can?" He sighed with relief. "I'll get a pen."

Viktor wrote the number – that of one David Yanovich – on the directory, and dialled without replacing the receiver.

"Well," said David Yanovich, when he had heard him out,

"if you've got that sort of animal, you'll have the money for treatment. Address?"

"Is the vet coming?" asked Sonya, as Viktor came back and sat down beside Misha on the floor.

"Yes."

"Like Dr Dolittle?" she asked sadly.

He nodded.

Half an hour later David Yanovich arrived: short, rather bald, with a frozen smile and kind eyes.

"Where's the patient then?" he asked, coming in and removing his shoes.

"In there." Viktor indicated the door. "Like some slippers?"

"No thanks." He quickly hung his mack on the hook, and briefcase in hand, made for the door, his socks leaving moist prints on the linoleum.

"Now then," he said, squatting down beside Misha.

He felt Misha all over, peered into his eyes, then, producing a stethoscope, sounded him front and back, like a normal doctor. Returning the stethoscope to his briefcase, he gazed at him deep in thought.

"Well?"

David Yanovich scratched the back of his neck, and sighed. "Hard to say, but clearly not good. It all depends, I'm afraid, on how you're placed financially. It's not my fee I'm talking about. There's not much I can do. He needs to go to a clinic."

"And what will that cost?" Viktor asked cautiously.

David Yanovich gestured helplessly. "It won't be cheap – that's for sure. If you take my advice, the Theophania Clinic's the place – $50 a day, but with the guarantee that they'll do everything possible. There's a hospital for scientists nearby, and their clinic rents time on their tomograph – an added guarantee of correct diagnosis. And quite a few good doctors from the hospital earn a bit on the side working at the clinic."

"Ordinary doctors?" Viktor asked in surprise.

David Yanovich shrugged. "Why not? You don't imagine animals are any different internally, do you? Their illnesses, yes. So I'll ring the Theophania from here if you like, and get a car sent."

"Please do."

Pocketing a mere $20 for attending, David Yanovich departed. An hour later another vet arrived who also examined Misha, sounding and feeling him all over.

"Right," he said, "we'll take him. And don't worry, you won't be conned. Three days diagnosis, and we'll know. If we can cure him, we will, if not . . ." He shruggged. "We'll bring him back, so as not to waste your money. Here," he handed Viktor a card. "Not mine, Ilya Semyonovich's – he'll be treating your pet."

The vet departed, leaving his card and taking Misha.

Sonya cried. The rain rained on. An unfinished *obelisk* protruded from the typewriter, but Viktor didn't feel like work. Legs against the hot radiator, he stood at the bedroom window, tears welling, as if in chain reaction to Sonya's, and through his tears, watched raindrops doing their best to cling to the glass. The wind set them quivering and away they shot finally, only to be replaced by fresh drops, and continue the senseless battle with the wind.

64

That night Viktor was unable to sleep. He could hear Sonya sobbing in the sitting room. The phosphorescent hands of the alarm clock showed that it was getting on for two. Only Nina was asleep, breathing heavily.

Naturally, she had been distressed at the news when she got back from Sergey's mother's. She had worn herself out vainly trying to comfort Sonya, and fallen asleep as soon as her head had touched the pillow.

Viktor felt strangely irritated that she should be sleeping peacefully. For an instant Nina seemed completely alien, utterly indifferent to him and Sonya, while Sonya seemed closer, and the two of them the more akin for their shared concern for Misha.

Looking at her, lying there with her back to him, he realized that it wasn't her sleeping peacefully that had caused his momentary irritation, but more his own peace-denying wakefulness.

Endeavouring not to wake her, he got up, put on his dressing-gown, went to the sitting room, and bent over Sonya.

She was sleeping, but uneasily, and still sobbing.

He stood for a minute or two, then went to the kitchen, shut the door behind him, and without switching on the light, went and sat down at the table.

The measured tick of the old alarm clock on the window ledge was amplified by the darkness and silence. It was surprisingly loud and he gazed, perplexed, at the tiny source of ticking lurking in the gloom. He wanted to silence it. He held it up to his eyes. The correct time, which it was the work of this simple, reliable mechanism to provide, did not interest him. Complete silence was all he wanted, but the tick grew even louder, and realizing that, stupid as it seemed, it was in fact time alone that was capable of stopping the clock, Viktor took it into the corridor, deposited it by the main door, and came back.

After listening hard and failing to detect so much as a distant tick, he felt reassured.

In the one lighted window of the block opposite, there was a woman.

She was sitting at a table reading. And although it wasn't possible to see her face, he felt a sudden warmth and sympathy towards her, as to a companion in misfortune.

He watched her sitting motionless, chin propped on hands, only occasionally lowering her right hand to turn a page.

For a moment it seemed brighter outside. A pale yellow half moon had emerged. But having revealed itself to Viktor, it hid again in unseen cloud.

He looked back at the lighted window. The woman was at the stove. She lit the burner, put the kettle on, then returned to the table and her book.

It was good that the rain had stopped, he thought, remembering the quivering drops on the window pane.

Turning to the closed door, he remembered Misha's habit of pushing it open, standing there, then coming over as he sat at the table and snuggling against his knee. If only it would open now, and Misha be standing there!

After sitting for half an hour or so, he stole back to the bedroom, and slipped under the blanket. With Sonya's sobbing still in his ears, he fell asleep.

Next morning Nina woke him.

"Someone came in the night again," she said, plainly worried.

"Brought something again, have they?" he asked sleepily.

She shook her head. "No, but they've left an alarm clock inside the door."

"That was me," he muttered in an effort to reassure her.

"Whatever for?" she asked in surprise.

"Because of its ticking," he said, dozing off again, oblivious to her bewilderment and questioning looks.

He woke at about 11.00. The flat was quiet. The sun was shining.

In the kitchen he found his breakfast and a note:

Back soon. We've gone for a walk. Nina.

After he had washed, he picked up the card left by the vet and rang the clinic.

"Can I speak to Ilya Semyonovich?"

"That's me," said a velvety voice.

"I'm the owner of the penguin . . . Misha."

"Greetings," said the invisible Ilya Semyonovich. "Well, how can I put it? Provisionally, it's flu, with serious complications. We're doing a tomograph this evening, and then we can be more precise."

"How is he at the moment?"

"No change, I'm afraid."

"Can I visit?"

"I'm afraid not. You must be patient. Ring daily and I'll update you," Ilya Semyonovich promised.

Returning to the kitchen, Viktor ate two boiled eggs, drank tea, and got out the typewriter from under the table. Sticking out of it was an unfinished *obelisk* on a certain Bondarenko, Director of *Broadway Private Funeral Services*. He smiled at the

bitter irony of it. He could imagine how *professional* his funeral
would be, with colleagues standing decorously beside a splendid,
gilt-handled coffin.

What did *he* have underlined? he wondered, no longer able
to remember anything from Bondarenko's file.

He found the three pages and looked.

> In 1995, at Belogorodok, in a common grave in the village
> cemetery, Vyacheslav Bondarenko interred a number of
> mutilated, unidentified corpses. There are grounds
> for supposing that among the interred were the bodies
> of Captain Golovatko of the Anti Organized Crime
> Department, and Major Prochenko of the Ukrainian
> Security Service. Bondarenko is supected of involvement
> in a number of similar interments in villages in the
> Kiev region over the period 1992–94.

With no sense of bitter irony, Viktor got up, made coffee,
and went out onto the balcony.

To take his mind off funerals for five minutes, he looked at
the windows of the block opposite, trying to determine which
had been the one with the light on. But now in broad daylight
they all looked the same.

65

The next morning also began with a call to the Theophania
Clinic. But Ilya Semyonovich wasn't there, and Viktor had nothing
to tell Sonya who was standing beside him.

"I'll try again in half an hour," he promised.

Without a word, she went over to the balcony door.

"How about going to the circus this evening?" Nina asked, bending down to her.

Sonya shook her head.

As Viktor was on his way to start work in the kitchen, the phone rang. Sonya and Nina stood and listened. He lifted the receiver, also expecting it to be the veterinary clinic, but it was the Chief, and he was evidently displeased.

"Philosophical masterpieces are not what I want," he declared, almost shouting. "Just do a simple professional job, and kindly be quick about it. I can't wait a whole week for just five or six texts."

Viktor nodded gloomily as he listened.

"Are you with me?" demanded the Chief in a calmer voice, as if wearied by his outburst.

"Yes," replied Viktor replacing the receiver. He had grown used to phone conversations with the Chief being too business-like to include *hellos* or *goodbyes*.

"Who was that?" asked Nina from the balcony door.

"Work," he sighed, returning the receiver to his ear.

He dialled the number of the veterinary clinic.

This time Ilya Semyonovich was there. "We need to meet," he said.

Viktor detected a note of doom in his voice. "Shall I come out to the clinic?"

"No point. We'll meet in town. *Old Kiev*, Kreshchatik Street, at eleven."

"How shall I recognize you?" asked Viktor.

"I don't think there'll be many there. Still, grey mack, tweed cap, thin, shortish, moustache . . ."

"What do they say?" Sonya asked impatiently.

"He's getting on," he lied. "I'm going to see the vet and find out exactly."

He was filled with foreboding. Otherwise why this meeting at a café in Kreshchatik Street? For good news there was always the phone. Maybe the vet wanted to talk money. Viktor had, after all, paid nothing so far, and it was $50 a day for Misha's stay in the clinic alone.

The thought that money might be the subject of their conversation in the café reassured him a little.

The sun was shining. By the entrance, two girls were jumping over stretched elastic, and he gave them a wide berth.

Down in the basement café Ilya Semyonovich was waiting, standing at a tall table on which was a cup of coffee. No one else was in evidence, not even behind the counter or at the coffee machine.

Ilya Semyonovich greeted him, and went and banged loudly on the counter.

"Another coffee," he told the woman who appeared from behind the scenes, then came back.

"So what's the score?" asked Viktor.

"He appears to have a congenital heart defect," said the vet. "Radical treatment for the influenza could kill him . . . But even without the influenza, his chances are virtually nil. Unless . . ." He looked expectantly at Viktor.

"Is it a question of money?"

"It is. But money apart, there's still a question of principle, pure and simple, which is for you to decide. I have no idea just how much your penguin means to you."

"One coffee!" shouted the counter woman addressing Viktor's back.

By the time he fetched it, she had disappeared.

"Just tell me how much," Viktor said, coming back to the tall table.

"All right. I'll put it as simply as I can." He took a deep breath. "Misha's only chance is a heart operation, or, to be more precise, a transplant."

"But how?" Viktor looked at him in despair. "Where do you get another penguin heart?"

"That," said Ilya Semyonovich, "is where the question of principle arises. I've consulted the professor of cardiology at the hospital for scientists . . . In our opinion the heart of a three- or four-year-old child would serve."

Viktor choked on his coffee, and spilt some as he put down his cup.

"Given a successful outcome, that could give him several more years of life at least. Otherwise . . ." He gestured vaguely. "But to cover your points: the actual operation would cost a total of $15,000. Which isn't too bad. As to a donor heart . . . You could try your channels over that, or we could try for you. I can't, at the moment, actually give a price for that. Organs have been known to turn up absolutely gratis."

"*Try my channels? How do you mean?*" he asked, dumbfounded.

"I mean that there are children's hospitals in Kiev, each with its life-support unit," Ilya Semyonovich said calmly. "You can get to know the doctors, not telling them the organ's for a penguin. Just say you've a transplant need for the heart of a three-to-four-year-old. Offer good recompense. They'll keep you informed."

Viktor shook his head. "No."

"Why not?" asked Ilya Semyonovich. "All right. You need to think it over quietly. You've got my number. The only thing is, don't be too long. It's your money-meter that's ticking. I'll await your call, then."

Ilya Semyonovich went, leaving Viktor alone.

Disinclined to finish his cold coffee, Viktor left too, and set off along Kreshchatik Street in the direction of the main post office.

The sun was shining, but he didn't notice. People were passing, but he paid no attention. Jostled by some young fellow in the underpass, he didn't so much as look back, and himself bumped into a gypsy woman trying to beg money from him.

Something was wrong with this life, he thought, walking with downcast eyes. Or life itself had changed, and was as it used to be – simple, comprehensible – only on the outside. Inside, it was as if the mechanism was broken, and now there was no knowing what to expect of a familiar object – be it a loaf of Ukrainian bread or a street pay telephone. Beneath every surface, inside every tree, every person, lurked an invisible alien something. The seeming reality of everything was only a relic of childhood.

Just beyond the former Lenin Museum, he stopped and gazed around rather oddly, as if seeking out hitherto unnoticed details of the familiar cityscape. He considered, beyond the park steps, the steel arch of the Two Nations Friendship Monument, the ruins of the Philharmonic Hall, a hoarding graphically awash with French shampoo: *Your Hair – The Envy of All!*

A 62 bus full of people drew up below the hoarding. Several people alighted, then it drove straight on, leaving an angry crowd behind at the stop, and turned right down Vladimir Rise.

He watched, then he too set off down the hill to Podol, passing the lower funicular station and the main river terminal. Vladimir Rise levelled off and ran into Pyotr Sagaydachny Street.

He paused outside the *Bacchus Bar*, and went in.

He ordered a glass of dry red and sat at a table. Sipping his wine, he sighed. Why did it have to be a child's heart? Why not a dog's? Or a sheep's?

At a neighbouring table a group of young men were lacing their beer with vodka.

Viktor drank more wine, relishing its astringency. Agitated, nervous thoughts gave way to calm.

A penguin did, after all, have much more in common with Man than with a dog or a sheep – penguin and Man both being erect creatures, bipeds, not quadrupeds . . . And unlike Man, the penguin seemed never to have had quadruped ancestors.

And he remembered Pidpaly's manuscript – the only thing he had ever read on penguins – remembered that it was the father penguins who reared and brought up their young, remaining faithful husbands year in, year out; that penguins were adept at orientating themselves by the sun; that they had an innate sense of community. He remembered Pidpaly's flat, the smell of smoke . . . And his thoughts returned to Misha.

He finished the wine and ordered another. The group of young men went, walking unsteadily. Viktor was left alone. He looked at the clock: 12.30. The sun peeped into the bar, silhouetting his glass on the table and providing the scattered crumbs with tiny shadows.

Misha must have the operation, he decided, emboldened by the wine. Let *them* do it all. There should be enough money. He could take some from the bag on top of the wardrobe. The fact that it was Sonya's didn't matter.

Back at the flat, Viktor went without lunch and lay down for a nap. Nina and Sonya were out.

Waking towards four with a muzzy head, he made coffee and sat down at the table.

When his muzziness eased, and the coffee's warmth had restored him just a little, his thoughts returned to Misha. But self-assurance had gone from him with the effects of the wine. Dragging his typewriter out from under the table, he tried to lose himself in work. He thought back to the Chief's phone call. The Chief was right. He must turn over a new leaf. And frozen into immobility, he sat at the typewriter before a white sheet of paper anxious to be typed on.

He picked up the folder and looked through the files. There was just one he hadn't dealt with. He began to read.

Nina and Sonya returned a little later.

"We've been at Sergey's mother's," Nina said, helping Sonya out of her coat. "She's worried. He hasn't phoned for two weeks . . ."

"How's Misha?" Sonya asked, coming into the kitchen in her socks.

"Go and put your slippers on," said Viktor sternly. "The vet's promised to cure him," he called after her as she went obediently to retrieve them from the corridor. "But he'll have to stay in hospital."

"Can we go and see him?"

"No," he said, "they don't let people in."

66

A day passed, but Viktor had still not rung the Theophania Clinic. He had completed his last *obelisk*, and was now awaiting the Chief's courier.

Nina and Sonya had gone for a walk somewhere, and taking

advantage of their absence, he counted Sonya's dollars. Just over $40,000. He refastened the fat wad with elastic bands and put it back. Then he counted his own money, the bulk of it earned by Misha. Almost $10,000.

"I must phone," he told himself, and at that moment the doorbell rang.

It was the taciturn courier, a man of pensionable age in an old drape overcoat, who took the folder, put it in his briefcase, produced another, nodded and hurried off down the stairs.

Viktor watched him go and went back into the flat, throwing the folder on the kitchen table. He went to the phone in the living room and again he dithered. Something was holding him back.

"I must phone," he kept telling himself, still rooted to the spot, just looking at the instrument as if it could ring on its own and say what was necessary.

At last he did dial the number of the clinic. He asked for Ilya Semyonovich, and learning that he was out, felt amazingly relieved.

He did not ring any more that day, but got down to work, and by the time Nina and Sonya returned had written three *obelisks*. Another two and he could ring the Chief – show him how fast he was working!

Next morning Lyosha rang.

"Very big funeral tomorrow, old chap."

"It'll have to do without him, I'm afraid," Viktor said wearily. "He caught a chill at the last one, and it's not certain at the moment whether he'll pull through."

He gave the horrified Lyosha a full account.

"Listen," said Lyosha, "if I'm to blame, let me sort it out. Where is he?"

Viktor gave him Ilya Semyonovich's number.

"Good. I'll get back to you," he said. "Don't go grieving."

That evening he rang back.

"It's going to be all right," he said reassuringly. "The boys are taking on the financial side and everything to do with the operation. He's a good fellow, your Ilya Semyonovich. He'll ring each day, and keep you informed . . . By the bye," he asked out of the blue, "could *you* come with me tomorrow? Taking the wake in after?"

"So it's me who's the penguin," Viktor said gloomily.

Back at his typewriter he felt suddenly both hopeful and distinctly alarmed. The *boys* – and he could guess the sort – had decided to pay for the operation, and were, on the face of it, looking out for a donor heart . . .

The present situation had the feel of a horror film about it, and Viktor didn't like horror films.

He shook his head to dispel the association, and returned to *the boys*. Why should they decide to take it on? Were they that good-natured? That fond of animals? Indebted to him in some way? Or to Misha?

Quickly wearying of questions, he determined to think of something else, but still his thoughts revolved around the sick penguin.

He suddenly remembered the television programme and the pretty presenter appealing for people to sponsor a plane with provisions to be sent to the Ukrainian research station in the Antarctic. He looked for the piece of paper he had noted the account and telephone numbers on.

A sudden happy thought struck him. If Misha survived, he must be sent home to the Antarctic on that plane. Viktor would offer to contribute on condition that they released his penguin amid the icy wastes . . . Make an offer they couldn't refuse.

Cheered by the idea, he tackled the remaining *obelisks* with enthusiasm, and two hours later had finished them.

That evening Ilya Semyonovich rang.

"You know it's all OK?" he said.

"Yes."

"I must say, you've got good friends. Your Misha's stable at the moment. We're preparing for the operation."

"Have you got all you need?"

"Not yet. A matter of two or three days, I think. I'll ring tomorrow."

Half an hour later, after her supper, Sonya asked how Misha was.

"On the mend," he said with relief.

67

Viktor delayed going to bed. Sonya and Nina must long since have been in the land of dreams, but he was still in the kitchen in the dark, watching the lights go out one after another in the opposite block.

He didn't feel like sleep. It was not a case of insomnia. He was simply enjoying the silence and peace of watching the city fall asleep. And he was no longer irritated by the ticking of the alarm clock, now back on the window ledge. His agitation was past. His thoughts, too, under the influence of this peace, had stopped racing, and were now flowing with the ease of an unhurried river.

After all these shocks, unpleasant discoveries and the dark suspicions they prompted, and moments better forgotten than understood and accepted as commonplace, his life seemed to be resuming its normal course. And normality was the only state from which to contemplate the future – a future to be achieved only by striving forward, without stopping to throw light on some mystery or going into any change in the nature of life itself. Life was a road, and if departed from at a tangent, the longer for it. And a long road was a long life – a case where to travel was better than to arrive, the point of arrival being, after all, always the same: death.

And off at a tangent he had gone, feeling his way past closed doors, but leaving behind him what traces of his contact they retained. All the same, they did stay with him, those traces of contact – in his memory, in a no longer burdensome past.

In the block opposite, only three lighted windows, and the one he sought not among them. Whoever was pottering behind those was of no interest. He wanted to see the woman he had watched during his last sleepless night. But even her absence failed to disrupt his peace.

He had, it seemed, divined the secret of longevity. Longevity depended on peace. Peace was the source of self-assurance, and self-assurance allowed one to cleanse one's life of needless upsets, twists and turns. Self-assurance allowed one to take decisions for the prolonging of one's life. Self-assurance led to the future.

He looked into that future and saw so clearly, as if for the first time in his life, everything that obstructed the peaceful path for him. It was, oddly enough, all connected indirectly with his beloved Misha. And although Misha himself had nothing to do with it, he had become an involuntary cause of complication in Viktor's life. Misha had drawn him into a mournful circle of people with an enhanced degree of mortality, and now Misha alone could free him from them. With Misha out of the picture, Lyosha and his binoculars would be also, as well as gilt-handled coffins. Of the two evils in Viktor's life, only one would remain – his work. But that was an evil he had long reconciled himself to – someone else's evil, to which, at the rate of $300 a month, Viktor imparted a philosophical dimension. It was an evil to which he was an indirect rather than a main contributor.

It was pleasing to picture Misha against a backdrop of Antarctic wastes. It was the only solution – to the advantage of them both. Freedom. Provided the operation went well. And even if *the boys* now shouldering the costs *were* to take exception to the disappearance of their penguin, what could they do? He was, after all, blessed with that mysterious *protection*, spoken of in awe by the late Misha-non-penguin and his enemy-friend Sergey Chekalin.

Seeming to discern the calm, measured rhythm of his future life, he smiled contentedly.

In the block opposite, the last window went dark, and the diffuse light of the moon was all the brighter.

68

Several spring days passed. Every evening the telephone rang and Ilya Semyonovich reported on Misha's condition, which was, like Viktor's – and that of the weather – stable. Nina and Sonya disappeared early each morning, Nina having conceived the idea of showing Sonya spring. They were studying it like a school subject. It was a game they both seemed to enjoy and Viktor enjoyed their absence for he was able to work in peace. *Obelisks* flowed fast and free, and he expected a call and words of praise from the Chief. But the Chief did not call. Nor, apart from Ilya Semyonovich, did anyone else. District Militiaman Sergey, now far away, had been the only one to make calls that did not tie Viktor down to something. Who else was there lurking on the shady side of his life? Lyosha, bodyguard of *big-affair* funerals? He would ring eventually. No doubt about that. And he wasn't so bad, either. Lyosha, too, was living at a tangent, having found his niche and occupied it. No mean achievement, perhaps, nowadays. And having done so, the thing was not to excite envy – lest, God forbid, someone thought the niche too good for you . . .

At about 3.00 Ilya Semyonovich rang.

"We operated last night," he said. "All's fine at the moment. No sign of the organ being rejected."

Viktor was delighted, thanked him, and asked when he would be able to bring Misha home.

"Not for a while, I think," said Ilya Semyonovich. "Six weeks is the rehabilitation period . . . But I'll keep you informed. It could be shorter. We'll see."

Viktor made coffee and went out onto the balcony, screwing up his eyes against the sun. An amazingly cool, gentle breeze was blowing. There was a pleasant feeling of freshness, and the early warmth of a still unsteady infant sun. An amazing feeling. The fragility of a light breeze and the continuity of the sun in combination. Warmth and freshness. That was what woke life, called life to the surface of the Earth.

The coffee was weak, but he didn't want it strong. Strong coffee seemed now to savour of winter, of having to struggle with lethargy, too little daylight, and a weary expectation of warmth.

He could now ring the Antarctic Committee. And he, lover of warmth, would be happy here, and Misha would be happy there.

Returning to the living room he paused for a minute by Sonya's framed family portrait with penguin.

He smiled and sighed, feeling a certain sense of pride in himself and his solution, and thought how much easier it was to decide someone else's fate than one's own. Particularly as all attempts at changing his own had only led to further undesirable, more burdensome consequences. All change, as it turned out, was for the worse, regardless of its nature.

69

The offices of the Antarctic Committee were in two adjoining rooms behind a door bearing the nostalgic legend *Party Office*, on the second floor of the admin building of an aircraft factory.

He arrived at about eleven, having rung in advance. To have mentioned his penguin over the phone would have been foolish – leading them to think he was either having them on or cracked. He had therefore presented himself as a potential sponsor.

At the factory gate he had a five-minute wait until a lean, grey-suited man of about 45 came down to collect him. This was Valentin Ivanovich, Chairman of the Antarctic Committee, who was, as befitted a raiser of funds, courteous and welcoming. Having first provided coffee, he opened the door to the adjoining office.

"You see, it's mostly provisions we get offered," he said, indicating rows of cardboard boxes and a corner filled with tins. "We take everything, even if the sell-by date's long expired. It's good to have the offer. Sometimes we're given money. The Southern Construction Bank has donated $300. Money's what we prefer, of course. We need fuel for the plane. We have pilots to pay for sitting idle."

Viktor nodded sympathetically.

Returning to the first office, Valentin Ivanovich got out some documents detailing the provisions and the amount of cash collected.

Viktor leafed through them, noticing that one sponsor had donated an enormous quantity of Chinese tinned stew.

"That's not all our stuff in there," Valentin Ivanovich added. "We store equipment and warm clothing separately. And we also have two drums of sunflower oil."

"When do you fly?" Viktor asked.

"Ninth of May, Victory Day as was. We're making intermediate landings, so we've had to give advance notice. But how, if I may ask, would you like to assist? Cash or provisions?"

"Cash," replied Viktor. "Subject to one condition."

"Go ahead," Valentin Ivanovich invited, staring hard.

"A year ago, when the zoo had no food for its animals, I adopted a penguin. And now I'd like to send him to the Antarctic, to his natural environment . . . That's really what I want."

For just an instant the bright blue eyes of the Chairman betrayed a flash of irony, but his face remained as grave as Viktor's own. They stared as if playing *who-looks-away-first*, but after a minute or two the Chairman lowered his thoughtful gaze to the table.

"And how much will you donate for this passenger?" he asked, without looking up.

"A couple of thousand dollars."

Viktor had no wish to haggle. So far all had gone well, the quizzical look – whether of irony or mistrust – having in no way influenced the business in hand.

For a minute or so Valentin Ivanovich pondered in silence.

"In cash?" he asked, looking keenly at him.

Viktor nodded.

"Good," said the Chairman, "we'll take your passenger. Could you produce the money in the next day or two, and the penguin at about nine on the day of departure? Take-off is at about midday."

Viktor's mood as he walked home along the sunny street was curiously one of anxiety. The ease with which he had decided Misha's fate set him thinking about his own. On the 9th of May he would be left alone. And although he would have Nina and Sonya at his side, their autonomous, apparently independent presence, wouldn't make him forget Misha.

Affection was not something he expected from Nina and Sonya, not being affectionate towards them himself. Was it then simply a protracted *we're-a-family* game? Maybe. But it appeared to suit Nina. Little Sonya didn't understand, of course. The presence of grown-ups was a natural feature of her life. Of her own parents she seemed to have no recollection at all. Perhaps he should try to grow fond of Nina and Sonya, get them to respond, so that their strange union became that of a genuine family.

70

April was drawing to a close. The city, made verdant by warmth, was preparing for the chestnut trees to blossom. But the pace of Viktor's life had been reduced. The last time the courier collected the finished *obelisks* he had left nothing in exchange. Viktor rang the Chief, and the Chief said that there would be no work for the time being. Viktor was caught unawares by this sudden hiatus. He had been wrong-footed. Thus far, all had gone according to plan: he had long since delivered the $2,000 to Valentin Ivanovich, and Ilya Semyonovich was reporting daily on the progress of Misha's convalescence. Now suddenly, this.

Nina had returned to the subject of buying a dacha, and was bringing home the weekly advertisers. He patiently studied everything she marked. It seemed to him they ought to get moving and buy their little house with garden as quickly as possible, so as to have it right for the three of them in the summer. But at the same time he fell victim to a certain passivity.

After the 9th of May it would all be over he thought, connecting his strange state with lack of work and anticipation of Misha's departure.

Sonya asked after Misha less and less often, and that pleased him. He was by now almost convinced that the disappearance of the penguin from her life would be achieved with a minimum of fuss. He was more fearful and sorry for himself, having no difficulty in imagining the occasions when he would soon miss his Misha.

But the decision having been taken, and therefore out of his hands, he was spared any premature self-pity.

Lyosha rang.

"First-rate, the whole thing!" he said. "In a couple of weeks we'll be drinking your penguin's health at someone's wake!"

Yes, thought Viktor, and for the first time in ages he managed a smile.

Nina came back from a visit to Sergey's mother with a post-office chit for a parcel.

They sat down to supper. It was early evening, getting on for six.

"Funny," Nina said. "it looks as if it's from Sergey, but it's not his writing. And there's $20 at exchange rate to pay. As if it's from abroad."

"We *are* abroad," said Viktor gloomily, applying a blunt knife to his chop.

"Mine's tough," complained Sonya.

"I'll cut it up for you," said Viktor, leaning over and sawing away.

"The knives need sharpening," said Nina.

"I'll see to it," he promised.

"Will you come when I go to the post office?" Nina asked later as they drank tea. "In case it's heavy."

"Of course."

That evening Sonya again fell asleep in front of the television.

They put her on the settee, covered her with a blanket and turned down the volume. They watched the latest Mel Gibson blockbuster to its bloody conclusion, before finally retiring to bed.

Next morning, having paid $20 at the rate of exchange, they received the parcel: a fairly heavy cardboard box with a diagonal FRAGILE – HANDLE WITH CARE strip.

"That's not his writing!" Nina declared, seeing the address on the cardboard box.

As Viktor picked up the parcel, there was a chinking sound inside.

Taking another look at the warning strip, he shook his head.

"Sounds as if something's broken," he said.

"$20 for nothing then," said Nina, far from pleased. "So we'll take it home first, and have a look. No sense in taking it straight to her. She'll only be upset if it's broken."

Back at the flat, they praised Sonya's latest drawings, then unpacked the box on the kitchen table and took out a strange, dark-green, four-sided vase with a little lid, wrapped round with sticky tape.

Was it copper? Viktor wondered, examining it.

"It's got something inside," Nina said. "And look! There's a letter."

It was a sheet of paper folded in two.

He watched while she read, stony-faced, lips moving, hands trembling. Saying nothing, she passed the letter to him.

Dear Sergey's Mother,

Militia Department, Krasnopresnensk, have asked me to write this on their behalf. Very likely because I, too, came here from Ukraine, from Donyetsk. And also because

Sergey and I were friends. He was a wonderful chap. I don't know what else to say. He died in the execution of his duty. It wasn't in Moscow it happened. He didn't want to go, but orders are orders. City MVD Finance gave us a problem: they would either pay just for burial – but way out beyond Orekhovo-Zuyevo – or pay for cremation. We from Ukraine thought cremation, as then he could still be buried at home. Please accept our condolences.

Nikolay Prokhorenko,
p.p. Militia Department, Krasnopresnensk.

Having read this, Viktor looked again at the four-sided urn. Nina slipped out into the corridor. He could hear her crying.

Gingerly he picked the urn up with both hands and gave it a gentle shake. A strange, dull, sand-like sound resulted. He put it back on the table.

As rattles went, one of the sadder sort, he thought gloomily. All that was left of Sergey.

From the bathroom came the sound of running water. A minute later Nina returned, wet-faced and red-eyed.

"I shan't tell his mother," she said. "It would kill her. We'll bury him ourselves."

Viktor nodded.

71

Several days passed. Time, continuing its snail-like pace, weighed heavily on him, and despite the warm sunny weather, he stayed indoors. A couple of times he dragged out his typewriter from under the table and tried to write, but thought and imagination seemed paralysed by the sight of the white paper.

He ought perhaps to have been reading – the popular crime report sections of the newspapers – in search of material and notables.

He remembered how he had winkled out the subjects of his first *obelisks* and wondered where they were now, those notables.

Standing on the window ledge where he had moved it to clear the table for lunch on the day they had received the parcel, was the dark-green four-sided urn. Whenever it caught his eye it made him think of Sergey, of New Year at his dacha, and of their winter picnics on the ice with Misha. And he felt a strange sense of happiness lost forever. Looking at the curious urn with its artificial dark-green patina, he could not believe that that was the new shell of Sergey's mortal remains. That, for him, was still simply a curiosity, a mute newcomer from another world. And its presence in the kitchen, while puzzling, roused no feeling of protest. It seemed alive, the velvety green of the patina, and the urn itself an animate object, in spite of its contents. And he could not believe it had anything to do with Sergey, his life or his death. No. If Sergey was no more, he *was no more*. In that urn or anywhere.

Towards evening Nina and Sonya returned.

"We had an uncle asking about you," said Sonya, busy

changing her shoes as Viktor looked out into the corridor.

"What uncle?" he asked, surprised.

"A young fat one," said Sonya.

His look of surprise was switched to Nina.

"Some friend of yours," she explained. "Just interested to know how you were at present, and what you were doing."

"He bought us an ice-cream," Sonya added.

For supper Nina roasted a chicken. And then, as they drank tea, produced a page of advertisements from her bag.

"Look," she passed it to Viktor, "seems ideal: Koncha-Zaspa, tenth of a hectare, and not expensive."

Two-storey dacha, he read, *four rooms, tenth hectare, new garden, $12,000.*

"Yes," he said, "we must ring."

Only immediately after, Ilya Semyonovich rang, and the dacha was forgotten.

"He's mobilizing, walking round the ward," said the vet.

"Can I fetch him?"

"Well, I think we should keep an eye on him for the next ten days."

"Would the 7th or 8th of May be all right for fetching him?"

"Yes, I think so."

With a sigh of relief Viktor replaced the receiver. Glancing towards the balcony he saw it was still light.

"Just going out for ten minutes for a stroll," he called from the corridor, putting on his trainers.

72

Two more days passed, bringing what was once Victory Day closer.

He did after all ring about the dacha in Koncha-Zaspa, and arranged to view it the coming Sunday. Nina felt sure it would be to their liking.

In this sort of weather any dacha would seem like paradise, he thought, standing on the balcony with his cup of coffee.

By midday the sun was scorching. There was a slight breeze, but even that was warm, like the wafting of a giant hair-drier.

After the ninth he would ring the Chief and get some work, he decided, otherwise he would be bored . . . Or maybe they would break loose, the three of them, go to the Crimea for a fortnight. But then what about the dacha? No, they must see to that first. And if they bought it, why go to the Crimea?

Nina and Sonya came back at about five.

"What have you been doing?" he asked.

"We've been to Hydropark," said Nina, "boating."

"And people are swimming already," added Sonya.

"We saw your friend again," Nina said. "He's a bit odd."

"What friend?"

"The one who treated us to an ice-cream and asked about you."

Viktor thought for a moment.

"What does he look like?"

"Fattish, about 30." She shrugged. "Nothing special . . . Sat at our table in the café outside the Metro."

"He asked did you love me," said Sonya. "And I told him you didn't much."

Viktor felt a growing sense of unease. Even among his former acquaintances there was no one fat and 30-ish.

"What else did he ask?"

Nina thought, looking at the ground.

"Oh – about your work. Whether or not you liked it . . . And if you were still writing stories . . . Used to enjoy them, he said. Oh, and could I show him something you'd written . . . Without your knowing . . . Writers were never keen on giving manuscripts to be read, he said."

"And what," he asked coldly, "did you say?"

"She said she'd have a look," said Sonya in her stead.

"I didn't," said Nina. "He said Kiev was a small place, and we'd meet again. I said nothing about manuscripts."

Who could it be, wondered Viktor. And why was he asking about him?

Finding no answer, he shrugged, went out onto the balcony, and leaning on the rail, looked down into the courtyard. The rectangle of asphalt was full of washing hung on lines stretched between white ferro-concrete posts. Children were playing nearby. On the left stood a white-painted skip at the base of which lay some old tin drums. Beyond, but not visible from the balcony, was the wasteland with the three dovecotes, where he, Misha and Sonya had sometimes walked in winter: *Plan View in Spring of Familiar Scene* . . .

He harked back in thought to the nosy, fat young man.

Maybe he was shadowing them, he thought, looking down into the courtyard again. How else could he know they were a family?

A couple of old men sat on the seat by the entrance, and by the next entrance people were also sitting. A number of youths were walking past the block opposite, quarrelling loudly.

Nothing and no one suspicious.

Reassured, he went back in.

73

That night sleep eluded him. Listening in the dark to Nina's calm breathing, and conscious of her warmth beside him, he fell to wondering who this pryer into his life might be, where he came from and he was after. And the curious question about loving Sonya.

Such thoughts were accompanied by a growing sense of alarm that rendered peace of mind and sleep ever more remote.

They *were* being tailed. And he must be too. So he would just go out less often.

Trying not to wake Nina, he eased himself out of bed, slipped on his dressing-gown, and went out onto the balcony.

The star-scattered heavens shed a pleasant freshness. The tense silence of the dormant city was oppressive. The windows opposite were all dark. And below, inactive for the night, the courtyard was a set without actors.

Still, if someone really was tailing them, they would be in a car, parked without lights at the entrance to the neighbouring block.

Leaning over the rail, he looked the length of the block, and seeing the entrance approach blocked by two parked vehicles, smiled ruefully at coming so close to persecution mania.

He returned to the bedroom, but not until first light did he fall asleep.

Next morning, restored by strong coffee to a state of cheerful irritability, he took a bath and shaved.

After breakfast Nina and Sonya got ready to go into town.

"Where today?" he asked Nina.

"Hydropark again. It's nice. They've got the amusements working."

As soon as they had left the flat he scanned the courtyard, face pressed to the kitchen window, then looked directly down to watch the entrance. When Nina and Sonya emerged, he scanned the courtyard again, and saw a short, solidly built man rise from a seat outside the opposite block, and follow slowly in the direction of the bus stop. After 20 metres or so he stopped and looked back. A *Moskvich* estate drew up. He got in beside the driver, and the car drove off.

Puzzled by what he had seen, Viktor quickly put on his shoes and left the flat.

The bus stop was deserted, the bus having left. He hitched a lift, and five minutes later was making his way down the Metro escalator.

The more he thought about this strange tailing and prying, the more puzzled he became. And that chap in the baggy football shirt and a car no heavy would be seen dead in – they somehow didn't tie up with his alarm and sense of danger at Nina's second mention of the nosy, fat young man.

Still, strange as it might appear, someone definitely was tailing Nina for the purpose of staging another chance meeting in town and asking more questions about *him*. Someone was onto him, and his only comfort was that close-cropped young men in tracksuits and the latest flashy imported cars had no part in this mystery.

That being so, he had nothing to fear. But the mystery remained, and had to be solved.

It occurred to him, sitting in the Metro train, that he was enjoying this game – or more precisely, this chance to clear things up for himself. His confidence had come back – as though he had once again been reminded of the *protection* he enjoyed, although he had never understood why. But given Misha-non-penguin and Sergey Chekalin's reverential mention of it at some point, it must be there, protecting him from something.

Bearing right as he left the Metro station, he stopped at a stand displaying dozens of sunglasses. Seated to the left of it, on a collapsible chair, was a girl of about 20, also in dark glasses.

Without stopping to think, he tried the rather old-fashioned drop-shapes, followed by some *Made-in-Taiwans*. When at last he had made his choice, he paid and put them on.

A smell of kebabs was in the air. Although it was a working day, the market area of Hydropark was fairly crowded. Most of the pavement tables were taken by people at a loose end. Finding one that was free, he ordered coffee and cognac, and still wearing his dark glasses, looked around.

No sign of Nina and Sonya, but against that he spotted another familiar face, a man of about 40 he had seen at several big funerals. He was sitting at a table outside the adjacent café with a tall elegant woman in a rather short belted blue frock. They were both drinking beer and chatting quietly.

Viktor watched for a few minutes, then took another look around.

The waitress brought his coffee and cognac and asked to be paid. When she had gone, he sipped his cognac and coffee, and forgot about Sonya and Nina for a while.

In four days' time he had to send off Misha. He wondered where the transplant heart had come from.

After sitting for half an hour, he went and strolled as far as the boat station, then back to the Metro and over into the second half of Hydropark, which also had its scattered groups of summer cafés. Here there were fewer people. He went as far as the bridge over the creek, beyond which there was nothing but beaches and sports grounds, then turned back. At a café still some distance from the Metro station, he sat down, ordered a Pepsi and again surveyed the scene.

They must be somewhere there, he told himself, taking in the faces, sizes and shapes of those sitting at dozens of tables.

His attention was caught by a little girl playing on the grass beside a path with wooden seats at set distances from each other, perhaps 150 metres away. On the seat nearest her, two figures were sitting, of whom he could see only the backs of their heads.

Leaving his Pepsi, he set off along the grass strip between two paths. Twenty or thirty metres from the little girl, he was no longer in any doubt – it was Sonya, either looking for something in the grass or studying it.

He stopped, and returning to the café, followed a path to the toilet from where he would be able to see who was sitting on the seat.

Outside the toilet he stopped and looked back, lifting his sunglasses to get a clearer view.

Nina sat quietly chatting with Baggy Football Jersey. Or more exactly, he was doing all the talking while she listened, nodding occasionally.

So as not to make himself conspicuous, he went into the

toilet, and when he came out set off back to the café.

He stole a glance in their direction as he went. Now *she* was talking and Baggy Football Jersey was listening.

Suddenly he felt a fool. It was not just that shadowing was deprived of its interest, but that suddenly the whole impetus of events seemed horribly banal. The fellow was obviously smitten, and making up to her. But seeing her always with a little girl and thinking her married, he was trying to get things straight and estimate his chances. To which end, pretending to be an old friend of her husband's was a sound tactic.

So what? he thought, climbing the steps to the Metro platform. Best of luck, Fat Man!

He returned to the flat well before Nina and Sonya.

"Had a good walk?" he asked.

"Lovely," said Nina, putting on the kettle. "Such weather! And you've been sitting indoors!"

"Still, the day after tomorrow we're going into the country. I'll get my air then."

"Day after tomorrow?"

"To view the dacha."

"Of course!" She waved a hand. "I'd forgotten. Like some tea?"

"I would. – See any old friends of mine today?"

"The same one again," she answered evenly with a shrug of her shoulders. "Kolya . . . Kept on about himself. How he'd wanted to be a writer even as a child, then had devoted himself to journalism . . . How his marriage had gone wrong."

"But no more questions about me?"

"No, but he was very insistent I should give him a photo of you. So he could see how you'd changed over the years. Promised us Italian ice-creams in return."

"Is he off his head?" he said, more to himself than to Nina. "What does he want my photo for?"

Again she shrugged.

"Did you arrange to meet?" he asked, giving her a searching look.

"No, but I did say I might go to Hydropark tomorrow."

"Right," he said coldly. "I'll give you a photo."

Nina looked up in surprise.

"What's wrong?" she asked in an injured voice. "Am I supposed to avoid old friends of yours?"

He went out of the kitchen, saying nothing, and made his way past Sonya playing on the living room floor with her plastic Barbie house. Shutting the bedroom door behind him, he pulled out an old portfolio from the cupboard of the bedside table and shook a bundle of photographs onto the carpet. Sorting through them, he put aside one showing him with Nika, a previous girlfriend. Replacing the rest, he took some scissors and trimmed away Nika. Standing in front of the mirror, he compared himself with the photo. Something had changed, but it was an elusive, inexplicable something. The photo had been taken four years before, in Kreshchatik Street, by a street photographer.

"Here," he said, returning to the kitchen and handing Nina the trimmed snapshot.

She looked at him questioningly.

"Take it. For next time he asks," he added, trying to put a little warmth into his voice. "And say hello from me!"

Nina looked at it with interest, and took it to the corridor where her handbag hung on a hook.

74

The next morning, as soon as Nina and Sonya had gone, Viktor fetched down the black shopping bag from the top of the wardrobe and took out the still gift-wrapped automatic. The cold, heavy metal seemed to sear his skin. Closing his hand around the grooved butt, he took aim at himself in the wardrobe mirror.

Suddenly he remembered how Misha would sometimes stand before this big mirror gazing fixedly at his reflection. Why? Was it out of loneliness? The impossibility of finding himself a mate?

He lowered his arm, feeling a disagreeable sensation in his palm, as if from the chemical reaction of two incompatible elements. Dropping the gun to the carpet, he inspected his hand. The palm was surprisingly white, as though deprived of blood by the coldness and weight of the metal.

With a sigh he stooped, picked up the gun, and thrust it into a pocket of his jeans. Another look in the mirror showed the protruding black butt and the clear outline of the weapon.

Opening the wardrobe, he found an old blue anorak with a hood, put it on and took another look in the mirror. Fine! Except that the sun on the carpet suggested the garment to be unsuited to a promise of summer warmth.

Zipping up his anorak, he left the flat.

Again Hydropark was crowded.

It's Saturday, he thought, sitting at a table of one of the pavement cafés.

Looking around, he was comforted to see others not dressed for the weather. Common or garden idiots. They couldn't all be concealing weapons! One man was wearing something like a nylon fur jacket. He was, it was true, much older than Viktor, and age may have been part of the trouble.

"Coffee and a cognac," he told the waiter standing stiffly to attention before him.

The little table-and-kiosk-filled square outside the Metro was suddenly thrown into shadow. Viktor was glad of the cloud. The weather was adapting itself to his dress.

Waiting for his coffee and cognac, he took a closer look around. No sign of Nina and Sonya, but knowing them to be somewhere about, he wasn't worried.

A quarter of an hour later he walked along between the tennis courts to the ruins of the *Okhotnik* Restaurant and back. After which he went under the bridge to the other side of Hydropark, to walk past the seats where Nina and the unaccountably nosy Kolya had sat the day before.

So what? he thought, still looking. He would very soon know why Kolya was interested in him and his photograph.

As the path became a track, Viktor turned back and made for the little bridge over the channel. He stopped in the middle and leant over the balustrade. Overhanging the channel somewhat gloomily on his right, was the *Mlyn* Restaurant. People were seated at tables on the spacious balcony, but those he sought were not among them. Parked below was a long silvery *Lincoln*, just like the late Misha-non-penguin's.

The sun reappeared, turning a black-and-white scene into colour. The waters danced and played, shot through with an emerald sparkle. The white concrete of the balustrade, now yellow, was not only rough to the touch, but warm from a kind of inner glow.

Heading back towards the open-air cafés he stopped dead,

having spotted Nina and Sonya. They were alone. In front of
Sonya was a tall glass containing three different-coloured balls
of ice-cream. Nina was drinking coffee.

Where, he wondered, looking around, was nosy Fat Man?

Selecting a table some distance away from them, he ordered
coffee.

They were chatting, and every now and then Nina turned and
looked in the direction of the Metro exit.

Some 15 minutes passed. Viktor finished his coffee and sat
on, lost in untimely memories.

When he looked again they were a threesome. Fat Man had
arrived, and the waitress was bringing coffee.

Viktor watched. Sonya sat saying nothing, while Nina talked
to Fat Man. He was smiling broadly, his moon-face growing
still rounder. From a pocket of his white summer jacket he
produced a bar of chocolate, which he offered to Nina. She set
about unwrapping it. It was, Viktor could see, stuck to the silver
paper, having melted. Nina licked some of it off and passed the
silver wrapping to Fat Man.

Disgusted, Viktor turned away, feeling a stab of pain in his
neck from the effort of keeping watch. After massaging it a bit
he looked back.

Fat Man seemed to be inviting them somewhere. He had got
up and was standing at the plastic table, talking, gesticulating
gently.

Nina and Sonya also got to their feet, and the trio started in
Viktor's direction.

He tensed, momentarily at a loss how to conceal himself, as
he sat leaning over the table, his back to the pavement where
they were about to pass.

Pushing back his chair suddenly, he bent down and pretended to re-tie a shoelace.

"Do you like the circus?" asked a sugary male voice directly behind him.

"Yes, I do," said Sonya, and Viktor bent still lower.

"We've been twice already," Nina was saying, her voice growing fainter. "Once we saw the tigers, the second time . . ."

He gave them another 30 seconds before looking the way they had gone and straightening up.

They were making for the bridge over the channel, but just short of it, they turned right.

Viktor set off in hot pursuit and arrived at the bridge just in time to see them enter the *Mlyn* restaurant.

He went up onto the bridge, and this time stood looking the opposite way towards Vladimir Hill. After about ten minutes he turned, and there they were, on the restaurant balcony, Fat Man in conversation with the waiter, Nina with Sonya.

He didn't see the hand-over of the photograph, but the bottle of champagne on their balcony table infuriated him even more than their sharing melted chocolate. His fury could not have been greater if he *had* actually seen the photograph pass into Fat Man's hands. Unlike the champagne and the chocolate, *that* was something he had anticipated.

The sun continued to shine, and Viktor was hot in his anorak, the discomfort of this only adding to his fury. He was now leaning over the balustrade, watching Sonya again. She was eating ice-cream while Nina and Fat Man did the same between sips of champagne.

When they emerged an hour later, Viktor set off behind them, staying well back. At the Metro entrance under the bridge they stopped, and he stopped too, keeping his distance.

Fat Man was taking his leave in rather modest fashion, without so much as a peck on the cheek for Nina. Viktor watched the ceremony with a malicious sense of irony, until Fat Man disappeared into the Metro, and Nina and Sonya made for the other side of Hydropark.

Viktor set off quickly after Fat Man, and spotting him on the platform, dodged behind a pillar.

They boarded a city train, entering the carriage by adjacent doors, and now he got a good look at Fat Man, standing sideways on to him reading one of the dozens of adverts stuck to the inside of the windows.

It was the first time he had seen him close to. He was wearing wide mouse-coloured canvas trousers and a white summer jacket over a dark-orange football jersey.

His appearance said nothing – he could have been anybody or nobody, so total was the lack of detail suggestive of either character or employment.

At Central Station he alighted. So did Viktor, and suddenly finding himself close behind Fat Man, he dropped back until the latter set foot on the escalator; then, with other passengers between them, Viktor did the same, keeping him in sight.

They crossed the platform of Central Station and came out by way of the underpass at the top of Uritsky Street. In company with Fat Man, Viktor waited for a tram, and travelled two stops, getting off when he did.

Fat Man looked once in his direction, but that was all. Either he didn't know Viktor by sight, or he wasn't particularly observant.

The street was fairly deserted and Viktor hung back at the tram stop. He watched Fat Man walk up a path beside a car park towards a multi-storey building somewhat removed from the road.

Viktor followed slowly along the same path, and seeing Fat Man heading for the entrance to the building, he halted and waited for him to go in.

In a flash he, too, was at the entrance, standing at the open door, listening, and noticing out of the corner of his eye the familiar blue *Moskvich* estate parked outside.

The entrance hall was empty and silent but for the hum of a lift. The service lift door was open, but above the closed door of the passenger lift a succession of tiny bulbs was lighting its unhurried upward progress. At last the hum ceased, and the bulb by 13 went out.

Entering the service lift, Viktor pressed the button for Floor 13.

Emerging on Floor 13, he was confronted by a graffiti-scrawled wall and abandoned cardboard boxes.

The landing door led into a long dark corridor smelling of dog.

He listened at doors as he passed. From one came the shrill barking of a wretched dog. At one end of the long corridor there was a window, but the light from it penetrated scarcely half way to the lift exit.

At the dark end of the corridor, he stopped and listened again. Outside one door stood a child's bicycle. Outside another, opposite, chained and padlocked to a pipe conveying water or gas to all floors, was a car tyre cover. He went and stood close to the door. Faint sounds were audible, a door creaked, a lavatory flushed.

His eyes having by now accustomed themselves to the semi-darkness, he took in the brown leatherette upholstery of the door and the black doorbell button. He had already wiped his feet on the crumpled cloth in front of the door, but seized by a familiar, partly understandable fit of indecision, he stood wondering whether it was worth trying to discover the reason for Fat Man's curiosity. What if he wouldn't say?

He felt for the gun, still heavy on his thigh, and was reassured, having made certain it was still there.

We're all entitled to satisfy our curiosity, he thought. And now it's my turn.

He gave the black button a determined press, and four bars of *Moscow Nights* resulted.

Shuffling steps came to the door.

"Who's there?" wheezed a man's voice.

"A neighbour."

The lock clicked, the door opened just a little, and a flabby man of about 50 in pyjama trousers and singlet looked out.

For a moment Viktor stood staring into a round, unshaven face.

"What do you want?" the man asked.

Barging him aside, Viktor found himself in the corridor. He quickly took in the layout, ignoring the stupefied master of the house, and there, peering out of the open bathroom door, was Fat Man.

"Who do you want?" Pyjama Trousers managed to get out.

"Him!" said Viktor, pointing.

Pyjama Trousers followed his gaze.

"Kolya?" he asked, aghast.

Kolya, clearly startled, shrugged.

"Who are you?" he asked slowly.

Viktor shook his head, surprised.

"What a question to ask!" he said.

He motioned Fat Man in the direction of the kitchen.

Fat Man led, Viktor followed.

"What do you want?" Fat Man asked, standing with his back to the window.

"To find out why you need my photo and take such an interest in my life."

Comprehension dawned on Fat Man's face. Staring thoughtfully at his uninvited visitor, he reached slowly into an inner pocket of his white summer jacket, produced the photo, and looked at it and at Viktor.

Viktor was emboldened by his obvious dismay.

"I'm listening!" he said, a note of menace in his voice.

Fat Man said nothing.

Slowly unzipping his anorak, Viktor produced the automatic, and without actually threatening him, let him get the message.

Fat Man moistened his lips as if they were suddenly dry.

"I can't tell you," he said in a trembling voice.

At the sound of shuffling steps, Viktor swung round, and looking into another frightened face, raised the automatic.

"Get lost," he said, and Pyjama Trousers retreated into the corridor.

"Well?" Viktor glared, his patience wearing thin.

"I was promised work . . ." began Fat Man. "This was my first assignment."

"What sort of work?"

"With a newspaper . . . Sort of interviews . . ." His voice trembled. "I worked in a different section . . . This was better paid."

Sort of interviews? Was that what *he* had been writing all these months? Was Fat Man his replacement?

That bleak conjecture had a numbing effect, and an old

suppressed fear reared its head, striving to take possession of his thoughts and feelings.

"What's the photo for?" Viktor asked icily.

"It wasn't essential. It was just that having learnt so much about you, I wanted to see your face."

"My face . . . What's my face got to do with you? When I wrote *sort of interviews*, faces were of no interest to me. Show me what you've written!"

Fat Man didn't budge.

"I can't. If they find out –"

"They won't!"

Fat Man marched along the corridor to a bedroom where there was a desk in front of the window with a typewriter on it. To left and right of the machine were orderly piles of paper – indeed, the room itself was excessively tidy. But the air was oppressive and stuffy, as though breathed for months without ventilation.

Fat Man went over to the desk, closely followed by Viktor.

His hands were shaking. He turned and faced his visitor.

"Let's have it!" urged Viktor.

With a heavy sigh Fat Man extracted a sheet from a green folder.

The brief but eventful life of Viktor Zolotaryov would suffice for a substantial trilogy, such as, it must be supposed, will in due course be written. Meanwhile, by way of a sad note to that future trilogy, it is his obituary that must be written.

Had he stuck to literature or journalism, he could safely have been described as an author *manqué*. But while clearly lacking purely literary talent, he possessed a manifest surplus of talent for the invention of subjects and plots. He did not go the way of more senior authors *manqués* – into quiet politics and a peaceful doze sitting as a deputy. But revealing his real interest to be for politics, he discovered a rather unexpected application for his talents.

A great deal concerning his life remains at present a mystery. And that includes the exact moment of his association with State Security Group A. But following this association, Viktor Zolotaryov became obsessed with a need to *cleanse* society. And already it is possible to identify some results of his abruptly curtailed politico-literary activity: 118 killings or deaths under suspicious circumstances, of persons, all, to use a Western term, of VIP calibre – from State Deputies to Ministers and factory managers – all persons of not-unclouded antecedents, on whom Group A had opened files. The impossibility – by virtue of Deputy immunity or judicial corruptibility – of bringing these persons to book, was evidently what, in the final analysis, led Group A agents to employ Viktor Zolotaryov. His *obituaries of the still living* became, uniquely, indents for future death, each supplying *per se* ample cause.

His appointment – through the good offices of our late Assistant Arts Editor – to be a freelance correspondent of this paper, proved ideal cover.

Much remains to be discovered, but already it can be stated that he not only made future death a basis for social justice, but even determined the date and manner of death – sometimes an unduly cruel one. Ballistic examination of the Stechkin automatic with which he shot himself, permits the supposition that he had personally taken part in at least one *social cleansing* operation, Deputy Yakornitsky having been killed with this weapon and hurled from a sixth storey.

The personal life of Viktor Zolotaryov was also more literary invention than real, the sole creature to which he showed genuine attachment being a penguin. So highly did he value his penguin, that on its falling seriously ill, he arranged for the transplant of a child's heart, buying it, literally, from the parents of a boy fatally injured in a motor accident, regardless of the ethical and moral questions involved.

Another mystery is that of his link with bosses of the criminal world, among whom he was known as *The Penguin*. A striking feature is the frequency with which he attended the funerals of persons he had assisted in killing, completing as it were, an original cycle: from file of future departed, to participation, with friends and relatives, in the departed's wake.

Now that the *social cleansing* operation he conceived and carried through has reached the public domain, there is hope that the full details will become known. A Committee of Deputies is already conducting an inquiry. The Head of Group A has been relieved of his duties, and while his name, like that of his successor, is kept secret, there are grounds for believing that nothing similar will recur, and that no organ of State Security will in future abrogate to itself the right to sit in judgement on anyone, criminals outside the law included.

Viktor Zolotaryov's contribution to the literature of

our young country is nil, but his contribution to the political history of Ukraine may well become a subject of research not only by a Committee of Deputies, but by his fellow writers also. And who knows, a novel on that theme may enjoy a longer and more successful life than that of Viktor Zolotaryov.

He looked up at Fat Man, and Fat Man looked at him, awaiting his judgement.

Viktor deposited the sheet of paper on the table without a word, oppressed by a sudden heavy burden.

He remembered the Chief's *When you do know what's what, it will mean there no longer is any real point to your work or to your continuing existence.*

The weight in his right hand brought his thoughts back to the automatic, which he now knew to be a Stechkin.

Fat Man was watching closely, his round face gradually losing its look of fear, his lips moving as if framing thoughts.

"Well?" he ventured at last, faced with a softened, no longer aggressive Viktor.

Viktor looked wearily at him. "Well, what?"

"Well, what I've written . . ."

"Dry as dust . . . lousy opening . . . newspapery . . . here!" He held out the gun to the flabbergasted Fat Man. "Something to remember me by."

Eyes riveted on Viktor, Fat Man held out both hands for it.

Viktor's right hand was its unencumbered self again. Giving Fat Man the gun was like throwing off an illness. Turning silently on his heel, he walked out of the flat.

75

Viktor sat until midnight with hundreds of passengers in the waiting hall at the Central Station, listening to muffled and unintelligible arrival and departure announcements.

He sat in his anorak, and froze.

He no longer felt afraid. It was not that he was resigned or had given up. After the shock of reading his own *obelisk*, the noise of the busy station resuscitated him. All right, his end was imminent and obvious: the same people who had created him in the image of a future *notable*, had already determined what that end should be – suicide – and when it should be. Having no idea who they were, he should have been in mortal fear of anyone sitting or passing near. But there was no point. Fear was for those who still had a chance of staying alive. Sitting there at the station, he could see no such chance, though he would have liked to prolong his life, if only by a day or two.

At the same time he felt hurt that his own *obelisk* should be the product of so obviously untalented a hand.

He, he thought, would have made a better job of it, but immediately rejected the idea as crass and obscene.

And why no mention of Nina and Sonya? Why just Misha? Someone must have known him better than he knew himself. It was obvious, too, that those who had compiled the file were better informed than he. They had even known, as he had not, the source of the donor heart.

The train arriving at Track 9 is the train from Lvov for Moscow, declared an indistinct tinny voice, and the women sitting around him sprang up, shouldering heavy sacks and lifting enormous shopping bags.

He felt ill at ease. Firstly, because he was in their way, and secondly, because when they had gone, the whole row would be empty. He got up too, and made for the station exit.

It was about one when he arrived back at the flat. He shut the door quietly behind him and took off his shoes.

Nina and Sonya were asleep.

Without turning on the light, he sat down at the kitchen table, and looked out at the windows of the block opposite. Only one was lit, on the first floor, over the entrance, which was, he thought, where the caretaker woman lived.

In a far corner of the window ledge he noticed a mayonnaise pot with a candle. It stirred a memory. Fetching matches from the stove, he put the pot on the table and lit the candle.

The nervy flame cast trembling shadows on the kitchen walls. For a while he gazed, fascinated, then, taking pen and paper, wrote:

> Dear Nina,
> In a bag on top of the wardrobe is Sonya's money.
> Look after her. Got to go away for a bit. Back when the
> dust settles . . .

The last sentence wrote itself, and he was about to underline it, but stopped and simply read it over several times. It had a soothing ring.

> All the best, – Viktor.

he added, pushed the note from him, and sat for a long while contemplating the candle flame.

The dark-green urn with lid still stood on the window ledge, its surface reflecting the gentle glow of the candle.

Style was a word beloved of bearded Lyosha. Maybe he, Viktor, should invent a style of his own. Do something new before suicide. Go where he had never been before and where no one would think of looking for him!

The candle lit a sad smile.

Quietly he went through to the bedroom and opened the wardrobe. From the pocket of his winter jacket he took his own bundle of dollars earned in conjunction with Misha. He went back to the kitchen and had another look out of the window. It would be cold, out there in the dark. Going again to the bedroom, he came back with a sweater, which he put on under his anorak. And shoving the weighty bundle of dollars into his pocket, he left the flat.

76

For $10 the taxi driver drove him to the door of *Casino Johnny* where his way was barred by a massive, dark-suited guard. Something about his mighty frame and aggressive manner moved Viktor to laughter. Flashing his bundle of notes and peeling one off, heedless of denomination, he stuck it in the guard's breast pocket. The guard stepped aside.

A girl cashier in a snow-white blouse with a pale-blue scarf around her neck dozed behind her window. For a night-spot it was too quiet. He looked around, puzzled, having imagined something very different.

He tapped on the glass. The girl woke, and looked in surprise at his anorak.

He proffered $100, and was handed a number of different-coloured plastic counters.

"This your first time here?" she asked, seeing his doubtful response. "They're instead of money. For use in the bar, and for placing bets."

He looked around, unsure where to go.

"That way," she prompted, pointing to a heavy green curtain.

It was another world he found himself in, more like what he had imagined, except that it was still too quiet. There were, by his estimate, no more than seven people in the whole place. A man was playing alone against the croupier at one of the roulette tables; at another, three men were playing. Two more were playing poker. There was soft music, and from a corridor, neon-signed *Bar*, a girl came in with a glass of wine.

Viktor went over to the table at which the lone man was playing. He might have been Japanese or Korean, and was placing his stakes in a subdued, embittered sort of way.

Viktor sat beside him, watched what he did, then made his first bet.

The tiny ball sped around, stopped, and the croupier slid some counters towards him.

He had won!

Roulette was something he had seen only at the cinema, and this was like a film he had never seen before. With sudden abandon, he placed all his counters on red, and won again, watched with evident mistrust by the Japanese-Korean.

Placing all his counters on even, Viktor won again.

This was tedious. Shoving the counters into a pocket of his

anorak, he went to the bar, ordered a large cognac, and as change for his counter, got back three of a different colour.

Toy money, toy prices, toy people – this was a Children's World indeed . . .

Returning, glass in hand to the tables, he sat down at the same one, staked a fistful of counters, and won again.

Beginner's luck, he decided.

The Japanese-Korean took himself off, and Viktor played on alone. Played and won. The plastic results of which began to weigh down both pockets.

"Look," he said, addressing the croupier, an elegant young man in white shirt and bow tie, "what do I do with these counters?"

"Change them back into dollars," was the answer.

Viktor nodded, and went on winning.

Then back to the bar. After which, the restaurant. A dumpy woman of no age or figure. A hotel room . . . All he could remember was the strength of her arms.

Next morning, head buzzing, Viktor woke alone. He got up and looked out of the window at the familiar square with its little market.

He wasn't going anywhere, he decided. He still had money that he wouldn't be needing . . .

Struck by sudden doubt, he took his anorak off the chair and felt in the pockets. To his surprise, the bundle of dollars and mass of counters were still there.

When he had washed and dressed he went down to the restaurant, and for a few counters had an excellent meal and more to drink. Back in his room, he slept until evening, then went down again, this time to the casino.

His second night was even more successful than the first. He went on winning, not caring what might happen to him. He realized subconsciously that to go on winning was bad. At the same time this seemed strange, since people played to win.

After a good spell in the bar, he proceeded to the cashier's desk. There was no one there, but another elegant young man of about 17, also in white shirt and bow tie, appeared, having evidently noticed him.

Viktor started shedding counters from the pockets of his anorak onto the shelf in front of the window.

Catching a flash of alarm in the young man's eyes, he stopped and stared.

The young man gave a barely perceptible shake of the head.

"You oughtn't to cash all that lot in," he whispered, "you'll never get away from here."

"So what do I do?" asked Viktor, at something of a loss.

"Play until morning, then phone some friends to meet you at the door."

"That's the local rule, is it?" Viktor said, drunkenly surprised.

"No," said the young man. "We play by the book, unlike most." He nodded towards the green curtain through which Viktor had entered the night before.

Leaving his counters at the window, Viktor went and looked through the curtain. In the hotel foyer, not five metres away, four thugs stood chatting. One gave him a cheery wink.

Gathering up his counters, Viktor played on, and towards dawn fell asleep on a comfortable black leather settee in the bar.

At about nine he was woken by someone who rummaged in his pockets for his key on its hefty hotel pear, and conducted him to his room.

For his third night at the tables he felt as if his powers were deserting him. He had a mist before his eyes and could hardly see where he was placing his counters. But he still kept winning, and in the end grew apprehensive, under the cold, lifeless gaze of the nattily dressed, neatly cropped croupiers and house security guards.

Towards morning one of them came over to him.

"Like us to see you home?" he asked, his face frozen in a waxen smile.

"*Home?*" For Viktor it was a word of menace.

"Don't worry, we'd drive you in the limo – with an escort, if you like. You could cash your chips, or leave them and come back."

"What's the date?" he asked suddenly.

"Ninth of May," replied Waxen Smile.

"And the time?"

"7.30."

Viktor tried to think. The 9th of May. Not just former Victory Day, but the day of Misha's flight . . . Only not now. Misha was at the Theophania Clinic, which was where they would be waiting, eager to close Viktor's dead hand around the Stechkin automatic.

"Could you, in an hour's time, take me to the aircraft factory?" he asked after a moment's hesitation.

They looked at him amazed.

"Certainly," said Waxen Smile. "With escort?"

Viktor nodded.

The man withdrew.

The limousine was enormous. He had never seen such a vehicle. It was like sitting in a room. The escort served him with a gin and tonic from a small refrigerator.

They drove along Victory Avenue, and through the tinted glass

Viktor could see people stopping to watch the limo pass.

He smiled contentedly, sipping another gin and tonic. He was still drunk. Pulling out a fistful of chips, he offered them to the escort. The latter accepted with thanks.

They pulled up at the factory gate and the escort enquired, "Where now?"

"Ask Valentin Ivanovich of the Antarctic Committee to meet me here."

The escort got out, and Viktor watched him walk calmly through the checkpoint and disappear inside the building. No one stopped him.

Five minutes later he returned.

"He's waiting," he said, indicating the checkpoint.

"You can go," said Viktor, getting out.

Valentin Ivanovich looked thoroughly alarmed, but seeing Viktor, heaved a sigh of relief.

"Phew! I didn't know it was you," he said. "Where's the penguin?"

"The penguin," said Viktor bleakly, "is me."

Valentin Ivanovich nodded thoughtfully.

"Let's go," he said. "We're loading."

December 1995 – February 1996

Penguin Lost

CHARACTERS IN THE STORY

From earlier:

Viktor Alekseyevich Zolotaryov	a writer
Misha	his penguin
Nina	niece of militiaman Sergey Stepanenko and partner of Viktor
Sonya	daughter of late Misha-non-penguin, adopted by Viktor
Lyosha	a guard
Igor Lvovich	sometime editor of *Capital News*
Ilya Semyonovich	a vet

In Kiev:

Andrey Pavlovich Loza	candidate for election to People's Assembly
Pasha	his aide

In Chechnya:

Khachayev	Chechen entrepreneur
Aza	his manager
Seva	slave to Aza

1

It took Viktor three days to recover from the four spent crossing Drake Passage. In which time, the scientists who had sailed with him from Ushaia in the *Horizon* were already acclimatized and working fast to complete measurements and analyses before the onset of polar night. Viktor kept to his quarters in the main block, emerging only to eat or to take a peek outside. He went un-questioned, and even made friends with a biophysicist researching the limits of human endurance, such as the crossing of Drake Passage would have provided ample material for, had he not spent the whole of it seasick in his bunk.

Vernadsky Base was soon got the hang of, and Viktor ventured forth, wearing the obligatory bright red with luminous yellow stripes, and entering name and time of exit on a board to the left of the door. Failure to return within the hour would, he'd been told, bring the whole base out on search. The base had known tragedy, and it was not hard to see why, after losing 16 men and two supply aircraft, the British had presented it to Ukraine, quite apart from the Devil's Island appearance of it, viewed from the shore. The one and only place to relax was the bar, but there being neither barman nor drink, you either brought your own or did without.

Viktor saw his first penguins when walking with biophysicist Stanislav down by the dinghy slipway, and compared with his Misha, now languishing in Kiev, they looked toy-sized. "These are

Adélie penguins," Stanislav explained. "We're not Antarctica proper, just an island." Their walk took them, via the noisy generator hut, to the set-apart magnetic research lab. "We've another Stanislav here," Stanislav confided, looking around uneasily. "In the sick bay. He's from Moscow. I mentioned you. He'd like to see you."

*

The ailing Muscovite, a big man of about 40, lay on his back, legs bent, the bed being too short. His massive face was of a pallor suggestive of the worst.

Biophysicist Stanislav slipped away.

"What are *you* here for?" the sick man demanded.

"Just to look round."

"Cut the crap! I'm Stanislav Bronikovsky, banker. Put on the spot and lying low. And you are?"

"Lying low, too."

"Good."

"Why so?"

"Makes us comrades in adversity. You might have come to do me in."

A long silence followed. Viktor rose to leave.

"Come when you can," said Stanislav abruptly. "We'll play chess . . . I could be of use to you."

From then on, Viktor became a regular visitor. He was not short of time, and it was cold outside, although less so than he had expected, a mere −15°. The living quarters were well heated, but the sanatorium was even better. They played chess, and as they did so, chatted about everything under the sun. It did not escape Viktor that occasionally Bronikovsky was sounding him out, but there was nothing strange about that. Bronikovsky plainly suffered from a persecution mania, and a highly developed one at that. Viktor would never have believed it possible that anyone might send a killer to the Antarctic in search of *him*. Who, after all, was he that anyone should be sent that far? But Bronikovsky was important and powerful, a Queen to Viktor's pawn. Bronikovsky's fears might be well founded. Added to which, his strange, undiagnosed illness was growing steadily worse, in spite of the expedition medic's antibiotic injections. The medic had thoughts of consulting the Americans at Palmer Base, but was put off by the 300 km separating the two bases. So, racked with stomach pains and eating nothing, Bronikovsky lived off his massive frame much as the camel lives off its hump. As his pallor became bluish, he whispered that he knew who was poisoning him, but left it at that, and played bravely on, losing in stony silence. Reaching under his bed, he produced a half full bottle of the Argentine vodka Viktor remembered trying and not liking.

"Look," he said, pouring two cups, "I've a proposition. It involves asking a favour." Viktor looked attentive. "Tomorrow a Pole called Wojciech puts in on his yacht to take me off, give me a new identity. But seeing me like this, he won't . . . So you go in my place, if you like, taking my wife a letter and a credit card which is yours to use on the way."

"Except that I'm not you."

"For Wojciech, the work of a minute."

Viktor thought for a moment, then nodded his agreement. Bronikovsky's pallid face registered a feeble smile.

2

A month or so later, Polish passport in one pocket, blue Ukrainian in the other, Viktor stepped from a train in Kiev, shoulder bag lightly packed with casino chips, notebook, and a packet of Polish pastries.

Emerging from the station, instead of proceeding in the normal way on autopilot to the bus stop and thence home to his flat, he stopped. His autopilot wasn't working, and his first few steps in the station yard were those of a novice moon-walker, while everyone else went rushing by, guidance systems in full working order.

Still, he had to go somewhere. In his pocket were the Ukrainian hryvnas which had sojourned with him in south polar regions, and provided there had been no geographical creep Russia-wards in his absence, he was able to afford the small pleasures of life. A bus journey, for instance. But where to?

Looking around and spotting a newspaper kiosk, he made towards it, the asphalt suddenly firmer beneath his feet. Of the many papers displayed he opted for Kiev's *Capital News*, and for some 30 minutes stood absorbed in its contents.

Life hadn't changed: foreign visitors delivering charitable aid to orphanages; two Ukrainian People's Deputies imprisoned in Germany for fraudulent banking; businessman's family shot dead in Kherson; opening of super garden-centre at Obolon; and on the last page but one, a couple of wretchedly written obituaries, all the more distressing for having been signed with Viktor's own pseudonym. The Editor-in-Chief, it appeared, was no longer his quondam patron Igor Lvovich, but one P.D.Weizmann.

For just one brief blissful moment he was back standing with

236

Penguin Misha at the grave of some departed bigwig, sun streaming down, while some nearest and dearest delivered words having no effect on him or Misha, who were outside it all, Misha part of the ritual, he part of Misha. And there they'd stand, unfeelingly waiting for it to be done with – as if *they* were immortal.

It would be good to be immortal. And to die young, cut off from physical time as if under a bell jar, yet seeing the trees on Shevchenko Boulevard, dogs cocking their legs, girls growing into women, while remaining the person one was. Foolish thoughts. But easier, pleasanter than wise ones.

Where was Misha now? At the Clinic? Resting between funerals? Baykov Cemetery would be the place to look – when the Mercedes turned up in force.

The grim icy waste that was home to Misha commanded respect – he'd not forgotten the searing cold to his cheeks. That was a country in its own right, giving not a damn what flags conqueror scientists sought to raise, secure in the knowledge that its native populace, its penguins, would remain free and unbowed come what might. The unprotected, paper frontiers of their "conquests" were the vanity and vainglory of the geography schoolbook for the patriotic edification of the children of a few countries bent on appearing bigger, colder, more inaccessible and of greater consequence than they actually were. Something else they vaunted were the penguins rounded up and brought back to their zoos to create the illusion of a twee-er, more accessible Antarctica. *Roll up, this enclosure's Antarctica. Breakfast at eight. Lunch at one. Muck out at four.*

As he tucked the paper into his bag, the sun broke through the louring sky, and just as unexpectedly retired again for a while. It was still summer, though autumn was on its way. As he was on his –

though to where had yet to be decided. Home to his flat and a bath was where he felt like going. His next priority being to find Misha, and make up for doing him out of his flight to Antarctica – a debt only he, Viktor, could, and would, repay.

From the window of his bus, streets and pavements were again lit by the sun. The elderly man in jeans and white football shirt seated next to him was immersed in an *Emigrate-to-Canada* brochure in the form of a quiz. A Higher Technical education earned you three points, an Intermediate – two points, Higher Arts – one point, and so on under each heading. A total of 15 or over put you in with a chance, so why not apply?

Assessing himself at eight points, Viktor sighed with relief. Maple Leaf Land was not for him. A paucity of chance offered more scope than a surfeit. From the bus stop to his block was about 30 metres, and the way led past a kindergarten, a school and a tiny square.

In no hurry, he stopped to watch a group of two- and three-year-olds playing trains, circling the sandpit on invisible rails, hands on the shoulders of the one in front, waddling like so many penguins.

He fell to thinking of Sonya and her father, Misha-non-penguin. Odd, Misha's outliving his non-real equivalent, as hopefully was the case.

With greater assurance and a spring in his step he walked on to the entrance to his block, newly-operative autopilot disorientatingly disengaged. Looking up at his windows, he felt heavily oppressed.

Mashka, the neighbours' cat, came flying down the stairs, and by the time he reached his own floor he was himself again. His metal door looked as impregnable as ever, except that beneath the existing keyhole another had been cut, leaving Viktor to finger his own now inoperative key uneasily, and to take in the new rubber doormat embossed with the English word WELCOME. Below, a door banged, footsteps followed, and he froze. A jingling of keys one floor down, the opening and shutting of a door, then silence.

Cautiously he made his way down to the entrance, and looked out, still in the grip of nameless past anxieties. Opposite, beyond the courtyard clotheslines, was the newly painted green door of the block where Old Tonya lived, one floor up. Mother of his friend Tolik, Old Tonya sold milk in the yard, as she had all her life, her *Milk-o, milk-o!* from six in the morning on serving to prepare him for his mother's *Up you get!* an hour and a half later.

Striding across the yard, he went up to her flat. "Why, it's little Vik!" she exclaimed happily, opening the door. "Thought you'd gone away. Come in." Neat in appearance, she took good care of herself, and though probably at least 60, had nothing of the old granny about her. Selling milk kept you young, did wonders for the complexion. "Like some broth?" she asked. "I bought a chicken, but broth was all it was good for."

As they made for the kitchen, he glanced into the sitting room and saw on the sideboard a portrait of the eternally young Tolik, her son. Tolik had fallen to his death from a tree. In those days there had been any number of fine old trees to build houses in, then look down on the petty world of adults building Communism. It was plain, even then, that what each was in fact building was his own private version of it, secretly competing to be the one with the most smoked salmon and Soviet champagne in his fridge at home. Another age entirely!

The broth recalled something of the distant past, too – the good homely childhood that had been his, with chicken legs of tooth-defeating toughness, and great yellow lakes of broth patterned with globules of chicken fat.

"There's a bit of cold rice," Old Tonya said, "Like some?" He nodded, and two spoonfuls of fried rice went plunging to the bottom of his broth.

"Where do you live now?" she asked.

"Over there."

"So you're letting the flat. I thought you'd sold it."

"A friend's niece and a little girl are there."

"Such a nice husband she's got – tall, militiaman or a soldier, from the look of him."

"Really? I didn't know about the husband." He looked anxiously across to his flat. "Could I, I wonder, use your phone?"

"On the fridge."

He dialled his number, and Sonya's clear voice answered.

"Uncle Kolya?"

"No, Viktor."

A slight pause, then, "*Uncle Vik! Where are you?*"

"Kiev."

"Is Misha with you?"

"No, but he's somewhere here in Kiev."

"Lost?"

"Yes, but I'll find him."

"You must, and bring him home. Auntie Nina's got a cat and it scratches. Misha never scratched."

"No," said Viktor sadly. "Is Auntie Nina there?"

"She's gone to the shops. Are you coming here?"

"Not just yet. And probably when Auntie Nina and Uncle Kolya aren't there. He lives with you, does he, this uncle?"

"Yes, and he's nice. Bought me roller skates. He's just gone away for a couple of days. He's going to bring me some mussels."

"So he's gone to the sea. What does he do?"

"Some sort of watchman – something special . . . But here's Auntie Nina. Like to talk to her?"

"I'll ring later," he said, replacing the receiver.

"Spend the night here, if over there's not on," Old Tonya said matter-of-factly, now standing by the stove.

"Thanks, Tonya, but if I may I'll just leave my bag, and collect it tomorrow."

"Of course."

3

Viktor walked along Kreshchatik Street feeling a need to unwind. Before leaving Old Tonya's he had retrieved from his bag the fruits of beginner's luck at the casino before his forced flight to Antarctica, and now the rattle of chips in his pockets revived a sense of reckless excitement. Still, more important than the chips, and safe in an inner pocket with his letter to his wife, was Bronikovsky's Visa credit card. Whether there were children he'd forgotten to ask, but would find out when he took the letter to Moscow and told what he had to tell. And there'd be tears . . .

First, though, he must find Misha, seek his forgiveness, do his best to put things right. Maybe there'd be another chance to fly him to the cold far south.

"Wanna play our sure-win lottery?" a boy of twelve in jeans, check shirt under thrown-over jacket demanded cheekily, pointing to a dubious band of players at a collapsible table.

"No thanks, I never lose."

"Wanna show us?"

"Why should I?" he asked, remembering that his luck at roulette had owed everything to fatalistic abandonment and nothing to skill.

Half an hour in a café, then on to Podol, where, to his disappointment, the Bacchus wine bar had now become a flashy window display of expensive clothes. Crossing to the other side of Konstantinov Street, he chanced on a tiny beer cellar which, to his delight, was selling Moldavian Cabernet by the glass!

And with time arrested, an ever-changing sea of flushed faces – Kievites drinking themselves silly – and substituting winey warmth for his modest experience of Antarctic cold, he again heard Sonya asking after Misha, complaining of being scratched by a cat.

"These seats free, mate?"

He nodded. The two men now sitting drinking and talking beside him, might as well have been on the other side of a wall.

A third glass being beyond his means, he returned to a street now lit by shop windows. A short walk, and he'd be at the Dnieper embankment. Fresh air by the river would inspire new life.

For the next hour or so he made his way slowly along the embankment to Metro Bridge, heedless of the speeding traffic, concerned only with the fact of being home again. That he was ousted from his own flat, he accepted. No longer a home, that was a new world and probably one he had no right to intervene in. Except for now feeling closer to Sonya, with whom he had in common the fact of belonging to nobody any more. Faced with a need to vanish every bit as presssing as Viktor was to experience later, Sonya's father, Misha-non-penguin, had left her in his care. *Back when the dust settles*, he'd promised, but those bent on killing him had got to him first.

From Metro Bridge, Viktor went by metro to Left Bank, then, on foot, to *Casino Johnny*.

Different faces, but same hotel foyer, same heavy velvet curtain, same booth for encashing chips, and a guard to be slipped a couple. Placing his bets at the nearest table, Viktor watched three drunken youths do the same. The tiny ball danced the wheel under the indolent gaze of a young croupier. Everything about him proclaimed the night to be young! Another three hours and the real fun would start!

Watched just as indolently by Viktor, the little ball stopped on ten, losing him his stake. Staking more chips, he lost again. The effect was sobering. The three youths fared no better, but took it calmly, as if that was what they had come for. But why was *he* here? Because last time, staring death in the face but playing to forget it, he'd discovered he couldn't lose?

He played a few more times but without success, as did one of the young men until ten chips were shovelled his way, while Viktor's got shovelled off to the enrichment of others.

Enough, he decided, dipping into his pocket for more chips, and stepping back from the table, watched the others for a while. A waitress served the palliative of complimentary champagne, and this he drank before going to cash his remaining chips.

"You've had luck," observed the cashier, as Viktor produced two handfuls of chips.

"10%'s yours."

The cashier counted. "You've $800 worth here."

"$800 then," said Viktor, knowing he was being done, but not prepared to argue.

In fact, as he discovered, checking in the toilet, he'd been given $760, but wasn't worried. Exchanging toy for real, he'd been bound to gain.

The one depressing thing was that his run of luck at the table was clearly at an end. This second casino visit was to be his last.

4

That here was a man with nearly $800 in his pocket was plain to see even in the night lighting of Kreshchatik Street by the look on his face, and the way he strode ahead, dodging no-one, making them dodge him. Twice some young girl over-scantily clad even for a mild summer night called to him as he passed. A little later, by Café Grotto, a third with a boyish haircut and massive shades parked on her forehead, challenged, "Not so fast – you could be missing something!"

Surprised, he stopped. She was petite enough to miss.

"Have you somewhere?" he asked.

The sunglasses dropped into position, leaving only a smile.

"Yep. Let's go."

"How much?"

Deftly she plucked the protruding wad of dollars from his pocket, folded it, and slipped it back. "This'll do, but put it away. Why show off?"

"I'm just careless. What's your name?"

"Svetlana."

"I'm Viktor."

"Come on."

Past Friendship Cinema they went, then up Lutheran Street, making as for Pechersk.

"What do you do?" she asked, not greatly concerned.

244

"Polar explorer," he heard himself say.

"So, labour camp?"

"No, in the Antarctic."

"On an ice-floe?"

"Sort of. We had a dacha-like set up. Penguin protection was my thing."

She laughed.

"Pull the other one."

"No, *really*."

"Well, Mr Explorer, here we are."

Gates of a kindergarten – sand pits, swings, main building, shrouded in darkness, and the prospect of sex *alfresco* a bit of a turn-off.

"Not to worry – I've a magic key," she said brightly, opening a side door and motioning him into an unnerving silence.

"It's all right. There's no-one here."

Then up to the first floor, where their soles squeaked on parquet. She opened a door, and in the dim light that penetrated from the street, he saw rows of child-sized beds made-down army fashion. The plumped-up, carefully aligned triangular pillows took him back to the Pioneer camps of his Soviet childhood.

"Don't just stand there," Svetlana said, pulling beds together. "Help create us a bit of comfort."

Five little beds pulled together made a normal double.

"So, out of your togs, Mr Explorer!"

"Is it still a kindergarten?"

"From 8.oo a.m. till 6.oo p.m., yes," she said, naked but for panties.

"And for the rest of the time?"

"Oh, for God's sake! What's wrong?"

"Nothing," he said, throwing off his clothes and getting down beside her.

"It's not a brothel, you know – mornings and afternoons I actually work here."

"Doing what?"

"What do you think!" she asked, kissing the finger tracing her lips. "I get the kids learning songs, play mazurkas, polkas on the piano, and they dance. Makes me wish I was them!"

"And get paid?"

"$15 a month in hryvnas. Still, it's not for its money you love your home."

"Meaning?"

She drew him to her.

"This, for my first five years, was home. They'd drop me at 8.00, my parents, and pick me up at 6.00."

"But why do this?"

"Sod off!" she exploded. "Who are you to tot up my earnings, not having paid a kopek! Let's get on with it!"

And pushing him over, she dived on top. "Explorer, my arse! Old windbag more like!"

"Only from being silent for so long!"

After which the dormitory echoed to bed noise, until, in the distant darkness, a phone rang. Just three rings.

"Someone wanting the headmistress. Like something to eat?"

"What's on the menu?"

"Semolina, knob of butter, dash of strawberry jam – ever since '73: Greedy gutses pick the butter and jam out and drink the rest, the sensible ones mix all together."

"Sounds good."

"So up we get. Jerries and washbasins just along the corridor."

They dressed and went down to the kitchen where Svetlana prepared semolina in the dark. Homely yellow light attended the opening of a fridge for milk, then the bluish flames of a gas ring contributed a semblance of comfort. But when it came to eating off a tiny table, petite Svetlana managed better than he.

"You fit in well here," he said lightly.

"And I like it because they're not nasty to the little ones, but make allowances, try to be nice, spoil them."

"And how do I spoil you?"

"It's you who's being spoilt, as way-out explorer, with semolina, but $50 will do."

He laughed. "Isn't that a bit much?"

"I hadn't thought in terms of an explorer discount, but if you insist . . ."

"I don't."

*

He woke to the ringing of an alarm clock somewhere on the floor, and reaching for it, realized it was in Svetlana's handbag. She, face deep in her pillow, was still asleep. Silencing the alarm, he examined her student identity card. Svetlana Alyokhina was her name, and she was in her third year at the International Business College. He went over to the window, stretched, feeling unusually fit, and looking out saw two elderly ladies advancing purposefully across the courtyard.

"Get up, Svetlana! People are coming."

"The alarm's not gone."

"It went fifteen minutes ago."

She leapt out of bed, dressed, then, helped by Viktor, moved the beds apart, restoring them to something like their former neat appearance.

They slipped out by way of a back door, meeting two hefty fellows on their way in with large cardboard boxes. Svetlana slipped past with a cheery "Hi!" Viktor stood aside.

"Who are they?" he asked catching her up.

"They rent the storeroom cellar. They sell computers."

She looked at her watch, then up at Viktor.

"And my hard-earned money?"

He gave her her $50.

"Sorry, but must dash." She kissed him quickly on the lips.

"How about another time?"

"What's your number?"

"No phone," said Viktor, not anxious for the call to be taken by Nina, Sonya or the militiaman-like guard.

"That's a feeble one! And before you blow your polar money, buy yourself a mobile!"

"Have you a phone?"

"But it's by Mummy's bed, and she hates being woken."

"I'll come and find you."

"That's the way. And when you do, you get a kiss."

When they got to Shelkovichnaya Street, she darted into the road, waved down a car and was gone.

He watched it out of sight, then set off down Lutheran Street.

5

The Old Kiev Cellar Café was just open and pleasantly cool. The woman in charge of the coffee machine was yawningly laying out yesterday's pastries.

The coffee was ghastly, seriously over-sugared, but fortunately not stirred.

Still in thrall to the night's experiences, Viktor wondered at petite Svetlana's possessing a student card. Maybe it was for the sake of cheap travel. Any kind of ID – from old MVD to Ukrainian State Security – could be bought in the Petrovka book market. A photo, a stamp, and the world, within reason, was your oyster.

He sipped his coffee, but it left none of the usual bitter tang. In its place was a taste of semolina and strawberry jam as remembered from childhood.

For the first time in his life he'd actually *bought* a night of happy passion – naturally, with no bad feelings, no qualms of conscience. *There'll be a time when you won't get it free and be too ashamed to pay,* Bronikovsky had told him. Not so. $50, yes, as a gift in recognition of moments of bliss. All so easy and homely. Rendezvous in a kindergarten where, when the children are gone, strange, romantic things can happen – computers in the cellar, semolina at night, and God knows what in the attic. Life with a cheerful touch of mystery somehow lacking before his trip to Antarctica, thanks perhaps to the isolation of a full, unsociable life as member of a disintegrating family, while feeding Misha, writing poignant advance obituaries, and shedding the odd tear. Added to which, his concern for Sonya, and, to the extent of providing her with money and the sense of being a housewife, for Nina. His own little world of his own, to which he'd had the key and from which, with the change of lock, he was now a refugee.

He thought of the kindergarten, also two-storeyed with sand pits and swings, where he had been a pupil, with semolina, strawberry jam and the same little melty butterberg for lunch. And after lunch a quiet hour and a song about a little hare to learn.

He worried about what Sonya, who had not been to kindergarten or played much with other children, was doing. Hers was a very different childhood.

Leaving the café, he rang his flat from a street phone.

Listening to the bleeps, he wondered what to say if Nina answered.

Happily it was Sonya who did, cheerfully announcing that Nina was out, Uncle Kolya hadn't come back and hadn't rung, and she'd let the cat out, who, though she scratched, was a good cat, and clever, clawing the door to be let in, and when would *he* be coming home?

He panicked.

"Don't know," he said eventually, "maybe in a day or two."

"Come when no-one's here," she suggested. "I'll make you an omelette. I can. Auntie Nina went away for two days once leaving just eggs and a roll. So I made myself an omelette. I'm grown up now. Seen Misha?"

"Not yet. I'm going to today."

"Give him my love and say he's to come back soon. It's dull without him."

"I will. And I'll come when everyone's out."

"And ring more often."

"Tomorrow morning then."

Ringing off left him depressed and with a sudden urge to go home, resume his old life, only with no more obituaries, no more funerals-with-penguin. But first, he must get organized, run Misha to ground. Then to Moscow, and Bronikovsky's wife or widow.

His prime duty was to Misha, and starting right now, he would do his damnedest, though it wouldn't be easy. Bad as it was, the coffee had done the trick.

6

At Theophania, a cool breeze, fitful sunlight, rustling foliage, singing of birds, and patients perambulating the grounds of the Hospital for Scientists, beyond which lay the Veterinary Clinic, where – and he blinked back a tear – he remembered seeing Misha mobilizing under strict medical supervision.

Today two white-coated assistants were walking dogs, one of which was limping.

On asking where to find the vet, he was directed to the first floor of the consultation block.

Passing what had been Misha's ward, he looked in. Only one of the child-sized beds was occupied, and the sounds emanating from the apparatus beside it, suggested that some four-footed creature was fighting for its life.

Ilya Semyonovich, the vet, was indeed in his room, and greeted Viktor pleasantly without immediately recognizing him.

"Do you remember operating on a penguin called Misha?"

"Of course. He was the only one we've ever had. Your name's coming back to me."

"Zolotaryov."

"That's it! People were here keeping a look out for you. For three weeks or so."

"What people?"

"Oh, I don't know – active, sporty-looking types. One stayed all the time, the other two came each morning, walked Misha, and left in the evening."

"And?"

"Misha made a full recovery, and men turned up in two jeeps to

251

collect him – nice polite chaps who settled up for his treatment and drugs. They asked after you, and I seem to remember, left something for you . . . No, I tell a lie – the ones who collected Misha weren't the ones who waited earlier. It was the ones who waited who left the envelope."

"Where is it?"

Sitting down at his desk, the vet pulled out one drawer, then another, from which, together with X-ray photographs, he pulled a brown envelope which he passed to Viktor.

"We never lose anything here, unless it's our sense of honesty. Only yesterday I had to sack some kennel maids for stealing dog food from the kitchen. *Not their fault*, of course," he smiled sadly, "genetic engineering's the only remedy for that."

But Viktor was no longer listening, having taken from the envelope a folded newspaper cutting and the word processed message:

"In your own interest, ring 488 03 00 before 20th of May."

There was no signature.

Unfolding the cutting, he was shocked to see looking up at him his former Chief, Igor Lvovich, edged round in funereal black. A brief obituary told of his tragic death in a motor accident on the Borispol Highway, his chauffeur-driven car having collided at speed with a tipper lorry loaded with sand.

Viktor folded the cutting and slipped it back into the envelope.

"When was it Misha was collected?"

"Quite some time ago. He spent six weeks here, so you can work it out from when you brought him in."

Viktor shook hands with Ilya Semyonovich and left.

Outside, he stopped for a moment. Veterinary assistants, hefty fellows, looking more like butchers in their white coats, were still walking dogs. One assistant stared back in a way that prompted Viktor to head quickly for the gate.

<h1 style="text-align:center">7</h1>

Short is the road from hospital to cemetery – even for the fit proceeding under their own steam. And proceeding by tram inspires thoughts about life and the sense of it, thoughts both prodigal of time and a distraction from the immediate. Leisurely, soporifically, the tram clanks along, then at the sudden sight of the red brick wall enclosing an overpopulated City of the Dead, thoughts of life and the sense of it fly up and off like so many sparrows. Almost reverentially the tram slows, and stops twelve metres short of the cemetery gate. Cawing crows. Gentle breeze. Old women selling wild flowers. Homeless urchins hawking flowers they've stolen from graves.

Arrived at the gate, Viktor paused. He foresaw no difficulty in locating the grave he had come to visit, though a good 15- or 20-minute walk was involved.

"How much?" he asked, going over to the hunchbacked old woman in an old blue quilted jacket standing with a boxful of flowering plants.

"Ten for five hryvnas."

Producing a 5-hryvna piece, he selected a clump of violets.

"Hang on," said the old woman, tearing in half a Marlboro carrier bag to wrap around the roots.

He walked slowly, letting his legs lead the way, and came at last to the now grassy mound, marking where Penguinologist Pidpaly lay. He put the violets down on the mound, seeing, as he did so, the good, gentle, ill-used old man he had known and done a little to help. Pidpaly had had charge of Misha at the zoo, until it could no longer afford a penguinologist or penguins . . .

Away in the distance the clank of a tram. He looked round. No-one was about. The only sound apart from cawing crows was now the whisper of the wind in the lofty trees. "I have no unfinished business", Pidpaly had told him shortly before his death. Would that he, Viktor, could say as much.

And buried somewhere here now was Igor Lvovich, cut off in life at speed on the Borispol Highway, when heading perhaps for the airport. He would have left any amount of unfinished business, to say nothing of a wife and a son in hiding in Italy from the horrors of Ukraine. Every story must end at a full stop, and none bolder and more final than that of death.

Some way off, in a little enclave, he spotted a skip filled with cemetery rubbish. There was a standpipe, a bucket and a watering can, both stencilled with numbers in red, and leaning against the skip, an old spade. Taking it, he planted the violets around the grave, watering them well in an attempt to create something of a memorial to Pidpaly amidst all the marble and the portraits in oval frames.

With a last regretful look at the grave, he retraced his steps, skirting a life-size marble statue of a man in modish tracksuit standing before a Mercedes radiator, also in marble.

Rastoropov, Pyotr Vitalyevich, 15.03.1971 – 11.10.1997
who might well have been one of the three thugs whose lavish interment Lyosha had been bodyguarding on the morning of Pidpaly's funeral. Lyosha, remembering him and Misha from a New Year celebration, had hailed them as they passed, driven them

home, and later made a lucrative business of hiring black-suited Misha out as a fashionable adjunct to mourning parties.

Faintly, above the clanking of far-off trams and the cawing of crows, he caught the strains of a funeral march, and spotted mourners in the distance.

As he got to the main avenue, flashy cars and a limo hearse drove in at the gate. Four identical black jeeps followed, from the last of which two men alighted to post themselves either side of the gate, while the cavalcade went on to the church and crematorium.

What's a Mafia funeral without a penguin? he thought suddenly.

Quickening his pace, cutting corners, he made towards the cemetery church, dodging headstones and railings, stumbling, literally, over names and dates with the church hovering, mirage-fashion, inaccessible, unattainable – like happiness after death. Even so he was in time for the carrying in, by elegantly attired males, of a costly, bronze-handled coffin in polished mahogany, while 40 or so mourners, of whom the few ladies wore long black gowns and dark glasses by Armani or Versace, prepared to follow. And for one brief moment a small black-and-white something went waddling in with them. His heart missed a beat. Misha! Yes, there had to be a penguin! He collided painfully with something, and nursing a bruised knee walked on. The mourners were now inside, then suddenly a ragged urchin sprinted out, pursued by a steward. Tripping him, Viktor continued on his way.

"Thanks," said the steward, catching up, having wrested a book from the urchin and banged his head with it. "There's no stopping them. Twenty Bibles we've lost. God knows what they do with them. They can't read. Whipping flowers and selling them back is all they're good for. They even take them to Kreshchatik Street."

Breathless, he fell silent, and watched by a guard, they entered the church unchallenged.

In the agreeable half-light of candles burning before icons and banked on stands, a wheezy priest was chanting monotonously, and but for the odd "This, Thy servant Vasily", unintelligibly. The steward slipped away, and Viktor, in the vain hope of seeing something of the deceased, joined those pressing around the fine coffin.

Later, as the coffin was borne out, he again glimpsed a tiny creature dodging in and out amongst the mourners. Tagging on to the end of the procession, he followed it along the avenue, craning to see ahead but attracting questioning glances that resolved him to contain his curiosity until they gathered at the graveside. He felt naturally, professionally at ease, as much at home in the presence of mourning strangers as priest or simple grave digger.

The late lamented Vasily's plot was no distance from the church. The coffin was lowered onto trestles draped in blood-red velvet, the highly polished mahogany lid removed, and the bandaged head, intelligent face and designer frames of the deceased revealed, as also his expensive suit, two rings, and what looked like a Rolex.

As he edged through the press of people, he saw, to his disappointment, a tiny boy in dark suit and a white shirt. So much for his penguin! And conscious of a yawning void within, he stood glaring at the boy, as if *he* was the cause of deception rather than Viktor's own eyes. With a nasty taste in his mouth and an urge to vomit, he continued to glare at the boy, unaware of being himself observed by two heavies and a grey-haired man, who gave a signal to the former.

Viktor's attention was strangely diverted by the men present reaching into their pockets as one and producing mobiles. Grey

Hair produced two, and approaching the coffin, placed one in the hand of the deceased. Stepping back, he dialled a number and the tango "Now going down is the weary old sun" blared forth. Grey Hair adjusted the emerald-green handkerchief protruding from his breast pocket, nodded, and two men replaced the lid, muffling the music.

The coffin was lowered into the grave, and the same two men, unusually presentably attired for cemetery employees, took spades, and sent earth thudding down onto the lid. Now, to the strains of the tango, friends and relatives of the dead man took a handful of brown clayey soil from the heap and threw it too.

Five minutes, and the tango faded into silence, buried with the dead. Viktor was saddened. Whose idea was it, this new ritual? Misha, Lyosha, where were they? Who were they, these new undertakers?

There being nothing to detain him, he turned away, but had hardly taken two steps before his way was barred by two men in identical black suits.

"Hold it," said one in a steely voice. "We'll drive you."

Seated beside one of the men in the back of a Mercedes 4 x 4, he watched mourners making for their cars. A woman in black passed, leading the tiny boy by the hand.

Grey Hair jumped in beside the driver.

"And who are you?" he demanded, looking back at Viktor as they joined the slow procession of cars leaving the cemetery. "Crashing a wedding for the drinks and eats is one thing. Crashing a funeral's quite another."

"I was looking for someone," said Viktor lamely.

"Looking for someone, eh? And did you find him?"

"No. He used to stand guard over funerals here."

"What was he called?"

"Lyosha. Chap with a beard."

Grey Hair exchanged glances with the man beside Viktor.

"Do you know him?" Viktor asked hopefully.

"He may do, or did," said Grey Hair, nodding at Viktor's escort.

"Chap who copped it in August," said the latter.

"The coffin bomb?"

"That's the one," said the escort.

"Some funeral!" said Grey Hair. "Why were you looking for him?"

"To find out what's happened to my penguin."

"Your penguin?" Grey Hair repeated, suddenly interested. "So it's you they were after."

"When was that?"

"In May, I think. 'Just conducting enquiries . . . Phone if you hear anything.' Actually produced a photostat mug shot of you!"

"Who were they?"

"Civvies, all smiles . . . Polite but persistent. Twice waylaid me leaving the house. 'Would I show your mug shot to my boys?' What the hell had you been up to?"

"Are they still around?"

"No idea. Shall I find out?" Grey Hair asked, reaching for his mobile.

"No, don't bother."

"If they are, they can't be looking too hard. I'm Andrey Pavlovich, by the way."

"Viktor Zolotaryov."

The Mercedes passed out through the cemetery gates and gathered speed. With the other cars they were now travelling along Gorky Street in the direction of Moscow Square. Viktor's thoughts as he looked out the window were of Lyosha, the coffin bomb, and the significance of "does, or did, know him".

"How many got killed?" he asked the man beside him.

"Five or six. But no-one escaped injury. Your friend Lyosha lost his legs, I heard. Might still be alive."

They drove on in silence through Moscow Square, finally turning into the private estate of Goloseyevo Park. Viktor glimpsed the lake with its sandy beach and mushroom sunshades. Five minutes later they stopped.

"We're here," said Andrey Pavlovich.

"Where?"

"At the wake," he said gazing thoughtfully at Viktor through half-closed eyes. "Come on, you've done the funeral, time now to drink to his memory."

8

Viktor found himself frisked. The contents of his pockets were carrier-bagged and he was motioned to join the others.

Most did not sit for long at the long table in the spacious lounge with its blazing fire, but having toasted the departed went their way. Eight or so stayed on. They were, Viktor gathered, at the house of Andrey Pavlovich, whose daughter Natasha, one of those still at table, was the departed's widow. Her husband had been shot while hunting, a drunken military party shooting in the same area, having mistaken him for an elk.

"As," declared Andrey Pavlovich, raising his glass, "might happen to anyone." At which point, one of Viktor's friskers entered to whisper in Andrey Pavlovich's ear and give back Viktor's carrier bag of possessions.

Andrey Pavlovich delivered a few brief words concerning the departed, and was followed by two others who stumbled through banalities culminating in the inevitable "May earth repose light as thistledown upon him".

"What a glum lot we are!" declared Andrey Pavlovich, flushed with drink, and ordering a minder to nip off to Kreshchatik Street "to get some music". Forty minutes later said minder reappeared with a crumpled, unshaven, pale and sickly busker, carrying a guitar and clearly ill at ease.

"This," Andrey Pavlovich announced, "is a house of sorrow – got any sad songs?" The busker nodded. Vodka and black bread were brought, and standing by the fireplace, he gave vent to a raucous, "Lonely gainst the dark of sky / Burns bright a lonely star."

Beaming with satisfaction and helping himself to vodka, Andrey Pavlovich came and sat beside Viktor.

"Bored?"

"Not at all."

"Good. You're an interesting chap, I see, and soon to go to Moscow."

"When I've found my penguin."

"Look, I'll help you over that, and you can do something for me on your courier run to Moscow. You must be a good man if those people trust you. One in a million."

"Could you find out about Lyosha?" Viktor asked, sensing that there was nothing Andrey Pavlovich couldn't do,

"I could," he said, raising his glass. "Here's to friendship!"

Viktor was about to clink glasses but Andrey Pavlovich prevented him. "Not done at funerals. We'll talk later," he added, getting up and returning to his place.

The busker was now singing of the hard life of the druggie. Time had flown, it was getting dark, but Viktor was asleep already, head rested on the table where, until thoughtfully moved aside, had been a plate of cabbage rissoles. Roused by one of Andrey's men, he saw, through bleary eyes, that the fire was out and he was alone. He was guided up to a tiny attic room containing a small divan with a black and red striped rug over it. On this he flopped down fully clothed, and pulling the rug over him, went back to sleep.

Feeling too hot, he woke and opened the window.

Later, he became dimly aware of voices in the courtyard below.

"Just see you don't upset him," Andrey Pavlovich called loudly to someone.

"I won't, I promise," a young voice answered. A car started, drove away, and there was silence.

Parched with thirst and restless, Viktor switched on the light, and finding himself still dressed decided to go down to the kitchen for some water. He made his way along a narrow corridor and down a steep wooden staircase. From the next floor wider stairs brought him to the familiar vast room with fireplace, whence he found his way to a kitchen dimly lit through uncurtained windows by light from the street. Opening a tall fridge, and screwing up his eyes against the burst of yellow light, he selected a carton of orange juice and a can of tonic water.

"Cut the light!" came a voice. Viktor swung round, and there, sitting at a small table in the corner over an open tin, a bottle of vodka and a glass, was the busker.

Viktor closed the fridge door, and waited for his eyes to grow used to the semi-darkness. A match flared briefly, leaving the glowing tip of a cigarette.

"Hungry?"

"Thirsty."

Finding a glass, he poured himself an orange and tonic. The busker was smoking, but strangely there was no smell of tobacco.

"Come and sit down. Have a drink," said the busker.

Viktor took a chair, sat opposite him and presented his glass.

"Nice place, this. Enough in that fridge to last a month. Every bloody thing you can think of – five sorts of frozen fish, crayfish, shrimps . . . Does himself well, does the Deputy."

"Deputy?"

"People's Deputy. We'll drink his health. Good type. Obliging. I asked, as a joke, if he had such a thing as a joint, and he gave me one."

"How do you know he's a Deputy?"

"One, being rich and being a Deputy go together. And two, in the bog there's an election poster of him promising the things he'll do. Saw him watching me from it when I finished spewing my guts up."

Viktor tossed back his soft drink and vodka, and struck with a sudden vague unease, crossed to the fridge. The top two shelves were all frozen fish and exotic seafood – exactly what Misha would fancy, supposing he were hidden here somewhere. On the other hand the lower shelves were equally richly stocked with joints, poultry, game birds, and, amazingly, a couple of turtles. Banging the door shut, he returned to the table.

"Well?"

"Bet you never knew sea tortoises were what Deputies ate!"

"You high, too, man?" he laughed. "*Sea tortoises!* A month back, when I skipped, hedgehogs were what I lived off."

"Skipped what?"

"Soldiering."

"So isn't it risky, busking in underpasses?"

"What I skipped was the Russian army. Here in Kiev I'm abroad."

"What's hedgehog like?"

"With salt, which I didn't have, not bad. Still, I should be off," he concluded thoughtfully, refilling his glass.

"Were you paid for playing?"

"Didn't like to ask, so this is by way of compensation."

Stubbing his joint out on the table, he got unsteadily to his feet.

"Where's my guitar? Ah, there you are, my lovely."

And as he stooped to retrieve it, the kitchen was lit by the headlights of a car entering the courtyard. The busker ducked down, Viktor leant forward over the table, then realizing he couldn't be seen from the window, went over and looked out.

Two men were unloading small but heavy, string-tied cardboard boxes from the Mercedes and stacking them on the brick path. Andrey Pavlovich went out, had a word with the men, then came back into the house. After which, soundtrack but no picture, just footsteps in the hall which died away then suddenly returned. The kitchen door opened, the light clicked on blindingly.

Andrey Pavlovich took the situation in at a glance.

"Couldn't sleep?" he asked rhetorically, then, addressing the busker, "The concert's done, life goes on." From a pocket of his crumpled white jacket he pulled crumpled notes and fanning them like playing cards, passed over two of 25-hryvna denomination. "So here you are, and off you go."

"I can sing more if you want," said the busker picking up his guitar.

"God forbid, old chap."

The busker tiptoed out.

"Sit down, we'll talk," said Andrey Pavlovich.

They sat at the corner table. For a while Andrey Pavlovich said nothing, then announced that he'd been interested to learn of Viktor's past activities – especially as obituary writer for *Capital News* under Igor Lvovich, he added, eyeing him as if to gauge his reaction. Not a word, though, about funerals-with-penguin.

Getting to his feet, Andrey Pavlovich made coffee and brought it to the table together with a sugar bowl.

"Make yourself at home," he said gently. "You'll be all right, and you'll go to Moscow – only maybe not for a bit. Don't worry, I mean it," he added, seeing Viktor's unease. "The thing is, with Igor Lvovich, alas, no longer with us, you are now without protection, in short, *exposed – to the elements . . .*"

Helping himself to sugar, Viktor stirred, tasted and sighed, as if mourning a freedom as yet not sufficiently savoured.

"We don't need much," Andrey Pavlovich continued, "a bite to eat, a spot of cash, a roof, and we're snug as a snail. Which brings us to Snail's Law: small snail, small shell, like you; big snail, big shell like me. Mine, if I outgrow it, I build afresh. No shell – you're a slug, and slugs come to a sticky end. Like me to build you one?"

"What use am I to you? You're a Deputy, the world's yours –."

"I'm not a Deputy, but I'm standing for election. But when I am a Deputy, your shell will be the sounder. You're a free man. It's only a temporary job I'm offering. You're a dab hand at writing obituaries, it seems. My lot are practically illiterate. You, with your imagination and your dodgy life, are just the man I now need to write me speeches and a manifesto. You're closer to the voters, know what they want – not that there's any need for that, though it looks good. Once I'm in, off you go: Moscow, New York, Santiago de Chile, wherever."

"What if you don't get in?"

"Wrong question! My opponent, known as Boxer, is damned

nearly bald and looks the bruiser he is. Not an attractive proposition. Oh, by the way, by morning – two hours from now – the boys expect to have word of your penguin. So you go and get your head down. You clever ones need more sleep than the rest of us, and live longer, so they say."

9

It was almost midday when Viktor woke, undressed and snug under his warm woollen rug, to the caress of the sun on his face. Swinging his feet to the floor, he sent a cut-glass tumbler rolling, and there, thoughtfully placed on the floor beside the divan, was a bottle of beer and a natty wooden-handled opener. As he drank, wishing there was more than one bottle, he suddenly remembered the promise of news of Misha by morning, a morning already well advanced.

He dressed and made his way downstairs, encountering not a sound, not a soul. Further inspection of the kitchen fridge yielded sausage and butter, which he washed down with beer – as good for clearing the head as coffee for the French – from a crate in the corner.

Two cars drove into the courtyard, and a thoughtful, worried-looking Andrey Pavlovich poked his head around the door.

"Come down to the basement when you've finished."

*

In the basement there was a large billiard table, and a bar with three tall, single-legged stools. A door behind the bar looked as if it might lead to a sauna.

Andrey Pavlovich, potting balls aimlessly, lost in thought, looked up and smiled.

"Any news of Misha?"

"He's not here in Kiev. But we've found your Lyosha. He might be able to tell you something. He's got a café, the Afghan, in Tatar Street. Nice spot."

"Can I go and see him?" Viktor asked doubtfully.

"Of course. You're not a prisoner, you're on the payroll."

"Not afraid I'll do a bunk?"

"You're not a fool. Besides, I'll have your two passports in my safe, safe from pickpockets. Terrible place, Kiev, for pickpockets! Mobiles, purses – they pinch the lot . . . Oh, and I wouldn't advertise to your old friends that you're back."

Viktor handed over his passports.

"Quick learner!" smiled Andrey Pavlovich. "This is now home – your *shell*, which you nip back into at the first whiff of danger."

10

Though the worse for lack of sleep, he kept going, cheered by the dazzling late-afternoon sun. He bussed to Kurenevsky Rise, then proceeded on foot to Nagornaya Street. No-one was about, just the odd car careering at speed, heedless of the Emmentaler-cheese-like surface.

Café Afghan was on the ground floor of some research institute, with a concrete ramp with a rail instead of steps. The double doors were open. Inside, a surprisingly low bar and no-one serving. The tables were more like occasional tables, but not a chair anywhere.

Behind the bar, a Siemens coffee machine, bottles, and glasses large and small hanging on hooks.

Viktor tapped with a coin.

"Just a mo'."

He thought he recognized the voice.

Doors behind the bar creaked open, and out, still bearded and with what little remained of him in camouflage battledress, came Lyosha in a wheelchair.

"Well I'm damned! Viktor! Fit?"

"And you?"

"Not jogging much, but come through to the back, get yourself a visitor's chair."

Taking one of the three collapsible wheelchairs, he wheeled himself to a table.

Lyosha joined him with coffee and sugar on a tray.

"Well," he said, sugaring his coffee and stirring, "win some, lose some."

"You're into philosophy."

"Not much else left."

"What happened?"

"A bit like bomb-disposal – one mistake, and if you survive, you never forget it. The mistake we made was not to check the coffin. Not content with killing one of ours, they somehow managed to get a bomb into his coffin. Killed my boss and his number one, and I got this. No legs, no money. Friends rallied round, and as you see, I've not been idle. I now actually run the place."

It belonged, he explained, to the Society of Internationalist Servicemen, and was therefore tax exempt. Not that anyone ever checked. Next door was a hostel for Afghan War veterans. They'd thought of organizing a veterans' sports club, but hadn't got round to it, though there were enough of them in wheelchairs to form a good one.

"What about Misha?" Viktor asked at last.

Lyosha scratched an ear.

"Yes, that was bad about him. The boss had been in a hole long before the last funeral Misha appeared at. $300,000-worth of smuggled booze was the start of it. Someone shopped us, the booze got seized, and no buying it back. Twice after that the same thing happened, putting the boss a million in debt to a chap in Moscow who runs petrol pumps here. So it was to him Misha went along with the other assets, and not a bloody thing I could do."

"And this Moscow chap?"

"He's back there. Lost his pumps to some People's Deputy. Got booted out."

"What's his name?"

"Really want to know?"

"I do."

Lyosha shook his head.

"Ilya Kovalyov, a.k.a. Sphinx. Bank in Moscow. Commercial Gas. If you know what that means."

"Money."

"Your own intelligence, your own army's what it means. Buy whoever you like, and do for anyone you don't . . . You know you've been *sought*, as they say."

"I do."

"Yet you still go about openly?"

"I'm trying to find Misha."

"That I call real love!"

As two men in camouflage battledress wheeled themselves in, Lyosha stiffened.

"Hi!" said one, pausing at their table and looking hard at Viktor. "Rung Potapych?"

"Here within the hour."

"So let's have some coffee."

"Come over to the bar," Lyosha said quietly, and there slipped Viktor a scrap of paper with his phone number. "Ring or look in."

Viktor folded and replaced his chair, gave a farewell nod, and left, watched by the two wheelchairers, one with one leg, the other with none.

11

That evening Andrey Pavlovich sat down with Viktor in the lounge and ordered a bottle of red Burgundy and cheese to be brought, which augured well for a first working session with his candidate. His intuition told him that, by and large, Andrey Pavlovich was a good man, and if nothing else, a man of his word, allowing him the freedom of Kiev. As to his passports, he'd soon have one back for his trip to Moscow. Thanks to Andrey Pavlovich, he'd found Lyosha and learnt where to continue his search. There was much on the credit side. The tart red wine and firm tart cheese created an atmosphere of welcome and trust.

"Tomorrow," Andrey Pavlovich began, "image makers arrive from Moscow. You're to listen in. Anything you don't care for, tell me."

"Will do."

"Having worked on a paper, you know about politics."

"Not to the extent of writing articles."

Dismissive wave of the hand.

"What you wrote *was* politics, *politics in action*. What I need to get the hang of is the politics of promises . . . Get it? Promises are what a political career starts with. So come on, what do I promise?"

"Who to?"

"The people, my electorate."

Viktor thought back to what little he'd skimmed of manifestos.

"Money for the poor, food for the starving, comforts and lower taxes for the well-fed."

"Not so fast," Andrey Pavlovich broke in, calling for pen and paper which were duly brought.

"'Money for the poor', he repeated as he wrote. "'The starving need food . . . The well-fed . . .' But how do we know who is and who isn't?"

"'Well-fed' is figurative," said Viktor quickly. "'The rich' is another way of putting it."

"Hang on. That smacks of simplification. 'Well-fed' and 'rich' aren't quite the same. The rich, when not dieting, tend to be well-fed. Against which, the well-fed aren't always rich. So where does that leave us?"

"With more well-fed than rich!"

"Making them the more important to us, since the few rich vote for themselves."

"And don't need to be promised anything," said Viktor, relieved to find him so receptive and beginning to enjoy himself. "Once elected, you never stop promising – you can't."

"Well, we'll see, though I get the point. Now let's recap. First, what to promise the poor. Nobody shells out money in the streets – any fool can see that."

"But they do, before an election, to secure votes. At least 10 hryvnas a head."

Andrey Pavlovich looked surprised.

"Bribery. Promises, a manifesto, that's what I need!"

"Promises re economy: new jobs, new factories, preferential credits for up-and-coming entrepreneurs . . ."

"That's the stuff!" exclaimed Andrey Pavlovich, pushing pen and paper towards him. "So that by this time tomorrow we've a manifesto for discussion and maybe to put to these chaps from Moscow. God knows what image makers do! Do you? They charge the bloody earth."

"Change your hairstyle, buy you ties, write your speeches . . ."

"Ah! Still, let's not overtax our brains. We'll play billiards – live like Tolstoy, spot of ploughing, then back to the novel!"

12

Trees, courtyard, city noise were lost next morning in a swirling milkiness of mist. Autumn had come, giving not a damn for the inconvenience it caused.

Standing at his attic window, Viktor took pleasure in the apparent absence of life. Sonya would be looking out at the very same mist, and he'd not rung her as promised.

An opened tin of olives in the kitchen and sausage from the fridge, provided a good breakfast. The house was silent, but in the hall he encountered Pasha, Master of Sport (Biathlon) and number one to Andrey Pavlovich.

"Is there a phone somewhere?" he asked, and Pasha with a lordly gesture pointed him to one.

A minute's worth of ringing tones, then Sonya's voice, and a happy "Uncle Vik!" as she recognized his.

"I think I've found Misha."

"Where?"

"He's gone to Moscow."

"What for?" She sounded both surprised and sad.

"To be in a zoo."

"Be what?"

"A penguin."

"How can he?"

"Why not?"

"I can't be a Sonya if I'm Sonya already!"

"In a zoo it's different, penguins are there to be penguins, elephants to be elephants."

Sonya capitulated, and they arranged to meet in an hour's time at the bus stop near her block.

13

By midday the fog had thinned, letting the wan autumn sun through. Hydropark had an air of summer inertia about it, as if this, the most southerly beachy islet, were several degrees warmer than anywhere else. For how else to account for the greater frequency of ice-cream kiosks per kilometre and the logicality of starting out with a chocolate candied fruit ice.

"You look older," observed Sonya, tackling her ice-cream.

"So do you."

"So what?" she smiled. "But so does Auntie Nina."

"How so?"

"She's forever grumbling and quarelling with Uncle Kolya."

"What about?"

"Not always coming home. Odessa's where he's from, and where he keeps going, promising to bring back mussels and forgetting."

"And what does he promise Auntie Nina?"

"Not to keep going, but he does."

"So Auntie Nina's fed up."

"She is. She's put his bag outside the door."

"So it's a merry old time you're having."

"We are not. She promised to send me to kindergarten, and to find me a nanny."

"But she hasn't?"

"No."

"I'll have a word with her."

"Best kick her out."

"Why?"

"She was supposed to take me for walks – that's what you got her for when Daddy went away and left me with you – but she hasn't for ages. Come on, let's hire a boat."

They went as far as Paton Bridge, with Viktor rowing and Sonya, ice-cream consumed, fingers duly licked, seated in the stern telling of her daily life, and inspiring a new feeling of guilt. For Sonya he was sorry, with Nina, angry. Not for the advent of Kolya from Odessa, but because Sonya, young as she was, had not forgotten what Nina was there for, and Nina had. So what next? Kick Nina and Kolya out, start afresh, just him and Sonya? Couldn't be done – not at the moment. Sonya would be better left poorly looked after than completely alone. The flat was his. He had the initiative.

"You tell her what's what!" Sonya said sudddenly. "Make her stand in the corner. And give Uncle Kolya the boot. She won't. She's afraid of him."

"Though she puts his bag outside the door?"

"Last time she took it back in when he started shouting."

"So he shouts."

"And smacks her bottom and makes her cry."

Viktor stopped rowing, resting his oars on the water.

"Are they ever nasty to you?"

"They don't bother me, except when they wake me up quarrelling . . . Or forget to leave any food."

"I'll speak to them," said Viktor gravely.

And Sonya smiled, reassured.

14

When Andrey Pavlovich returned at midnight, Viktor was ready with a 6-page manifesto. Compiling it, he had worked off his anger and irritation over Nina and her Kolya, and rereading it, was surprised to find that it convinced even him.

Clearly depressed, Andrey Pavlovich took the pages with no great enthusiasm, but very quickly became engrossed.

"Nice bit of work!" he declared eventually, looking more relaxed. "Tomorrow morning the image makers arrive, and we start work in earnest. So no sloping off!"

Viktor nodded.

"Bit off colour today, are we?" he asked with sudden concern.

And Viktor found himself relating the situation at his flat.

"Poor chap, but you've only yourself to blame," said Andrey Pavlovich. "'Thou shalt admit to thy home neither stranger, nor semi-stranger, nor semi-intimate' – Snail's Law, Article 3."

Viktor shrugged.

"Either you're no judge of people, or just can't be bothered. Who, out of that lot, really matters?"

"Sonya."

"Right. So tomorrow – no, tomorrow we'll be busy – the day after tomorrow, you shall have back the keys of your flat."

"But how about Sonya? She can't live there alone."

"We'll think of something. Meanwhile you stay put."

15

Next morning the image makers turned up in a black jeep, travelling light with sports bags and three cardboard boxes containing "a state of the art computer, their mobile brain," as head imager Zhora, a man in his thirties, put it. With him were Slava, the computer expert, and twin brothers, bright-as-buttons Sasha and Vova, in their young twenties. Desiccated, round-shouldered, pebble-bespectacled Slava, though about 40, still had the look of a brilliant schoolboy.

"No computers?" Zhora asked in amazement, touring the house in search of where to establish himself.

"My games I play live," said Andrey Pavlovich.

"But information, where do you store it?"

Andrey Pavlovich tapped his forehead.

Zhora looked disappointed.

The old nursery on the first floor was declared suitable and the image makers took up their bags and computer. Viktor, introduced as "aide to Andrey Pavlovich", Zhora treated with interest and respect, shaking hands and introducing him to the others. They lunched together in the lounge, off cheese, sausage, fresh rolls and coffee. Andrey Pavlovich sat in for five minutes, then disappeared.

After lunch, Viktor accompanied Zhora outside, where the latter produced a packet of Gauloises and lit up.

"Been here long?" he asked.

"Not very."

"But clued up."

"I think so."

"Your boss, what's he like?"

"All right."

"Fond of money?"

"I wouldn't say so."

"Good. What does he pay you?"

"Enough."

Zhora betrayed signs of weariness.

"Don't worry. We're battling on the same front, you and I. It's just that to do a good job I need to know . . . Every client has his little oddities . . . His submerged rocks . . . It's nice to know . . ."

"As I said, he's all right."

"Any serious oppo?"

Viktor shrugged.

"No war in progress?"

"How do you mean?"

Zhora ground his Gauloise into the gravel with the stub toe of his designer shoe and unnecessary vigour.

"'How do I mean' means, any casualties to date?"

"Only a hunting fatality."

"Involving?"

"Andrey Pavlovich's son-in-law."

"Uh-huh . . ." Zhora thought for a moment. "That's the kind of thing to keep me up to speed on – I'll make it worth your while."

"Will do."

This exchange with the notion of their "battling on a front together" left Viktor with a nasty taste in the mouth. But elections, as now practised, *were* war – no longer simply a seizing of territory, but a killing off of opposition, as in big business, on a front of anyone's choosing.

"Loitering?" demanded Andrey Pavlovich, emerging from the house and encountering Viktor. "Pay our image makers a call. They've got your manifesto."

*

Where the cot had been, there was now a desk with computer. Slava was busy with leads, Zhora recumbent on the couch with Viktor's manifesto.

"This OK by the boss?" he asked.

"Yes."

"Bloody good! So we bung it on computer, print it off, knock up posters . . . And make ourselves a nice little bit on the side."

"How so?"

"On computer I've got 50 or more manifestos: party, non-party, populist, what-have-you, you name it. But your ideas are quite new ones on me . . . A client of ours standing for Mayor of Gomel recently, came up with pledges of the subtlest. But they're a simple lot in the place, so I told him straight: Promise money – money for jam's what they understand. Which he did, and now is Mayor of the place. Get the idea?"

"No."

"Yours is an up-market manifesto – Moscow, Kiev quality. Kiev is where he's standing for?"

"Not sure."

"Hasn't he said?"

"No."

"Not good! How is he today?"

"He's all right."

Zhora took himself off, leaving Viktor with Slava, who was working at his computer. The twins were not in evidence.

"Do you really have 50 manifestos on computer?" Viktor asked.

"More."

"Might I see a couple?"

"Afraid not. Information of commercial value. Manifestos cost money."

"You don't sell them, do you?"

"What else?" Removing his spectacles, he polished them with a handkerchief. "There's hardly one we can't use three times over. The main things to clear off before the successful candidate starts implementing them."

"Why?"

"No, not seriously. But a golden rule of the image maker is 'Never be there for the result'. The client gives you hell if he loses, his rivals give you hell if he wins."

"Where are the twins?"

"Zhora's sent them somewhere."

16

"What do you make of our image makers?" Andrey Pavlovich asked later that night as they played billiards. Unusually for so late an hour, he was sporting razor-creased dark trousers, a white shirt and bow tie.

"Not sure."

"Would you trust them?"

"No!"

"Interesting. And you're right," he added, having cued. "You can't trust those you pay a lot to. Especially when they show such a taste for luxury. Wanted the best sauna in town laid on for them today. 'To relieve stress.' Have you seen any sign of stress?"

"No."

"Nor I, but I've laid it on. You keen on saunas?"

"Haven't had many."

"Like the experience?"

"Yes."

"Pasha, switch on the sauna," he shouted up the stairs.

★

Later, as they sat naked and sweating in the cosy sauna sandwiched between the billiard room and the underground garage, Andrey Pavlovich dashed a mug of liquid onto the heated pebbles, scenting the dry heat with lavender.

"Every activity, be it sex or a shower or a game of billiards, has a pleasure potential never fully revealed until the very last," Andrey Pavlovich said languidly. "The sauna's is inexhaustible. Whatever activity you pursue thereafter is an Aladdin's cave of delights."

At 2 a.m., again in razor-creased trousers, white shirt and bow tie, he set off for his rendezvous and Aladdin's cave.

"Tomorrow," he said, "I'll be like a squeezed lemon!"

*

Pasha drove him in the 4 x 4, and Viktor was alone in the house, or had the sensation of being alone, but with no inclination to sleep after the invigorating sauna.

Switching on the light in the attic, he lay on his bed, and thought of Antarctica, Bronikovsky and Misha, then of Andrey Pavlovich's promise to restore his flat to him. Try as he might, he could find no qualm of conscience nor shred of pity concerning Nina, not even as niece of his late lamented militiaman friend Sergey. Sonya was all he cared about. We'll think of something, Andrey Pavlovich had said, and Viktor was sure that he would. So for a while he would surrender his freedom of choice, and live quietly under Andrey Pavlovich's roof, until such time as the unwritten contract of his simple, if imprecise, employment reached its natural termination point.

Before settling down to sleep he got out Banker Bronikovsky's letter which so far he had scrupulously not read, but now felt that he should, to see if there was any urgency about it.

> Darling Marina,
>
> A thousand apologies. I'm far away, and clearly here to stay. The bearer of this will tell you all. I just have one or two last – really *last* – requests. Get hold of Fedya Sedykh and tell him it's not me who's to blame for his troubles. It was Litovchenko who framed me. Why should I depart this life blamed for the sins of others! Simply tell Mother I'm abroad,

280

lying low, and shall be for some time. My brother you can tell the truth, which is, alas, that when you get this, I shall be no more. In some strange way they've got at me even here. Through the cook. All night I'm in agony but by morning it eases. I wish the sods had gone for something short and sharp, instead of making sure I suffer. Sorry, I'm on about myself again. The money should last quite a while. The bearer will give you my credit card and PIN. That's it, then. A big hug. There'll be thousands at my funeral – all king penguins, says he, joking to the last. All my love, Stanislav.

Viktor lay thinking again of the Antarctic, Bronikovsky, and hosts of penguins wanting only their prodigal son Misha to return for their happiness to be complete. The sooner the election was over, the sooner he would be free to search. By both a happy and an unhappy coincidence, he would be delivering the letter to Moscow, where Misha was!

Some time later a car drove in, and through the open window he heard voices. The image makers and their driver were back from the sauna. Zhora sounded well lit up.

*

Next morning Viktor breakfasted alone. At nine, Andrey Pavlovich, still in dark trousers, white shirt and bow tie, popped his head around the door, weary but smiling.

"Make me a nice cup of coffee," he said, and disappeared.

He was soon back, now in a tracksuit. Gratefully he took the coffee, and spooned in sugar. "How's it going?" he asked.

Viktor shrugged. "You've not given them anything more to get on with."

Andrey Pavlovich smiled. "Or anything less. Don't worry. Just asking. Your main task now is to keep an eye on them. You might learn something. Back in good time, were they?"

"At about four . . ." Then, taking breath, he added, "How long is it to the election?"

"Two weeks."

"Not long, then."

"Don't worry – I've been meeting my electorate. The problem at the moment is my dilatory opponent – no posters, just leaflets in post boxes. Not a word against me. I don't like it."

"Maybe he's a decent chap."

Andrey Pavlovich gave him a withering look. "Elections are a competition to see who can outspit the other – it's for him to prove I'm no good, and for me to prove he's no good."

"Which you're not actually doing."

"Not my job," he snapped, "I've men doing that, 40 of them! Keep my nose clean, wear a tie, shave, that's what I do."

At that moment Pasha came bursting in with a rolled up poster which he handed to Andrey Pavlovich.

"Know where he's getting this printed?" Andrey Pavlovich demanded, face contorted with rage.

"Belaya Tserkov."

"Bloody idiots. So now what?"

"May I see?" said Viktor.

The poster showed a crew-cut, visibly brainless, mildly disdainful-looking man banally promising a solution to the housing problem within five years by dint of State investment.

"You don't get it, do you?" said Andrey Pavlovich. "Photos, Pasha!"

They were enlarged picnic photographs showing a man not unlike Andrey Pavlovich's opponent.

"His brother?"

"No, him!"

And comparing the scarred right cheek and bruiser's broken nose of the photo with the classical profile of the poster, Viktor saw the reason for Andrey Pavlovich's anger.

"You've got half an hour to come up with something, Pasha," Andrey Pavlovich said sharply. "And you, Viktor, rouse our image makers. They've got half an hour to decide how to put that bloody scar back!"

With which he left, banging the door behind him.

"A fine mess we're in!" said Pasha. "How are we supposed to know what they're printing where? We're not State Security."

"I'll wake up Zhora," Viktor said, getting to his feet.

"Damn Zhora!" Pasha said grimly. "What do you think?"

"We could, at a pinch, stick the scar back on."

"Look, you're paid for the brainwork, I'm the muscle. So get on with it."

Glancing through the other prints, Viktor was struck by one full-face portrait showing scar and broken nose to maximum advantage, with the plus of an animal-at-bay expression much at variance with the smug Hollywood smile of the airbrush portrait.

"You couldn't bring me a coffee," he said, and Pasha, seeing the problem as good as solved, betook himself to the stove.

Before and after – that was it! The whiter-than-white technique of the telly soap powder ad could be applied to faces as well as shirts!

"Got anywhere?" asked Pasha, bringing the coffee.

"I think I have, and without our image makers! All we do is enlarge the scar-broken-nose-horrible-expression one, superimpose some cosmetic house name, and stick it up beside the existing poster."

★

Andrey Pavlovich was slow to get the idea, but when he did, his eyes flashed with Young Pioneer fervour.

"Cosmetics," he said, thinking aloud, "there's money in them. Some could go towards our friend's election expenses. Pasha, ring Potapych. Get him to find out if he is in fact financed by some cosmetics firm.

"Nice work!" he continued, turning to Viktor. "Image makers still asleep?"

Viktor nodded.

"By the way . . ." he reached into a pocket. "Key to the new lock. You still have the old one, I take it."

Viktor stared, at a loss for words.

"You'll find Sonya, and this Nina, now formally engaged as her nanny, and happy to be so."

"And Kolya?"

"Enjoying my hospitality. Not here, elsewhere. Undergoing 'educative treatment'. I'd have a good look round your flat when you go, in case he's left something. He was on a hard drugs run between here and Odessa, then switched to plastic explosive. Price has gone up fivefold, thanks to the elections."

"When can I go?"

Andrey Pavlovich consulted his watch.

"In two hours' time. Pasha will drive you. Not as warder but for protection!" he added with a laugh, seeing Viktor's expression. "I need your brains."

17

Red Army Street, Tolstoy Square, brief traffic jam, then fifteen minutes freeway to the turn-off past the rubbish collection point and pathetic Eiffel Tower dovecotes of the waste area, where, less than a year ago, Viktor, Sonya and militiaman Sergey walked Misha in the snow, friendly stray dogs intervening.

For a moment there was the strange confused sensation of finding himself lowered, in special diving suit and protective submersible, into the past. And if he felt frightened, he had only to pull on an invisible air line leading up to reality and they would pull him up, remove his helmet, let him get his breath back and make up his mind whether he really did want to go down into the past.

They drew up right outside the block. It was not the first time Pasha had been here.

"I'll wait by the transformer hut," he said.

*

Holding his two keys but eyeing the bell, he hesitated. If he rang, Sonya or Nina would open, and though the place was his, let him in like a visitor.

So he both opened and rang. The first thing he saw was a saucer of milk for the cat that scratched.

Sonya, wearing a denim tunic dress embroidered with roses, looked out into the corridor.

"Hi," he said.

"Hi."

"Alone?"

"No."

He took his shoes off, looked into the sitting room, and was brought up short by the unfamiliarity of pink wallpaper, green tapestry throws over the armchairs and couch, and a pink crochet-edged tablecloth. He raised the cloth a little and was relieved to see the old polished surface smiling up at him.

"Don't you like it?" asked Sonya from the door.

"No."

"Doesn't like the improvements, Nina," Sonya called, opening the door of the bedroom.

Nina, in towelling dressing gown, was sitting moist-eyed and miserable on a double bed where the single had been. Biting her lip, she nodded a response to his "Hello".

"You're like two cats!" Sonya said suddenly.

"Go and play with your cat," said Viktor.

"She's out."

"Well, go anyway."

She went, leaving the door wide open. Viktor pulled it to.

"How is it?" he asked, finally breaking the silence.

"'How is it?'" she repeated tearfully. Everything I've got together, all my happiness, destroyed in 30 minutes, trampled on!"

"Whatever do you mean?"

"Don't pretend! You organized it. I know. People warned me, but like a fool I didn't believe them."

The cord fastening her dressing gown emphasized that she had put on weight. He had no wish to argue or talk, and seeing him suddenly sad and distant, Nina fell silent.

"No, I'm sorry . . . I shouldn't have said that," she said after a while. "But I was so frightened when they came yesterday. And as I said then, I accept – there's nothing here I lay claim to or want."

"All right, but could you make some tea."

Nina went off to the kitchen, and he looked down from the window at the wasteland with its rubbish collection point and dovecotes. Way over on the left he could just see a bit of the fence of the kindergarten where, as a little boy, he had buried his first hamster. It was cold. It would be another month before the heating came on and made its way laboriously up to the 4th floor. The door opened. He turned.

"Tea's ready, Auntie Nina says."

The kitchen, thank God, was unchanged, almost.

"Where's Sergey?"

"Who?"

He nodded to where the urn with the ashes of his militiaman friend had stood.

"On the balcony. It was in the way."

"Bring it back."

She brought it in, wiped it clean with a dishcloth, placed it on the windowsill near the stove, then sat on the little stool once reserved for Misha's food bowl.

"You should go through the flat, and anything of Kolya's put into a bag," Viktor said. "If it's wrapped, leave it wrapped – it might be dangerous."

"Oh, God," she whispered. "I'd no idea."

"Sonya will help – won't you, Sonya?"

"Of course I will."

"How about money?"

"Not a lot left," said Nina nervously. "What with decorating, buying furniture, and the dacha . . ."

"Dacha?"

"At Osokorki on the Dnieper. You'll like it."

He said nothing, got up, and in so doing kicked against

something made of glass. Looking under the table, he saw any number of empty champagne and vodka bottles.

"Get rid of them," he snapped, making for the door. "I'll ring this evening."

Before joining Pasha, he collected his bag from Old Tonya's.

"Your tenant got carted off by the militia," she said. "What had he been up to?"

"Militia? In uniform?"

"The special sort of militia. He was just on his way in when they swooped. They had him down flat on his face like on telly."

"You saw the whole thing?"

"Not much I miss living up here right opposite. They'd turned up in two cars an hour earlier and waited. You could tell something was up."

18

The evening was spent discussing Viktor's plan with the image makers. Slava took to the whole thing immediately, but Zhora kept spinning things out, either because his professional pride was hurt at the idea's not being his, or because something else was bothering him. But Andrey Pavlovich stood firm as a rock, and rather than risk overdoing it, Zhora finally capitulated, then proceeded to explain to Slava that morphing and printing would take longer than he thought. Andrey Pavlovich and Viktor could see his game, but kept their thoughts to themselves until, at nearly midnight, Zhora and the twins set off by taxi for a night club, leaving bespectacled Slava to strain his eyes further.

"Can you do it by morning?" Andrey Pavlovich asked, looking closely at the familiar portrait now scanned to screen.

"I can try," he said dully.

"By, say, four or five?" Andrey Pavlovich asked, placing a $100 bill on the keyboard.

"Maybe sooner," said Slava, pocketing the note.

"Let's play billiards," said Andrey Pavlovich, turning to Viktor. "You see," he added when they were out of earshot, "the dollar, timely invested in technology, becomes the engine of progress!"

*

Their play was soon interrupted by Pasha's gravely announcing that Potapych was on the phone and would like to speak to Andrey Pavlovich.

"We're going to hear a tape," said Andrey Pavlovich when he returned, and a few minutes later they were driving away on what proved quite a journey.

The streets being empty, and assuming a nil response to a Mercedes 4 x 4 proceeding at speed, Pasha drove accordingly – Artyoma Street, Frunze Street, then, somewhere beyond Spartak Stadium, off left into a private estate. They stopped in front of tall iron gates.

"Flash your lights," said Andrey Pavlovich.

A light went on in the courtyard, the gates opened, and they drove in.

A man in camouflage fatigues conducted them into the house, where a robust sixty-year-old in jeans and dark blue sweater showed them into a mahogany-furnished lounge.

"Masha, lay the table," he ordered, then turning to Viktor and Pasha, "you warriors can wait here, while we confer."

289

Masha wheeled in a trolley of eats, Pasha helped lay the table, and a bottle of brandy, two of vodka and glasses were produced from the bar.

Ten minutes later Andrey Pavlovich returned grim-faced and weary, followed shortly after by their still-smiling host. Inviting them to table, he set about pouring cognac.

"Not for me till after the election," said Andrey Pavlovich, and was given mineral water.

It was not exactly a cheerful occasion. Pasha looked questioningly at his master before accepting a second cognac. Viktor stuck at one, as did their host.

*

On the way back to Goloseyevo, Viktor fell asleep. Roused by Pasha on arrival, he got out, yawning, his one aim being to get back to sleep in his little attic room, only to be jollied into action by a "Make coffee all round", from Andrey Pavlovich.

"No sleep for us tonight," he declared, and went for a cold shower.

Pasha went up to the nursery to see how Slava was getting on, and returned with the news that he'd nearly finished. It was then 2.30 by the kitchen wall clock.

Andrey Pavlovich entered, now in a dressing gown, and carrying a radio cassette player.

"Right," he said dryly, "I declare the present night sitting of the revolutionary committee to be in session. All got coffee?"

He switched on the tape recorder.

. . . Incriminating stuff's what we're after, really incriminating, OK?

Yeah, but how? With not one bloody computer and staff all doggily devoted?

Doggy devotion comes dearer, that's all. You pick your man, bring him to

290

the sauna, and we talk . . . "Is there anything about his nibs his opponent shouldn't know?" isn't a bad line to start with. "To beat your enemy, you must know his weapons." – Lenin. And you've got just two more days, after which . . .

But . . .

But nothing, Zhora. That arsehole who doesn't comb his hair, he's the one to go for.

"I'll buy you a comb," said Andrey Pavlovich, seeing Viktor's look of concern.

No joy there – he's dead from the neck up.

Switching off, Andrey Pavlovich turned to his coffee.

"Nice turn of phrase they have, our image makers."

"Bastards to a man!" cried Pasha, and receiving a quizzical look, modified it to, "Well, bloody swine, then!"

"Cost me an arm and a leg, that tape," said Andrey Pavlovich, "but we'll save on image management."

He turned to Pasha.

"Ring Tolik to help lift that lot from the nightclub, deprive them of sleep and deliver at the Dump for me and Viktor to interview tomorrow. Search their kit, and bring in a good computer buff for tomorrow evening."

Before setting off, Pasha splashed his face with cold water.

19

It was 8.oo before Viktor got to bed. He slept late, heavily and headachily at first, but towards midday he was on the Dnieper, alone, walking anxiously around a pool of unfrozen water edged with footprints, waiting vainly not just for Misha to surface but militiaman friend Sergey as well. As if to spite him, there were no fishermen, just the dark patches of their iced-over holes.

He woke, still tired, and surprised to hear not a sound. He remembered promising to ring Sonya and Nina, but his watch said it was time for a late lunch.

In the empty kitchen he helped himself to sausage, cheese and butter from the fridge, and made tea instead of coffee.

On the table in the lounge he found the new portrait of Andrey Pavlovich's opponent.

GRAZZIOLA COSMETICS IMPROVE

NOT ONLY THE FACE!

read the glaring caption. Heartened, he toyed, as he ate, with ideas for Andrey Pavlovich's campaign. The President's lady ran an aid-the-children fund, which prompted thoughts of another possibility – not terribly original, but original was not what voters went for. What appealed was the instantly recognizable. Like charitable concern. That said more about the character of candidate or deputy than any political process or activity. "Charitable" hinted at a possibility of hand-outs, whether deserved or not.

Some proposal for Andrey Pavlovich was what he needed. He could then buy press space for it and win popularity.

His thoughts turned to Tatar Street, Café Afghan, and the young disabled – too young to have fought in Afghanistan – who gathered there. True he'd seen only three of them, Lyosha who had lost his legs here, in Kiev, being one. Still, to be disabled young was both bad and honourable enough to have public appeal.

Andrey Pavlovich returned shortly before five, clearly not having slept, but cheerful, unstressed, unyawning and back stiff as a ramrod. The image makers had given some account of themselves. Zhora and the twins ran a lottery swindle in Zhitomir; Slava, the computer buff, was a simple lad from Kursk. They had decided to cash in on the election, make a handsome profit on the side. Amongst their effects were a silenced automatic, cocaine, and a mobile phone capable of being used as a bug.

"What will you do with them?"

"Slava I've let go. The others will suffer. How I've yet to decide. We'll go and visit tomorrow."

Judging his moment, Viktor ventured a suggestion he had in mind.

Andrey Pavlovich showed interest.

"How many disabled? What do limbs cost?"

"I'll find out how many. Maybe Pasha could look into cost."

Andrey Pavlovich nodded. Charitable concern – he was all in favour of. And instructing Pasha to wake him in two hours, went to put his head down.

20

In Central Universal Stores, Kreshchatik Street, he treated himself to a cheap Chinese umbrella against the drizzle. The cheerful bustle of the place provided a pleasant distraction from the little-relished prospect of visiting Lyosha at Café Afghan. He had a sudden urge to find Svetlana and go again to the kindergarten at night. But reality, or more accurately his sense of it, won the day, and opening his umbrella, he made for a pedestrian underpass, hitched a lift, and fifteen minutes later mounted the ramp to the café, which this time was busier.

"Fetch yourself a chair, so I don't get neck-ache looking up," Lyosha said. "Like a coffee?"

"I would."

"Hey, Whiskers, how about my cappuccino?" a voice complained.

"On its way."

Viktor's idea was coldly received.

"I'll ask around," Lyosha said dully. "But what does he get out of us, this candidate of yours? Our vote?"

"No more than that there should be a journalist and a photographer there when the limbs are handed over, if it gets that far. So the electorate becomes aware."

"Never thought *you* would worm yourself into politics."

"Other way round. Trapped in a bog of them, and soon to get out."

"Really?" Lyosha sounded doubtful. "Still, hang on, I'll see what the boss man says. It's a good thing he's here."

He returned five minutes later.

"In principle," he said, "the boss man's pro, but he'd like something from your man in return. Artificial limbs are like evening dress, not something we wear every day. Get us a low-level billiard table, and he can hand over as many artificial limbs as he likes, so long as we don't have to wear the damned things."

Viktor laughed.

"You could be on, he's keen on billiards."

"Try him, and let me know. Have this card – my number's changed – and it's got my mobile. Give me a ring. We'll have to meet, with your boss and mine there. It's not long to polling day. Like a cognac?

"Do you know," he went on, raising his glass, "I remember those

funerals of ours as the best time of my life . . . You won't understand
. . . But here's to the past! It always is better than the present . . ."

"And worse than the future."

"Who can say?"

He tossed back his cognac.

"What is it?" Viktor asked, savouring his.

"Martell. Friendly humanitarian aid. Once made me dream I was
walking again. I woke to find my legs still aching . . . Still, drink up
and get moving – this lot's rather anti the sound of limb."

21

No sooner had he arrived back, feeling he'd done well and
expecting praise, than Viktor found himself speeding through Kiev
with Andrey Pavlovich and Pasha, both equally taciturn, in the 4 x 4.

"Stop!" Andrey Pavlovich ordered suddenly. "Let's you and I have
a look see, Viktor."

They were on Victory Avenue opposite the stone animals
guarding the entrance to the zoo from which he'd rescued Misha.

"Forget the zoo, this is what we've come to see." It was a
hoarding displaying the variant portraits of Andrey Pavlovich's
opponent, plus caption.

"What do you think?"

"It works!"

"Damned good idea for which my thanks, and these," said
Andrey Pavlovich, handing him a wad of $100 bills.

"Drive on, Pasha."

"Where now?" asked Viktor.

"The Dump. How about your disabled?"

"They've come up with a counter-request."

"Is it expensive?"

"They'd like a billiard table of a height for players in wheelchairs."

"No problem. Mine's due for replacement. We'll run it over to them, cut the legs down . . ."

★

The Dump lay deep in a private estate off the Pushcha-Voditsa road. It was surrounded by a tall metal fence topped with coils of barbed wire, and comprised a metal hangar and a three-storeyed brick-built building with windows emitting warm, cheery light.

A man in combat fatigues opened the forbidding metal gates, and announced their arrival over an entry phone. The metal door of the building buzzed open and they were received by three similarly clad guards.

Andrey Pavlovich was taken aside for a *sotto-voce* conversation, and five minutes later, all three of them were conducted down steep steps into a broad, brightly-lit corridor with to right and left rusty iron doors at regular intervals.

"Who first?" asked their escort.

"The twins," said Andrey Pavlovich.

Leaving Pasha outside, Andrey Pavlovich and Viktor entered a prison cell with two wooden benches, a table and a slop pail. Handcuffed together, the twins were sitting up, evidently woken from sleep by the clang of the door.

"So, how are my cagebirds?" inquired Andrey Pavlovich. "Any complaints?"

They shook their heads.

"Who was it you were talking to in the sauna?"

"Zhora knows him, we don't."

"We'll go and ask him then."

Next door they found Zhora, visibly battered and chained to a ring so low in the wall that he was forced to kneel.

Andrey Pavlovich squatted in front of him.

"Remembered yet who you were talking to in the sauna? Time – like money for your board, *my money*, $50 *per diem* – is short. No sense in wasting it. Infringing Snail's Law's bad enough. Refusing to talk's even worse."

"Law? What law?" Zhora mumbled.

Andrey Pavlovich slowly straightened, shaking his head. He looked for Viktor's response, but Viktor was more or less asleep.

"Due for discharge," he told the escort. "Pumped full of dope and dumped in the Dnieper . . . Ignorance of the Law's no defence. Come on, Viktor."

They stood outside for a while listening to Zhora's shouts, then went back in.

"The Godfather," Zhora confessed.

"Who's working for Boxer."

Zhora nodded.

"Good. Sorry to have troubled you."

"This Law? What is it?" Zhora croaked.

"Article 5 is what applies: intruding into another's home for the purpose of ousting him. Punishment: death by drowning."

The iron door clanged shut again.

"Forget the dope, just bung him over South Bridge one night," Andrey Pavlovich instructed their escort. "And if he makes it ashore, good luck to him."

"And the twins?" Pasha asked as they drove back.

"Impress on them – and I do mean *impress* – that the next time
they show their faces in Kiev it's curtains. Let them play smart arse
in Zhitomir, or Moscow. Sloppy sort of place, Moscow."

22

It was three in the afternoon when Viktor woke. His attic window
showed the blue sky and bright sun of Indian summer.

Meeting Pasha on the stairs, he asked what was happening.

"The Chief's gone to bed for an hour. You're to stay, not go out,"
he said.

Viktor brewed coffee, took it to the kitchen table, then went to
answer the phone in the hall.

It was a TV presenter exploring the possibility of a debate
between Andrey Pavlovich and his opponent on National Channel 1.
He was not available at the moment, Viktor told her, and would ring
her back.

The more he thought about it, returning to his coffee, the less he
relished the idea of a TV debate. A ding-dong verbal exchange with
Boxer might well become physical.

Andrey Pavlovich was quick to see the point.

"You could suggest having our close advisers in attendance. All
of Boxer's share the same good looks."

"That should do the trick. Still, in this last week we must get on
with promotion."

Andrey Pavlovich rang a number on his mobile, inquired how
canvassing was going, listened, then repeated to Viktor what he'd
been told.

"200,000 of your manifesto leaflets distributed; 90,000 rations to pensioners; lists drawn up of all in need and entitled, if I'm elected, to financial assistance; three schools given computer rooms; and lots of less spectacular things. Not forgetting the plus of the artificial limbs. Will that do?"

"Yes, I'm sure it will," said Viktor, much relieved.

"And while we're at it, suggest that that TV woman of yours films me handing the limbs over."

"So we've actually got some?"

"In the garage. Four crates from some Swedish charity."

"But we've taken no measurements."

"No time. And they won't give a bugger anyway – simply take what fits and leave the rest."

"How about the billiard table?"

"We've settled that. Lay on transport and deliver."

Half an hour later, freshened by a wash and shave, Viktor rang the TV lady, who declared herself only too happy to film the hand-over of artificial limbs for a slot on the news. An hour later four hefty men turned up with a covered lorry and loaded the billiard table and crates of limbs. Viktor climbed in beside the driver, and away they went to Café Afghan.

23

Polling Day minus 7

With half an hour to go before the actual presentation, the crates were opened by an undersized creature reeking of vodka and onion to whom Pasha had slipped ten dollars. Viktor kept up-wind until he had finished, then examined the bubble-wrapped, sticky-taped contents. The leg-and-knee-joint he unwrapped struck him as unusually small, and then it dawned on him: child-sized! And so was the whole consignment! Accompanying documents in English showed the limbs to be the gift of the Save-the-Children-of-Rwanda-Fund, Salzburg. Heaven alone knew how they had ended up in Kiev.

He turned anxiously to Pasha, who was now showing the crate-unpacker the legs of the billiard table and explaining what had to be done. The latter, looking scared and anything but confident, was nodding thoughtfully. The task proposed was not one of which he had daily working experience.

Hearing that the limbs were too small, Pasha panicked, and Viktor felt suddenly back on even keel again.

"We stick them back in their crates and present the crates," he said.

The TV crew were a little late, Andrey Pavlovich a good fifteen minutes. In the end it was decided to film the crates being carried into Café Afghan, which involved carrying them out again, and here the evil-smelling unpacker-packer came into his own, three takes of the carrying in being needed. At last, clean-shaven, tweed-suited Andrey Pavlovich, grey hair gleaming with lacquer, shook hands with the young, legless, manifestly grateful manager of the café. Lyosha, too, had his hand shaken for the camera. Directing the cameraman, a thickset fellow in sleeveless, multi-pocketed jacket, was a tall, leggy female with an attractive but off-puttingly predatory sort of smile. The half hour of filming completed, Andrey Pavlovich handed her an envelope, and she graciously handed him her card.

"We didn't want the bloody things anyway," said Lyosha, learning that the limbs were for children "Best take them back. The billiard table's what matters."

When Andrey Pavlovich declined to take them back, it was decided to add them to the rubbish littering a hillside above Nagornaya Street. Pasha's man helped.

24

Polling Day minus 6

This time Nina answered the phone.

"How are you both?"

The warmth of her response surprised him. "You should come back. Sonya's been asking for you."

"Is she there?"

"No, outside with the little girl from the next flat."

"I'll be there in a day or two."

Drinking his coffee, he pondered her affability. Maybe she was scared he'd kick her out.

Andrey Pavlovich had left early with Pasha. The house help arrived and set about washing the floors. Later the computer expert called in by Pasha turned up to examine the image makers' computer. Viktor showed him up to the nursery, then returned to the kitchen. The solitude and relative silence appealed to him. He was glad he was not needed that morning. He found himself thinking of Andrey Pavlovich's Snail's Law. For the time being he, Viktor, was himself snug in the shell of a good solid house. Here was calm, quiet, an even tenor of existence. Outside much was astir, and would be for the next six days. After which the lucky snails would be handed new shells, Deputy shells, commensurate with their degree of official immunity, while the unlucky would have to go their separate ways, back to hide and act as if nothing had happened . . .

Viktor looked out at the desolate, tyre-marked gravel yard and the well-pruned lilac along the fence. The sky was blue and cloudless. A tiny swallow swooped low, then darted skywards – a sure sign that rain was coming.

His attention was diverted to the computer expert, who having passed through and out into the yard, was lighting up, looking anxiously about him. Pulling out his mobile, he dialled a number, spoke insistently, listened, nodded, then ground his cigarette into the gravel and came back into the house.

Shortly afterwards the computer expert passed through and out again, this time wearing his jacket, carrying his briefcase, and apparently in a hurry to be off.

Up in the old nursery Viktor found the computer still on, and making no sense of the file names displayed and selecting one at random, he brought to screen the image of a People's Deputy particularly active in the last Supreme Council, a lawyer and much publicized dispenser of gratuitous advice on anything from the privatization of a former collective farm perk plot to the purchase of small-business real estate. There were various icons which, duly clicked, revealed the makes and numbers of vehicles he used, his home address, names and home addresses of his two drivers, his daily routine. On the point of clicking RELATIVES AND INTIMATES, he desisted, vividly reminded of the safe in his late Chief's office. The Chief, then in hiding and about to flee Ukraine, had sent him to retrieve some air tickets. In so doing, he noticed a bundle of the advance obituaries he himself had written to order for the Chief's paper, each, he discovered to his horror and amazement, now endorsed with the date of future publication!

On the face of it, this computer had amassed in it infinitely more detail than any jealous husband cuckolded by the Deputy could ever have gleaned. And here it all was ready to be exploited to some as yet uncertain electoral purpose.

Feeling in need of a cleansing bath, Viktor left, leaving the computer on.

On his way downstairs, he heard a car drive in.

It was Pasha, with the news that Andrey Pavlovich would be late.

His growing anxiety was not something he wished to share with Pasha. Pasha might well be already conversant with the means and methods of electioneering, but he had no urge to become so himself. Indeed, he felt particularly grateful to Andrey Pavlovich for not directly involving him in his campaigning. The Dump showed something of what was involved. Just how many, he wondered would be deemed dumpable in this campaign – as, when thought appropriate, the subjects of his advance obituaries had been.

"Think he's going to want me?" he asked Pasha.

"Doubt it. He's got several election meetings. The last in an out-of-town sauna where he's not likely to need you."

"So I'll go and get a bit of air."

"You do that," Pasha encouraged.

*

He arrived at Svetlana's kindergarten shortly before six, and inquired where he could find her. "She's only here till two," he was told to his surprise. "She does music up to lunch, and Quiet Hour."

Disconcerted, he returned to Kreshchatik Street. He looked into a café, but put off by all the strange faces, came out again. What was wrong with him? Fatigue? A sense of impending danger? The dangerous knowledge he possessed?

"The full story's what you get only if and when your work, and with it your existence, are no longer required," his better informed late Chief had said, implying "the less you know, the longer you live". Yet he, Viktor, was still alive – something the Chief, omniscient as he was, could not have foreseen, not having a Misha to give him a seat on a plane.

Singing a Ukrainian folk song in the pedestrian underpass was a tall lean young man with a Nescafé tin at his feet into which Viktor dropped a hryvna. As he walked on, the young man went out of tune, prompting the thought that he would have done better to give his hryvna to one of the many old women not singing, but propping up the wall, each holding out an emaciated hand.

25

Half past seven saw Viktor standing outside his own flat wondering which of his two keys to use first, and as reluctant to play unwelcome guest as to play unwelcome flat owner. Tiring at last of just standing, he pressed the bell, and as if Nina had been watching through the peephole the door opened immediately.

"Good that you've come," she said, ushering him in.

Was it, he wondered, no longer convinced of her sincerity, and was relieved to see Sonya emerge from the kitchen. Sonya he knew better – he'd known her longer. Sonya's smile was genuine.

"Like some black pudding?" she asked looking up at him. "Auntie Nina got it for the cat, but the cat doesn't like it. I do though."

"I would."

"Eat it all up, and I'll show you a secret."

Her not asking about Misha hurt. Had she really forgotten him?

After supper – fried potato and black pudding, promptly served and piping hot – they retired to the sitting room. Sonya produced a grimly official-looking folder, and undoing the tapes, passed it to Viktor.

It contained drawings, yes, but not the sort he'd been expecting. All were of the same little black and white penguin, and headed in Sonya's uncertain hand:

> LOST! PENGUIN MISHA
>
> REWARD 5000 HRYVNAS
>
> Phone . . .

"There really is a reward – Auntie Nina's paying it," Sonya insisted, seeing how sad he suddenly looked. "All we have to do is stick them on lampposts. We'll get five penguins straight away for that money, Nina says, and from as far away as Moscow. The main thing will be to tell which is him. But I'll know at once. Will you help me put them up?"

"Of course."

Nina said little that evening, but looked at him with a sad sort of warmth, as if to convey that here was still home, that Pasha, Andrey Pavlovich and the Goloseyevo villa no longer existed, and that the only problem was Misha's disappearance.

"Can't you stay?" Nina asked warily, when the time came for him to go.

He stiffened and sighed.

"But you were the one who disappeared. You were the one who went away. It was terrible for Sonya and me on our own."

"It wasn't terrible for me," Sonya broke in. "It was terrible for her. Yesterday she cried!"

A betrayal that earned her a look of dislike and regret.

26

Polling Day minus 5

It was a night of thunderstorms. Every so often Viktor got up and watched the lightning from his attic window, thinking of Sonya and Nina, of Nina crying, of the thirty Penguin Lost notices, and of the image makers' computer. He'd mentioned the specialist's strange behaviour to Pasha, but not of having himself accessed one of the files. Should he tell Andrey Pavlovich that he had? When he woke next morning there was no thunder, but the sound of some disturbance downstairs, which, turning to face the wall, he chose to ignore.

When at last he went in search of breakfast, he found Andrey Pavlovich sitting, pale with fatigue, in the lounge.

"Wonderful night, then this bloody lot!" he said moodily, motioning Viktor to a chair. "That damned computer! State Security, hordes of them, down on us like a ton of bricks. And nothing to do with me! Never touched the thing! Sodding image makers! I'll shove the prat who put me onto them headfirst down the boghole! And the way they talk, those State Security buggers! 'Just one fingerprint, and that's your lot!' Let's have a whisky."

Viktor fetched tumblers and a bottle of Black Horse.

"Ice?"

"Just pour. Another bloody thing: Security demands a list of every visitor in the last three weeks. Still, five more days and I'll be elected, and sod the lot of them."

"But I'm afraid I did touch the computer," Viktor confessed, and told Andrey Pavlovich what he'd seen on it.

"Silly man! Still, you weren't to know, any more than I was. I'll have to see what our lot can do to put the lid on this."

306

27

Polling Day minus 4

Although Andrey Pavlovich was away touring Kiev in the 4 × 4 with Pasha in an effort to smoothe things over, indications were not promising. Two taciturn minders were now patrolling and keeping watch outside the house. Viktor, who came in for their indifferent gaze as often as he made coffee in the kitchen, noted that they were in mobile contact with someone, probably Pasha.

At four in the afternoon a silver Chrysler hooted at the gates and drove in followed by a Mercedes 4 × 4. Observing the seven newcomers from the kitchen window, Viktor had no difficulty telling who was who. The four with earphone attachments were bodyguards, the soberly suited pair – the drivers, and the well-groomed Baby Face in long raincoat and stylish square-toed shoes was the big man. Baby Face addressed Andrey Pavlovich's men, who listened dutifully. The one with the mobile made as if to make a call, but experiencing some difficulty, hurried in to the phone in the hall. Viktor in the kitchen heard every word.

"Pasha, tell the boss to come back now, Kapitonov's here."

Twenty minutes later, Andrey Pavlovich arrived, got out and joined Kapitonov in the Chrysler. Kapitonov's minders then positioned themselves at the four corners of the vehicle and stood looking outwards.

"What's up?" Viktor asked as Pasha came into the kitchen.

"Nothing good. They're piling on the pressure. A deal's in the air. Big stuff. Someone'll get sold down the river."

For two hours the ear-wired minders in their identical macs stood guard over the black-windowed Chrysler. Assailed by the nasty thought that it might be him who was being sold down the river, but seeing no immediate chance of escape, he withdrew to his attic, and gazed out at the gathering dusk. From 40th Anniversary of October Avenue there was the hum of traffic, nearer at hand, a cawing of crows, but of human voices not a sound. Hearing engines start up, he went down to the kitchen and looked from there. Pasha was closing the gates after the Chrysler and the black 4 × 4. The yard was empty.

"Admiring the great free world?" asked Andrey Pavlovich, clapping Viktor on the shoulder. "Pasha's getting the sauna going. Let's go and sweat. Meanwhile, have a look at this."

It was a blue identity card in the name of Andrey Pavlovich, Aide to People's Deputy Kapitonov, Dmitry Vasilyevich. The photograph bore the stamp of the Supreme Council. The authorizing signature was dated two weeks ahead.

"So that's me," said Andrey Pavlovich, pocketing it, "a hired man, and in danger of becoming a fall guy. Anyway, sauna one hour from now! By order, Aide to People's Deputy Kapitonov," he added with a rueful smile.

*

"Up like a rocket, down like a stick!" observed Andrey Pavlovich, as they sat drinking beer in the snug, wood-panelled pre-sauna booth.

"I was banking on your winning," said Viktor, thinking it might now be harder to enlist his help in the search for Misha.

"Got above myself, trying to be a two-headed snail. And along comes a genuine two-head and cuts me down for size."

"Isn't a two-headed snail a bit like a two-headed eagle?"

Andrey Pavlovich laughed.

"Except that eagles don't have shells, and a two-headed snail's got two: an everyday criminal and an everyday state official one."

The sauna was pleasantly hot, and they sat on the upper bench. Andrey Pavlovich ladled water onto the heated stones, filling the cabin with scalding steam. Throat and nostrils suddenly afire, Viktor moved down a bench.

"Something wrong with your fire-proofing?" Andrey Pavlovich inquired.

"I need to acclimatize."

"As you did to Antarctic cold." Then after a while, he asked, "Keeping the little house in order and strangers out, are we?" He ladled more water. "If I were you, I'd stay submerged for a bit."

"Keep my head down?"

"Up to you. The minor, highly vulnerable post of Aide to Aide to People's Deputy Kapitonov is yours if you want it. Though with protection on the thin side. So better Moscow at the moment, where no-one's after you."

"There's still trouble over the computer, then?"

"Not exactly. Just that for the time being the material's been sat on. When it will be released and who by is uncertain. It might pass its sell-by date. And it might not . . . Still, come and have some beer."

With the drop in temperature Viktor's mental processes revived, but his physical lethargy lingered. Andrey Pavlovich was speaking of his daughter and her three-year-old son whom Viktor had mistaken for Misha at the cemetery, both now in Cyprus for safety over the election period. On the credit side – as he'd rather forgotten amid the present troubles – a military, chauffeur-driven Volga had been in collision with a minivan on Park Avenue. Both passengers in the Volga had been killed, one of them being the man who had mistakenly shot his daughter's husband.

"Was it really an accident?"

"They don't come any realer," smiled Andrey Pavlovich. After two more bottles of beer they went up and sat in the lounge, Andrey Pavlovich in his tiger-striped bathrobe, Viktor wrapped in a terry towel. Pasha said he'd bring them coffee. Outside it was dark and raining.

The hall phone rang, and soon after, Pasha brought both coffee and the news that friends had just rung to say that finger-prints were to be taken in the morning.

Quickly they drank their coffee, and Viktor went and dressed.

Andrey Pavlovich brought him two passports and dollars in an envelope.

"So, off you go. Pasha will drive you where you want. Oh, and have this."

It was a visiting card adorned with the Ukrainian trident, the stamp of the Supreme Council, and the legend "Aide to People's Deputy".

"If you need help in Moscow, ask at Peking Restaurant for Bim. Say hello to him from me."

28

There was warmth and matter-of-factness about their leave-taking. Involuntary as had been his sojourn with Andrey Pavlovich, there had been nothing of incarceration or forced labour about it. Ahead lay Moscow, where he would have no such safe, snug shell to protect him. But what mattered – and was all that mattered – was to find Misha, get him back to the Antarctic. And after that, start living? For himself and Sonya? But doing what for money?

Questions that could be set aside for the moment. There'd be something. There *was* a future and life would reveal it.

Pasha dropped Viktor at the entrance to his Khrushchev-era block, gripped his hand, and with a meaningful "Keep your end up!" drove away.

Craning his head back Viktor looked up at the windows of his flat. They, like all the other windows, Old Tonya's included, were in darkness.

Taking off his jacket and shoes in the passage, he went on stockinged feet to the kitchen, and put on the light. The carrier bag containing his two passports, the banker's credit card and letter, and his dollars, he deposited on the table.

He made tea, sat by the window, and contemplated the urn containing the ashes of his friend Sergey, now in its rightful place on the window ledge by the gas stove. He remembered the picnic they'd had on the Dnieper ice and Misha wrapped in a towel so as not to catch cold. Suddenly in need of something stronger to drink, he looked in the cupboard, found an already opened bottle of Smirnoff and fetched a glass.

He remembered the night he'd sat here in the kitchen writing Nina and Sonya a note saying he'd be back when the dust had settled. Maybe he should do the same again, and head for the station.

The sudden squeak of the door made him jump. Misha had been in the habit of thrusting the door with his breast and quietly plip-plopping in while Viktor was working at his obituaries. Swinging round, he saw not a ghost but Sonya's sleepy face looking round the door.

"Why aren't you in bed?" he asked.

"Why aren't you?" she asked, now coming right in. Her pyjama jacket had an embroidered penguin.

"I'm not here for long – I've got to go away."

"But you promised to help me stick my notices up."

"Is Nina asleep?"

"She takes something to make her. Sitting up late watching TV makes her eyes ache."

"What does she take?"

"That."

"Vodka?"

"I don't know what it is, but it's to make her sleep."

Uneasily aware of Sonya's scrutiny, he helped himself to some more.

"Do you have to be made to sleep too?"

"No."

Getting up he emptied his glass into the sink, and turned as if expecting praise.

"Where are you going away to?" she asked blinking sleepily.

"Moscow."

"Let's do the posters first."

"We could do them now while there's nobody about, if you like."

"Yes, let's."

"Rinse your face then, and put your clothes on. But quietly. Don't wake Nina."

Fifteen minutes later they left the block, Sonya carrying the file of posters, Viktor a tube of glue.

"Shcherbakov Street is busiest – that's where we'll go."

They set off through the deserted, sleeping city, passing the kindergarten he had attended, and his old school, No 27, Sonya gazing around and up at the sky, as if she had never seen the city at night before. In Shcherbakov Street, they stuck their first poster at a trolleybus stop. Further on they came to an election billboard.

"Let's put one here," said Viktor indicating a portrait of Andrey Pavlovich's opponent, and Sonya glued a penguin to his airbrushed features.

The night air was invigorating. He was enjoying his walk with Sonya and the feeling of doing something to find Misha, though Kiev was not where he was. When he'd found him in Moscow, he would bring him back for Sonya to hug and play games with before he flew off to the far south.

Having postered three more trolleybus stops, they were about to tackle another election billboard, when the silence was shattered by the siren of a speeding ambulance, and they watched it out of sight.

Sonya handed him a poster from her file, he smeared the back with glue, and handed it to her, just as a bright red BMW drew up and three young men got out, one carrying a metal scraper.

"What's that you've got there?" a voice demanded.

"Penguin lost notices," said Sonya calmly.

The man shone his torch, then laughed.

"It looked like you were flyposting," he said, and joined his companions who were already tearing and scraping off Andrey Pavlovich and his opponent.

"You won't scrape ours off?" Sonya asked.

"No fear. Your penguin's safe. He's not standing for election!" said the man with the scraper.

Work completed, they returned to their car, and drove on to the next hoarding.

"What did he mean about posting flies?" Sonya asked, and he tried to explain.

By the time they reached Nivki metro station, she was yawning, and he carried her home. Before getting into bed, she gave him her five remaining posters, and he promised to put them up in Red Square in Moscow.

29

Noonday sun greeted his arrival in Moscow, bleary-eyed from lack of sleep. He'd been woken several times in the night by customs and frontier guards – whether Russian or Ukrainian it was hard to tell with both speaking Russian – demanding, with a fair show of politeness, his passport, or to know the extent of his luggage. His Polish passport was happily out of harm's way in a trouser pocket together with credit card, dollars and crumpled letter to banker Bronikovsky's widow. The trousers had spent the night rolled beneath his pillow, while his Ukrainian passport lay, concealed by a newspaper, on the compartment table. Hence the dishevelled, somewhat dispirited state in which he stepped down onto the platform.

"Porter?" shouted a red-faced hale-and-hearty pushing past with his trolley. "Ten roubles a load."

Viktor shook his head, shouldered his sports bag, and stood looking about him, daunted by the practicalities of the task ahead – where to sleep, how long a stay to plan for, how he would buy back Misha when he found him. Best get on with delivering Bronikovsky's letter – that was manageable, just a question of ringing the number on the envelope. And after that, he could look up Andrey Pavlovich's friend Bim. Thus resolved, he set off along the platform with the other passengers, closely scrutinized by armed Special Forces men in bullet-proof vests.

He rang the banker's widow, and encountering an answerphone, told it he would ring again at six. He then changed 20 dollars, treated himself to a portion of fried chicken at a stand-up bistro, and watched the people. He washed the chicken down with a Pepsi, then paused at a newspaper counter. All seemed well – the station atmosphere seemed even to have a calming effect, until suddenly the Special Forces men were back, eyeing faces, then making a beeline for two dark-skinned men, probably Azerbaijanis, queuing for hot-dogs. Feeling he'd seen enough of the Special Forces, he left the station, boarded a trolleybus at the first stop he came to, and pressing his face to the window, looked out at a Moscow almost unrecognizable since his last visit eight years before. What he remembered were meat-dumpling snack bars, beer-shops, the October metro station, Hotel Kosmos near the Achievements of the National Economy Exhibition, the Garden Ring. They were on the Ring now. It had seemed immutable, but now he didn't know it at all. The very windows of the flats were different. "Been here before? Never!" was what it all said.

He got off at the next stop and continued on foot. Clouds were gathering, and from force of habit he walked faster, as if to beat the rain, and gain the shelter of some roof. Spotting the nostalgically old-world sign of a dumpling snack bar, he hesitated, but for the barest moment, impelled onwards as if by energy pent up during the rail journey.

As rain fell, it turned surprisingly cold, and feeling the inadequacy of his windcheater, he looked around and on the other side of the street spotted, under a faded old-fashioned signboard, what was either a café or a canteen where he could cheaply and warmly sit out the rain drinking tea.

He crossed the road. Club Café, which had a teenage ring about it, turned out to be an Internet café with young people seated at computers, drinking Coca Cola.

Sitting behind a counter, engrossed in his computer, was a fat young man in designer spectacles, with cash register, coffee maker, microwave, Cola, Pepsi and fizzy drinks in plastic bottles to hand.

"Any tea?" Viktor asked.

"In bags."

"Tea please."

Reluctantly the fat young man got up.

"Forty-five roubles," he said, presenting Viktor with his tea. "Computer No. 9."

"How do I use the Internet?"

"Where are you from then?"

"Kiev."

The fat young man grinned, then explained simply and clearly.

Left to himself, Viktor tried "penguin", clicked the mouse, and was quickly informed of 520 results, which, being of no great interest, he tried "Antarctic" getting more than 200. Then, by way of testing the computer's patience and endurance, he typed in "Bronikovsky", which produced just eight results, of which the third, on the evidence of a *Criminal Gazette* extract, turned out to be the right one. Bronikovsky, then chairman of his bank, had disappeared while under indictment for having improperly transferred some $32,000,000 abroad. One director had hanged himself, another had been found dead in a forest bearing signs of torture. Revolted by the bloody details, clearly relished by the reporter, Viktor spent the remaining fifteen minutes ogling semi-nude Moscow Beauties, and thinking of Svetlana.

The rain was no longer so heavy, but he hardly noticed.

<h1 style="text-align:center">30</h1>

In precise Moscowese, Widow Bronikovsky had explained how to get to Kutuzov Avenue and her apartment, given the keypad number and warned him of the concièrge he would have to contend with. Her cheerful air was at variance with the news he brought. The letter would come as a shock, but there was no backing out now.

The concièrge was typical Special Forces, with rubber truncheon, handcuffs, CS gas spray and holstered automatic at his belt, though whether loaded with gas or bullets it was hard to tell.

"To see who?" he demanded.

"Bronikovsky, Apartment 26."

Taking in Viktor's general appearance and sports bag and eyeing him with mistrust, he asked to see what was in the bag, then retired to his booth and picked up the phone.

"Lift on the left, 6th floor," he said, emerging a minute later.

Outside and inside the lift were posters in English. The one forbidding smoking was easily read, but the Land Rover, without customs clearance offered for sale by some foreigner for $10,000, took longer to work out.

Arrived on the 6th Floor, he at once saw the banker's massive oak bronze-handled door with caller-video. He pressed the button.

The door opened. A Korean woman bade him enter.

He was about to hand her his windcheater, but thinking better of it, hung it up himself.

"I've come to see Marina," he said.

"That's me," said the Korean with a dazzling smile.

The vast lounge housed equally vast mahogany furniture. A massive round table set with twelve chairs formed the centrepiece.

"Olya!" she called, and a leggy, moon-faced blonde in black dress and small white apron appeared, the archetypal maid.

"Coffee, tea, hot chocolate, Viktor?"

"Coffee, please."

They sat in armchairs facing a broad window with a half-drawn blind.

Viktor handed her the letter.

While she read, he looked about him, noting a couple of photographs of Marina and her husband on board a large yacht somewhere in the Mediterranean. He glanced across at her. No longer smiling, she was engrossed in the letter, lips moving slightly. At last she dropped it on the magazine table beside her, and gazed at it for a while.

Viktor placed the credit card beside the letter. Her nails, he saw, as she reached for it, were varnished black, matching her jumper suit and shoes. An emerald on the third finger of her left hand gave life to this otherwise funereal ensemble.

"You must join me in a drink," she said suddenly with almost manly assurance.

"We'll have the bar in," she told Olya, when she brought Viktor's coffee and orange juice for her mistress.

When the bar trolley was wheeled in, Viktor opted for cognac, uncomfortably conscious of the gaze of Marina's dark slant eyes. Marina asked for whisky, then told Olya she could go.

"Do you smoke?" she asked.

Viktor said he didn't.

"You must suffer me to," she said, lighting a long thin cigarette.

Viktor drained his cognac.

"Help yourself, and pour another for me. Is this all my husband gave you?"

"Yes."

"There was nothing for anyone else?"

"No."

Viktor felt he should go, but to leave her digesting the news he had brought savoured of cowardice. Surely she must break down. A Slav would be screaming and sobbing and needing first-aid or comforting. Marina's reaction was out of keeping with the news she had received. Why this doubt about what her husband had given him? Why no interest in his meetings with her husband?

"Wasn't there perhaps another something – something for another woman?" she demanded, transfixing him with her eyes as a cobra might its prey.

"No, I swear there wasn't," he replied, his voice no more than a whisper.

"The rotten sod!"

"I'd better be going," he said getting to his feet.

"Have you anywhere to stay?"

"No."

"Stay here, then. Olya will make up a bed in my husband's study . . . So he spoke of no-one but me."

"He spoke only of you, and what I've given you is all that he gave to me."

"Pour us more drinks."

This time they clinked glasses.

"To friendship!" she said, then went over to the integrated bureau area, returning with a fine fountain pen and several sheets of paper.

"See if you can write it," she said, indicating her husband's signature on the credit card.

He looked at her in amazement.

"Come on, have a go."

It was fairly straightforward, and in ten minutes he had mastered it.

"That's it," she said tossing back her whisky. "Now sit back and relax. I'll be a quarter of an hour."

Parched with thirst, he examined the bottles on the trolley, and lighting on a lone tonic water, drained it gratefully.

He looked out at the lanes of traffic below, of which, up here, there was not a sound. Returning to his chair, he helped himself by way of a change to a generous amount of ouzo, which he downed in two gulps.

Marina returned, no longer black but in dark-green, full-length skirt and blouse, nails now a bright shade of green and not yet quite dry. The emerald ring had been replaced by a plain gold wedding-ring-like circlet. Dark green shoes completed the outfit.

"Let's go," she said, giving her nails a last blow and picking up the credit card.

Awaiting them at the entry was a dark green Lexus driven by a middle-aged, simple-looking man in a smart dark suit. Viktor sat with Marina in the back and they set off along Kutuzov Avenue.

Feeling chilly, Viktor was about to put on his windcheater, but a look from Marina dissuaded him. What served for Antarctica or passing as just another reluctant pilgrim of the post-Soviet era, was not appropriate sitting beside an attractive woman in a Lexus. Moscow was a good deal brighter and more colourful at night than Kiev the day before. Eventually they stopped. The chauffeur opened the door for them. The restaurant was the Prague.

A table for two was reserved for them on the first floor. Leather-bound menus and the wine list were brought. An exquisitely dressed blonde acknowledged Marina in passing. Marina smiled and returned to her study of the menu. The waiter waited.

Such were the prices that Viktor found it hard to concentrate –
hors d'oeuvre upwards of $50. For which sum he could have dined
more pleasantly with Svetlana off semolina, the latter free of charge.

"What are you going to have?" asked Marina.

Like a drunken swimmer, he surfaced, slowly.

"I'll order for you," she said.

The waiter became all attention.

"A dozen oysters. Black-caviar pancakes. Steak *à la mexicaine aux
galettes*. And for me, salmon salad, then marinated partridge and
chicken liver on the spit, with vegetables."

Turning to the wine list, she ordered a first growth claret at
20,000 roubles – as near as damn it $800 – prompting speculation
as to what the Moscow fee for a funeral-with-penguin might be,
until cut short by the arrival of oysters and a half lemon.

Now the wine waiter was at his elbow, displaying the label,
drawing the cork and pouring a little into his glass.

"Taste it," said Marina. "If you don't like it we'll have something
else."

As wine went, it was clearly an improvement on Moldovian
Merlot, but doubting whether it was worth the money, he passed
the glass and the responsibility of deciding to Marina.

Marina laughed, drank, nodded, and the waiter poured.

Viktor was successful in opening his oysters, but was dis-
appointed to find that lemon did nothing to improve their taste.

"I should have ordered vodka with these," he said, emboldened
by the earlier cognac and reacting to the pretentiousness of the
place, and to his infinite relief Marina immediately ordered a carafe.

The vodka disposed of the taste of oysters well before the black
caviar pancakes arrived.

"Have you children?" she asked.

"An adopted daughter. Her father was my friend. He got murdered."

The slant eyes showed interest. "How old is she?"

"Six next birthday," he said, unable to remember when that was. "Have you any children?"

"No. Maybe I shall have. Who knows?"

He learnt in the course of the meal that she had been born in Ukraine of Soviet Korean parents who grew water melons there. She had married Stanislav in Donyetsk, where she had been studying accountancy, and he and some friends were setting up an investment company. When it crashed, he moved to Moscow and created a commercial bank. Now that had crashed.

She finished her wine, followed it with a little vodka, called for the bill, and slipped Viktor the credit card.

Now the blonde from earlier was at their table, giving Viktor a somewhat unsteady perusal, before addressing Marina.

"Glad to see it's all working out." She smiled archly. "We're going on to the Metropol. Care to join us?"

Marina shook her head.

"Give me a ring some time."

The waiter presented a counterfoil in the sum of 58,320 roubles. Viktor did his imitation of Bronikovsky's signature. Marina produced a $25 tip.

*

The Lexus conveyed them to Marina's, where they sat in the lounge drinking Olya's strong, spicey and, so far as Viktor was concerned, unwelcomely invigorating coffee.

"Ever tried what the coffee grounds show?" Marina asked,

inverting her cup. "Well, come and see."

What they showed were two naked, sexually explicit silhouettes, male and female.

"To the bedroom," said Marina.

A night of vigorous love-making ensued, and after breakfast, a day of the same, with time together in a vast triangular bath by way of intermission.

At supper, as if remembering something of importance, she got to her feet, went over to the bureau, and took out a wad of $100 bills, most of which she sealed into an envelope.

"The chauffeur will take you to a certain young lady, one Kseniya. Tell her Stanislav left this envelope for her. Otherwise the truth – that he's dead, and so on – though not about us. Don't hang about. The chauffeur will be waiting. So shall I."

31

Despite the late hour there was no dearth of traffic.

"Much further?" Viktor asked.

"Ten minutes – it's off the Ring."

They stopped at last outside a tower block.

"15th floor, flat 137," announced the chauffeur.

Viktor got out, grateful now for his warm windproof. No keypad, no concièrge here, just a lift with dim, grill-protected bulb, stench of tobacco and walls stripped bare and scrawled with the usual obscenities. Eventually he reached the 15th floor.

As he rang, he looked at his watch. 1.30 a.m.

"Who is it? I'll call the militia," came a frightened voice.

"I'm from Stanislav."

The door opened, revealing a sleepy-faced young woman in a dressing gown over night attire, standing barefoot on brown linoleum, a piggy-eyed pit bull terrier at her side.

"Come in."

Closing the door behind him, he slipped his shoes off and went with her to the kitchen. The pit bull terrier withdrew into the darkness.

It was a small kitchen with a tap leaking onto a stack of unwashed crockery and three pots of aloes on the windowsill.

"He asked me to give you this."

"Has something happened to him?"

"I'm afraid it has. He's dead."

"Is it money?" she asked, through tears.

He nodded.

"He wouldn't have sent money. I've never needed his money . . . Would you like some tea?"

Without waiting for an answer, she cleared and wiped the table, and put the kettle on.

Hearing steps in the passage, Viktor swung round in surprise. Kseniya hurried out.

"It's all right, Mummy, just someone to see me. You go back to bed, Mummy," he heard her say.

"I've had to take her in," she said, coming back. "She can't cope – sclerosis, her joints are agony . . . Are you from Moscow?"

He explained who he was, and said that he'd known Stanislav only slightly.

"Pity. He was a good man. Just naïve. Thought money would solve everything. Bought me a flat on the Arbat, and when I wouldn't move, said he'd take me to a psychiatrist," she said, looking at a photograph of Bronikovsky on horseback.

"Promised to teach me to ride, give me an Arab racer – always the grand lord. When he left, I was pregnant, but nothing came of it."

The dog could be heard worrying at something in the corridor.

"Why do you have a big dog like that?"

"Bosik? I took him in as a stray. He's a dear. Have you any children?"

Why did she and Marina ask the same thing?

"An adopted daughter."

"And where is she?"

"With her nanny."

"I think I'll adopt too. A son. Though with no Stanislav, it'll be tough . . . I always thought he'd leave her . . . It was *she* who sent the money?"

Viktor said nothing – he didn't have to. She went over to the window, looked out at the night, then turned off the gas under the kettle.

He was about to offer some word of reassurance, but judged it right not to. She was grieving, as no woman would grieve for him.

Hoping to divert her, he told her about Misha. Did she, he wondered, know of a banker known as Sphinx who had a private zoo? She didn't, never having moved in such, or indeed any, circles, and she found it odd that bankers should have funny names, like gangsters and dogs – her own was at that moment cheerfully noisy in the passage.

Told of Misha, she listened with interest and was upset at Sonya's now being without her friend.

Lighting suddenly on the envelope of money, her gaze hardened.

"I would take nothing from her . . . But Mummy needs medicine. She's got cancer."

Time, Viktor judged, to be going. In the passage, he found Bosik chewing one of his shoes.

"Drop!" said Kseniya, darting forward, rescuing the shoe and returning it to Viktor.

"I'm terribly sorry."

Viktor went his way, deeply depressed and with a decidedly uncomfortable left shoe.

In the lighted Lexus the driver was reading a book. Viktor got into the back seat, and they accelerated away along a deserted street with lights at amber.

"Could be trouble," said the driver over his shoulder, referring to two jeeps on their tail, and as Viktor turned to look, one overtook and cut in, forcing the Lexus to slow to a halt, while the other closed up behind – a manoeuvre his driver could have avoided, having the better car.

The door was opened by a thickset tough in a blue tracksuit.

"We'll deliver," he told the driver. "Don't worry, and tell the boss lady not to."

He turned to Viktor.

"Out you get."

There was nothing for it but to obey.

32

Viktor opened his eyes on inky blackness, tried to get up, but was physically incapable. In an attempt to distinguish dream from nightmare reality, he opened his mouth, said "Ah!" But between his making the sound and actually hearing it, there was an appreciable time lag. He had another go. With the same result, except that the sound now took over a minute returning. Something pricked his hand. He raised his head in an effort to see what. So there was hope. He could now move his head. It only remained to decide where he was and what had happened.

A pillow. He was in bed. Suddenly he remembered – two men in blue tracksuits, one in a sweater. While the men in tracksuits restrained him, the third had injected a vein on the inside of his elbow. It still hurt. Worse, it was stabbingly painful, as if the vein was obstructed by something. And echoing and re-echoing in his head, as if from far, far away through an infinity of intervening walls, the same questions. "Did you actually see him dead? Where did you get that credit card? What are you doing here? Did you actually see him dead?"

The inky blackness thinned. Walls . . . A tiny room . . . A window beyond which it was night. A door opened creating a rectangle of brighter light. He raised his hand to shield his eyes, and felt again the pain of the injection.

"How are we?" asked a familiar voice, and lowering his hand, he saw almond-eyed Marina in a wine-red housecoat. Her nails will be wine-red, he thought, but they weren't, they were their natural colour.

"How did I get here?" Again it took a surprising time for the words to become audible.

She pulled a chair up to his bed.

"They brought you back."

"What happened?"

"At a guess I'd say you got pulled in for questioning. What's that in your hand?"

She prised open his fingers, looked at the paper they had been clutching, and laughed.

"It's the counterfoil for the meal we had. Someone thought Stanislav was back and raised the alarm. So you see the danger of forging dead men's signatures."

Her cold indifference to her late husband was in contrast to Kseniya's reaction.

"How was she?" Marina asked, as if divining his thoughts.

"Tearful."

"For long?"

"No."

"She took the money?"

"Not willingly. She knew it wasn't from Stanislav. He would not have given her money, she said."

"Little fool! How about a drink?"

"I'd like a cognac."

She brought cognac and glasses.

With an effort he raised himself into a sitting position and drank.

"So you knew all about her."

"How could I not, with him sending his driver out to her with food. Somewhere beyond the Ring! Just imagine – our Mercedes S600 driving up outside her grubby high-rise for all the world to see! Should have got her a flat in Tverskaya Street nearer his bank, and nipped out in the odd break. He shamed me."

"He did give her a flat on the Arbat, but she wouldn't accept it. Maybe it was true love."

"True relaxation, more like. Naïve, warm-hearted country bumpkin – the clapped-out old banker's dream! No pretensions. No demands. Just boundless gratitude for being noticed. Still, enough about him!"

She handed him her husband's credit card, still warm from her housecoat pocket.

"You have this. I've money of my own, I don't need his."

Viktor took the card, but being naked, had nowhere to put it.

"Olya and I undressed you, and by now she'll have your things laundered for you. And so, when you've recovered, it's back to Kiev."

"I've got to find my penguin first. And with this card I should have enough to buy him back."

"If you haven't, ring me."

33

Woken next morning by the warmth of exploring hands, he responded accordingly.

"Do you know, with a bit of fitness training and massage, one could make a decent job of you," Marina said. "You're not, like my husband, past it, though not exactly a box of fireworks."

Their parting verged on the emotional.

"Whenever you're in Moscow, be sure to ring," she said drawing her housecoat about her and closing the door.

Going down in the lift, he felt like an astronaut returning to earth, guinea pig term completed. He regretted the less positive side of his exploitation, of which the discomfort of his left shoe was a painful reminder.

The lift doors parted, and with a nod to the concièrge/security guard, Viktor left the building.

Kutuzov Avenue was a continuous two-way stream of cars. His

watch showed 11.30. It would soon be time for lunch, and the place for that was the Peking Restaurant, where he could enlist the help of Andrey Pavlovich's friend Bim. He was never going to find the banker unaided, and even if he did, would only be kept at arm's length by his bodyguards. Someone to speak for him was what he needed, someone after the style of Andrey Pavlovich.

34

The Peking Restaurant was packed, mainly with Caucasians. Viktor hung his jacket on the back of a chair, sat down, and anticipating a long wait looked around for service. The next minute a young man of eastern appearance presented him with a menu, volunteering that it would be easier and quicker to take the business lunch than order *à la carte*, which, trusting Moscow to know best, Viktor did.

He made short work of the sweet-and-sour soup, spitting unchewable bamboo shoots into the bowl. *Porc à la Sé-Tchouen* with rice followed, then green tea. Inner man satisfied, he turned his thoughts to the matter in hand.

"Where would I find Bim?" he inquired into the tactfully inclined ear of the waiter.

"He will join you," was the calm reply. "Will that be all?"

"Yes, thank you."

He drank his green tea and observed the four men at the next table also enjoying a business lunch, and helping it down with vodka. The unhealthy pudginess of their amply-ringed fingers suggested the possibility of early deaths.

"You asked to see me?" said a pleasant-looking man in a

nondescript grey suit, seating himself at Viktor's table.

"Andrey Pavlovich of Kiev said come to you if I needed help."

Bim smiled. "How is he?"

"Standing as People's Deputy he was fine. Now, having been demoted to Deputy's aide, he's less so."

"Not to worry. All part of life's rich tapestry. What's your problem, then?"

"I'm afraid there's a bit of a preamble."

Bim nodded, and Viktor told the story of Misha, the funerals-with-penguin and his own forced flight to Antarctica, omitting his obituary-writing as past history. Mention of Sphinx gave Bim pause for thought.

"The Gas Commerce Bank is no longer with us. But your penguin will be legally Sphinx's. Snatching him back's not on. But a buy-back or swap for a pretty girl might be. Negotiation's called for. Leave it with me. I'll try for an appointment with him – or his boys if he's too high and mighty – for this evening."

He consulted his Rolex.

"Look in at about 8.oo. Meal on the house, then, all being well, we'll motor."

*

Light of step and light of heart Viktor strode along Tverskaya Street towards Red Square, indifferent to the fine drizzle, except in so far as wet was penetrating his shoe.

As drizzle turned to downpour, he popped into the People's Bar for a cognac, and discomforts forgotten, marvelled at anything of the People's being quite so clean and orderly. When the rain eased, he went his way, and looking into a shoe shop, was outraged at the telephone-number-like prices.

35

He returned to the Peking Restaurant, footsore but with a feeling of relief. Bim was standing by a palm in the foyer, smoking a thin cigar which, seeing Viktor, he stubbed out against the palm, and replaced in a wooden case.

"This way," he said, leading the way to a remote table bearing "Reserved" and "No Smoking" notices. "And best stick that in the cloakroom," he added, as Viktor went to drape his jacket over the chair. "Eats on the way. What are you drinking?"

"Cognac, please."

An elderly waiter appeared instantly to take their order. Bim re-lit his cigar.

"Is the banker coming?"

"Not so fast. Greetings, by the way, from Andrey Pavlovich. You're to look him up when you get back."

"How is he?"

"Fine, and free again," came the reply in a stream of cigar smoke.

"He got arrested, then?"

"Heavens no! Free because the Deputy he was aide to, pegged out enjoying a call-girl the day after the election."

Not knowing what to make of this change of fortune, Viktor looked blank. Bim smiled, and at that moment his aniseed vodka and Viktor's cognac arrived.

They had just knocked back their first, omitting the formality of a toast, when an elderly man, slim and with an unnaturally bronzed face, quietly took his place at their table. Expensively and tastefully dressed, he was clearly concerned not to look his age. Needlessly adjusting the blue bow tie worn with a white shirt, undoing the leather-covered buttons of his single-breasted jacket, crossing his legs and resting his right elbow on the table, he greeted Bim in silence, then turned attentively to Viktor.

"I'm Eldar Ivanovich, and I'm all ears."

"Tell him all that you told me," Bim prompted gently in the manner of a schoolteacher.

Reluctantly Viktor retold the story of his penguin, abbreviating it out of sheer weariness.

"Ah!" exclaimed Eldar Ivanovich when he'd finished. "I see now what I'm here for."

"Eldar Ivanovich acted as liquidator for Sphinx," Bim explained. "You've got questions, he's got answers. I'll sit quietly with my aniseed vodka."

"It's all straightforward," said Eldar Ivanovich. "Some of his property, his real estate, is still here in Moscow, but not his zoo where your penguin was. That was taken by Khachayev."

"Who's he?" asked Viktor, seeing the prospect of success receding.

"Khachayev is who Sphinx lost his shirt to. Khachayev ran the casino. He and Sphinx were in some business together, but Sphinx came unstuck. Later, when things hotted up for Khachayev, he packed everything in and skipped it to Chechnya."

"Is that where Misha is now?"

"I wouldn't be too sure. Somewhere in North Caucasus, with Chechnya a strong possibility. And that's about the extent of my help. Unless," he added with a wicked smile, "you'd care to follow him there."

Chechnya, penguin, penguin, Chechnya – somehow the words refused to match up. Under the stolid gaze of the other two, Viktor helped himself to vodka and drank.

The elderly waiter delivered an enormous dish of rice and smaller servings of meat, shrimps and fish. Earthenware bowls were set before them, and a metal stand of sauces and spices brought from a neighbouring table. Bim served himself a heap of rice, topped it with meat generously sprinkled with brown soy sauce, finished his aniseed vodka and ordered plain. Viktor asked for more vodka, and in a mood of funereal gloom set about eating.

As they ate and drank conversation flowed more freely. Eldar Ivanovich confessed to having had plastic surgery and to be now undergoing sun-ray treatment for the good of his skin. Bim demonstrated the making of a cocktail called "Border Clash", using vodka, soy sauce and half a lemon.

Viktor tried one, but as a result of his mood or state of fatigue, got no special kick out of it.

"Do you know," said Bim after a fair number of "Border Clashes", "if it was your brother or son carted off to Chechnya, I'd understand, and like any Russian I'd go all out to find him. But to be cut up over a penguin is neither manly nor Russian . . . So how say we drink instead to a victory of Russian arms?"

"You don't understand, because I didn't tell you," Viktor protested, beginning to slur. "He'd had a heart transplant. The donor was a child. He was all set to fly to the Antarctic to end his days there. But I robbed him of his place on the plane."

"Well, now I've heard everything!" exclaimed Eldar Ivanovich, exchanging meaningful looks with Bim. "And if this isn't just drug talk, let me tell you: Chechnya's a damned sight closer than the Antarctic. Two nights, and I can have you there, if that's what you want. But is it?"

Viktor sighed. The talk was getting wilder and wilder. There was no point in his speaking further of Misha, and all he held dear.

Eldar Ivanovich thought for a moment, then rang a number on his mobile. "Arthur, old son, got a run on tonight? Pop over, then. The Peking."

"Listen, Viktor," he said turning to him, "you've got one minute to decide. A no-nonsense yes, and with Bim as my witness, I will, at my own expense, get you to Chechnya to find this heart-transplant penguin of yours, if you're not shot first."

This, though it took Viktor time to grasp it, was for real. The wicked gleam in Eldar Ivanovich's eye fired him with sudden desperate determination, and with only seconds to go, he breathed "Yes."

"And there were Bim and me thinking *we* were the only real men left," said Eldar Ivanovich, preparing another "Border Clash". "My advice to you for the next half hour is drink yourself senseless. Better than sleeping tablets or jabs. So here's to liberating your penguin, and the victory of Russian arms!"

They clinked glasses.

"And, as both sides are using them, there's bound to be!"

Either *he* was starting to sway, or everything else was. Putting his empty glass down and gripping the table with both hands, he managed to steady it, and felt calmer. Eldar Ivanovich was mixing another "Border Clash" for him. Bim was telling the waiter to bring tea and mineral water.

He was finding it harder and harder to keep his eyes open, but for the moment was equal to the struggle and contriving to hold the restaurant in his field of vision, only it was a diminishing field from which waiters and neighbouring tables were gradually slipping. He saw a young man in a short leather jacket arrive at the table. Taking him aside, Eldar Ivanovich pointed once or twice in Viktor's direction. What happened next he neither saw nor knew, his eyes being closed. One after another his senses switched themselves off, yielding to alcoholic befuddlement. His head lay on the tablecloth beside his bowl of sauce-laced shrimps and rice.

Brown Jacket drank a little vodka, made a call on his mobile, and 20 minutes later, crew-cut men turned up to half-arm, half-carry Viktor out. "He's got a jacket in the cloakroom," Bim called. "You'll find the ticket in his pocket."

36

What befell him in the next six hours escaped him entirely. As often as he managed to open his eyes in response to some violent physical jolt, what he saw was unfocused and without shape. He was given something bitter to drink from a throw-away glass, and fell back into the depths from which he had been struggling to rise.

Meanwhile the minibus, a typical bull-dog-nosed product of the Pavlovo Motor Works, drove slowly and steadily on, windows hung with the homely plush curtains of the long-distance trains of yore, two feeble headlamps lighting the way. In the blacked-out passenger compartment twelve men of varying ages were asleep. Two others armed with thermos flasks of drugged tea saw to it that they remained so.

Coming to the warning STATE VEHICLE INSPECTION POST 300m, the driver retrieved from his feet a plate reading SARATOV – NOVOCHERKASSK which he placed against the windscreen. But the SVI hut on stilts was in darkness, its officers either sleeping or elsewhere.

On the left, the dawn of a new day was breaking.

"Twenty kilometres on there's a bit of forest for a halt," one of the men told the driver.

Half-sitting, half-lying on an upholstered double seat in a world of utter silence, Viktor came to. Straightening his aching back, he looked about him. Of the dozen or so other passengers, some were still asleep. Across the gangway an old man was eating meat from a tin, indifferent to Viktor's awakening.

The driver had disappeared. They were parked in a forest. He could hear birds.

He got to his feet, made his way to the open door and looked out.

Sun shafting through pines. Shading his eyes, he was overcome with a paralysing sense of unreality. Where the hell was he? Beyond Bim, Eldar and talk of Sphinx, he remembered nothing. He checked his pockets. Passports and credit card were still there. He got out.

A short way off three men in leather jackets were sitting round a fire toasting mushrooms speared on twigs.

Going round to the front of the bus he read the destination board, then, in the grass at his feet, noticed a tiny snail slowly climbing a blade until, bending under his weight, it returned him to the ground.

Novocherkassk was near Rostov-on-Don. Both were North Caucasus.

"Here!" called one of the men by the fire.

He went over and was given a tin of meat, an aluminium spoon and a hunting knife.

"There's no bread."

Squatting on the ground, Viktor opened the tin with the knife and ate.

By the fire a ring tone sounded, and putting a mobile to his ear, one of the men spoke in a language Viktor did not recognize.

Just then his companion from across the aisle stepped down from the bus, hurled his empty tin into the trees, wiped his mouth on the sleeve of his quilted jacket, squinted up at the sun, then came and joined Viktor.

"Got the time, boy?"

"Half past twelve."

The old man nodded, sat on the grass beside him and watched the trio enjoying their mushroom kebabs.

"Been there before, boy?"

"Where?"

"Chechnya."

He shook his head. He wanted to ask about Chechnya, but hesitated to betray the extent of his ignorance.

"Have you?"

"No." The old man looked around. "Could do with some water . . . It's meant selling the cow and slaughtering the two pigs to pay for this . . . So I'll be glad to die . . . I've decided to trick them," his voice dropped to a whisper, "by taking my son's place. They've promised to let him go if I'll work the debt off. I've nothing to ransom him with, even *they* can see that. Bloody parasites," he gestured towards the fire, "they've bled me dry. The old woman's left with damn all except potatoes to live on."

Absorbed in watching two tiny snails engaged in the senseless blade of grass ascent he'd seen earlier, Viktor asked who the men by the fire were.

"Two are Chechen. The driver's Russian like us."

"Are the others for Chechnya?"

"They are, boy. Some looking for the missing, some hoping to bargain . . . I'm being taken as an act of kindness. They told me first I couldn't go till November, then gave me this date. And you —

who've you got over there, a brother?"

"No," said Viktor, looking into weary, deep blue eyes, "a friend."

It occurred to him suddenly that a miracle was what he'd been expecting of his restaurant meeting with Bim and Eldar Ivanovich, rather as, when a child, he'd been told by his father to close, then open his eyes. Now it was to see with amazement the effect of Bim and Eldar Ivanovich's magic. But would he, knowingly, have set off for Chechnya in search of Misha? Or sought an opportunity for so doing? Yes, should have been the answer, but to his shame he could not say that it would have been, or yet wouldn't.

One of the two tiny snails on the same blade of grass dislodged the other and climbed on, until dislodged by Viktor.

"God send you find your friend," said the old man, getting to his feet.

"May I ask your name?"

"Matvey Vasilyevich. Just going for a piss."

Viktor finished his tin, took the spoon and hunting knife back, thanked the man and asked when they were moving on.

"When it's dark."

"Is it far?"

"Weren't you told?" asked the man in surprise, and with the merest trace of foreign accent.

"No."

"Well, seeing you're one of Eldar's, I'll tell you . . . I'm Rezvan."

Their destination was Achkhoy-Yurt, he said, and they'd be there the day after tomorrow. The seven road blocks were no problem. They did the run every week. They had friends amongst the Russian Feds with their own interest in promoting trouble-free transit. At Achkhoy-Yurt the Green Cross would get to work. They were a good lot, Chechens prepared to trace the missing, dead and captured, help negotiate, and whatever.

"Last time we got out eight for one ransom," Rezvan added proudly. "True, we lost one, though. His fault. Wouldn't be told. Fatal in the mountains. Given a photo have you?"

"Photo?"

"Of who you're looking for?"

Viktor ignored the question.

"Can I get back with you?"

"You've a choice, but we're the cheaper. $300 is the Fed charge by helicopter."

Again the musical ring tone, and producing his mobile, Rezvan moved away.

Returning to the minibus, Viktor drew the plush curtains towards him, and resting his head against the window, fell asleep.

37

As darkness fell they continued their journey. The passenger compartment was unlit, and Viktor's eyes soon tired of counting oncoming headlights. After sleeping during the day, he was now in a state of nervy wakefulness. Added to which he was feeling increasingly hungry. Rezvan's Chechen companion came round with a thermos of drugged tea which Viktor refused and later wished he hadn't, artificially induced sleep being preferable to abnormal alertness.

Matvey Vasilyevich was asleep, head against the window. Luckiest of their number was a tall dapper man in an Alaska jacket stretched out on the rear bench seat, snoring loudly, while the rest dozed in semi-recumbent postures. At last he relapsed into a state verging on sleep which, though far from ideal, left him registering no more than the noise of the engine, the snoring of other passengers, exchanges in Chechen and terse remarks to the driver, until at last he slept.

Pulling onto the verge, the minibus flashed its warning lights. Ten minutes later a Volga drove up. Two men in battle fatigues heaved two fat sacks into the minibus, then, as the Volga drove off, returned carrying Kalashnikovs.

Light went on in the passenger compartment, the Chechens shook sleepers awake, and pulling from his sack a warm camouflage top and trousers and tossing them onto Viktor's lap, told him to change into them. The driver replaced the destination board with one bearing the letters MoES in red, which also adorned Viktor's jacket. They now all looked more or less alike, except for Matvey who with his desiccated, deeply lined face, continued to look very much himself, Ministry of Emergency Services disguise notwithstanding.

Transformations complete, the minibus drove on, the rear bench seat now occupied by the two newcomers. Ahead, the lights of a village. The road was utterly deserted.

38

His far from deep slumbers were fitfully invaded by distant conversation, first in Russian, later in impenetrable Chechen, by which time he was aboard a yacht way, way out at sea, gently rocked by the faintest of breezes. Suddenly the wind strengthened, the sails filled, the boat heeled sharply over throwing him against what proved to be the seat in front. The bus had braked.

The men with Kalashnikovs were gone. Rezvan was now alone on the passenger seat talking to his companion, who was driving. The Russian driver was no longer with them.

The narrow earth road through the forest was not for vehicles, but to Viktor's amazement their mini climbed with a will, even with the engine sounding at times at last gasp. It was now light. Somewhere above the densely wooded mountain slopes the sun was shining, and what little of it penetrated to the forest floor seemed the brighter for having done so.

For a brief moment the road levelled out, and with a sigh of relief the driver pulled up and looked at his watch.

Rezvan produced a walkie talkie, spoke into it, waited, and receiving an answer in a burst of static and nodding to the driver, addressed the passengers.

"Which is it to be – blindfold or drugged tea? So if you fall foul of Fed Security, you can't rack your brains remembering which tree or tree stump you passed."

Variously expressed, passenger response was unanimously against drugged tea.

Rezvan grinned.

"Just as well, as we're out of it. Have your kit on the seat beside you."

The driver handed round black blindfolds, telling them to help each other and not cheat. Viktor blindfolded Matvey Vasilyevich, then himself.

The minibus set off again.

At each of the five or six stops that followed, Rezvan ordered everyone to stay blindfolded, then shouted who was to collect his things and get off, this being the stop requested. Outside were always Chechen voices, once there was yelling and the revving of a lorry or armoured troop carrier.

The names he shouted were fairly ordinary – Medvedyev, Pishchenko, Kartashov, Polenin, Dmiterkin – and others that he didn't remember.

It was a good three hours before they stopped again, having been climbing almost continuously. He tried to reckon how many were left on the bus. Three or four, perhaps, apart from himself. He began to wish he'd asked Matvey Vasilyevich's surname.

Resting his head against the soft plush curtain, he fell asleep again.

The bus stopped.

"You, and Vasilishin," came Rezvan's voice, followed, as Viktor raised a hand to his blindfold, "Keep it on, just get up and out!"

He felt for his sports bag, now the heavier for his clothes, and edging forward, stumbled, only to find an arm supporting him from then on.

"Two steps forward march," ordered a Moscow voice, and he obeyed.

"One of Eldar's," he heard Rezvan say.

The deafening beat of helicopter rotor-blades prompted Viktor, seated back to a tree, to look up, though to little purpose. Seated beside him, breathing but not saying a word, was Vasilishin. The blindfold heightened physical awareness, especially of the discomfort of his chewed left shoe, which wriggling his toes did nothing to ease. Two or three male voices approached, then went away – one, to his confusion, speaking both Moscow Russian and Chechen.

He dozed until woken by three helicopters flying over, one after the other, or was it the same one circling? Then silence, then the crackling of a fire.

"You can take your blindfolds off."

Screwing up his eyes against the sudden light, he found that it was night and that his companion was Matvey Vasilyevich. He held out his hand, and it was firmly shaken.

Sitting by the fire were two men, one tall, crew cut, the other, shorter and plainly a native of the Caucasus, busy stirring a pot.

"We eat, then bash on," said Crew Cut. "Which we can't by daylight without one lot or the other trying to kill us, or Special Forces shinning down from helicopters . . . Come and sit down."

Which, a waft of boiled mutton whetting the appetite, they did.

Crew-cut Petya was from Zagorsk, something he'd lived down by adopting a Moscow accent, which, in the silence of the Chechen night, rang out so odd and alien, as to be in danger of stopping a bullet any minute.

Maga, the other man, was a Dagestani from Khasavyurt, here, as he explained in the very opposite of Moscow Russian, for the money.

"Good money?" asked Viktor.

"For some, not for others."

They spooned the mutton stew straight from the pot, eating small dry cake-like loaves with it.

Before they moved on, Petya stamped out the fire and for good measure urinated on the embers.

Following a steep and tortuous path, they came out onto bare, moonlit mountain. Petya and Maga set a cracking pace, and Viktor kept up, gritting his teeth against increasing pain in his left foot. Looking back, he saw that Matvey Vasilyevich was managing, though with difficulty.

Soon the track narrowed to no more than a ledge bounded on the right by vertical rock, on the left by a void, slowing progress and calling for care.

Following close behind the pseudo-Muscovite, Viktor found himself thinking of Kiev and Snail's Law, some article of which he was very likely offending against – possibly that of having, so to speak, drunk himself out from under the protective shell of Bim, in ignorance of what, beyond finding himself with no fixed shell of abode, the end would be. Here different laws applied, of which he had yet to learn.

He walked with a lighter step, temporarily forgetting the pain in his foot, just as for a while he had forgotten Matvey Vasilyevich.

They came to a ravaged village. Maga led the way through the ruins to where some houses were still intact.

"Take the old un on to Duda, shall I?" Maga asked Petya.

"Then come to Arbi's."

"Good luck," said Matvey Vasilyevich, giving Viktor his hand.

Viktor was sad to see him go. Somehow he'd expected that they would be kept together.

"Come on," said Petya.

The tiny street led downhill, and at last they came to a tiny house tucked away amongst the ruins. Smoke rose from the chimney. Telling Viktor to wait, Petya went in.

Standing watching the smoke, he became increasingly aware of the cold and its effect on hands, face, thoughts and breath.

On his flight to Argentina the pilot had announced "We are now at 10,000 metres. The air temperature −45°. Those who wish to acclimatize can open the windows." Everyone had laughed. Thanks to the champagne, there had been a lot of laughter. What was the altitude and air temperature here?

The door creaked open. Petya motioned him to enter.

41

Viktor was allotted a corner curtained off with a camel-hair blanket, with, against the wall under a tiny cracked window, a trestle bed topped with two striped mattresses. On a bedside table a candle threw light on walls and ceiling. On the wall, two copper plates and a black-ribbon-draped photograph of a young man in Soviet Army uniform.

The old Chechen whose house it was spoke no Russian, and having shown Viktor to his corner and pointed to the bed, he left him.

Dumping his bag on the worn carpet, Viktor sat on his bed and took in the silence. From beyond the camel-hair blanket, which was decorated with a brown tiger, came a muttering and rustling. Peeping out, he saw the old man standing looking into an open cupboard. On the dressing table there was a candle, and the walls were hung with a great number of photographs in old wooden frames. Of what it was too dark to tell.

"Good night," Viktor said softly, at which the old man swung round in alarm and shook his head.

*

He was woken next morning by someone knocking loudly at the door of the house. Brilliant sunlight was streaming through the tiny window. Pulling on his trousers and scorning his shoes, he emerged from his corner. The old man, in grey dressing gown and black boots, was standing at the open door talking to Maga.

"You can wash out here," Maga broke off to say.

Edging past them and treading cold stone, Viktor saw a blue washstand with an enamel bowl. Splashing his face and gargling in ice-cold water, he looked round for a towel, but there was none.

The cold was intense, in spite of the bright sun, and returning to the house, he dried his face on the camel-hair blanket, put on his shirt and his MoES tunic.

Maga motioned him outside.

"Got some photos?"

"No need. There can't be more than one penguin in Chechnya."

Maga looked puzzled. He repeated the question several times, thinking he'd misunderstood, and finding he hadn't finished by giving a dispirited shake of the head.

"Where do we look?"

"He was brought here from Moscow by a businessman called Khachayev, so where Khachayev is, he'll be."

"This isn't a Russian village, you know, where everyone knows everyone else. What are you prepared to pay?"

The question caught him unawares. "Quite a lot."

347

"I'll do my best, though penguins aren't exactly my line."

"What is your line?"

"We've our Green Cross, a bit like your Red, only privately run. We trace dead and prisoners, and we help negotiate. We've a fair fixed tariff."

"How did Petya get here?" Viktor asked suddenly. "Desert?"

"Posted 'Missing'. Look, I'll see what I can find out about this Khachayev. No joy, and that's my lot. I've a living to earn. Anything you need?"

"Boots. My shoes leak."

42

Viktor spent two days in his corner, going out only to wash or relieve himself. The old man brought him disc-like loaves, dried meat and cheese from the two goats he kept. Maga advised him not to show himself outside any more than he had to.

Conversation with the old man was out, even in sign language. Viktor tried to convey something about himself by way of the photographs on the wall, but in vain. The old man was simply not interested. All Viktor gathered was that he was sleeping where the old man's younger son used to sleep. This son had died during military service, but how and where was not to be discovered.

After two days Maga returned carrying a large but not heavy canvas bag, and sitting down on Viktor's bed pulled out a pair of dirty black boots for him to try.

They were tight and the soles bore traces of yellow clay.

The next pair was on the large side but passable. He tried walking

in them. The left one slopped a bit, but puttees over his socks would
take care of that.

"Fine," he said "How much?"

The question incurred a look of displeasure.

"Take them as a gift. The owner never had the full wear of them."

"Killed?"

"Natural death's uncommon here." Then in a tone more sug-
gestive of failure than success he added, "I'm onto Khachayev. But
he's unapproachable. Thirty-man bodyguard. The one road
exposed to fire. Doesn't deal in prisoners. Sees nobody. There's just
one possibility. He has a business here. I could get you a job. The
past two or three months he's been short of labour."

"What sort of business?"

Maga shrugged.

"I don't know. Probably oil. Or gas. You'll have to go and see."

"I'll do that."

Maga looked distinctly unhappy.

"You will? Then you'd better pay in advance. For a normal job I'd
get $500 for this week's work."

"For doing what?"

"Inquiring, negotiating. That old man you came with has given
Petya $500 to trace his son."

"Leave me to myself for a moment."

Maga ducked out under the blanket and was soon in conversation
with the old man, and by the sound of it complaining.

Viktor delved into his sports bag to check how much he had. $570.

He called Maga.

"Here's $200 to be going on with. Now tell me about Khachayev."

"He's recently returned from Moscow, where he has a casino and
several jewellery businesses."

"About here's what I want to know."

"What he said the moment he arrived was that he was here not to fight but make money. His business dates from the beginning of the war. It was supervised by his younger brother, but now he's been packed off to Turkey, and Khachayev's in sole charge. He's as well in with the Feds as he is with the Chechens, and he's declared an exclusion zone. His *ashore* area, or something, where no outsiders may carry arms."

"'Offshore' more likely."

"Could be. Where no-one dares go. Anyone carrying arms will be shot on sight, he says, regardless of nationality."

"You could get me a job there, you said."

"I could try."

"So what next?"

"I take you, and leave you somewhere while I negotiate. Which I do well. But guiding and negotiating come at a price."

"How much?"

"$500 or $600."

"$500 was your normal charge, you said, so I give you another $300."

"OK, so give."

"Not till you've got me there."

Maga shook his head.

"And if you're killed on the way I've got to go through your pockets for it . . . Not nice. Looks like looting. Give me now. I won't let you down. I'll even tell you which pocket it's in, in case it's me that gets killed."

"Right," said Viktor.

43

Maga called for Viktor at six in the evening.

"I'd leave that here," he said, eyeing the fat sports bag lying ready on the floor. "The old man may be able to use something out of it."

Viktor shook the old man's hand, thanked him, and tried to indicate that he was leaving the bag as a present. Maga duly translated, throwing in something on his own account. The old man then presented Viktor with two scraps of red towelling bearing the Olympic symbol and half an Olympic teddy bear. Pointing to Viktor's new boots, he said something which Maga translated as "May Allah preserve you!"

Dusk was falling, though the sky was still bright.

As they picked their way through the ravaged village, Viktor remarked on the absence of power lines.

"There never were any. No gas, no telephone, no school. They wanted us to quit the mountains and live down there."

"Why no weapon?"

"To better my chances of staying alive. There are people who don't shoot the unarmed. I'm no guerilla. Peaceful civilian, that's me. As having no weapon shows. Feds included."

Arrived at the narrow ledge, they halted. Maga looked up at the sky and shook his head.

"Something wrong?"

"Wind. We could get blown off."

"But there isn't any."

"It's coming. Still, let's go." And muttering to himself in Chechen or Russian, he led off along the ledge.

The night sky was darkening appreciably, the light more from the stars than the increasing sallow moon. It was a place for care and concentration, with the added danger of the occasional falling stone or rock.

"Ten days from now, I'm off home," Maga announced suddenly.

"To Dagestan?"

"Khasavyurt. I take money, see my parents, show I'm still alive. I've three sisters still to be married off, and my parents are far from well – you get the idea. The only place to buy medicine is Makhachkal, and it costs the earth . . ."

Stopping, he listened.

"Get down! Press in against the rock!"

Viktor did his best to do both as two helicopters flew by, beaming their searchlights on trees far below.

"Who are they after?" Viktor asked, he expected rhetorically.

"Basayev, Nagayev, Raduyev and other racketeers. You from Moscow?" he added, getting to his feet.

"No, Kiev, though I came on here from Moscow."

"Some place, that! I've been!"

"Not now, not if you're from the Caucasus. It's all 'Show your papers!' And harassment."

"So you wouldn't see me for dust! But the girls! Mine has the most wonderful eyes. Same in Kiev?"

"No," said Viktor, thinking of Marina.

"You can see why Chechens hate Russians, Chechen women being not much to look at and ageing early, whereas Moscow boasts the belles of Russia . . ."

44

With dawn came a mighty wind that even the warm MoES uniform was not proof against, and coming to a village, they sought shelter in a wooden barn.

"I'll have a breather, then go on," said Maga. "You stay here."

There were several spades and a tall stack of firewood. The floor was strewn with straw.

"Shame we can't make a fire," said Maga. "Still, I shan't be long – we're practically there."

Left alone, Viktor tried to sleep, but without much success. Day was breaking, but only dimly through the dirty window. The gale was shut out. Uncomfortable on his seat of firewood, he kept going to the door and peering out, seeing no more than a wooden fence and trees beyond.

Trying to make himself comfortable on the floor, he felt something dig into him, and reaching into the straw and wood chippings encountered the ice cold though heavily greased metal of a Kalashnikov, and exploring further, the rough casing of hand grenades.

★

"Still there?" came Maga's voice.

Viktor let him in.

"All's well! You're sold into slavery! We can go, they're expecting you."

"How do you mean, slavery?"

"It's the way they put it here. Chechen men don't work, slaves work for them. If I'd offered them you without charge, they wouldn't have trusted me. They'd have taken you for Fed Security."

"How much did you get for me?"

"A good price, don't you worry. $220. They offered $100 to start with, but I ran them up. They're short-handed."

"What do I have to do exactly?"

"You'll find out. You're going to Khachayev's, and that's what you wanted. It's all quiet there – no shooting in his ashore area. Brought you something to eat."

And they stood by the dirty window, eating dried meat and flat round loaves.

"There's a Kalashnikov and grenades hidden here," Viktor volunteered.

"Where?"

"Under the straw."

"You can tell your boss, increase your credibility," said Maga cheerfully, adding, as an afterthought, "No, don't – I'll stick them somewhere else, maybe sell them on."

When they had eaten, they set off. For three hours they followed a forest track in silence and complete darkness. Coming to a road, they looked for and found the continuation on the far side. The track began to climb, growing increasingly twisty. Viktor asked Maga to go a bit slower.

"Not much further – under a kilometre."

Coming to a large pipeline they followed it, now downhill.

"What is it?"

"Oil. Friendship Pipeline. We follow it, and in an hour we'll be there."

"Under a kilometre, you said!"

"Roughly I meant."

In fact it was another two hours before they came to a large white A painted on the pipe and stopped.

"See – A for Ashore!" said Maga, and picking up some metal object, struck the pipe twice. "Let's go and sit down over there."

Over there, was to a tree where, surprisingly, there was a bench.

They did not have long to wait before a bearded young man in quilted jacket appeared and inspected Viktor, first without, then with, a torch.

"Best give him your weapon," he said, indicating Maga. "Otherwise . . ."

"Hasn't got one," said Maga, getting up and holding out his hand for something.

My price, thought Viktor.

"All the best," Maga wished him, and set off back along the pipeline.

45

Hardly able to keep his eyes open for sheer fatigue, Viktor followed quilted-jacketed Seva, yet another of the Russians posted as "missing".

"I'll let Aza see you, then you can get some sleep," he said as they walked. "We're not working today. No raw material."

A little way into the forest they came to a log cabin. Seva pushed open the door, let Viktor in ahead of him, then knocked at one of the several doors opening off the passage.

"Aza! Addition to the workforce," he called.

The door opened, revealing a plump, bald-headed little man in a blue tracksuit. His round face, prominent nose, button eyes and shaggy brows were of the Caucasus, but not Chechnya. He yawned, looked briefly at Viktor, then turned to Seva.

"Not got a gun, has he?"

"No. He's very tired. Wants to sleep."

"So he can," he said, nodding at the door across the passage. "You've aired Dzhangirov's?"

"And kerosened."

"They could be bringing custom tomorrow night. One of the Feds came," said Aza and taking another look at Viktor, went back into his room, closing the door.

Viktor's small room had two roughly fashioned beds with mattresses and red quilts. Under the window was a little table, and in the middle of the floor a small stove made out of a metal keg with a flue that went straight up into the ceiling.

46

Viktor woke, still weary, to a strange smell. The little room was warm and dark, the only sound from the stove, whose glow seen through its slotted door was reflected on the floor. The other bed was empty. And but for the smell hanging heavy in the air, he might have succumbed to an illusion of comfort. It could have been kerosene.

He pulled on his boots, then removed them to wrap his feet in the strips of cloth the old Chechen had given him. The door opened, and behind the beam of a torch, in came Seva.

"Sleep all right?"

"Yes, but what's the smell?"

"Home-made kerosene. We've a whole barrel. Chechen barter. Just the thing for mosquitoes, though too much, and you get a headache. Not to worry, it's soon got rid of. And with winter coming, mosquitoes are out. So, to work!"

"Doing what?"

"Getting heat up."

The sky above was clouded and starless. A stiff breeze barely perceptible at ground level was stirring the tree tops.

"Splendid! Just the weather we need!" said Seva. "You've no idea just how lucky we are."

Viktor followed Seva and his torch into the darkness, bending, taking care, or watching out for roots where and when told, until they came to a large shed. Seva unlocked the hefty padlock, opened the door wide "to air the place a bit", and as they stood there Viktor noticed that this pipeline was much smaller than the one he and Maga had followed.

"This is tapped into the main oil pipeline," Seva explained shining his torch along it and suddenly illuminating a white-painted HAVE A GOOD FLIGHT! He spat in disgust.

"Forgot to paint that out. Dzhangirov got pissed like the fool he was and wrote things. Hang on, I've got some paint left."

He fetched a tin from the shed, broke off a fir branch, and with Viktor holding the torch, used it to black the letters over.

"Where does the pipe go from here?" Viktor asked.

"Into the shed and up through the roof of it. Come on, I'll teach you valve control."

Striking a match, he lit several candles in shallow tins on the floor, and on a table at the far end. The shed was spacious, 20 metres in length and almost as wide. The pipe entered at ceiling height, to be connected to an enormous iron coil sprouting flow valves and dials. Leaving the coil, it passed into a great reducer drum on iron legs, beyond which and another flow valve, it tapered gradually to a diameter of 50 cm before branching into a dozen smaller pipes welded to the closed end of an enormous cylinder resting on the ground like a crude space rocket. The far end was also closed, but capable of being opened or even removed, like a door. The scale of the installation was impressive, although for the time being its purpose was a mystery.

"Tomorrow's Fat Friday, so let's get to work," said Seva.

At his direction, Viktor operated the heavy wheels of the flow valves, while Seva played engineer, hopping from dial to dial with his torch.

"Bit more. Bit more. Back a bit. That's it."

The coil came alarmingly alive, hissing with the menace of a rocket about to destruct.

At the final flow valve where the pipeline branched, Seva took over.

"A mistake at this point, and it's goodbye!" he whispered, eyes on the dial. Adjustments completed, he stood back, breathing deeply.

"Must relax a minute after that," he said in a shaky voice.

It was not the moment for asking questions.

Still visibly shaken, Seva opened a tiny vent in the rocket-like section, and lighting a roll of paper, thrust it deeply in as though into the jaws of some fearful beast. A mighty bang followed, and Seva leapt back with the alacrity of a gymnast, again breathing deeply with relief, then closed the vent and checked the dial.

Viktor touched the cylinder, expecting it to be hot, but it wasn't.

Waxing expansive, Seva explained that it was an inner cylinder that was heating, but that this outer one got hot too, so that when there was snow, the grass stayed green within 50 metres of the shed.

The temperature in the shed was rising.

"We heat for another 20 minutes, then ease back and wait for custom," said Seva.

47

20 minutes brought a considerable rise in temperature. Seva, seeing Viktor about to take off his jacket, stopped him, threw open the door, and after adjusting the final flow valve, suggested a breath of air.

Seva lit a cigarette, and Viktor watched the dense smoke from the chimney being carried quickly away and dispersed by the wind. Seva took one last drag, stamped out his cigarette, and went with his torch to meet the custom. At a loss what to expect, Viktor withdrew into the trees, and from there saw two men carrying on their shoulders what looked like a rolled carpet. They followed Seva into the shed.

"Hi! Viktor!" bawled Seva from the door. And when he came out from the trees. "No skiving off, or you go the way of Dzhangirov!"

*

"What way was that?"

"Never you mind. Let's get on with it."

On a blanket on the ground at the far end of the furnace was the body of a man, but whether Russian or Chechen was impossible to tell, so pulped was his face. The men who had brought him were Chechens.

"Have these against the heat," Seva ordered, handing Viktor boxing-glove-like gauntlets.

Each taking a handle of the outer door of the furnace, they pulled, and beyond the blast of hot air Viktor saw the door of another cylinder, clearly the one into which the heater jets ran.

"One, two, three, and tug," said Seva.

They tugged, and with the heat came a distinct odour.

"Pop him in," Seva told the Chechens, who after some hesitation proceeded to do so, head first.

"Pull his boots off!"

One of the Chechens got them off and threw them into a corner.

"Look back in two hours," said Seva, shutting both doors and opening the flow valve.

Outside, he produced a heavy silver cigarette case, and selecting a cigarette, lit up.

"May I see?" Viktor asked.

The inscription read:

IN APPRECIATION OF CAPT. KHVOYKO'S

SMOKE BREAKS, FROM HIS MATES, GROZNY, 1997.

It was repeated on the other side in Georgian.

"Where did you get it?"

"From the Feds in lieu of dollars. Never know your luck – look at this."

He displayed his watch.

"Rolex?"

"And not your Chinese crap either. On the back it's got 'To our idiot Tobacco Factory Director on his birthday from grateful colleagues.' So, work hard and you, too, will be rich."

48

The two hours allowed for the incineration of the corpse seemed to drag on for ever. Viktor kept looking at his watch, thinking the time was up, but his watch said differently. Now and then, above the noise of the furnace, the wind could be heard and the shrieks of night birds. Suddenly there were footsteps and Aza appeared carrying a ledger-like book and a pencil, and sat down beside them.

"Got his name and date of birth?"

"Not yet," said Seva, striking a match and lighting a cigarette. "And what's the point? They'll be false anyway. It's the Feds who always tell the truth."

"False or not – I don't give a toss. That's on their heads. The main thing's to get a name and bung it down. Tidy paperwork's the need for any job – ours especially."

"Well, get it when they come for the ashes," snapped Seva.

Fifteen or so minutes later the Chechens returned, looked into the shed, and finding nobody, looked around and espied the three sitting under the trees.

Seva got to his feet.

"All done. Let's have his name and date of birth."

"What for?" one asked.

"The record. State requirement. Then if anyone comes looking, they'll find here was where he was cremated and be reassured."

"Well, if that's the idea, Ilyas Zhadoyev, date of birth '83, Nizhniye Atagi," said the Chechen with little trace of accent. "Anything else?"

"That's fine," said Aza, opening his ledger.

To Seva's instructions, Viktor shut off the flow valves in reverse order. They opened the outer furnace door, allowed the heat to be dissipated, then opened the inner – the question now being not so much one of heat as of odour.

"Bucket!" ordered Seva.

Viktor placed the bucket beneath the opening of the inner furnace, and Seva, using a long-handled tool, scraped out the furnace contents into it.

How little, how insubstantial! Viktor thought, reminded of the

urn containing militiaman friend Sergey's ashes which he and Nina
had received as a parcel out of the blue. Where was all the rest?
Where was what had made him a live, physical presence? Where his
experiences, principles, joys?

Something metallic fell into the bucket.

"First catch," said Seva, extracting a small nugget of gold and
slipping it into a pocket. "His ring."

As the ashes, when bagged, seemed on the short side, and since
these Chechens were a decent lot, Aza got Seva to top them up with
some from a petrol drum in the corner, before handing them over.

Aza was given a number of banknotes, Seva and Viktor a
crumpled $5 apiece.

"The Feds should have been here by now," Aza said finally. "But
hang on, you two, and call me if they do come."

49

Next morning Viktor awoke with a headache, the result both of the
lack of sleep and the all-pervasive smell of kerosene. On top of
which, the odour of cremation lingered as an unpleasant taste in his
mouth. In the other bed was Seva, head pressed into uncased
pillow, now snoring, now calling out in, or commenting on, his
dreams. And as he jerked from one side to the other, his face was
coated with what looked like soot, and Viktor, passing a hand over
his own face, encountered something similar.

The only sound was of steady rain.

Suddenly it all came back – three Feds with the corpse of a
comrade and a bottle of spirits, morose tin-mug toasts to the

departed, committal to the furnace, and the two hour wait while it did its work. Seva had sent him to fetch Aza, and Aza had come with his ledger. But apart from Kineshma as place of birth, he remembered nothing beyond that their disbursement of roubles or dollars had been so meagre that Seva dispensed with the normal top-up of ashes. Other Feds turned up – regulars this time, not conscripts – dragging evil-smelling sacks. Grubby, unshaven, they'd watched him and Seva put the sacks into the furnace, and then hung about sweating profusely in the blistering heat, obliging him to stay too, hardly able to breathe and longing for fresh air. But at last they left the shed, slipping Seva dollar bills and something else which he later displayed in the light of his torch: three signet rings and a lady's ring set with a stone.

The regulars did not claim the ashes.

"All they want is to get shot of Chechen bodies," Seva explained, later adding the raked out ash to his secret stock.

Gradually the headache eased, but not the unpleasant taste in his mouth.

Looking around the kitchen for something to fetch water in, he came across some enamel Winnie the Pooh mugs and plates stamped KINDERGARTEN PROPERTY, and wondered how Sonya was. Still thinking of him? And of Misha?

He opened the tall cupboard and was surprised to find that it also did service as a wardrobe. Hung on hangers from a bar were two army greatcoats and a militia uniform. There were various small white sacks which felt as if they had been starched, tins without labels, a litre bottle of sunflower oil. One of the bags contained oatmeal and vermicelli. Suddenly ravenous, he took a saucepan and went outside for water.

50

Two weeks passed, and then the first snow fell.

The white flakes had a cheering effect, stirring memories of last winter's walks with Misha.

He had grown accustomed to their nocturnal employment and all that went with it. Every now and then explosions and automatic fire could be heard, and military aircraft and helicopters flew overhead. The war, like the night incineration of corpses, ground on without respite. More often than not it was the Feds who brought bodies, either in sacks or with heads concealed, and on two occasions the bodies were those of young women.

Chechens were something of a rarity. Cremation, Seva said, was not the Muslim tradition. So anyone the Chechens brought would be from another country, and if a Muslim, then from as far away as Saudi Arabia, Yemen or Turkey, where the ashes could be sent for burial.

Chechens and Feds gave only small dollar tips, but the latter more often than not gave watches or gold rings, and Viktor, knowing how such things were come by, was happy to pass the gold to Seva. Sometimes towards dawn, when Aza had retired to bed taking his ledger with him, Seva would fetch an iron mould from under the tree nearest the shed, and from somewhere else, a heavy gold brick. This he returned to the mould, and laying his new gold on top, placed the mould in the furnace.

"Don't want anyone recognizing some ring or trinket one day," commented Seva. "Gold's more precious than dollars."

There were questions he would have liked to ask Seva – about his future plans, how he proposed to get away from here and Chechnya – but was in no mood to ask. Time was passing, and without his learning anything of Misha or Khachayev. Twice he'd tried to sound out Aza, but Aza wasn't to be sounded out.

"What do you want to know about Khachayev for?" he asked, and Viktor, not wanting to tell him about Misha, didn't say. It was, he kept telling himself, only a question of hanging on. As boss of the crematorium, Khachayev must, some time, put in an appearance.

So he waited – simply living, working, eating from enamel bowls, drinking from enamel mugs, once kindergarten property. The mugs and bowls even had a cheering effect, reminding him not so much of his own childhood as of that night in Kiev with Svetlana and semolina.

51

Invariably cheerful, Seva became doubly so on Thursday, when Aza offered a reduction in the rate for cremation. How great a reduction, Seva and Viktor never knew, but more custom meant more tips.

This Thursday Viktor woke earlier than usual at getting on for twelve. They had gone to bed on the early side, having completed the last cremation by five. The Feds had given them a bottle of vodka and – an unusual departure – some recent Russian newspapers. Flopping out on the stove bench, Viktor had fallen asleep, thinking how next day he would read every last word and maybe something about Kiev, a plan that came to nothing, or more accurately, went up in smoke. Following the first snow, he and Seva had been taking it in turns to get up early and put more wood in the stove. Today he found Aza consigning the last of the newspapers to the flames of the passage stove together with some logs. Boiling on top of the stove was a saucepan of water into which, with Viktor watching in amazement, he poured two one-kilogram packets of salt, popped in a number of cloth bags and proceeded to stir them with a fork.

"Are they for lunch?" he asked.

"No," said Aza in all seriousness. "Winter brings the mice in. Chechen mice are a hundred times worse than Russian, but they don't like salt."

He went on stirring the boiling bags, then, with a nod in the direction of Viktor and Seva's room, said, "Don't go modelling yourself on him. He's greedy. Thinks I don't know. But I do." And he left it at that.

Outside, snow, deep-blue sky and keen conifer-scented air. It was as if the whole cremation shed area had been deodorized. Seva came out wearing the smile that only exhaustion was capable of removing. The fate of their newspapers left him unmoved.

"How about a drink?"

Viktor shook his head, not feeling like vodka, and wanting the pure air and the joy of breathing it to last.

"OK. Healthy spirit in healthy body! Another time. In three days it's my birthday."

"How old will you be?"

"Nineteen."

"Just a boy."

"But still teaching you, old grey beard, how things are done. And with more earned than you've ever dreamt of!"

*

At six the sun sank behind the mountain top, providing the signal for Seva and Viktor to set off for the shed, and half an hour later the furnace was roaring.

First to arrive were two Chechens carrying a body wrapped in a greatcoat, followed at a distance by another man.

"Where's Aza?" asked one.

"Not here yet," said Seva, and was brusquely sent to fetch him.

The bearers, tall powerful fellows with stubbly black beards brought the body to Viktor in the shed.

"Open the furnace!"

Viktor took his time. These Chechens had an air of insolence about them that he'd never before encountered. Most were submissive, these were anything but.

"We'll have to wait for Aza."

"Look, new boy," said one menacingly. "Open up – we haven't got all night."

Viktor opened the furnace. The body was that of a man aged about 20 – pale, emaciated, check flannel shirt, jeans, gold star earring – clearly a civilian and apparently Russian.

"What are you gawking at? Friend of yours, is he?" demanded one of the Chechens engaged in sliding the body into the furnace. "Come on, get cracking!"

Viktor closed the inner and outer doors and adjusted the flow valve.

"Give what's left of him to the old bloke outside. And be polite and humane!" said the same Chechen making for the door.

"Name and date of birth?" Viktor called after him.

"The old bloke'll tell you."

Aza and Seva entered, Aza, as always, carrying his ledger, but muttering in Azerbaijani, clearly very put out.

"The old man outside will tell you the name," Viktor said.

"He's told us," said Seva answering for Aza.

Sniffing the hot acrid air, Aza made a wry face, and left, saying he'd be back in an hour.

"What's biting him?"

"They didn't pay. Maybe we'll come in for something," said Seva, pulling a packet of cigarettes from his camouflage jacket and heading out of the shed. Viktor followed, seeking relief from the sauna heat.

Watching the falling snow, he thought again of Kiev, and Sonya waiting for winter and snow. He even thought of Nina, waiting for he knew not what, though obviously not for him. A bit of stability in life was very likely what she was waiting for – a man at her side, a roof over her head, a bit of money. Oh, and a dacha with a garden to grow things in.

He shrugged, but went on thinking of her, doing his best to understand, which, with this distance between them, should have been easier. Except that he still saw her only as a chance outsider. But for militiaman Sergey, she would never have come into his life.

Melting snow ran down his face.

"Is it you, Viktor?" said a voice he knew.

"Matvey Vasilyevich!" All became suddenly clear.

"Well, there we are," said Matvey Vasilyevich after a while. "It was my living son I came here for."

"I'll leave you," Seva said quietly.

"Just sixteen, and they give him a gun 'to scare Russians off with', and he goes and pulls the trigger . . . Can you call that war?"

Viktor shrugged, asking himself the same question. He was not here to fight a war. He was here for no good reason at all. Fate – Misha-the-Penguin's, not his – was why he was here.

"Found your friend?" Matvey asked suddenly, as if divining his thoughts.

"No, but I shall."

The old man nodded approvingly. "Good for you," he whispered. "With friends like you, my son might still be alive."

*

Later as they stood watching Seva rake out the furnace into a bucket, something clinked. His face brightened, but quickly resumed the expression appropriate to the task.

Viktor remembered the gold star earring, but not any rings.

"Wait in the fresh air – I'll bring out the ashes," said Seva.

Five minutes later he handed the old man not the usual knotted black plastic sack, but a fine Aeroflot Duty Free carrier bag.

The old man pulled out and proffered two grubby one-dollar bills. Seva accepted one, and when Viktor made no move, the second also.

"Where now?" Viktor asked.

But the old man was far away, tears streaming down his cheeks, hearing, seeing nothing.

"Where now?" Viktor asked again.

"Not far. An hour and a half along the pipeline, then on. Any idea how I'm supposed to bury him? Ordinary grave? We always have coffins. We don't have cremation."

"In a grave," said Viktor, not wanting to make things more difficult than they were. He, after all, had not yet decided what to do with the urn of Sergey's ashes – or had, to the extent of deciding to do nothing, beyond keeping him warm and cosy in the kitchen, always there to be talked to.

Matvey Vasilyevich embraced him. Seva respectfully withdrew.

"Stay no longer than you have to," said the old man. "Find your friend, and go. There'll be no peace here."

Seva's birthday celebration began at midday, the idea being to get it over before dark, then recover. On the table were the Feds' bottle of vodka, three enamel Pooh Bear mugs, three bowls of boiled potatoes, dried meat bars and a half-litre jar of damson purée, the last two Aza's lordly contribution to the feast.

Seva poured a modest measure of vodka all round, then waited.

"Your health!" said Viktor, breaking the silence.

They clinked mugs, producing for Viktor a sound unnervingly like the dropping of a certain metal into a bucket.

"Have another," said Seva. "Good stuff. Almost as good as Smirnoff."

They drank and ate, dipping the meat bars into the open jar of purée.

Aza took the bottle and poured round another modest measure.

"First hand to pour, pours all!" protested Seva.

"Just Russian prejudice!" laughed Aza, "like your nonsense about unlucky black cats and empty buckets! You're a big boy now. You're 19."

"The next pour's mine, or it's bad luck. I've tried. Break the rule, and next day a splitting head."

Gesturing assent, Aza raised his mug in a toast. "May you grow in wisdom!"

"To higher education, then!" Seva corrected with a laugh.

"With a bit of education and your low cunning you could run the whole show."

Seva let this pass – maybe no offence was actually intended – and Viktor, fearful of the party's ending in a drunken brawl, was much relieved, and even ribbed Seva himself.

Vodka and food soon ran out, but the festive mood endured. Seva looked questioningly at Aza, and Aza, getting the message, went to his room and returned with a bottle of Armenian cognac.

"Go ahead, drink. I'm going for a walk."

Opening the bottle, Seva helped Viktor and himself to half a mugful.

"No half measures!" he said, smiling broadly. "I've saved the best toast for the cognac, you see. Here's to the future!"

They clinked mugs, producing the same unnerving sound.

Downing his cognac in a single gulp, Seva surveyed the empty table, and spotting the jar of damson purée, took a swig and wiped his lips with the back of his hand.

"What will you do next?" he asked, looking keenly at Viktor.

"How do you mean?"

"Next – in the future."

He had said nothing to Seva of his intentions, and wasn't inclined to start now. Anyway, it looked as if Seva was more interested in revealing, on this his birthday, plans which he had hitherto kept secret.

"I'll be off from here very soon," he whispered, glancing at the half-open door. "I've sent my parents money from here, and do you know, they've actually got it. I rang them."

"Where from?"

"A satellite phone. They've got one hereabouts, only not where you can get at it. I'm getting transport home. It's all agreed. Not a word to Aza, though. He'll shop me. They have it in for us, Azerbaijanis do."

"What transport? Chechen?"

"Chechens got the cash to my parents, taking 20%. This time it's the Feds promising help."

Viktor's expression must have betrayed his doubts for Seva fell silent, but was quickly his old self again, dispensing the last of the cognac.

"Don't give a sod whether you believe me or not. But here's me coming back from the war with dollars and gold. And you?"

"What will you do with the gold?"

"Cut it in three – buy myself a two-room flat, buy myself a bride and buy myself a bakery. Good money in baking, and I'm used to heat."

"The bride being Uzbek or Kyrgyz."

"No, gypsy. They don't let their women marry Russians, but will for money. Maya's her name, and she's wonderful."

Viktor could just see him in a white cap taking freshly baked bread from the oven. Stranger things happened. The thought of bread made him hungry.

"Now let's drink your health," said Seva, raising his mug, and then, "Have some purée!"

"Do you know Khachayev?" Viktor asked, wiping his mouth and returning the near-empty jar to the table.

"Seen him a couple of times. It was his place I phoned from. I got taken to mend his telly. The next time was when he came here. One of his Moscow pals had got murdered."

"What's he like?"

"Good man. Not like the rest. All for a drink and a laugh. Typical Muscovite. The wife's Russian, but she's in Moscow."

"What's his place like?"

"A bloody fortress. Crawling with relatives and bodyguards. I got taken to the telly, then up to a room with a balcony where the phone was, then back here. And now I'll go and lie down for a bit. Wake me when it gets dark."

And Viktor was left with the thought that if he had seen Misha he would surely have said so.

53

Vodka and cognac proved a heady mix, but long before darkness Viktor's sleep was broken by a small Chechen in a sheepskin coat, come in search of Aza. Told to wait, he limped over to a fallen tree trunk and sat, and as Viktor did his best to sleep against Seva's rhythmic snoring, there were voices speaking in Russian, one of them Aza's.

"I can swap three, maybe four Russian soldiers for Zara, tell him," said the Chechen.

"What use will they be to him?" said Aza. "He's in a cleaner line of business than you. Get the money. Soldiers are out."

"Listen, I beg you – Zara's my brother! He was a fool to do it, yes, but he's young."

"Clear off! I tell him nothing," snapped Aza.

"Foreigner, you're evil!" said the Chechen wearily. "Not a tear will there be when you meet death."

Sitting up and looking through the window, Viktor saw the Chechen limp away, watched by Aza.

*

The heating of the shed to sauna level, did nothing to improve Viktor and Seva's headaches.

"I feel bloody," said Seva as he checked the gas pressure. "Lousy way to end a birthday. Damned damson purée! If my guts hold it, I'll be lucky."

Outside the air seemed warmer, as if the wind was now from the south, and Viktor was surprised to see the snow gone from in front of the shed.

Shining his torch, Seva consulted his watch.

"6.30 and not a customer in sight."

Half an hour later four regulars the worse for drink turned up, and learning it was Seva's birthday, made presents of cigarettes, another watch, and to his special pleasure, gold earrings.

"Just the wedding thing for my little gypsy," he said, tucking them into a trouser pocket.

The body, Viktor thought, was either of someone very young or very small, not that of the limping Chechen.

Pulling a bottle of vodka from an inner pocket, one of the soldiers took a sample swig.

"The real stuff," he said, passing Seva the bottle. "You first."

Seva was presented with a crust of rye bread to take a bite of.

"Look," said the soldier who was clearly in charge, "the lads know the form, they'll bung it in."

"Not till I fetch Aza," said Seva.

"Bloody hell, no! Have another swig!"

Viktor seemed to see movement in the sack, and as he watched, had an open bottle of vodka thrust under his nose and a round, unshaven, toothlessly smiling face peer into his.

"Drink to pal Seva's health!"

"Cut it!" roared the soldier in charge. "Job first. Get the sack in the furnace before that bloody Azerbaijani comes at the double!"

The three stood gawking.

"You and you," he detailed, "there's the shed, get on with it!"

Lifting the sack as if it weighed nothing, they set off. Seva made as if to follow, but the soldier in charge detained him for another swig.

"You stand fast. Not needed. They'll be back in a mo, and then we'll have another drink. Best you keep clear," he added with a laugh.

"How about payment?"

"Payment's on collection, mate, and we won't be collecting this lot of ashes. Sell them or do what you like with them. They're all yours," he added with a laugh.

Swinging round, Viktor saw the men had closed the shed doors after them. Whoever was in that sack was, as he feared, alive! He rushed to the shed.

Hot as it was, he seized the handle of the outer door of the furnace and did his best to open it, when something made of glass was broken on his head and vodka ran over his face.

"Silly sod!" said a voice.

Afer which it was down into a bottomless well and nothingness.

<h1 style="text-align:center">54</h1>

He came to, feeling an agonizing pain in his foot. Opening his eyes, he tried to reach up to his right temple under its tight bandage, but couldn't. His hands were bound behind his back, and so tightly that his fingers were dead. He was in a deep pit. Adjusting his posture, he took the weight off his foot and eased the pain. Looking up, he judged it to be some three metres to the surface.

Something icy touched his cheek. It was snow.

55

Near frozen to death, he was hauled from the pit by two Chechens, who dumped him in the snow outside a two-storey house and disappeared. Unable to turn his head, all he could see was a Russian jeep with two Kalashnikovs hung from the driver's wing mirror. Somewhere behind him he heard men conversing quietly in Chechen, then one spoke over a walkie-talkie. After that, silence, until two young Chechens came and dragged him into the house and a bare room where they sat him on a wooden bench and themselves on another under the window. They were, he saw now, no more than 16. One was staring at the wooden floor, the other twirling a Tula Tokarev automatic.

The door opened and a thickly stubbled Chechen aged about 40 appeared, stared at Viktor, and said something in Chechen. One of the youths left the room and returned with a bottle which he put to Viktor's lips and tilted. The tingle on lips and tongue suggested home-brewed vodka or *chacha*.

"Have some more. Bit chilly, isn't it?" said the Chechen in perfect Russian.

He sipped. His head cleared, deepening awareness of his feeble fetteredness and the head-bandaged wound, now throbbing so painfully as to make him grimace.

"What's wrong?" asked the Chechen, bringing a stool and sitting in front of him. "Not to your taste?"

"It's my head."

Rising, the Chechen stripped off the blood-stained bandage, and looked closely.

"Dear, dear, dear! Not done anything to it, have they!"

Grabbing the bottle from the youth, he poured vodka into the wound.

Viktor winced and groaned.

"Be a man. Sit and bear it."

He took another look, then got the youth to replace the bandage.

"Why, knowing the customer's always right, take the Feds on?"

"They were drunk and and they were burning someone alive."

"Did you see who?"

He shook his head.

"Weren't *you* drunk?"

Again he shook his head.

"Weren't you celebrating your little friend's birthday?" the Chechen asked with a tight-lipped smile.

Viktor shrugged.

"His idea was that if you had any sense you wouldn't be here. Now, what I want to know is, why were you asking about me?"

So this at last was Khachayev in person. He tried to concentrate, collect his thoughts, but was foiled by a fresh wave of pain.

"Sent by our friends of Fed Security to sort me out, that's you, isn't it?"

Viktor shook his head, gesture being easier than speech.

"Let's not beat about the bush. I've no great desire to hear you scream. Moscow lifestyle, man of education, father of children, that's me. Don't make me get tough, and supply Russian TV with yet another Chechen atrocity to be outraged by. Where did you get my name?"

It was now or never, Viktor thought.

"When you came from Moscow, you brought a penguin called Misha . . ."

"I brought a wife and children, too. Fed Security knows that.

What it doesn't, is that they're no longer here. And it won't be you who tells them."

"I'm from Kiev," said Viktor. "I looked for you in Moscow. You see, it's my penguin. But he came into the possession of a certain banker, and then into yours."

"Rather like you," he laughed. "Why do you lot keep coming? I'm not fighting. I've not interfered with you. And in Moscow I minded my own business. An ordinary teacher of Physics and History, that's me. Reared on your great Russian literature, and Gorky, its glory. What about you?"

"Kiev's where I'm from, not Russia."

His eyes showed a glimmer of interest. "So you're Ukrainian. Well, have you got a Gorky?"

Viktor had not the strength to rise to that one.

"Some nations – we Chechens being one – have an inborn sense of their own worth – in the genes, in the blood. Which others need tyranny and an ideology to achieve . . . And I tell you this, you've only to swap tyranny and an ideology for democracy, and that's it! Nations that do, are slaves of their own impotence again. An inborn sense of national worth is more powerful than any political system. Which is the one reason why you Russians fight us. We've got it, you haven't."

"We aren't fighting you."

"Who are you Ukrainians fighting?"

"Nobody."

Khachayev shook his head. "Bad. Fighting amongst yourselves, then . . . Now, let's have your story."

"I've told you the truth. My passports are back there in the hut."

"How many?"

"Two. My real Ukrainian and a false Polish."

Khachayev laughed. "You'll never guess how many I've got! A passport proves damn all. Mine says I'm Russian, born Ryazan."

Distant bursts of automatic fire sent Khachayev rushing from the room, shouting an order to the two youths as he went.

The youth with the automatic took aim at Viktor's head.

Viktor closed his eyes. The shot deafened him. He sat, ears buzzing, not knowing if he was alive or dead, until he heard Khachayev shouting in Chechen, and opening his eyes, saw him haranguing the youth, having taken the automatic from him.

The walkie-talkie broke in. Snapping a reply and barking some order, Khachayev strode out.

Thrown back into the pit, Viktor heard further automatic fire in the distance.

56

That night Aza and others came with torch and rope ladder, and soon Viktor was sitting on his bed in his room, with Aza, pale, anxious and concerned in the candle light, sitting on Seva's bed handing him a Pooh Bear mug of steaming tea.

"Drink, there's work to do."

"Where's Seva?"

Aza smiled but said nothing.

"Had enough tea? Like some vodka?"

Viktor shook his head.

"Let's go, then."

It was snowing lightly, and Viktor followed Aza on automatic pilot, aware of two faceless men treading the snow behind them.

In the chilly shed, Aza lit candles, and while Viktor was wondering where the others were, they entered carrying a body.

"Get it going," said Aza handing him a box of matches.

"Where's Seva?"

"Gone," grumbled Aza.

Viktor went through the drill, and got the furnace going.

"We've to speed up," said Aza, "and be through by morning. The boss is coming."

"Be through what?" Viktor asked, but Aza had gone.

The corpse was clearly Chechen, as were the men with it who, until they spoke, he had taken for Feds. They shot the corpse head first into the furnace, and as Viktor closed the doors he heard their receding footsteps. He thought they had gone, but a few minutes later they returned with another body which they laid on the ground.

"Any more?" asked Viktor, beginning to grasp Aza's call for speed.

"Three."

"What time is it?"

A Chechen lit his watch for Viktor to see. 11.30! Not, as he'd been imagining, getting on for dawn!

57

Dozing, he dreamt an uneasy dream in which he was both himself and a tiny yacht, subject to the elements but still capable of happiness. He had sailed off, neglectful of sail and wind, and as himself was sitting open-eyed on deck looking at Seva and militiaman Sergey, who were sitting silently beside him looking at each other, waiting almost disinterestedly for something to happen – land to appear or Misha to come back. Yes, come back, though no-one in this dream knew from where, not knowing where he'd disappeared to. Out of the watery depths, most likely, popping up like a cork. But nothing was happening. Rousing himself, he checked the pockets of his warm Emergency Services trousers and jacket, and from an inner one pulled a sheet of paper folded into four – a child's poster depicting a lost penguin and offering a reward. Oblivious to his fussy searching of pockets, Seva and Sergey sat quietly on.

Refolding the poster, he tucked it away in his pocket, and instantly forgetting it, now joined in waiting for Misha. Eyes fixed on the deck, he missed the gradual dissolving into thin air of Seva and Sergey, leaving him completely alone.

"Where," demanded someone surfacing in the warm sea, "does the ash go?"

He shrugged, a hand seized him by his right shoulder throwing him off balance, and overboard he went, hitting disconcertingly solid water.

"Give him a slap," said another voice.

He opened his eyes. Standing over him were the two Chechens, one holding the raking tool.

"Where does the ash go?"

"Carrier bags – behind the metal drum," he said, pointing.

"What's wrong with a bucket?"

"Who's coming to collect?"

"Dump it under a tree, we were told."

"Well, do that," said Viktor, puzzled by such indifference to the disposal of Chechen ashes.

*

The tiny bead of gold in the last of the three buckets of ash and charred bone he emptied next morning, which set him thinking of Seva and his dream of a good life. At that moment a green Russian jeep appeared, with Khachayev driving, Aza beside him, and two young Chechens bristling with weapons in the back. Motioned to get in, he sat with the Chechens, and the discomfort of a hand grenade pressed against his thigh.

For a long while they followed the winding forest track, climbing steadily, coming at last to a deserted village and open iron gates.

Aza and the bodyguards jumped out, and Khachayev turned to Viktor with the bleak expression appropriate to addressing the condemned.

"Well, I trust that today we shall finish our conversation. As you can see, I'm not now in the mood for cock-and-bull yarns."

"What's happened?"

"Seems you were right. Some Fed regulars raped and beat up a Chechen girl, and shoved her in my furnace. Alive. Chechen guerillas caught up with them, got the truth out of them, chopped their heads off, then burnt your friend Seva alive. So we shot the guerillas. You burnt the bodies. And I've enforced my neutrality. All very logical."

At that moment Aza appeared and came over to them.

"One's a write-off – TB. The other's not fit, but they're offering good money."

"How much?"

"A thousand."

Khachayev thought for a minute.

"Fetch him. They've a week to pay, tell them."

The bodyguards returned with a lean, ginger, whispy-bearded, hook-nosed young man in tattered army uniform, looking, under his stubble, much like an Ingush or a Dagestani.

For the return journey he was squeezed in with Viktor and the two Chechens on the back seat. It was impossible to talk to him across the Chechens. He seemed dead to the world, and for the latter part of the drive he slept.

By the time they reached Aza's hut it was dark. Aza and the soldier got out. The rest of them drove on.

58

At Khachayev's

But for the candlelight, wartime iron-plated door with spy hole, two impressive locks and armed guard, it might have been a first-floor flat room in any city.

Khachayev said something that sent the guard scuttling down the wooden stairs, then lit a fat candle in the middle of a massive round table. Later, a generator roared into life. The bulbs of the chandelier flickered feebly, then grew steadily brighter, finally lighting the whole room.

Snuffing out the candle, Khachayev sat down at the table, motioning Viktor to sit opposite.

Viktor looked with surprise at the piano, the sideboard-cum-drinks cabinet, the portraits of Gorky and Shamil. The one jarring note was provided by the automatic and two Kalashnikovs reposing on an occasional table.

"How about a spot of Dutch courage?" said Khachayev, removing his camouflage jacket, throwing it on the couch and making for the drinks cabinet. Wearing jeans and a grubby blue sweater, he looked most unlike a Chechen or guerilla.

"Let's, to make it easier for you, start at the beginning," he smiled, returning with a bottle of Martell and cut-glass tumblers. "Who are you?"

Viktor told all, from advance-obituary writing and funerals-with-penguin to Banker Bronikovsky. Of the latter's widow and his own meagre existence he made no mention, but enlarged on the events of Andrey Pavlovich's election campaign and their experience of image makers.

Khachayev listened, nodding, pouring cognac, and when the bottle was empty, fetched another.

"Not a dull life you lead," he said, going over to the couch to retrieve a ringing walkie-talkie from his jacket and respond to the call.

"And all very interesting," he continued, returning to the table and placing the walkie-talkie beside the bottle. "But can you substantiate any part of it?"

"I could by ringing Andrey Pavlovich."

"Ring the US President, if you like. What's this Andrey's number?"

Khachayev crossed to the phone and dialled.

"Answerphone," he said wearily, replacing the receiver.

"Try my flat," suggested Viktor. "Nina will vouch for me. She knows about my penguin."

"Number?"

He dialled.

"Hello, Nina? . . . Where? . . . Who are you, then? Sonya?"

He passed the phone to Viktor.

"Sonya, it's me, Uncle Viktor!"

"In Moscow?"

"No, a long way away. I've found Misha, but they may not let us go. It's not easy to explain."

"Not let you go? How do you mean?"

"Speak to the other uncle here. Perhaps he'll believe *you*."

He passed the receiver to Khachayev.

"Sonya, this uncle you've been talking to," he said, eyeing Viktor, "do you know him well?"

"He's my Daddy."

"Daddy or uncle?"

"Daddy. So *you've* got Misha."

"Yes. But which: uncle or Daddy?"

"Are you going to let them go?"

"Who?"

"Uncle Viktor and Misha."

"Hang on, first you tell me –"

"No. You promise you will let them go. Misha's got a bad heart, in case you didn't know."

"All right, I promise, but –"

"Give your word, swear on the head of your mother!"

"I give my word, I swear on the head of my mother I will let them go! Now will you answer my question!"

"Viktor's my second Daddy. My first went away and disappeared. But where's Misha? Is he with you?"

"No."

"*When* will you let them go?"

"Soon. But that's it for now. Goodbye, Sonya."

"Can I speak again to Uncle Viktor?"

"Not at inter-city rates!" he snapped, replacing the receiver, then felled Viktor with a punch.

"You have set me up," he said, with no special rancour.

"How?"

"She – that little girl – got me to give my word."

"But will you keep it?" Viktor asked warily.

"The word of a Chechen is worth a hundred of your promises . . . Do you understand?"

In fear of another outburst of temper and hopes of relieving the tension, Viktor reached into his inner pocket, took out Sonya's poster and laid it on the table.

Picking it up, Khachayev examined Sonya's penguin under the far from steady light of the chandelier, then spoke into his walkie-talkie.

"Aslan will take you back," he said.

Viktor made as if to retrieve the poster, but Khachayev shook his head, opened the door and gave him charge of the guard.

59

Aslan yawned. "Give him half an hour in the dog cage, then take him to Aza's," Khachayev had said. A funny sort of order, but as he'd learnt in the Red Army, an order was an order, and still was. Just that the amount of ferrying involved left so little time for sleep. But should the Alsatians make a meal of this Russian – as might be the idea – the run to Aza's would be out, and sleep back on. But no, he'd have the body to take, to Aza's, blood and all. Without Khachayev's furnace there'd be Fed graves and headstones in the Chechen forests, there'd be monuments – such as he'd stood guard over in Treptow – federalizing Chechnya, destroying it. Khachayev had the right idea.

Another half hour and they were there. The main gates were shut, but as there was a side gate giving access to the cage, he saw no need to rouse the place and go into explanations.

At Aslan's approach the dogs pricked up their ears, sniffed the air, but did not bark. They, like Chechens, were cunning. Without a sound they'd get you by the throat, and that was it.

Aslan opened the door a little and squatted down. Dzhoka trotted lightly over, sniffed him, looked him in the eye.

"How about some nice Russian meat?" Aslan asked, resisting the urge to stroke him. He and Dzhoka were equals. Told to seize, they seized.

Aslan woke Viktor and led him to the cage, which was, Viktor saw though half asleep and through a flurry of snow, a metal cage about the size of Khachayev's sitting room containing a number of roughly-fashioned dog kennels. Aslan jostled him through the door, and sleepily he took several steps forward. The door closed behind him, and turning he was in time to see Aslan glance at his watch and light a cigarette before heading back to the jeep.

Viktor stood alone in the falling snow, hardly daring to breathe, rooted almost tree-like to the spot, with five Alsatians regarding him from their kennels. If one charged, the others would follow. Had he time to escape? He didn't dare look round at the door to see how it was fastened – the slightest movement might be his last. This, then, was how Khachayev kept faith. But similarly placed, might not he have done the same?

But the dogs had not charged.

Out of the corner of an eye, he saw something move. Without turning his head, he squinted to the uttermost, and saw, waddling to a food bowl by the kennels, a *penguin*. Bending, it picked something from the bowl. It wasn't at all like Misha. It was some other penguin, shorter, thinner.

"Misha!" he called softly, all else forgotten, and the penguin looked at him through the falling snow.

Still the dogs did not move.

The snow eased.

He called again, louder.

The penguin took several steps towards him, stopped, fixed him with his tiny button eyes for a while, then advanced and stared up at him.

Seeing the dogs still sitting or standing, Viktor took a deep breath and slowly eased himself down to the penguin's level.

The penguin came closer.

Heedless now of the dogs, Viktor reached out, stroked its breast, and feeling a long scar, knew at last that it was Misha.

With Misha pressed against his knee, the past with all its warmth and sense of life worth living came flooding back. He reached out to smoothe Misha's flippers, but drew his hand back, deterred by a sudden growling. Absurd though it seemed, the dogs were being protective. The absurd was here amazingly real. Life here was ruled by it.

"Time to go," came a voice.

"Are we taking the penguin?" he asked, turning to Aslan. "Khachayev promised to release him."

"Hasn't said anything to me about it. Come on."

Would surprises, the survival of this Russian not least amongst them, never cease?

Viktor straightened up, and watched in amazement as Misha, or what remained of him, shuffled off to one of the kennels, and ducking awkwardly, entered it.

No sooner were they clear of the village than Viktor fell asleep on his back seat. Glancing back at him, Aslan concluded that since the dogs had not set tooth in him, this was a Russian of the harmless sort. They weren't wolves, Khachayev's Alsatians – gutless slaves, and the sick were safe from them.

60

Woken by the cold, Viktor found himself lying fully dressed on his own bed at Aza's, where Aslan must have deposited him. Seeing the window wide open, he jumped up and shut it. The bed that had been Seva's was empty. He sat down for a moment on his own, then went and had a wash.

The place seemed deserted, but outside, a fabulous carpet of snow sparkling in the sun sent spirits soaring, and thoughts back to the dog cage, finding Misha, and Khachayev's promise to Sonya. Well done Sonya!

He smiled. Now he had simply to wait for him to act upon it. Nothing difficult about that. It was like seeing in orders that your demob was due. Bubbling with energy, he had a sudden urge to turn cartwheels, fling himself down, do press-ups – anything to let off steam, demonstrate that life went on. Passing the half-open door of Aza's room, he took a peep inside, noting with interest the settee upholstered in leather cracked with age, the file-laden school desk, the occasional table with decanter and glasses, the ancient Sony radio.

On top of the files was Aza's ledger. Viktor went in and examined it. The names and places of birth were a geography lesson in themselves. Of the recent entries, 856 and 857, had dashes in lieu of both. 857 would have been Seva. To keep records was to breed secrets. He thought back to that dream where he, Seva and Sergey had been together on the yacht. Seva, yes, but why Sergey?

Idly he leafed back through the pages, and there, for 13th of February 1997, in Aza's round childish hand, he read with incredulity: Stepanenko, Sergey, Kiev.

He banged the ledger shut and for a long while sat at the desk, reliving the picnic he, Sergey and Misha had enjoyed on the Dnieper ice, and their eventful New Year celebration at Sergey's dacha, when Sonya had been with them.

How very strange that he, having no idea of the existence of this private crematorium, should still have been both directly and indirectly linked with it by the urn on the window ledge in his kitchen in Kiev!

61

Two hours later as Viktor lay, vitality spent, staring at the ceiling and awaiting demob, Aza returned.

"Up we get! Here's Ginger to be taught the job. Work's on its way. So teach him, or burn."

Ginger, Viktor learnt, as they crunched their way through the snow to the shed, was Vasya from Archangel in the far Russian north.

"How about food?" he asked.

"Vermicelli, and come Fat Friday, army tinned meat."

"Why fat?"

"Because Thursday night's a discount burning."

"Of what?"

"Best I explain when we're there."

And when there, Vasya listened open-mouthed, but quickly cottoned on.

"Better a hot furnace than a cold pit," Viktor threw in at some stage.

"So you've been there."

His nod earned him greater deference.

"So it's feet first?"

"Other way round. You use the legs to shove."

"How about a bit of heat now?"

"Not till dark, because of the smoke."

When darkness fell, Vasya proved a quick learner.

"And when's Fat Friday?"

"We'll ask Aza," said Viktor, having lost count.

62

Fat Friday fell two days later, producing a half-litre tin of pork to augment their vermicelli soup.

"We had this when we were stationed at Mozdok," Vasya said in surprise, examining the tin.

After breakfast Viktor retired to bed, only to be woken at midday by the noise and vibration of two Sukhoy fighter bombers passing low overhead.

Outside he found Aza taking his ease on a felled tree trunk.

"Has Khachayev said anything about me?"

"Should he have?"

"He's letting me go. He's given his word."

"If he's given his word, he will let you go."

"Where were Seva's ashes put?"

"Drum in the corner."

"Perhaps they should be sent to his home. Have we an address?"

"We have, but no postal service. Not unless you fix something with the Feds and pay for it."

"I could, I suppose, or I could take them and post them from Kiev."

"I'll give you his address. His are on top in the drum. No-one's been added since him."

"I need a bigger bag," Viktor said, thinking of having to carry Misha.

"I'll give you some canvas. You can make one."

Returning to his room, he got out a Marlboro carrier bag from under his bed, folded it neatly and put it in his jacket pocket. Vasya was asleep, and to judge from the movement of his lips and the half-smile on his face, dreaming pleasant dreams.

He made his way to the shed and the well-filled drum of unclaimed ashes, got his carrier bag ready and fetched a spade. He half-filled the bag, and thinking that wasn't quite enough, dug into the ashes again, this time striking something solid. He shovelled this spadeful into the bag, then plunged his arm in and fished out Seva's gold brick, weighing a good seven kilos, if not more.

He left the shed with the carrier bag in one hand and the gold brick in the other. Outside, he put the carrier down on the snow and wiping some of the ash from the brick, saw that it had precious and semi-precious stones embedded in it. He pushed the brick down into the ashes, and carried the bag in his arms for fear the handles would break.

63

Another Fat Friday came and went, and Viktor lost his appetite. He and Vasya had worked well together, harmoniously even, and Vasya had come on well, doing and saying nothing to irritate him. His response to Viktor was that of raw recruit to hardened old soldier. He did exactly what he was told, and Viktor made a good superior. As Vasya had put it early on, after life in his Mozdok unit and freezing and starving in the Chechen pit, here, offshore, with the nightly sauna of the shed, was a holiday. Only from time to time, the excessive dryness of the heat produced an unpleasant taste in the mouth forcing them out into the chilly night for a quiet chat with, whenever the Chechen sky cleared itself of cloud, a pause for silent contemplation. The stars of this winter sky were of the same magnitude as those of southern Ukraine or northern Archangel. They were common to all those stars, though Chechens refused to concede as much, despite having sun and moon in common with Russians and Ukrainians.

Feds came and went with their corpses. Chechens put in a rarer appearance. Vasya's pockets bulged with small dollar bills and rouble notes, at night a source of anxiety with the thieving of army life still fresh in his memory. Of his own anxieties and growing sense of grievance concerning Khachayev and his promise, Viktor said nothing.

Then, stoking of passage stove completed and with Monday inclining to an early sunset, Viktor was about to join Vasya, who was sitting outside smoking, when the familiar jeep turned up, Aslan driving, Khachayev in the back.

Dismissing Vasya to the furnace shed, Khachayev, in Viktor's room, sat on Vasya's bed and producing a half-litre bottle of cognac, lit the bedside candle.

"Any glasses?"

Viktor brought Pooh Bear mugs.

"Pity no penguins," said Khachayev, pouring for them both. "Now listen. You go first solo, together's not on. From Taganrog you make your own way, and I'll call within a fortnight."

"You've got my number?"

"And Andrey Pavlovich's. So drink up!"

He poured Viktor another.

"Good luck!"

Viktor felt suddenly he couldn't care less. Thoughts, wishes ceased to exist. The future became a haze. Another minute and his past would vanish, he would no longer remember who he was, where he was from or his place of birth. There were now two candle flames where there had been one. The bed rocked beneath him like a raft or yacht in heavy seas. He rolled forward, then back, banged his back against the wall, then his head in a way that made the wound in his temple throb.

"Put him in the jeep," Khachayev ordered Aza and Aslan who came running to his call. "And don't forget his things. Probably under his bed."

"It's heavy," said Aza, dragging Viktor's home-made bag out.

"Open it."

Putting it on the bed, Aza undid the three greatcoat buttons fastening it, and was about to rummage inside, when Khachayev passed him the Pooh Bear mug.

"Stick that in and do the bag up. We don't poke about in other people's things."

Aza put the bag on the floor behind the driver, Khachayev got in beside Aslan, and the jeep drove off, retracing its furrows in the snow.

*

Three hours later the jeep stopped and switched off its headlights. Three helicopters flew over towards the mountains, Khachayev followed the sound, leaning back against the jeep, grim-faced. A little later, a minivan displaying a red cross on a green background drew up, two Russians in battle fatigues got out, exchanged greetings, then transferred Viktor and his canvas bag to their minivan.

"Three boxes of Spanish disposable syringes and some super antibiotic three days from now," said one of the Russians. "Bring them?"

"Yes," said Khachayev, "but first get this chap away, safe, sound, and with his gear intact exactly as I've promised."

The Russian nodded.

Shortly after, the vehicles went their separate ways, each retracing its own tread marks in the snow. Overhead, the clouds parted and a steely wedge of moonlight shone forth.

64

For the sake of physical and psychological wellbeing, some frontiers are best crossed in the state of unconsciousness that was Viktor's entering and leaving Chechnya. But the ticket clerk at Taganrog station took one look at him, and shook her head, sorely tempted to inform this young man that two weeks ago a nephew of hers had died of a drugs overdose in Nikolayev.

Having more than an hour to kill, he spotted a beer kiosk, and beside it, an inebriated old man selling dried fish.

Totting up his roubles, Viktor decided he could indulge himself. Still unsteady on his feet, he bought a bottle of Baltika and a dried fish. The beer went down easily, the fish less so. A second bottle left him inclined to stay on here by the beer kiosk, until an idle glance at the clock betrayed that he had ten minutes to catch his train.

"Hi, don't forget your bag!" cried the dried fish man, and Viktor, slowed by the weight of it, only just made the train in time.

65

Kiev was freezing. The sixteen-hour journey largely spent sleeping, had banished the effects of whatever drug he had been given. Squatting, he felt in his bag, encountered cold metal, and had a good look. The gold brick lay at the bottom, no longer wrapped, with, he had been amazed to find, the Pooh Bear mug. That the brick should have survived road block checks and got through customs at the Russo-Ukrainian border, beggared belief. It was all there: credit card, both passports, and a wad of the small-value dollar bills regarded with suspicion in Kiev and usually rejected.

Washing his hands in the station toilet and seeing himself in the mirror, hairy, head in filthy bandage, he marvelled that he'd not been pulled in by the Taganrog militia.

He washed his face, and had another look in the mirror. He must get home quick before he did get pulled in. But what was this? Three medals pinned to the breast of his jacket! Someone's idea of a joke. On the point of removing them, he thought better of it, shoved his hands into his pockets and in one of them found a card – a creased and grubby army pass in the name of Kovalyov, Sergey Fyodorovich, Sergeant. The photo could, at a pinch, have been him.

Leaving the toilet he came face to face with a military patrol, an officer and two cadets. One cadet, on the point of saluting Viktor and seeing that his officer wasn't, desisted. Not everyone in camouflage battledress was a genuine veteran.

The patrol went its way.

"Drive you cheap," offered a freelance driver outside the station.

"$10?"

"Fine."

He was about to take Viktor's bag, but Viktor forestalled him.

66

"God!" exclaimed Nina aghast, opening the door as Viktor stood on the WELCOME mat searching vainly for his keys. "Come in."

Underfoot, a cat mewed.

Sitting on the floor, he removed his boots, and unwound his discoloured puttees.

"Where ever have you been?"

Lashes black with mascara, not a hair out of place, she wore a blue sarafan and fur slippers, and looked a good ten years older.

"Taganrog. Where's Sonya?"

"At her friend Tanya's on the second floor . . . Not a happy family," she added, with a note of maternal concern that was new to him. "The brother's on the militia register of offenders, the father who's a car park watchman, drinks . . . But what have you done to your head? Banged against something?"

"Someone banged it for me. Is there a bandage anywhere?"

"Yes." She hurried out to the kitchen.

Viktor ran a bath, deliberately not looking in the mirror. The long-forgotten sound of running water was wonderful.

"Nina!" he called, addressing the little window above the bath, "How about some tea? And is there anything for lunch?"

"Soon will be," came her gentle, compliant voice.

Stripping off his clothes, he at last stood in front of the mirror contemplating his long unwashed body and filthy bandage. He was about to take that off too when he spotted the disposable razor, brush and soap, and decided to shave.

Once in the bath, he felt like immersing himself completely, but didn't because of the bandage. These last few hours, curiously, his wound had pained him not at all.

From the kitchen came other long-forgotten domestic sounds: table-laying, the clink of a saucepan.

The kitchen door squeaked open as Nina came into the corridor.

"Don't touch that!" he called, hearing a clink of metal from his bag.

"Don't worry, just moving it under the coat pegs."

Now someone was knocking at the outer door when they could have rung.

"Auntie Nina! Tanya's bitten my finger! I want something on it!" came Sonya's voice. "And whose bag is that?"

"Daddy's. He's back."

The bathroom door opened, as he'd forgotten it could be from the outside, and there, open mouthed, in red knitted leggings and green sweater, she was.

"So they did let you go! Hi! Where's Misha?"

"Coming."

"Did they hurt you?"

He nodded.

"Like me!" She held up her right index finger, brown with iodine. "We were playing doctors. I was seeing to her teeth."

"Come and help me," called Nina, "let Daddy have his bath."

"I'll do his back!"

"Next time," said Viktor.

Sonya shrugged and left the bathroom.

*

They ate in silence. Sergey's urn, he was quick to notice, was where it belonged, on the window ledge by the gas stove, and the effect of it was calming. Even so, as he munched sausage and fried potatoes, his eyes returned to it, as they did not to Nina, now dressed, with make-up renewed.

Sitting between them, Sonya looked curiously from one to the other, but kept her peace.

After lunch Nina removed the bandage, swabbed the wound with hydrogen peroxide, dressed it, and seeing how it pained him, said he must go to a doctor.

"What day of the week is it?"

"Tuesday."

67

The half-hour drive in snow to Theophania cost him 20 hryvnas.

Entering the gates of the Hospital for Scientists he made his way to the Veterinary Clinic. An attractive girl in glasses and a sheepskin jacket was walking an emaciated Alsatian having trouble with its back legs.

"Come on, Caesar!" she was coaxing.

Following the well-trodden path to the entrance, he went up to the first floor and knocked at the veterinary surgeon's door.

Just as at Viktor's last visit some months earlier, white-coated Ilya Semyonovich was seated at his desk.

"You've been before – with a penguin. Where's he now?"

"Some way off at the moment."

"So?"

Viktor raised a hand to his bandage.

"Could you examine me?"

"It's a long time since I switched from humans to animals."

"You're the only medical man I know."

"Sit on the couch."

Removing the bandage and putting on his glasses, he bent low over the wound.

"How long have you had this?"

"Several weeks."

From a glass-fronted cabinet Ilya Semyonovich took tweezers, cotton wool and disinfectant.

"Be brave, this'll hurt," he warned, dipping the tweezers in disinfectant and probing the wound.

Viktor clenched his teeth, closed his eyes, his whole body racked with pain.

"Got it! Lie back for a bit."

As he lay staring at the ceiling, the agony abated, leaving him with an intense burning sensation in his right temple.

"Well, Mr Emergency Service, think you'll live?" Ilya Semyonovich laughed. "You get up and see what I found."

It was a piece of bottle glass the size of a two-kopek piece.

"There'll be a scar, of course. It was deep, near the bone. Come and see me in a couple of days."

"What do I owe you?"

"Let's put it this way: humans I now treat as a hobby, free of charge. But also I'll accept no complaint concerning the treatment. You came of your own free will."

68

That evening, while Nina and Sonya were watching some Mexican TV serial in the sitting room, Viktor shut himself in the kitchen, got his typewriter out from under the table, dusted it off and inserted a sheet of paper. He had an urge to busy himself with something, get away from a tangle of conflicting thoughts – thoughts leaping now to Chechnya, now to a remoter past, only to come suddenly up against the question "What now?" It was a question suspended in weightlessness, and he had the feeling of being similarly suspended, looking down to check that his feet were on the floor and the law of gravity operative.

He stared at the white sheet of paper, but his brain refused to function. It was becoming internal, this weightlessness, prior to becoming external again, and beginning to irritate. At long last, he did actually type the words "What now?" and felt better for it. Materialized, turned into text, the question ceased to occupy his thoughts.

By way of the sitting room and Nina and Sonya watching TV, he betook himself to the bedroom, and closing the door behind him, snuggled under the double feather duvet. Dreaming later of another body beside him, he moved away to the edge of the bed.

★

Next morning he slept till 11.00. Nina had gone out, but Sonya, catching him as he emerged in underpants and singlet from the bedroom, tackled him about Misha.

"He'll be here soon," he reassured her.

Happy, she went back to practising her letters.

He went to the kitchen, put the kettle on, and seeing the typewriter, was about to put it back under the table, when he noticed that the paper had other typing on it, and read:

> What now? you ask, Viktor. I don't know. I'd still like us to be a family – you, me and Sonya. I will, if you want, bear your child, then all will be better. It will. Someone I know also had problems with her husband until they had children. Promising to obey, and begging your forgiveness over Kolya.
>
> Love, Nina

Pulling the sheet from the typewriter, he read it again, shaking his head as if to dispel some delusion.

Whatever had come over her? Bear him a child? What nonsense!

He replaced the sheet in the typewriter intending to type a reply, but returned the machine to its place under the table instead, and looked out of the window.

The snow was dazzling in the sun. A middle-aged woman was pushing a pram past the block opposite. He stared for a while at Old Tonya's window, recalling his childhood. It was now he felt the lack of roots, or simply of threads linking his today with his past. It was like being torn from life by one's very flesh, like existing in some virtual, non-real world. Being seen or merely noticed by too few to feel real himself, perhaps no more than a spectre registered here, at this flat, with no right to quit its walls.

God, but he must go somewhere! Enjoy himself, breathe the frosty air! Break out of here, recover his Kiev, his own proper element! Look someone up! But who?

He thought of Lyosha, who was no longer taking himself anywhere, and would always be found in the same place.

Hanging in the corridor was his MoES jacket. It went against the grain to put it on, but it was all he had.

69

Walking, free of the encumbrance of towelling puttees and overlarge boots, along less than busy wintery Kreshchatik Street, he had the feeling of being home at last. Looking into Central Universal Stores for a bit of warmth, he was amazed to see New Year decorations on display. Recapturing the feel of a city was clearly not enough in itself. Where it and its life stood in time had to coincide with one's own account of time.

Returning to Kreshchatik Street, he looked back at the Trade Union House tower with its non-stop display of data by courtesy of Adidas: −12°C . . . 13h36m . . . 17 Dec. . . . He waited till the cycle of data and images was complete, then set off in the direction of Independence Square.

*

Café Afghan was open but empty. The low tables and absence of chairs no longer struck him as odd. What was new was the second room. Stamping the snow from his boots, he went in.

The second room contained the low billiard table, and against the wall were three one-armed bandits of American films of the '70s, looking thoroughly at home. Inserting a 50-kopek piece, he pulled the lever that set the three drums spinning. Two plums and one banana was the result. Returning to the first room, he tapped the coffee machine with a coin.

"Coming!" said an unfamiliar man's voice, and shortly after, a man in a wheelchair appeared, aged about 40, wearing a tracksuit. He had all his limbs but the use only of some.

"Is Lyosha about?"

"What do you want with him?"

"We're old friends. I'd like to see him."

The man grimaced.

"Lyosha's gone off the rails. Taken to drink."

"Where is he?"

"Hostel next door."

*

Lyosha's door was not locked. Stale air, squalor, empty bottles greeted him. In one corner, an overturned wheelchair, in another, a bed, and Lyosha, fully dressed, one empty trouser leg dangling to the floor, asleep, head deep in a pillow.

"Lyosha!"

Lyosha turned his head to the wall. Red face, tangled hair, tangled beard, he looked the typical destitute vagrant.

Viktor shook him by the shoulder. "Come on," he urged.

Lyosha turned onto his back, and looking up at him, reached down for a bottle. "What the hell are *you* doing here?" he asked raising it to his lips.

"Come to see you."

"Like a drink?"

"No."

"Then go and get me some. I'll pay you back. Just had a rise in my disablement pension."

"Hang on. I'll be back."

The driver of the ancient Moskvich was either anxious to oblige or very hard up. For ten hryvnas he not only agreed to drive a disabled passenger, but also to help Viktor carry him up four floors. The folded wheelchair went with difficulty into the boot.

"Where are you taking me?" Lyosha demanded.

"To my place. To get you straight."

"What for?"

"To get you back in shape."

"Balls! What do you really want? The election's done!"

"Nothing," said Viktor with growing irritation. "I owe you! You got my penguin a job."

Lyosha looked at him in amazement. "Did I? I remember getting the money for his operation."

"Look, I want to help. You're the only one left here I can help."

"Like me, I've no-one. So let's be friends and play chess," he said bitterly.

"No, sod you, it's clean you up, get you straight, then bung you back in your filthy hole!"

For the rest of the way neither spoke.

70

There was no-one in, and the first thing Viktor did was run a bath, while Lyosha sat in the corridor staring dully at a saucer of milk.

"Swapped the penguin for a cat?"

Ignoring the question, Viktor helped him undress and then into the bath.

"Don't worry – I'm at Tanya's," announced Sonya poking her head in, then darting away.

Viktor passed Lyosha the loofah and the soap. "Have a bath while I get us something to eat."

The sound of splashing made him think of Misha and his cold water baths, as he took macaroni from the kitchen cupboard. And where was he now? Still with the dogs? And when would Khachayev make good his promise? They were now both a bit like Misha, he and Lyosha, helpless, waiting . . . For what? Food? Warmth? Though warmth, in Misha's case, was out.

Viktor helped Lyosha dry himself, get into an old tracksuit of Viktor's, and, with an effort, wheel himself into the kitchen.

By the time Nina returned, they were eating macaroni.

"This is Lyosha," said Viktor. "He'll be staying for a bit."

"Sleeping where?"

"We'll decide."

"Trouble there," Lyosha whispered, when Nina had gone.

"It's my flat. Like some tea?"

"No vodka?"

"No vodka."

"So, tea, damn you – with plenty of sugar."

★

Sonya having refused the visitor her couch, Lyosha's bed, to which he raised no objection, was two armchairs pulled together in the sitting room.

Waking next morning to a strange sensation, and opening half

406

an eye, Lyosha found a cat licking his face. He blew at it. The cat turned lazily away. Raising himself on an elbow, he saw Sonya asleep on her couch, recalled yesterday and Café Afghan. Then, ears strained to the silence, stealthily lowered himself to the floor and crawled, baby-fashion, only on his stumps. Thirsty, he drank what remained of the cat's milk in the corridor, then pressed on to the kitchen. Here, reading the sheet left in the typewriter, he had instantly the feeling of assisting at a funeral which, unlike those he'd officiated at, involved nearest and dearest. He wished he could help. Opening the fridge, he found no vodka.

71

Lyosha's first few days of settling in were not easy, though some small distraction was provided by Sonya's directness. Which tram was it sliced his legs off, she asked. A Number 11, he told her, driven by a blind woman.

"Does it hurt where they're cut off?" she wanted to know.

"Usually it does, for quite a time, but with me it soon didn't."

"Do you know," she said after a moment's thought, "you'll make a good husband."

"How so?"

"By staying at home, not going mucking about. Have you any children?"

"No."

"Well there you are, you must get married."

Nina and Lyosha exchanged hardly a word. Meeting him, she smilingly withdrew to kitchen or bedroom, thinking heaven alone knew what. Amazed at her compliance, Viktor began to think more warmly of her, but still did not turn and embrace her in the double bed they shared at night.

Today, without a word, she set off for the post office with his parcel for Seva's parents, while he went to Theophania, where Ilya Semyonovich dressed his wound, declaring reassuringly that in a day or two he could leave off the bandage.

So life was slowly ordering itself. His one source of anxiety being the absence of any message from Khachayev.

"Will Misha be here for New Year?" Sonya kept asking. "Because if he is, he'll have to have a present."

And it was of New Year presents that he was thinking as he got down his bag from the top of the cupboard, and checked that his gold brick was safe. The film of ash still adhering to it prompted him to run the hot tap over it in an effort to wash away the horror and sorrow of its provenance.

Before returning the brick to the bag and the bag to the cupboard top, he rescued his Pooh Bear mug and took it with him to the kitchen, where he found Lyosha seated in his wheelchair at the table reading yesterday's papers bought at his request by Nina.

"Do you know," he said, "life, as Comrade Stalin was wont to say, 'is now jollier, more joyous'. For three months I didn't touch a newspaper, and started drinking. And now see what they write! In Russia 10,000 die annually from drinking home-brewed vodka, and in Ukraine 4000. How about that, then?"

"Another good reason for not drinking."

Lyosha laughed.

"As if one were needed. Getting champagne for New Year?"

"I shall be," said Viktor.

"Present for Sonya?" he asked, seeing the Pooh Bear mug.

"No, it's mine."

72

New Year minus 4

Changing his thick wad of messy $1 bills – uneasy tender in these parts – for a measly 230 hryvnas and recognizing the obvious, he returned to his flat for the banker's credit card.

As the cashpoint delivered the modest 1000 hryvnas requested, he half expected someone to snatch the notes from him. But there was no-one in the gently falling snow, only a man breaking the ice outside his fish restaurant with a crowbar.

Sonya, Nina, Lyosha, and maybe Svetlana, were the ones to buy presents for. His mood, as he entered Central Universal Stores, was expansive.

First, the toy department. Sonya, while clearly past the stage of Barbie Dolls, had not yet so clearly entered any other. He tried to remember what toys of hers he'd seen in the flat. Certainly no dolls. Ah, bitten finger! Hospitals, dentist . . .

The Doctor Doolittle stuff failed to appeal. What did, was a big plush penguin on a top shelf for 95 hryvnas. Making a further round of the shelves he lighted on a Doctor Kit, a plastic bag containing plastic syringe, tweezers, stethoscope and enema equipment.

After paying, he tried attaching the bag to the penguin, but without success.

For Nina he bought a large but inexpensive Turkish make-up box.

Next to Cosmetics, Gifts, with a tall girl dressed as the Snow Maiden.

"Come on, you men," she called, "just the present for the woman you love!"

And though he had at the moment no such woman, he was drawn to the little table displaying dainty coffee cups and saucers.

"Come on, don't be shy, read what the coffee grounds foretell."

By now a group of men had assembled.

"Demonstration coming up."

Transferring a spoonful of dregs from coffee pot to cup, she inverted the cup on its saucer and paused, conjuror-fashion, before displaying the very same erotic images he had seen in Moscow.

"Six cups and six saucers to the set, each with its own special surprise. See what the future holds in the way of love, money, happiness."

Were love and happiness different things, he wondered, and decided they were.

"Do you sell them separately?"

"Of course. One cup, one saucer 7 hryvnas, the set, 42 hryvnas. Which subject?"

"Love."

Her fingers, as she gift-wrapped the cup and saucer, were amazingly long and slender.

"Happy New Year!" she said, handing him the parcel.

For Lyosha the Bavarian beer mug for 200 hryvnas seemed just the thing – or would have been but for its connection with drink. Better the neutrality of the brown leather pocket book with a small appointments diary and calculator.

In the end, he bought nothing for Svetlana, not wanting to look her up, at least not at the moment.

*

Back at the flat, Sonya was taking Lyosha a cup of tea. She liked serving him in his helplessness, and he, though really far from helpless, was not averse to acting up.

"Two spoons, please. Though better three."

"Sugar's bad for you. One and a half's what you're getting, and you be thankful it's not just one. Have you any idea how many illnesses are due to sugar?"

"Diabetes for one."

"Is that in the tummy?"

"No, the blood."

"Tummy ache's another – you get that from the sugar in chocolate."

Drinking his tea, Lyosha looked out of the window. He was not very comfortable sitting at the kitchen table. He and Sonya were then of a height.

It was snowing. Lights were going on in the block opposite. Their light in the kitchen was on already. Turning to Sonya, who was sitting by the stove, he noticed the green urn on the window ledge.

"What's in that pot?"

"A friend of Uncle Viktor's, who died somewhere in Moscow. Auntie Nina put him out on the balcony, but when Uncle Viktor came home, he put him back here."

Lyosha fell silent, gloomily recalling the funerals that were once his job, the wakes, expensive coffins and the wonderful peace of the cemetery. Joyless beauty. Tranquillity.

"Drink up before it gets cold!" ordered Sonya. "Like me to make you a sausage sandwich? It's good sausage."

"Yes, please."

411

That evening, when they had eaten and were sitting in front of the telly, the phone rang, making Viktor jump.

Nina answered.

"For you," she told Viktor.

"Viktor?" asked a man's voice. "Got something for you . . . 10K and it's a swap."

"10K?"

"$10,000. Ring you where at noon tomorrow. And don't try anything. Cheers!"

"Who was it?" Nina asked anxiously.

"Misha's back."

"Hooray!" shouted Sonya, then saw Viktor's look of dismay.

"What's wrong?" Nina asked.

"It's the money. I thought they'd bring him free."

"You mean Misha," said Lyosha.

"Yes."

And suddenly Viktor saw what to do.

"I'll be late," he said, leaving the flat.

73

Roofs blanketed in snow, the odd fir tree hung with fairy lights, Goloseyevo was pure fairy tale.

At Andrey Pavlovich's, a good three metres of fairy-light fir. Pasha's 4 × 4 parked on the gravel suggested that he would be in if Andrey Pavlovich wasn't, and Pasha it was who opened the side gate in response to his button press.

"The Chief was only just talking about you!" he said happily. "Coffee?"

"Please."

"He'll be back in half an hour," said Pasha as they sat together in the kitchen. "Now he's a Deputy, he's almost always home before midnight."

"Deputy? Last time he was just an aide."

"Got in on the by-election. And really chuffed. Nice people there, he says, as well as a few, as there are everywhere, to drop by night over some bridge."

A car hooted and Pasha dashed out to open the gates for an official black Mercedes from which Andrey Pavlovich in a smart dark, almost ankle-length overcoat emerged.

The Mercedes drove off, and Pasha shut and locked the gates.

"Aha!" cried Andrey Pavlovich, looking into the kitchen. "Pasha said I'd a visitor. Welcome back! We must celebrate, like men!" he declared divesting himself of his overcoat and standing in his dark smart suit.

"Coffee's for the morning, for now it's cognac. Here or upstairs?"

"Here's more democratic," said Viktor, thinking the kitchen more appropriate to the favour he was about to ask.

"Cognac, Pasha!" he called, joining Viktor at the corner table. "And well said, now I'm a Democrat! National Demo's what I started as, but all that matters to that lot is talking Ukrainian – independence, economics, they come second. But what have you been up to in Moscow all this time?"

Viktor told him the whole story.

"Ten thousand, eh? Why don't we knock them off, free your penguin and give the money to charity?"

Viktor said nothing. Andrey Pavlovich bit his lips thoughtfully.

At this moment Pasha appeared with a bottle of Hennessy and suitable glasses, poured and quietly retired.

"Well, what do you see it as – loan or gift?"

"Loan."

"I take it you've something to secure it with?" he said with a mischievous smile. "Shares? A controlling interest preferably."

"I've a credit card, but don't know how much is in the account. And I've a great deal of gold."

"Is it clean?"

"No."

Andrey Pavlovich shook his head.

"Not something to offer a People's Deputy. Right, we'll have our drink and think of something."

He leant forward.

"Where did you get that scar?"

"From a Russian soldier's vodka bottle."

"Were there any Ukrainian hostages?"

"Just Russians."

"Pity, or we could have ransomed them. Russians we leave to the Russians. That scar! Wear it with pride! The door to People's Deputy's wide open to a scar like that! Now, what do we do about your penguin?"

"They're ringing tomorrow at noon."

"You're a good chap," said Andrey Pavlovich. "And with your brains it's high time you had a proper job earning real money. All well at home?"

"Yes."

"Hang on a minute."

He left the kitchen, and came back with an elastic-banded bundle of $100-bills which he placed on the table in front of Viktor. He was about to replenish their glasses, but seeing the look of alarm on Viktor's face, hesitated.

"What's up?"

"First hand to pour, pours all," said Viktor with Seva's birthday and its consequences in mind.

"Superstitious, eh? So be it. Pasha! Refills!"

"My security, when do you want it?" Viktor asked, when Pasha had gone.

"When, naked and hungry, I come to you asking for shelter, that's when," laughed Andrey Pavlovich. "No, take it as your first year's salary as my Assistant for Humanitarian Affairs. After all, you *are* our charity expert. Remember the artificial limbs?"

But Viktor was no longer listening. Misha and the means of ransoming him were what mattered. And why not work for his Andrey Pavlovich again? It would be better than sitting waiting for something to turn up. He must get back into life, earn some money . . .

"And your first job is to find some run-down orphanage, pick 20 or so deserving kids and have them here by noon on December 30th. For a tree and presents, you having alerted the press. Pasha will have got you phone numbers. Any problem?"

Viktor shook his head.

"Not kids from Kiev, though – the big boys are onto them. Pasha!" he shouted, "take Viktor home, and see the Chechens don't get him."

He turned to Viktor, who was stowing away the dollars in his MoES jacket.

"Still got my number?"

"I have."

"And here's $300 for clothes. Let this be the last time I see you in military uniform!"

74

New Year minus 3

Next morning the cat got under his feet as he was on his way to the bathroom, and again as he was putting on the kettle in the kitchen. Lyosha was getting up from his bed of chairs and into his wheelchair, awkwardly, and sighing loudly. Sonya was lying on the couch switching the TV channels in search of cartoons. Only Nina was quiet, lying gazing at the bedroom ceiling, thinking uneasily about the day ahead, how crowded the flat was with Lyosha, and how much worse it would be when Viktor brought Misha.

Viktor sat in the kitchen in a state of nerves. He checked yet again that the dollars were safe. He looked at the clock. 7.30. Quite early. It was still dark outside, except for the over-bright yellow light of the windows opposite.

Feeling hungry, he decided not to wait for the others. Lyosha was in no hurry to come to the kitchen. He had wheeled himself to the balcony door and was watching the winter morning appear slowly out of the darkness. He was waiting for Nina to use the bathroom, then it would be his turn. Sonya was always last up.

After his fried eggs, Viktor felt a little calmer. Time was advancing, slowly. Three more hours to the phone call.

*

At noon precisely the phone rang.

"Got the money? Then it's 8.00, Hydropark. Cross the footbridge below the Mlyn restaurant and wait till you see a car flash twice. Got that?"

"Well?" inquired Lyosha.

"8.oo. Hydropark."

"I'll come with you."

"Best you wait here."

Lyosha sighed.

"Mind you pick up something nice for Misha to eat."

"We'll do that."

Viktor then rang Andrey Pavlovich and got Pasha.

"Glad it's you. I need some help this evening."

"The Chief said you'd ring about twelve to tell where."

"So, outside Mlyn Restaurant at six."

"I'll be there."

75

At Hydropark metro station Viktor was the only one to alight. The train sped on to Left Bank, and for a while he stood by the digital clocks looking about him. Beyond the well-lit platform, all was darkness. One clock said 17.45, while the other indefatigably recorded how many minutes and seconds had elapsed since the last departure.

Checking that the weighty wad of dollars was safe in the inner pocket of his jacket, he headed for the exit. With kiosks and cafés all shut, the desolate little square filled him with sadness and nostalgia for summers spent heedless of the future. The clink of glass betrayed a vagrant checking waste bins for bottles to claim the deposit on.

Arriving at the footbridge he was cheered to see the restaurant windows lit. At least someone was about on this winter island of summer relaxation. He crossed the bridge, and saw the familiar 4 × 4 waiting outside the restaurant.

He and Pasha went in for a snack and a coffee. Pasha proposed to conceal himself on the Mlyn side, watch events, and if they took the money without producing Misha, step in.

"So, not to worry," he said, showing his silenced automatic, and Viktor felt easier in his mind.

At 8.oo he stood on the far side of the channel, solid darkness behind, before him the odd solitary street lamp, the distant light of the metro platform, and a hum of traffic – life hurtling by, indifferent to the lifelessness of Hydropark at night in winter.

Headlights flashed twice, and reassuring himself that the dollars were in place, Viktor walked to the middle of the bridge.

A car door slammed, two men in sheepskin jackets advanced, collars raised, faces wound with scarves under ski caps.

"The money!" demanded one.

"And my penguin?"

"In the car."

Viktor handed over the dollars.

"Correct," said the Chechen, having counted them, then added "How about a couple of thousand for yourself? For the address of someone in petrol or gas."

"I've no friends in that line."

"They needn't be friends."

"Sorry."

"Please yourself."

The two strode back to the car. A door banged, the engine started, the headlights went on, and left standing in the snow as the car reversed, was a small figure.

"Misha!" he cried, dashing forward, and slowly, at an old man's shuffle, the penguin came to meet him.

Squatting and embracing his penguin, Viktor wept, warmly regarded by Misha's black button eyes.

★

At a supermarket on the way home, Viktor bought half a kilo of fresh salmon and a bag of king prawns.

"Terribly thin, isn't he?" said Pasha after several looks over his shoulder. "On telly they're all so plump."

"You'd be thin, kept in a kennel and fed on gruel."

"Bastards!" said Pasha. "Should be shot."

76

Having another job to do, Pasha dropped Viktor at his block, giving him his card – "Security Aide to People's Deputy" – with a mobile number.

Carrying Misha like a child, Viktor made his way up to the 4th floor.

The door was opened by Sonya wearing a denim tunic and white leggings.

"Hooray!" she cried, clapping her hands, "Now we kick the cat out!"

Putting Misha down in the corridor, Viktor removed his jacket and shoes, and squatting beside Sonya, wagged a finger.

"No, we can't. One because we don't kick pets out, even if they do scratch. And two, Misha's a visitor, and sooner or later he's going home."

But Sonya wasn't listening. She was staring at Misha, and Misha was staring back, as if recalling the past.

"Me and Auntie Nina went to the supermarket and got him some cod's liver."

"He won't eat tinned things," said Viktor, immediately wondering if now perhaps he did.

"If he doesn't, I will. I like it. Now let's go to the kitchen – we've been waiting half an hour."

A bottle of champagne, bowls of salad, a smell of roast, something sizzling in a frying pan on the stove – a celebration was in the making.

Sitting in his usual place, Viktor watched Misha make his way hesitantly to his food bowl on its stool beside the stove.

"See, he remembers!" Sonya cried happily.

Lyosha, busy opening the champagne, let the cork escape, hitting the ceiling and dropping behind the stove.

"Some for me!" cried Sonya, as Lyosha poured.

"You're too young," said Viktor.

"I'm not. I've had it before – haven't I, Auntie Nina?"

In the end, Sonya was given just a little, and they drank to Misha.

Misha looked round from his bowl of salmon and still frozen king prawns, and stared at Viktor.

77

29th December

Next morning Viktor rang Regional Social Security, and inquiring as Deputy's aide – a tip of Pasha's – got the telephone numbers of orphanages.

The director of one was blunt and to the point: supply of children would involve a fee of $500 plus cost of transport. Downing the receiver on him, Viktor dialled the next number, and this time met with success. The Deputy Director, a woman with a good, clear, warm voice, was genuinely pleased to hear from him. It would be a real treat for the children, she said, and told him how to get to her. For the last 12km it was earth road, and it would be well to send a good tough vehicle. Viktor said he would be there by nine tomorrow.

Flushed with the success of his first assignment, he decided to take Sonya and Misha for a walk.

"Do you think you could you take me too?" asked Lyosha.

"Of course."

While Viktor carried Lyosha down, Nina brought the wheelchair and joined them in their walk.

An old woman beating dust out of a rug, gazed transfixed at the penguin, before taking in the legless man the young woman in the long blue overcoat was helping to push. The young man in the camouflage jacket she knew – she'd seen him grow up. The little girl must be his daughter.

"Let's go to the dovecotes," said Sonya.

At the dovecotes, a burly man was walking an Alsatian, towards which Misha set off at speed, swaying comically as he went. The Alsatian stopped dead in its tracks, pricked its ears, and as Misha came up, leapt away.

"Get that thing out of here!" shouted the dog's master. "It ought to be on a lead!"

"Why? He doesn't bite," Sonya declared, hugging Misha to her.

78

30th December

The road to the orphanage proved long and hard. The coach ordered by Pasha had seen better days and made heavy work of it, skirting potholes and worse in the asphalt, or rather what remained of the asphalt laid in Soviet days on the earth road. They were heading as for Chernobyl, but 15 km short of the no-go zone, they turned left.

"Some place, this!" said the driver, shaking his head at a 30 kph speed-limit sign. "You couldn't do 30 here in a tank – it'd shake the ruddy turret off!"

Coming to the one-street village of Kalinovka and a hut bearing the sign *Post*, they stopped, and Viktor went in and asked the way to the orphanage.

"Carry on to the end of Lenin Street and you'll see it on the left. A two-storey building," said a woman in a headshawl, looking up from the *Pension Gazette* spread open in front of her.

The red-brick box of the orphanage standing in a newly planted garden, looked like the one and only piece of building undertaken in the past 20 years. In front of the main door was a snow-free area paved with square flagstones, bordered by wooden benches, and appoached by a snow-free path.

"So you've found us!" Galina Mikhaylovna said happily, coming out to meet them. "The children told me you'd arrived – they've been looking out for you."

And now Viktor saw them – a great many of them, aged from six to 13 or 14, running out to look at the bus. At least 30, against the 20 asked for.

"You are bringing us back, aren't you?" Galina Mikhaylovna

asked. "I've let Cook go home as there'll be no-one for lunch, and she'll bring back something for supper – she's got a horse and cart."

"Of course we are," said Viktor, calling Pasha on the mobile the latter had presented him with.

"Forty-two not 20, and I'm bringing them all."

"Only 20 presents."

"Get some more. Andrey Pavlovich will pay."

"Will you, if he doesn't?"

"All right."

*

A beaming Andrey Pavlovich, a tree ablaze with fairy lights, and a red sack bulging with presents, greeted the children who came streaming through his gates. Grandfather Frost and the Snow Queen trod out half-smoked cigarettes under their red boots, and hurried forward.

"Well done!" Andrey Pavlovich whispered in Viktor's ear. "Now nip back with Pasha for your little one and the penguin. One more or less will make no difference."

By the time they arrived, festivities were in full swing, Grand-father Frost and the Snow Queen leading the dance around the tree to music from a ghetto blaster.

Seeing Viktor, Sonya and Misha arrive, Andrey Pavlovich, who was in earnest conversation with Galina Mikhaylovna, broke off and stopped the music.

"Children, a big hand for our special guest, a real live penguin!"

The children clapped, then ran and crowded round Misha.

"But you mustn't touch," said Sonya protectively.

At a signal from Andrey Pavlovich, the disc jockey restored the music.

423

A Channel 1 TV-car drew up, a girl and two cameramen got out, and preferring not to watch, Viktor went into the house and up to his old attic room. He sat on the bed. Still the same cover, as if there'd been no-one after him.

Last New Year they had spent at militiaman Sergey's dacha. There'd been no Nina then. Who there had been was bearded Lyosha, still with legs, seeing Misha for the first time. All just one year ago.

From below, children's voices singing,

> "In the forest grew a fir tree,
>
> in the forest there it grew . . ."

He went to the window. It was snowing lightly. He might still have been in Chechnya, celebrating New Year in the furnace hut, if not himself already amongst the ashes.

Going down to where Grandfather Frost was handing children their presents, Viktor saw it was just after one.

"They'll be missing their lunch," he told Andrey Pavlovich.

"Take them to McDonald's," said Andrey Pavlovich, giving him 200 hryvnas. "In consideration of what you've done for my image. Over New Year you're free. Report in on the 2nd. Earlier, if you're bored."

Presents distributed, the music stopped. The driver started up his bus. The children ran to the open doors.

"I can't thank you enough," Galina Mikhaylovna told Viktor. "You've no idea what it means to them – their first visit to Kiev."

"And now," said Viktor, "we're going to McDonald's."

Her eyes filled with tears. She tried to speak but couldn't.

"Us, too?" asked Sonya.

Finding three in seats for two and standing room only, Viktor asked who would have Misha on their lap.

"Me, me!" came from all sides.

Gently he deposited him on a little girl with fair curls peeping from a blue knitted hat.

The bus moved off.

79

The flat was amazingly warm, cosy and quiet, even with snow beating against the window, and Viktor felt far from sleepy.

Nina slept soundlessly, lying at the very edge of the bed so as to leave him the maximum amount of room and be out of reach.

For a while he stood looking at her, thinking, as he had been ever since yesterday's festivities, of the word "orphan" used by Sonya as they hitched their way home from McDonald's.

"Is it true they're all orphans, as one girl said?" she'd asked.

"Yes."

"Like me and him."

At which the driver, unaware that the "him" was Misha, looked round in surprise.

Sonya, Viktor explained, wasn't an orphan, since she had him, Auntie Nina and Misha.

"How about Uncle Lyosha?"

Viktor shrugged.

He remembered Galina Mikhaylovna's long farewell handshake.

"Do come and visit us," she begged. "There's a little river nearby. It's lovely in spring. There are beavers and coypus. We could put you up for the night."

He would, he promised, knowing that he wouldn't. In his place Khachayev would never have given a promise he had no intention of keeping, it occurred to him as he stood there in the dark. It had been so easy, that promise, and made solely to keep Galina Mikhaylovna happy all the way to Kalinovka in the back of beyond.

Taking his dressing gown, Viktor tiptoed through the sitting room and shut himself in the kitchen. He turned on the light, screwing up his eyes against the sudden glare.

He thought of getting out his typewriter, but then remembered the noise it made. Instead, he fetched a sheet of paper, and sitting in his usual place contemplating the blank whiteness of it froze into immobility.

The scrape of the kitchen door opening made him jump. Misha was standing there staring hard at him.

"Want something to eat?"

Still the penguin stood and stared in the manner of a Higher Presence observing him, his doing and his thinking.

On his sheet of paper Viktor wrote "Misha", looked at him, then added, "Repatriate". A little later, of its own volition, his hand added a question mark.

80

The first thing Sonya did on waking was look around the flat, pout, and bid Lyosha, head still under blanket, a chilly good morning.

"What's up?" he demanded sleepily.

"Don't you know? It's New Year's Day."

"Tomorrow, not today."

"But tonight's when Grandfather Frost comes. And where's he to put presents? No tree. Untidy flat. It's like we're not proper."

Lyosha looked astonished, seeming to hear something of Nina, although not in so many words.

"Tell Daddy. There's still time to buy a tree," he said.

"I shall!" she declared angrily.

"Uncle Viktor, where are you? We've got to buy a tree!"

"Here," he answered from the kitchen, and Sonya came running.

*

Their tree they bought outside the local food store from a tattered vagrant in a green scarf wound with festive tinsel, for three hryvnas. It was small, under two metres, and they carried it between them, Sonya leading, crown grasped in a mittened hand.

All took part in decorating it, Lyosha unpacking the shoeboxes of decorative balls and stripping off the newspaper in which they were wrapped. They were all rather in each other's way, and Nina managed to smash two balls. Only when there were no decorations left did they they see the obvious – that the fir resembled an over-cropped apple-tree, the saving difference being that the decorations were not so weighty.

"It's the most beautiful ever!" said Sonya. "But where's Misha?"

"He was in the kitchen," said Viktor.

She darted off, and returned shooing Misha before her.

"Come on, we've done our best for you!" she urged. She was, he saw, now taller than Misha.

Waddling up to the tree, Misha looked under it.

"There'll be nothing till midnight," Sonya explained. "Uncle Viktor's going to buy something, give it to Grandfather Frost, and while we're celebrating, he'll quietly lay it under the tree."

*

427

The time to New Year sped amazingly. It was dark before four, and a heavy fall of snow made it more so.

Nina switched on the television. It was a repeat of an old Soviet black-and-white comedy about combine harvest operators. Collective-farm girls were singing their heads off, watched by no-one, their songs penetrating to the kitchen where Nina was seeing to the meat, Lyosha peeling potatoes, as instructed, and the cat mewing in anticipation.

Sonya having dashed off to her friend below, Viktor found himself at a loose end, alone with Misha on his camel blanket bed by the sealed-up, but still draughty, balcony door in the sitting room.

"How are we?" he asked squatting down in front of him.

Misha stared, first at him, then, as if making a point, at the balcony door.

"I'm just going to move you clear for a bit," said Viktor, tugging Misha's bed away from the door.

Misha hopped off, and watched.

"Just a minute, then we'll cool ourselves outside."

Going to the kitchen, he complimented Nina and Lyosha for their work on the tree, got his Pooh Bear mug and a miniature cognac from the kitchen cupboard, and stole out.

Neither Nina nor Lyosha turned to look.

The balcony door opened with a sound of tearing draught excluder, and in with a great blast of cold came snow that fell and melted on the floor.

"Out you go, Misha!"

Obediently Misha went, cheerfully stamped himself a space in the snow, then looked back, as if expecting Viktor to join him.

And rather than lose face, Viktor did, in his light shoes, and once outside, put mug and cognac down in the snow and shut the door on the catch behind him, wishing he was still wearing his good, thick MoES uniform.

Squatting in the warm light from the sitting room, he poured cognac into his Pooh mug.

"To you, Misha," he said, raising the mug to him. "To your escape, and a happy, happy future!"

Misha listened attentively, then, as dogs started barking below, stomped to the balcony rail and peered into the dark, snowy depths. Viktor joined him at the rail. The barking continued, but there was nothing to see.

Out here in the snow, with barking in the darkness, his left shoe leaking and a lively sense of discomfort, was like being back in the Chechen mountains and a war he had played no part in, but which had played its own in both their lives. The two of them were like veterans rejected by a society that had missed out on this both distant yet not so distant war.

Suddenly, and for the first time for as long as he could remember, his pity having been all for Misha, he felt sorry for himself. He felt, too, the old familiar sense of guilt towards Misha that had sent him to Moscow and Chechnya. Anyone else would have regarded that as now atoned for, forgotten the whole thing, and got on with his life, seeking that little bit of happiness, sorrow, love, and wealth of free time that most people are entitled to. Except that he was not anyone else.

Pouring the last of the cognac, he drank, and thinking suddenly of Lyosha, curiously fell to wondering what had happened to his ancient Mercedes.

Hearing a tap on the window, he turned and saw Nina.

"You'll freeze to death!" she shouted.

Kicking the snow from his leaking shoes, he came in and shut the balcony door, leaving Misha still looking for dogs, though their barking had ceased.

"We're out of mayonnaise," complained Nina, and glad to change his footwear and dress for the cold, he betook himself to the still-open food store where everyone was buying spirits.

Someone had rung, she told him on his return – a man who would ring again in ten minutes.

Andrey Pavlovich, he decided.

At nine, Sonya, back from her friend's, checked the tree for presents and undismayed by there being none, offered to help in the kitchen, where all was well in hand.

Viktor settled her to watch Disney cartoons on TV, moved Lyosha's bed chairs and bedding to the wall to make more space around the sitting room table, then helped Nina lay it.

At 10.30 they came to table, all except Misha, who was disinclined to leave the balcony. Sonya was yawning, but managing to keep awake. Nina poured herself a full wine glass of Fizz, then went to check the state of the roast, the smell of which all were savouring.

"It needs another twenty minutes," she announced, returning.

"Let's switch to Moscow TV, and clink glasses with them," suggested Lyosha, eyeing the magnum of Russian pink champagne.

Viktor switched channels, and there was Yeltsin wishing "his dear Russians" a hiccuppy Happy New Year.

"Cut the sound," Lyosha pleaded.

Viktor did, restoring it only to clink glasses to the Kremlin chimes.

For the Kiev New Year, Viktor carried Misha in from the cold for the feast of cod fillets, his on a plate like theirs, decorated by Nina with two slices of lemon.

Another switch of channel, and now, until muted by Viktor,

President Kuchma.

Viktor consulted his watch and brought another bottle of champagne to the table.

"Nearly time."

Sonya, despite fits of nodding off, made the Ukrainian New Year, clinking her glass of Fizz with the rest as midnight sounded. After which she found Misha's beady little black eyes staring so that it was hard to look away.

"Why isn't he drinking?" she asked.

Viktor shrugged, then got to his feet. In the corridor he nearly trod on the cat lapping milk from her saucer. Taking a teacup rather than a saucer and filling it with cold water, he dropped in a few ice cubes.

"There you are," he said putting it down for Misha, much to the latter's satisfaction.

"I'll sleep in your room," Sonya said wearily. "Wake me when Grandfather Frost comes."

They were now drinking cognac and vodka – Viktor from his Pooh Bear mug.

"You should give that to Sonya," said Nina. "She likes it."

"I can't," Viktor said, more than a little intoxicated.

He looked to see if Lyosha was drunk, but Lyosha, leaning back against the upholstery of his wheelchair, looked fit and alert. His face wore the pensive smile of a man lost in introspection or memories of the past, glass of vodka untasted, the one jarring note the state of his beard. Short, it suited him, of Tolstoyan length, it aged him. He must help him trim it, Viktor thought, remembering suddenly how he had shaved poor dying penguinologist Pidpaly in hospital. Last year – now, in fact, the year before last, during which all of them at table – Sonya, Lyosha, Nina, Misha – had been with him at one time or another. It hadn't really been all that bad, that life, just a question of conforming to it. And it wasn't over yet. Some had gone out of it, others had come into it, and some, like him, had returned to it.

The phone rang, and relieved to see the door where Sonya was sleeping as good as shut, he went to answer it.

"Well, Viktor my boy, Happy New Year!" said a faintly familiar voice. "Tried to get you yesterday evening, but no joy. Lasting happiness to you and yours! See you soon!"

"Thank you, but –"

But the caller had rung off.

It was a voice he knew, had heard more than once, but the rejoicing on TV, the howling blizzard, and Nina serving him and Lyosha more roast, were a distraction. On top of which, there were things to be done, and telling Nina and Lyosha not to look, he fetched his bag of presents, and laid them under the tree.

He put a hand to the icy air entering by way of the unsealed balcony door, and snatched it back as if cut by a knife.

81

Waking to find himself wedged between Nina and Sonya, he tried in vain to remember when and how their celebrations had ended. Extricating himself from the bed, he went over to the window. The blizzard was done. He remembered putting presents under the tree, but not Lyosha and Nina unwrapping them. Clearly memory had its limits. He must go and investigate.

Quietly snoring on the sitting-room couch, Lyosha lay still in his tracksuit. The television was off, but the table was still a mess of plates, bowls, glasses and tumblers. By the radiator next to the balcony door, the glint of empty bottles, but Misha was not on his blanket.

Viktor went to the kitchen, and switching on the light, saw him under the table with the typewriter, not asleep, looking thoroughly lost. Lifting his head towards the light, he fixed his beady eyes on Viktor.

Viktor stooped in front of him.

"You feel lousy too? How about going for a swim? Like we did with Sergey."

Misha turned away and looked at the typewriter.

"Don't believe me, do you? Just you wait!"

He dressed, put on his MoES tunic, slipped a left-over half-full bottle of cognac into his pocket, put on snow boots, and with Misha cradled in his arms, left the flat. No-one was about, and the city so deeply and infectiously asleep as to set Viktor yawning, and also Misha, who was standing beside him on the snowy pavement.

The faint yellow dots of distant headlights appeared and grew slowly larger and brighter. Stepping into the road, Viktor raised his arm. The ancient Moskvich crawled cautiously towards him and stopped. He went to open the door, but it was locked.

"Where do you want to go to?" a man's voice asked through the lowered window.

"Dnieper Embankment," said Viktor, trying to see the man's face.

"Cost you 30 hryvnas, seeing it's New Year's Day," said the still unseen driver.

"OK."

They got out just beyond Metro Bridge. No sign of dawn breaking. He looked to see the time, but discovered he'd left his watch at home.

"Come on, we'll find you an ice-hole," he told Misha.

It was somewhat alarming to be down on the frozen river in –10°
with the far shore invisible in greyish – hopefully, morning – haze.
Something else he'd left behind was his fur hat, but the effects of
champagne and cognac, and the security of having a supply of the
latter, did something to mitigate the loss.

Together they set off across the ice. Slowly. Not from fear, but
because Viktor found a slow pace more manageable, and Misha was
not in a hurry. Indeed, every so often he stopped to look up at his
master, falling behind as he did so, then catching up in order to do
so again.

"Soon be there," said Viktor, plodding on.

But like the darkness, the ice continued unbroken. He halted,
stared about him, but saw only ice. That was strange. Hydropark
should be there somewhere. Squatting beside Misha, he confessed
quietly, earnestly, that they were lost, but that it would soon be
light. He swigged his cognac, felt its bitter-sweet warmth suffuse
his body, slowing thought and movement even further. The bottle,
as he replaced it, struck against what proved to be his mobile.
Lighting its tiny window, he dialled 060 and an electronic woman
announced that it was 06hrs 08 mins.

"It's a pity they don't tell you when dawn is," he said to Misha.

They pressed on, and in the chilly twilight, encountered a
fisherman seated on his box over an ice hole.

"Any luck?" Viktor asked.

The man, in sheepskin jacket with turned-up collar, made no
reply. On the ice beside him, short of the frozen-over hole, lay his
rod and an empty bottle of vodka.

"You see – what's good for penguins is death to us Ukrainians,"
he told Misha, as horrified by the idea of himself suffering such a
fate as he was fearful of the future in general.

82

It was completely light by the time they drew up outside their block in an ancient, L-plated Zhiguli, and Viktor paid the driver, a pale, bespectacled youth, the 45 hryvnas he asked. It was excessive, but New Year was when those out to earn a bit extra found fares willing to pay over the odds.

Everyone was still asleep. The clock showed 9.45. The cat was mewing over her empty bowl in the corridor, and to keep her quiet Viktor filled it with milk. He then got a fillet of frozen cod, and put it in a sinkful of hot water to thaw.

Time for his own breakfast, he decided. Their walk on the Dnieper ice had left him tired and hungry. He fetched his unfinished plate of roast from the sitting room, and he and Misha settled down to breakfast.

Sonya, who was the first to wake, looked into the kitchen with her presents.

"Actually new roller skates were what I wanted," she said.

"You should have told Grandfather Frost."

"He ought to have guessed!" she snapped. "By the way, I'm hungry too."

"Like me to make you some semolina?"

"Semolina? No, thank you. I'll get something from the table."

She was soon back, sitting on a stool with slices of dried-up Dutch cheese, rings of smoked sausage and two pickled cucumbers on her plate.

By 11.00 everyone was up and about. Nina washed up before opening her presents, then gave Viktor a manly hug, kissing him on the lips and cheek.

Viktor, having by now somewhat recovered from his early morning excursion, made Nina coffee, telling her to read the grounds when she'd drunk it. Nina drank so fast she burnt her lips, but the images, when revealed, made her laugh and forget it. Sonya wanted to see, but Nina wiped the side of the cup before she could.

Lyosha tried his calculator and examined the diary.

"Any use?"

Lyosha shrugged.

"It will be if you find me something to do."

But for me, no presents, thought Viktor, and beyond an anonymous phone call, no best wishes either.

He had an urge to be alone. Tomorrow he'd be at work for Andrey Pavlovich, but today was still a day off.

"The new year's what your first day makes it!" came suddenly to mind, and so far the outlook was not good. He thought of the fisherman frozen in the pose of Rodin's "Thinker", and no doubt by now removed to some morgue. He decided to go for a walk.

83

Kreshchatik Street was already a little livelier. Two great orange snow ploughs were at work, and a few pedestrians window-gazing at the unaffordable. Viktor went, as his steps led him, to the Old Kiev Cellar Café, which was shut. Turning back, he slowly made his way past Znamya Booksellers, Central Universal Stores and what was once Friendship Bookshop. At the corner of Proreznaya Street he paused, tried to remember when he'd last read a book, but couldn't. As a boy he'd liked Jack London, as a young man, Khachayev's

Maksim Gorky. The time of books had then ended, and the time of newspapers dawned. He'd had a go at writing something of his own, but work for *Capital News* had put the kibosh on that, teaching him to write fluently and with due respect of those who had died.

That fisherman dead on the Dnieper ice was equally worthy of respect, though, not having known him, he could not say in what particulars. However much he may have boozed, abused his wife, banged doors, there was something fine, perhaps even enviable, in the manner of his death.

Viktor looked up at the Trade Union House tower to check the time, but got only the Adidas advert, of which he'd seen more than enough. In quest of an open café, he set off up Proreznaya Street, and found the Cyber, where teenagers were playing virtual war games and the supervisor, deep in a back number of *Top Secret*, deigned eventually to notice him.

"Any coffee?"

"Could be."

"Internet working?"

"And why shouldn't it?"

"Coffee and Internet, then."

"Computer 6. Coffee on its way."

"Penguin" produced a mass of search responses, "Vernadsky Base" included, but what caught his eye, was "Antarctic SOS". He clicked on.

A photograph showed two bronzed, tough, tall 50-year-olds, and a resolute, attractive, equally bronzed blonde, and a fine sea-going yacht with, in three languages: "Croat crew seek like-minded spirit for voyage to Anatarctica, sharing expense." The e-mail address being Mladen, he wondered which of the men Mladen was, and who the attractive young lady might be.

Helped by the supervisor, he printed out the advertisement, registered an e-mail address of his own, then e-mailed Mladen, expressing interest but making no mention of Misha. The new year's what your first day makes it, he thought. Things were looking up.

84

Woken by something between a cry and a sob, Viktor eventually got up to investigate. Lyosha and Sonya were asleep in the sitting room, but Misha was missing from his bed by the balcony door.

Viktor found him in the kitchen, pressed into the corner between the stove and the wall, body heaving as if he were sobbing.

"Misha! What's wrong?"

Misha turned. His cheek was bleeding. Sensing another presence and spotting the green eyes of the cat under the table, Viktor grabbed her by the scruff of the neck and threw her out of the flat. Then, fetching cotton wool and ointment, he ministered as best he could to a willing patient.

Sonya appeared in her white flannel pyjamas and sleepily took the scene in.

"The cat scratched him," he explained.

"We must kick her out," said Sonya.

"We mustn't do that. It's just that she's jealous of Misha."

"Could I have some Fizz?"

He poured them both some Fizz.

"Do you know, Uncle Lyosha's keen on Auntie Nina."

He looked at her in amazement.

"It's true. He's always asking her about something or other. And

438

she's told him about the dacha at Osokorki, and about Uncle Sergey in the urn."

Viktor shrugged. "You must go to bed. I'll sit up with Misha for a bit."

Misha was now standing with his back to the stove, looking puzzled and aggrieved, the latter by virtue of the ointment on his cheek. Before returning to bed, Viktor saw Misha to his, and having shut the sitting room door, let the cat back in.

85

At 11.00 next morning the virgin snow outside the Goloseyevo villa revealed that those within had not yet ventured beyond its bounds, and that he, on this yet-to-start second day of the New Year, was the first to visit it.

A red-faced Pasha, dressed as if just back from a ski run, lack of tracks notwithstanding, opened the side gate to him.

"The Chief's still in bed. Come and have a coffee."

Viktor kicked the snow from his boots and removed them in the hall.

"He didn't get back till 3.00 this morning. What a time! You've no idea! Vasya – he's another of his aides – made a list of people to wish Happy New Year to, 73 of them, People's Deputies, State officials. Had to be done. That's politics. He *has* to have a drink with them, talk about the weather and entry into Europe, though some of them make him want to puke. He's happier talking to me now, whereas in the old days he'd nothing to talk to me about."

"Maybe I should come back later."

439

"No, wait. He told you to come, didn't he?"

"Yes."

"So you're at work, and you've got to wait. Don't imagine he needs me every minute of the day. Very often I sit for a couple of hours doing nothing, but I'm on duty. You have to get used to it."

Drinking his coffee, Viktor wondered if he really wanted to get used to it. Having a job to do was all right, might even be interesting, but waiting for orders was different.

"Did you have a good New Year?" he asked.

"Usual sort of thing. All sorts coming with greetings and presents, sitting for five minutes knocking back their drink, then off. Each with his own list of a hundred to visit. But all quiet by four. So we had a gin and tonic and watched porn on video."

His mobile rang. The caller's number as revealed in the window commanded instant respect.

"I'll tell him to at once . . . He's resting at the moment, but I'll wake him."

"Who was that?" Viktor asked, when Pasha returned.

"A two-headed snail. Potapych. Now Special Presidential Adviser, if you please."

★

"Before I forget," said Andrey Pavlovich, as they sat with coffee in the sitting room, "there was a plain-clothes man inquiring about you. My fault for including you in document distribution lists. Wanted to know what I knew about you. I think I reassured him, but watch out. Still, back to business. Remember what I retain you for?"

"Humanitarian matters."

Anton Pavlovich laughed. "And how! Those artificial limbs were

440

the goods! Now here's a whole lot of begging letters for you. Take them home, bin the crap, but anything that strikes you as worthwhile and not too costly, let me know and we'll consider it."

★

"Sorry, I'd like to drive you, but I'm delivering more presents," said Pasha, helping to pack at least three kilos of letters into a carrier bag.

"Not to worry, I'll make it," said Viktor.

86

Over coffee in the Old Kiev Cellar, Viktor made a start on the bundle, reading carefully at first, then skimming with growing mistrust. Kiev feminists requesting money in support of their magazine and for return tickets to a Women's Rights conference in the USA. The Old Kiev District Council Veterans were more modest: cost of repairs, estimate for 6000 hryvnas enclosed. The Children-our-Tomorrow Benevolent Fund simply wanted $25,000 paid into its account, number supplied. An infant music school needed to have its instruments tuned.

He ordered another coffee and a large cognac.

Two requests from children's homes, but they, too, wanted money transferred to accounts. Lottery-fashion, he drew one of the many remaining letters at random. It was from a war veteran seeking assistance in publishing his memoirs.

Dumping the whole carrier bag of letters in the first litter bin he encountered, he set off for the Cyber café.

As he walked up Proreznaya Street, he had a strange sensation of being followed, and concluded that he was – by a man in a long black overcoat and grey wolfskin hat with earflaps, on the other side of the street. When Viktor entered the café, the man walked on towards Adidas, taking a mobile from his pocket.

The e-mail message awaiting Viktor ran: "Hi! Glad to hear of your interest in joining our expedition. We sail from Split 8th of March. Contribution required: $10,000. Look forward to your confirming. Best, Mladen Pavlich."

He e-mailed back his confirmation, inquiring the name of the yacht and details of what he should bring. Split, informed the Internet, was, *inter alia*, a popular venue for events: Croatian Basketball Championship, from 6th of January; Chess Tournament, February; European Arm-wrestling Championship, 3rd–9th of March.

"What's arm-wrestling?" he asked, distracting the supervisor from his screen.

The supervisor demonstrated.

When he left the café and headed back to Kreshchatik Street, the man in the wolfskin hat was nowhere to be seen. At the Proreznaya–Pushkinskaya Street junction a Mercedes S600 drew up beside him. A rear door opened.

"In you get, Viktor," urged the voice of his supposedly deceased former chief, Igor Lvovich, Editor of *Capital News*. "Have some champagne. I've already wished you a Happy New Year, but we've still to clink glasses."

Viktor got in, Igor Lvovich tapped the chauffeur's shoulder, and the Mercedes glided forward.

"Prior to my death in the motor accident, word reached me that you had shot yourself," said Igor Lvovich. "Then, it emerged, it was not you but another obituarist, a novice at the job, nothing like you. So as you see, all has turned out for the best."

He laughed, seeing Viktor's expression of total disbelief.

"Nor was it me who burned to death on the Borispol Highway, but a suitably clothed, suitably documented, spruced up vagrant. So here's me, dead and buried, yet not. And happening to hear that one Comrade Zolataryov, a.k.a. 'The Penguin', is walking about, large as life and complete with penguin, I say to myself, we must meet . . . After all, you're one of the best, already Aide to a People's Deputy – I'm in the picture, you see – and as Gorbachov would put it, rightly so. Here's us, a vast country, but catastrophically short of men able to think and act, or simply think. Functionary-wise, we're a wilderness!" he declared, accompanying the words with a dismissive gesture. "Our problems far exceed the number of men capable of coming up with solutions. You can see for yourself. That Deputy of yours, for instance. Pasts are no longer considered. All's forgiven, all's forgotten! Just so long as a man can string two words together!"

He paused as if to give Viktor a chance to speak, but Viktor could do no more than stare. It really was his old chief, though fleshier of face and with bags under his eyes from liverishness, sleepless nights or unhealthy living. On the other hand, he was more expensively suited, and his Rolex was not a Chinese fake.

"I'm starting a new paper. *Ukrainian Courier*. First issue ten days from now. Buy it. Read it. You might have some thoughts. I'd like your advice. I value your opinion. I could in due course make you editor-in-chief . . ."

Consulting his Rolex, he told the driver to switch on National Radio 1, and a few seconds later the chimes reverberated over the quadraphonic stereo system.

"A sucker for the exact time, that's me," he smiled.

From a tiny bar between the two front seats he produced a bottle of champagne and glasses, and briefly lowering the window at the touch of a button, shot the cork out. "Happy New Year!" he said with a merry twinkle in his eye, and they clinked glasses.

Dropped off in Pechersk between Arsenal metro station and Square of Glory, Viktor plodded in the direction of Caves Monastery, numb from the shock of this encounter, and as little able to comprehend it as to clear his head of Igor Lvovich's "So here's me, dead and buried, yet not".

87

That evening Sonya again confided suspicions concerning Lyosha's feelings towards Nina, who was at that moment pushing him to the bathroom to wash and clean his teeth.

"So what?" Viktor asked.

"So he's a guest and you shouldn't allow it!" Sonya responded in amazement.

"Sonya," he urged. "Keep an eye on things, yes, but where grown-ups are concerned, don't meddle."

Sonya sighed and swept out.

88

Early next morning Viktor spent Andrey Pavlovich's clothing allowance on a warm Finnish jacket with hood, high winter boots, jeans and an emerald green pullover, and returned to the flat to get into them.

"Very smart," said Lyosha.

Nina, poking her head out of the kitchen, said nothing.

"Not found anything for me yet?" Lyosha went on to ask. "If I sit doing nothing much longer, I'll be back on the vodka."

"Bear with me. Everyone's still celebrating."

His mobile rang in the pocket of his MoES jacket in the corridor. It was Pasha. The Chief would like to see him within the hour.

★

"Well, let's be hearing what you've got me," said Andrey Pavlovich, settling Viktor in an armchair.

"Nothing, actually."

"How so?"

"It was all such feeble stuff – nut cases or con men trying it on."

"But where the hell does that leave me, with a TV 1 interview the day after tomorrow advertising my generosity?"

"How about helping the orphanage we laid on the tree for?"

"What do they want?"

"Nothing."

"So?"

"That's why we could help."

"Good point. Get on to them sharpish, find out what they need . . . Ring from here . . . You do have a phone at home?"

"Yes."

He rang from the phone in the hall.

"Galina Mikhaylovna?"

"Yes, who's that?"

"New Year, McDonald's, remember?"

"So you've not forgotten us!"

"I'd like to know what you need. I might be able to help."

"Oh my! I really don't know . . . Bowls, mugs for the kitchen perhaps . . . The children have to eat in two shifts. Unbreakable would be good . . ."

"And on the teaching side?"

She gave a deep sigh.

"This is so sudden . . . Our text books are old . . . We've no TV – we had one, but it packed up a year ago . . . You must forgive me – it's shameful, begging like this . . . When I should be applying in writing with the approval of District Education . . ."

"No need! Will you be there tomorrow?"

"Where else? I live next door. House with the green fence."

"Till tomorrow at about 12.00, then."

Andrey Pavlovich approved the purchases, telling Viktor to see what else the orphanage might need, and Pasha drove Viktor to Darnitsa where, in Children's World, he bought 50 Pooh Bear enamel bowl-and-mug sets, the mugs identical with his from Chechnya. At Radio House, Lesi Ukrainki, a boxed Samsung television was added to the Pooh Bear cartons already on board.

89

As they turned off onto the snow-covered earth track, it was like entering an untravelled snowfield, and Sonya, sitting on the back seat with Misha, was wide-eyed at the beauty of it. When Viktor had said that he was going to the orphanage, she had insisted on going with him and bringing Misha. After all, she and Misha knew everyone there, she said. From time to time Viktor looked back at the two of them. The children would be delighted to see Misha. Good for Sonya! She had been quite right to insist.

Pasha gave the impression of feeling his way, relying on the marker poles and bare trees bordering the track for guidance. His face was tense, but every now and then something of his own pleasure in the scene shone through.

It was good to be doing good, Viktor thought, and he had Andrey Pavlovich to thank for the opportunity. For all the dark past hinted at by Igor Lvovich, and for all its showiness, Andrey Pavlovich's benevolence sprang as much from a genuine desire to do good as from recognition of the need to adhere to some set of principles – like his pet Snail's Law – in order to make fewer mistakes and keep clear of trouble. One had a choice. There was a Constitution that promised much but achieved little, its articles pathetic and unrealistic. The right to free medical care ended when old age and sickness began. Penguinologist Pidpaly, for instance, who could only be got to hospital by bribing ambulancemen. Snail's Law promised nothing, beyond punishment for its infringement. And therein lay the life-attested truth and effectiveness of it.

At the orphanage they were received like old friends. There and then the children wanted to eat from their new bowls and drink from their new mugs. Water was brought from the well, bowls and mugs were rinsed, and 20 minutes later, all were consuming buckwheat porridge, and Pasha was taking snaps with his simple camera. Misha, temporarily at a loose end, buckwheat porridge not being to his taste, stood keeping Viktor under observation.

A stout old lady in an apron went around filling the new mugs with fruit juice from an enormous teapot.

"My Uncle Viktor's got a mug like this, but he won't let me have it," he heard Sonya informing one of her new friends.

"But, I will," he intervened.

"Honestly?"

"Chechen word of honour," he said, but the point was lost on her.

The new television set was connected up, and with the help of one of the older boys adjusted and made to work.

"They're not really that big," Viktor confided to Sonya, after a Big Mac advert.

90

It was growing dark as they followed their own wheel tracks back to the main road, and just as they reached it, Viktor's mobile rang.

"How did it go?" Andrey Pavlovich asked.

"Splendidly. Tears of joy all round."

"As it should be. Tight-lipped smiles go with taking bribes. But listen, you're not finished yet. Just write it all up, today's beneficence, when you get home; see me tomorrow and we'll decide where to place it."

Sonya, he saw, was dozing, while Misha, head now on a level with hers, was gazing into the gathering dusk, raising his flippers in response to the lights of oncoming cars.

Back at the flat, they found Lyosha and Nina playing chess in the kitchen, or rather, Lyosha teaching Nina how to play.

"Is she good?" Viktor asked.

"I'd have made $100 a night if we'd been playing for money,

which we weren't, and didn't even in the old days, not having any dollars."

"Good man," said Viktor.

Lyosha looked a little surprised, and while Nina gathered up the pieces, Viktor went to put the kettle on, still smiling.

"We've been waiting supper," said Nina. "I've fresh sausage in the fridge, and can do you buckwheat porridge straightaway."

As he washed in the bathroom, he was joined by Sonya.

"See, it's like I said, he's keen on Auntie Nina."

"So?"

"So *you're* in trouble," said Sonya, tossing her head and marching from the room.

Supper went well. Even the cat looked in, but seeing Misha, withdrew to the corridor.

★

When all were in bed, Viktor settled down in the kitchen, brought up the typewriter, put paper in, and sat and stared.

After a while Misha rolled in like a drunken sailor, after barging the door open with his chest, and pressed against Viktor's knee to be stroked.

It was strange being asked to write for a newspaper again, and straight journalism at that, with the sense and feel of the event as fresh in his memory as the joyous laughter of the children. And before he knew it, he was typing away, and in half an hour the article was finished. It was short, just four sides, about doing good and the need there was for it, a context in which Andrey Pavlovich was the more easily and sincerely portrayed, and his donation of a billiard table and artificial limbs lightly alluded to. Viktor read it through, and was just putting the typewriter back under the table

449

when Sonya came in, sat on her stool and gazed at him intently.

"What's wrong? Want a drink?"

She shook her head. "What's that you've written?"

"About where we've been. For a newspaper."

"So you're back to being a journalist."

"No."

"Maybe I'll be a journalist when I'm big. And sit up in the kitchen when everyone's asleep."

"You mustn't – you wouldn't want to be a soldier and go to war."

"No, I wouldn't."

"You'd have to, as a journalist. You'd be taken on by some paper, given a pen instead of a gun, and told, 'There's the enemy, you go and write nasty things about him'. And you would, until you got killed or hurt."

"Are nasty things what you've been writing?"

"No. I've written about the orphans we visited today."

"And you can do that without having to be a journalist?"

"Yes."

"Good," said Sonya, "I'm going back to bed."

*

Early next morning, well before breakfast, he dressed, and without rereading it, rolled his article into a cylinder and slipped it into an inner pocket of his jacket.

It was snowing lightly, and with their little globes of light colouring the flakes yellow, the street lamps looked like dandelions. People were emerging from their blocks into the wintery dark and hurrying to work. There was something strange and unusual about these shadows bound for the bus stop, something of the Soviet past with its work discipline, punishments for lateness, and Heroes of

Socialist Labour. Life had somehow re-established a daily rhythm. Factories were back in operation. Earth was again revolving, and all upon it astir and flourishing. Only clearly a different, parallel life – not his or even impinging on his. Daily rhythm was the refuge of all who neither noticed, nor cared to notice, what they didn't like, convinced that what they read in papers or saw on telly couldn't be true. Or more precisely, were glad not likely themselves to be murdered, being, not in business or seriously in debt, disinclined to fall victim to the new reality. And there they were, getting up, going to work, just as another, parallel world was going to bed.

At Independence Square, he popped into McDonald's for a coffee and a doughnut, watched the world go by, then went on to Goloseyevo.

Arriving at 9.30, he found Andrey Pavlovich up and about in his tiger-pattern towelling dressing gown. Pasha not being in evidence, Andrey Pavlovich made coffee, which they drank in the kitchen.

"Odd sense of humour you've got, Viktor! *Group of Friends?* What sort of a signature's that?

"Force of habit, it's the pen name I wrote under."

"Well, cross it out and be yourself."

"I'd rather not."

"Then think of a different pen name."

For *Group of Friends*, he substituted *Sergey Stepanenko*.

91

Viktor sat late at night in the kitchen before a bachelor still life of vodka, jar of gherkins, sliced sausage and a newspaper open at an article, complete with photo, describing the charitable activities of State Deputy Andrey Pavlovich Loza. He read it through, and finding it exactly as written, he turned back to the front page, noted the patriotic yellow of *Ukrainian* and blue of *Courier*, sighed, and poured himself vodka.

Getting to his feet, he clinked his glass against Sergey's urn.

"Your first publication – congratulations!" he whispered.

Pouring another vodka, he kept an eye on the door, expecting at any minute to see Misha standing there. Tonight, though, he seemed in no hurry to appear, as if reluctant to intrude on Viktor's thoughts.

And certainly the paper and his article under the by-line of *de facto* deceased Sergey, both published by *de jure* deceased Igor Lvovich, his former Chief, provided food for thought. There was material there for something – a drunken theory, or a short story.

He mused, as he drank, on the fact that every week was losing him more of his freedom, or what remained of it. He was losing space in his own flat, and in process of losing himself, if he hadn't done that already. Still, it wasn't all gloom. He had Misha and Sonya, and was alive, *de jure* and *de facto*, and more validly vital than Igor Lvovich with his photograph-adorned grave already at the cemetery. The vodka, instead of making him drunk, was inspiring a desperate sense of loneliness. There was an air of menace in the silence of the flat, as if an ambush or trap were about to be sprung. His eyes returned to the door, and with a sudden urge to see what it concealed, he opened it, went out into the corridor and listened. Silence.

He looked into the sitting room. Lyosha was asleep and snoring gently.

"You awake?" he whispered foolishly.

"What's up?"

"Come and have a drink."

"What's wrong?"

"Nothing. I've had an article published. Come and celebrate."

Viktor carried him through to the kitchen and sat him at the table. Misha came plip-plopping after them to make it a threesome.

"This isn't like you," Lyosha said, clearly concerned.

"I'm out of sorts. Not happy."

"I see, hence the vodka cure. Which I tried for being unhappy. Actually, if there's anything other than vodka I'd rather have it."

Moved, Viktor jumped to his feet, looked in the fridge, then in the wall cupboard, and returned with a bottle of cognac.

"How about this?"

"Fine."

Viktor poured the vodka from Lyosha's glass into his own. They drank, and ate sausage and gherkins.

"Fed up with me – that's it, isn't it?" Lyosha asked abruptly. "After saving me from drink and taking me in . . . And, yes, I do fancy your Nina . . . But don't worry – I am not that sort of a shit."

"Hold on! Why shouldn't you fancy her?"

"Because you and she sleep together."

"I one side of the bed, she the other. So let's drop that one."

Viktor replenished their glasses. "Know anything about arm wrestling?"

Lyosha nodded.

"Care to demonstrate?"

Lyosha did, leaving Viktor to nurse his right arm. "I thought chess was your thing," he said. "Your health as better man!"

"You said something about finding me work," said Lyosha, sipping his cognac.

"I believe I have. Give me a couple of days."

92

Out of the blue next morning, Igor Lvovich telephoned, full of praise for Viktor's article, but disappointed that Viktor had not read more of his *Ukrainian Courier*.

"You must – I value your opinion. Again, you see, our paths converge."

While Nina was still showering, Lyosha viewing winter through a balcony door obligingly vacated by Misha, and Sonya applying mascara to her brows from Nina's make-up set, Viktor prepared to breakfast alone. He cut bread, fried an omelette, and was about to eat when he saw Misha eyeing an empty bowl, and gave him the last piece of cod from the fridge.

He'd no sooner finished his omelette than Sonya in denim pinafore dress and white tights appeared, and making sure the bathroom shower was running, whispered in Viktor's ear:

"It's all right – they had a most terrible row yesterday, really shouting."

"Who did?"

"Auntie Nina, Uncle Lyosha. So you've no need to worry."

Viktor laughed, and Sonya looked hurt.

"Who shouted most?" he asked, concerned.

"First Auntie Nina, then Uncle Lyosha, then both together."

"So all's well."

Again a hurt look and something approaching a glare.

"Look," he said gently, "if Auntie Nina and Uncle Lyosha row, it's because they mean something to each other. If they didn't, they wouldn't."

"So they're still keen on each other?"

Viktor shrugged.

"Oh, you're impossible!"

"You still love me, don't you?"

"Of course I do, you're my Uncle-Daddy."

"So that's all right, then." He patted her on the head. "And if you like, today or tomorrow, we'll go to a café and talk."

"I'd like that."

Enter Nina in Viktor's dressing gown, hair in a towel.

"You off somewhere?"

"Work"

"The bath outlet's leaking. We need a plumber."

"Lyosha can ring Maintenance."

She nodded. "Seen the cat?" she asked, as if reminded by the sight of Misha.

Viktor shook his head.

"She asked to go out last night, and isn't back," said Nina whisking off to the bedroom.

*

En route to Goloseyevo, Viktor checked at the café for e-mail and was pleased to find one from Mladen.

The yacht was the *Vesna*, and he was to bring light but warm clothing, and over and above his contribution, spending money in dollars. Any last minute purchases could be made in Split before sailing.

This he acknowledged, then, consulting the Split website, noted that while Great Britain, Rumania, the USA, Holland and other Western countries were competing for the European Arm Wrestling Championship, the old Soviet Union was not.

From the Internet café he walked freshly fallen snow to the Old

Kiev Cellar, bought a coffee and sat down to think. His head, even after a night's drinking, was clear and bursting with ideas.

Coffee forgotten, he got to his feet, thumbed a lift, and 20 minutes later, arrived at Andrey Pavlovich's.

93

Sipping coffee and looking perplexed, Andrey Pavlovich was so slow to cotton on that Viktor almost lost hope of gaining his interest.

"Look," he said, "what I take on, must be big – football club, basketball club, something like that . . ."

"But they've all been bought and are damned expensive to run. This is cheap, cheerful, and benevolent – support for the sporting disabled!"

"How many to a team?"

"Five or six including the captain, plus trainer."

"Trainer? Do they need any training?"

"Of course, and he sees they keep fit and don't get drunk."

"Let's have another look at that sheet of yours."

Viktor gave him the computer print-out.

"I'll think about it, test the water," said Andrey Pavlovich. "You go about your business. I'll get back to you on your mobile."

*

Viktor was in a café on P. Sagaydachny Street when Andrey Pavlovich rang.

"Where are you?"

"Podol."

"Where in Podol?"

456

And when told, he said, "Stay put," and 30 minutes later turned up in an ankle-length sheepskin and a deerskin cap.

"You're dead right," he declared, ordering coffee and cognac from the waitress. "I spoke to a friend. 'You're a brain,' he told me, 'worth good money', – as if I didn't know!" He slapped Viktor on the shoulder. "So yes, we'll have a team, and you're responsible, OK? We start a club, qualify as Arm Wrestling Federation, with me as President, just as soon as we've decided on a name and aims. So?"

"Disabled Arm-Wrestlers Club?"

"No, trendier – Chechnya Veterans, say."

"Except that Chechnya's Russia and we're Ukraine."

"How about Afghan Veterans? Should be the odd veteran there."

"Sounds better, certainly."

"Got a team yet?"

"I've got a captain. Knowing the pay would help."

"What do you suggest?"

"Captain $150, team $100 each."

"Let's call it $300 and $200, leaving my indebted trainer till later. Let me have the team list by tomorrow. I'll then register us as a club and get us legal for the coming championship."

<h1 style="text-align:center">94</h1>

Hearing that he might well find himself team captain, Lyosha was a changed man. Viktor carried him, then his wheelchair, down to the ground floor, and hitched a lift to Tatar Street and Café Afghan in a car with room for the chair in the boot.

Viktor let Lyosha go in alone, giving him half an hour to recruit a team before himself turning up, and duly found him sitting with six other wheel-chairers over a bottle of cognac at two tables pulled together. Taking the guest wheelchair from behind the counter, Viktor was received wide-eyed as he joined them.

"The boys are happy," said Lyosha, "but they've one or two questions."

They were simple enough. Would expenses be paid? Their hostel places kept safe for their return? Their pensions affected?

Viktor didn't always know the answer, but did his best to keep his end up.

"Do we get a uniform?" asked a one-legged man with a crew cut.

Viktor nodded.

"Advertising what firm?"

"Don't know yet, but something good."

Lyosha finished by making a list of their names. There were seven in all, including himself. Still, one extra wouldn't break Andrey Pavlovich, and the team would have a sounder look about it.

Nagornaya Street being something of a dead end, traffic was sparse, so instead of trying to hitch, he used his mobile to call a taxi to take them home in comfort.

He carried Lyosha up first, went down for his wheelchair, and by the time he'd removed his outdoor clothes, Lyosha had broken the good news to Nina and Sonya, and Viktor felt somewhat mortified by Nina's manifest joy.

Sonya, more matter of fact in her reaction, pouted. "Will this mean your going off every day to compete?"

"Not every day," Viktor said, answering for him. "Sometimes it'll mean travelling, sometimes flying."

"Can I go and fly too?" she asked, turning to Nina.

"I'm afraid not," said Viktor.

"Who can, then? Misha?" she demanded, unwittingly touching on the secret plan he was reluctant to confide to her and Andrey Pavlovich, and reminding him that it was high time to solve the problem of getting Misha to Split with the team.

After supper, Nina made herself coffee, using the cup Viktor gave her for Christmas, and spent some time studying the grounds with a thoughtful, mildly flirtatious expression unusual with her, but not unbecoming.

Seeing that Misha was not with them, Viktor fetched him from his bed to a plate of frozen fish.

"Still no cat," announced Sonya. "I expect the dogs have eaten her."

At the word "dogs" Misha perked up and took an interest. But conversation flagged. Lyosha swung round in his chair, and with Viktor and Sonya looking on, Nina got up and helped him through the door. In the ensuing silence, Misha returned to his fish and his own thoughts.

95

Two days later, clearly enthused by the way their plans for the club were progressing, Andrey Pavlovich invited Viktor to dinner, asking him to come on the early side so that they could talk. The table was laid in the sitting room, with an orderliness suggestive of a woman's touch and to that extent surprising. And no sooner were they settled in armchairs, than a woman of about fifty in headscarf and voluminous faded dress tied round with an apron looked in.

"Andrey Pavlovich, I've done my best to crack it," she complained, "but . . ."

"Let me have a go," he said, getting up.

An almighty crash, a woman's scream, then silence, and Andrey Pavlovich came back to his seat.

"All's well," he said, "I've got us sponsors. We get our strip in a few days' time. The paperwork's complete. We're as good as legal already. I'll get off notice of our intention to participate to the Jugs direct from our Supreme Council Sports Committee."

"Croats, not Jugs."

Airy wave of the hand. "Same thing! Passports. The boys will need passports. We'll have a journalist accompany you to write you up. How about an emblem? Thought of one? What have Dynamo got?"

Viktor shook his head.

"Well, get thinking. We've the souvenir stuff still to do, and there's not much time."

"How about Misha?" suggested Viktor brightly.

Enter the housekeeper with a bowl of salad, which she placed in the middle of the table. "Bring the cold *hors d'oeuvre*, too?" she asked.

"Please," said Andrey Pavlovich, then, turning to Viktor, "A penguin! Yes! Your penguin! And a big red A for Afghan Sports Club! Oh, by the way, I forgot to say, we've a guest for dinner. Sorry. One of those things . . ."

The table was, Viktor now saw, laid for three.

"Marvellous cook, this woman," said Andrey Pavlovich. "Came recommended, and all for $200 a month!"

★

The guest proved to be Igor Lvovich, sometime Editor-in-Chief of *Capital News*, and central to their repast was real turtle soup.

"Unnerving, having a new pair of eyes in the house!" said Andrey

460

Pavlovich, holding poised his tumbler of Hennessy. "Got her to start by checking the fridge and freezer. Half an hour later, she brings me a frozen turtle. Hell of a shock, till I remembered: present from Head of District Tax Inspectorate. 'Make a good soup, this will,' says she, 'I've got a recipe.'"

"The real thing," said Igor Lvovich approvingly, having conveyed a spoonful to his mouth and wiped it with his hand. "Had it in Mexico once, though not so fatty. Couldn't have been fed right," he added with a smile.

Andrey Pavlovich smiled also.

But Viktor, far from at ease, did not smile. Igor Lvovich's presence was, he suspected, destined to have some bearing on his future, something he could definitely do without. Decide for himself was what he wanted, be sole captain of his fate.

"You'll be sending your special correspondent with them, I take it."

Igor Lvovich's nod suggested that the subject had been broached already.

The alacrity with which Andrey Pavlovich filled Igor Lvovich's glass, plus his general state of agitation and apology for there being another guest, betrayed a degree of dependence on Igor Lvovich, as well as of inferiority. Viktor's role, it appeared, was to sit, mark and inwardly digest the discourse of his betters, which he did, drinking cognac and enjoying a remarkably fine pork chop with apple sauce, while absorbing information from circles he did not aspire to.

"Two years from now we'll be electing a President," Igor Lvovich was saying, as if himself determining the date. "Time to unite, form a single powerful block, be a bit more amenable . . ."

It would be no bad thing, he continued, if Andrey Pavlovich were to join the founders of his new paper, especially as his aide – big smile for Viktor – was appearing in it already, and free of editorial interference at that.

The cognac had the effect of extending intervals between words in a delivery that was slow enough already. And at "He'd make a good Editor-in-Chief, your aide here – he's bright enough . . ." from Igor Lvovich, with another big smile, it dawned on Viktor that the whole performance – *haute cuisine*, cognac – had been contrived to create the impression of his having an important part to play in some new game, yet to be revealed, a nod and complete trust in these two infinitely superior entrepreneurial big boys being all that was required on his part.

Before he knew it, he was drawn onto the thin ice of their conversation. What future did *he* see for Afghan S.C.? How did he rate its chances? The likelihood of its scaling national heights? How best to popularize it? And as if already Editor-in-Chief of the *Ukrainian Courier* he let himself be drawn. Split, he explained, was the opportunity to get started, create sporting contacts that would put the team on the international arm-wrestling circuit. They wouldn't disappoint. No half measures for them.

He concluded, of course, by mentioning the team emblem sanctioned by Andrey Pavlovich, a penguin, of which the live original would accompany the team everywhere as mascot.

"Good PR!" observed Igor Lvovich.

At about midnight, his Mercedes S600 turned up.

Viktor declined a lift on the pretence of having something to discuss with Andrey Pavlovich, and in consequence had to pay some taciturn sod of a taxi driver 30 hryvnas to jump lights at amber, ignore them at red, effing and blinding every time some flashy imported car spattered his with slush in overtaking.

96

The nocturnal peace of his flat did nothing to diminish his growing sense of irritation as he sat in the kitchen, too out of sorts to resort to drink. He had an urge to break something, hammer the table with his fist. But why wake the others? What rankled was finding himself again married off without his consent – this time to the editorship of an electioneering rag. And though as editor he'd be less likely to get knocked off than any of his foot soldier reporters, the odds would shorten the more militant his paper became. Which was why Igor Lvovich had had to hide his family abroad and feign death in a car crash. He looked down at his typewriter, for years a true and faithful servant, concerned only to make a writer or at least an essayist of him. Or had it, like woodsman's axe or mechanic's spanner, been no more than an essential tool? It would, he judged, just go through the window vent, and standing on Misha's stool, he eased it into the silent darkness. When at last it hit the asphalt, it made no great noise.

As the kitchen door squeaked, he turned, expecting to see Sonya, but it was Misha standing staring in the doorway, before advancing on the stool from which he was accustomed to eat.

"Sorry I woke you," Viktor said, squatting and stroking his head. "Shall I tell you what I've done?"

Recoiling from the smell of cognac, Misha fixed him with a beady eye.

"I've disposed of my past," Viktor whispered, "so as not to repeat it."

Misha nodded, as if in approval.

"Soon we sail, but first we fly."

97

Café Afghan was all excitement when it came to trying on kit. Things really were happening, and a feeling of unity prevailed. The round café tables proving unsuitable for training, Viktor quickly got $500 out of Andrey Pavlovich for the purchase of three solid, rectangular ones in oak.

Conveying Lyosha to the daily training sessions wasn't easy, but Viktor didn't complain. During Viktor's absence in Chechnya, Lyosha had been involved in some sort of money difficulty at the café, which had led to his taking to drink. Now he was team captain, all was forgiven, the small sum of his debt included. It was even suggested that he should return to his old room in the hostel, which was as on the day he left it. Viktor waited anxiously for his response. Yes, and he'd no longer have to carry his bearded friend plus wheelchair up and down four floors of stairs. But Lyosha turned the offer down, with a plea for the room be kept open for him. All of which, as Viktor saw at once, had its explanation in Sonya's shrill "keen on Auntie Nina!"

Andrey Pavlovich kept calling on his mobile to ask after the team. Their passports and visas were ready in his safe. The organisers had faxed confirming the team's entry and requesting payment in advance for their accommodation, and that had been dealt with.

From Igor Lvovich he heard nothing further, and was not sorry. The disappearance of his typewriter having passed unnoticed, Viktor wondered if perhaps his old Chief had dropped from his life with it. The notion of ridding oneself of a person by disposing of some object connected with him was appealing, fairytale-ish — provided it was the hero who did the disposing.

464

More e-mails were exchanged with Mladen, who was anxious lest Viktor's ready money for the journey be seized by customs, while Viktor, having no ready money to get through customs, just a gold brick, had that to worry about. The balance of his credit card account, as Andrey Pavlovich had obligingly discovered, was $27,000.

"Not exactly on the bread line, are we?" had been Andrey Pavlovich's comment.

"I'll give back Misha's ransom."

"No need. Work it off."

Which, in his capacity as trainer, Viktor proceeded to do.

*

Andrey Pavlovich phoned a few days later to say that TV Channel 1 were coming to cover the team's preparations.

Drawing 500 hryvnas on his card, Viktor booked a private-visit barber to shave and trim his bedraggled-looking team. Most submitted willingly to his ministrations, impressed by the Mazda he arrived in. The only one to balk, until presented with the choice of losing either his beard or the captaincy was Lyosha. The clean-shaven American superman that resulted, went down well with Nina, as Viktor later saw.

*

When Sonya and Nina were in bed, Viktor confided to Lyosha that he, Viktor, would not be coming back from Split, and didn't know when he would.

"So it's back to the hostel for me?"

"Not necessarily. But who would there be to do the carrying?"

"Nina?" he said tentatively, as if thinking aloud.

"Have a word with her. And will you do me a favour? Get

465

something through customs for me at the airport – maybe in your luggage, I don't know yet."

"Fine, so long as no unpleasant consequences."

"Not with this," said Viktor, showing his Aide to People's Deputy card.

98

Two weeks later, with a thaw heralding the approach of spring, Viktor made flight reservations for the team and the *Ukrainian Courier* correspondent, and learnt that for the conveyance of small animals plastic containers with air holes were available.

Lyosha announced happily that he had spoken to Nina. He would be staying on at the flat, where he would be more comfortable, and she would help with the stairs.

"Fine," said Viktor, though with mixed feelings. "But don't neglect Sonya, will you? You could try teaching her chess."

"She plays already. And she's good."

Next morning, while Nina was showering and Lyosha waiting his turn for the bathroom, Viktor called Sonya, who was quick to join him in the kitchen, closely followed by Misha.

"Do you remember what I said about going to a café and having a proper talk?" Viktor asked, having served Misha frozen hake. "Well, say where you'd like us to go, and in half an hour we'll go there."

He watched while she thought, certain that it would be McDonald's.

"Uncle Viktor," she said at last, "I'd rather go to a restaurant, where there's a big choice of ices."

"Except that restaurants are shut in the morning."

"We can wait till this evening."

"I might be busy then."

"All right. Let's go to McDonald's."

An hour later they were there. Viktor ordered a Fishmac and coffee, Sonya a Happy Meal. Her present this time was a little cowboy from some American cartoon.

"Listen," Viktor said, "there's something I want to tell you about, something serious."

Screwing up her eyes, she became all attention.

"Misha and I are leaving and I want you to stay and be flat senior."

"But Auntie Nina and Uncle Lyosha are older than me."

"In years, yes, but this is different. You're to go on pretending to be little. Be naughty, demand things, but watch what's going on. Whether they quarrel or shout."

"They don't any more. Twice a day they have coffee in the kitchen, and talk. Once they even asked me to go out. But I listened at the door and heard everything anyway."

"And what was it? No, don't tell me," he added quickly as she took breath. "You mustn't listen. It's bad."

"Then you don't ever find out anything!"

"You must learn how to ask if you want to know something. Anyway, I'm leaving you as flat senior. I shall ring and you'll tell me what's what. And another thing — ask them to take you to the puppet theatre and children's films more often. All three of you should go together. And when you're there, make sure you get bought an ice."

"When will you be back?"

"Don't know. Not for a while. I'll ring."

"And often."

99

The team was conveyed to Borispol International Airport in a special coach affording lift access for wheelchairs, and bearing the legend "Japan's gift to the Chernobyl Fund". Andrey Pavlovich led the way in the black Mercedes 4 x 4.

The plastic container for Misha which Viktor hoped not to have to use, as it seemed on the small side, stood empty on the floor. Misha was seated by a window immediately behind the driver, and for the moment Viktor's anxieties centred more on the gold brick reposing in Lyosha's bag amongst the luggage which Viktor had loaded, helped by Isayev, the *Ukrainian Courier* correspondent.

At Borispol, the coach swung right past the lifted barrier to stop at the VIP Terminal behind its screen of snowy trees. Andrey Pavlovich handed their passports to a smiling and attractive brunette in smart Border Guard uniform. A young steward appeared, and they were conducted into a pleasant lounge with tables and armchairs, where two waitresses offered a choice of tea, coffee or spirits. Two of the team looked to Lyosha for a lead. Viktor ordered a gin and tonic, Andrey Pavlovich a whisky, the others suitably confined themselves to fruit juice or tea. One of the waitresses paused in passing to stroke Misha, who was standing beside Lyosha's chair.

"Is he your mascot?"

Lyosha nodded.

"The Lugansk basketball team always have their tortoise."

Andrey Pavlovich handed back the passports, and the team was called to the boarding gate. Their flight being under the aegis of a People's Deputy, customs formalities were dispensed with, the disabled members of the team attentively helped to their seats, and their chairs folded and taken to the hold.

Viktor and Misha had the comfort of three seats between them. He and Misha had a long journey ahead of them, the crossing of Drake Passage the toughest part of it. Last time it had been comparatively calm. But how about this time? The *Horizon* had been a large vessel, a yacht would be different.

"What would you like to drink?" inquired the stewardess with the bar trolley.

"A gin and tonic, please."

"And for the penguin?"

"Mineral water."

"Bubbly or still?"

"Still, please."

Misha gazed into the glass on the little table before him, as if hopeful of spotting a fish, then calmly lowered his beak and drank.

100

Five hours in another special coach took them from Zagreb to Split, and just as the sea and high-rise buildings came in sight, Viktor's mobile rang.

"Good flight?"

"Splendid. The coach is just coming into Split."

"See you win! Otherwise don't come back! Talk to you soon."

★

The second floor of the hotel, where the team were accommodated, was well adapted to their special needs. Viktor and Isayev, who found themselves sent to the 13th floor, did not have a great deal to say to each other. Regarding him as the long arm of Igor Lvovich, Viktor had at once erected his own private and invisible Berlin Wall against him. The others he trusted completely.

Sun was streaming through the window of his room. Split was much warmer than Kiev. Here it was spring already. He set about running a bath, but when Misha made plain that he expected to take precedence, turned the hot tap off and the cold on.

From his balcony he had a splendid view of the sea. A snow-white liner lay at anchor a little way out. Down below, handsome yachts were moored at long jetties. He dialled Mladen on his mobile.

"Yes?" was the stern challenge.

"Viktor Zolotaryov from Kiev. About our trip to the Antarctic."

"Ah!" The voice softened, "Good to hear you. *Dobro došli!* Welcome! Where are you at the moment? Right. I'll drive down. Be outside in ten minutes. Old dark blue Mercedes. Oh, and bring some cash – we need to buy stores."

Viktor recovered his gold brick from Lyosha's bag, and as he slipped it into his own, it encountered something metallic which, to his amazement, proved to be his Pooh Bear mug.

He dialled the flat.

"Was it you put Pooh Bear in my bag?" he asked, when Sonya answered.

"A present from me. I know it means a lot to you."

"Well, thanks," he said gently.

"How's Misha? Was he airsick? Auntie Nina says everyone is."

"Tell her everyone was, except me, Misha and Lyosha."

"Really?"

"Really. But I've got to go. I'll ring you."

"Big kiss for Misha."

Misha was playing happily in the bath, and before hurrying out, Viktor kissed him from Sonya.

101

It was indeed an old Mercedes, a '70s model, but Mladen, in tracksuit trousers and football shirt, had a lean and powerful look, although clearly a man of 60.

A short drive brought them to a small picturesque village overlooking the sea. Drawing up before light green gates, Mladen hooted, and soon a tall girl in jeans and sweater emerged, together with a man in a grey suit and blue bow tie, looking even older than in the Internet photograph, who introduced himself as Radko.

"Vesna," said the girl, giving him her hand.

"We'll go to the yacht, then to the ship's chandler's," said Mladen getting back into the car. "You've got some money?"

"I've got a credit card."

The yacht, moored in a nearby bay, was smaller than he had imagined, or seen call in at Vernadsky Base. From the bay they drove back to Split and a ship's chandler's on the waterfront.

Ropes and tackle depleting Bronikovsky's credit card account to the tune of $3,800 were duly loaded into the boot of the Mercedes and transferred to the yacht.

"Leave me the card and I'll see to the stores," said Mladen examining the signature on the card. "That's your hotel, over there," he added, pointing. "0600hrs on the 8th is when we sail. I'll look you up tomorrow at about 11.00"

"Could you make it 2.00? My team's in for the arm-wrestling, and I've got to be there."

Mladen and Radko exchanged meaningful glances.

"I could," said Mladen.

"One other thing," said Viktor, his voice trembling. "I'd like to bring my penguin and let him loose in Antarctica. I've been there before."

"We'll talk tomorrow," said Mladen impassively.

They shook hands, and Viktor, crossing to his hotel, imagined them staring mistrustfully after him. Maybe the credit card would help redress the balance.

102

The Championship opened with dinner at 8.00 and a speech by the Senior Umpire, a Dutchman with an unpronounceable name. The Deputy Sports Minister of Croatia read out a list of the countries competing, the team leader of each rising in acknowledgement. Lyosha, when it came to mention of Afghan Sports Club, shot both arms up, as did the rest of the team, Viktor and Isayev with them, waving in response to a great surge of applause in genuine, and generous tribute to the one disabled team competing. It was easy to be moved but at the same time hard not to regret the subterfuge – *his* subterfuge – that had much to do with their presence here. Still, if Ukraine were to emerge champions, subterfuge would be offset by Ukrainian verity. Andrey Pavlovich, a success as politician, might do something useful for the country. Igor Lvovich might turn his electioneering rag into a decent and objective newspaper.

One glass of astringent Dalmatian wine all round, after which, to Viktor's relief, Lyosha insisted on Pepsi.

Dinner was soon over. Tomorrow, at 0900: Ukraine v Rumania.

*

Viktor lay listening to the gentle Adriatic through the open balcony doors, when there was a knock.

Getting up, putting on the light – it was, he saw, 11.00 – he opened the door and there, to his amazement, was Vesna, in a short lilac-coloured dress.

"May I come in?"

He turned to the chair with his discarded clothing for something to put on.

"No need," she said, "I'm not staying. Get back to bed. Where's your penguin?"

"On the balcony."

She went out, and squatting beside Misha, spoke to him in Croat. Returning, she slipped out of the little she was wearing and into Viktor's bed.

"Don't get the idea that I like you," she whispered, as they lay together afterwards. "Whatever people say about my father, he gave me a proper upbringing, and I can't tell a lie."

"Then why all this?" he asked, turning to face her.

"This?" Vesna repeated with a note of surprise. "For you, to keep you alive. . ."

Getting up, she slipped into her clothes and left without another word.

103

In a vast school sports hall hung with sponsorship posters and banners, the Ukrainian arm wrestlers faced the Rumanian at six sturdy tables under their national flags, the eyes of the other teams, and no few spectators.

The competitors were awaiting the signal to begin, which came in the form of a single hand clap by the Senior Umpire. Instantly arms tensed and strained, and somehow the spectators became tense and strained with them. The umpire darted this way and that, keeping all six duels under observation. At the table furthest from the entrance the Rumanian began to force the Ukrainian's arm back, then the latter recovered and exerted pressure on his opponent.

To Viktor, absorbed in watching the duel on the first table, it didn't seem quite fair to pit the able-bodied against those unable to bring their full weight to bear, being legless.

But as if to allay his doubts, a tow-haired Afghan Veteran forced the Rumanian's hand back until it lay palm uppermost on the table. The umpire raised the victor's arm, shouted something, and the spectators who were nearest applauded. In his excitement Viktor got to his feet, looked around for someone to share his delight with, and looking beyond Isayev with his camera, spotted Mladen sitting talking to a young man in a fashionable denim suit.

The final score was 5 : 1 in favour of Ukraine. A half-hour followed, in which two tracksuited young men changed the table flags to those of Holland and Poland. For no good reason Viktor expected the Dutch to win, but in the event, the Poles did, and Viktor was almost as pleased for them as for his own team.

The days's events were over by 1.00, and before lunch in the hotel restaurant, Viktor went to a supermarket and bought some Adriatic fish for Misha. This he served him on the balcony, where he could enjoy the sea view as he ate. The team were already at table, but waiting for Viktor before starting, as if in expectation of a toast or a speech. So he praised them for today, wished them five victories tomorrow. For Lyosha, their Captain, he had a special word of thanks, and Lyosha nodded gravely in response.

*

At 2.00 Mladen appeared, and drove Viktor to a little Balkan tavern, where the meal, washed down with raki, proved superior to the celebratory one enjoyed with Lyosha and the team. Mladen asked what Viktor had done in life. Viktor said merely that before entering sport he'd worked as a journalist, then steered conversation to life in Ukraine.

At the end of the meal Mladen plonked down Viktor's credit card.

"All done, $10,000 stake included, for which *hvala lepo*, many thanks!"

*

On the way back to his hotel, Viktor drank coffee and cognac on a café terrace, and thought of Vesna – her masterful performance of the previous night, and the prospects of a repeat – a woman such as would, as Nekrasov put it, "Stop a bolting horse, or dash into a blaze . . ." His mobile rang.

"How's it going? Enjoying the sun?" inquired Andrey Pavlovich.

"We've just beaten the Rumanians!"

"Good lads, keep at it! If they come out champs, tell them, I'll give them a $1000 apiece and up their pay."

"I'll do that."

475

"Speak to you tomorrow."

Downing his cognac, Viktor ordered another.

The gentle lapping of the Adriatic provided a pleasant background to the measured, everyday life of the place. Girls and young men strolled past. The next café along was crowded with elderly men drinking raki and watching a football match on television. It was the sort of background his life had lacked. He liked it.

104

The *Vesna*, with three cabins, saloon, galley, shower and WC, was more spacious than it looked – a home on the water, subject to the winds and the controlling hand of man.

Viktor decided against saying goodbye to the team, and especially to Isayev. But at his request, Mladen got his friend Mirko to bring Lyosha to the bay in his car. Mirko helped him into his wheelchair and then down to the bay.

"So tomorrow it's between us and Poland for gold or silver," said Viktor holding out his hand. "See you keep up the good work."

Lyosha raised both arms and they embraced.

"And good luck to you," he said.

Viktor's eyes filled with tears. This, it seemed to him, was goodbye, not only to Lyosha but to his whole life, Kiev, Sonya, his past . . .

He turned to the yacht and Misha, standing in the stern regarding them.

"I must go," he sighed.

*

When they were well out to sea but with Split, the hotel and even, he fancied, the ancient Mercedes still in sight, he called Lyosha on his mobile.

"Fed up already?" asked Lyosha.

"8th of March! International Women's Day! Best wishes to Nina and Sonya from me."

"Hell! I'd forgotten. Thanks. I'll ring them."

"And ring me tomorrow."

"If I can get through."

★

Down in his cabin, he changed his Afghan S.C. wear for a check flannel shirt which he tucked into his trousers. He was now, he felt, free of his homeland, free of his past, but not, with luck, free of a future.

"Childhood souvenir?" asked Vesna, looking in and seeing his Pooh Bear mug.

Viktor nodded.

"Come on deck, I want to show you."

On deck she pointed to Misha standing motionless in the bows intent on the vessel's course, for all the world like a little boy playing Skipper.

"Know the story of Wee Rolly Roll?" he asked.

"From school, yes."

"Well, that," he said gloomily, "is how I feel. 'I've got away from Grandpa, got away from Grandma, got away from Wolf, got away from Hare . . .' The question is, am I going to get eaten by Fox?"

"We'll see," she said, going below.

Watching Mladen and Radko sail the yacht, he wondered why they didn't ask him to help, seeing how far they had to sail.

Misha insisted on staying on deck, as if expecting to sight Antarctica at any minute.

*

Only half asleep, he became aware of someone trying to open his bolted door.

"Me," whispered Vesna.

"So you're scared," she said, perching on his bunk.

"What did you mean when you said 'We'll see?'"

"Dad and Radko have been declared war criminals. We're Bosnians, not Croats, and it's not Antarctica we're bound for, but Argentina, where my father has friends. The plan's to dump you overboard."

"Misha, too?"

"Look, we're not there yet. Wee Rolly Roll couldn't swim, you can. Trust me. Try and get some sleep," she said, getting to her feet.

105

Woken next morning by shouting and hammering, he lowered his feet to the heaving floor, and sleepily went to unbolt and open the door. In burst Mladen, face red with fury, yelling over his shoulder for Vesna.

"Is it true?" he roared.

"What?"

"That you slept with her in the hotel?"

"Yes."

Mladen swung a mighty blow at him, but it was Vesna who fell to the floor. Viktor sprang forward, but Mladen rushed out, bawling

"Bloody fool that I am!" and clutching his head. Viktor knelt beside Vesna whose left eye was already swelling. Having clearly taken the blow aimed at him.

"It'll be all right," she said gently. "And I don't sleep around . . . You're the only man I've slept with . . ."

He helped her to her feet, and soaking the end of a towel in cold water, let her press it to her eye.

Agitated pacing of the deck overhead moved suddenly to the companionway, and Mladen and Radko appeared in the doorway, the former looking genuinely contrite, the latter at a loss.

Mladen looked closely at his daughter, then at Viktor. "Where did you get that scar?" he demanded.

"Chechnya."

Mladen looked relieved. "I got these in Bosnia," he said, pulling up his blue-and-white-striped vest to display scars and a gold Orthodox cross so roughly cast as to prompt the question why at all? "Not Jewish, are you?" he asked abruptly.

"Ukrainian of Russian parents."

"We Slavs must stick together," said Mladen slowly, as if reciting a lesson, reaching out and drawing Viktor to him.

"My son, I rejoice for you," he went on, voice trembling with emotion. "But let her down, and I'll kill you . . . If she lets you down, over to you . . ." As Mladen eased his embrace, Viktor came near to losing his balance. "We'll have the marriage this very day," said Mladen, "and at 0600 tomorrow you come on watch and I'll show you what's what."

"Dad's no murderer," said Vesna when they were alone. "Just a patriot. What he says, he means."

"Like you."

"Yes."

106

That same evening the *Vesna* dropped anchor off a tiny island. Mladen and Radko put on dark double-breasteds, white shirts and ties. A table was brought up on deck and heaped with their supplies. Misha was given tinned tuna. Radko played his accordion and sang, the others singing with him. The words might be lost on Viktor, but the gypsy rhythms and with them a sense of unbridled freedom was not. Hailed by a passing yacht, Mladen, silencing the music, shouted back that they were celebrating a marriage, only to come under the scrutiny of four brawny men and two sun-bronzed women who shouted something as they passed.

"*Gorko*, let's see some action!" cried Mladen, at which Viktor and Vesna locked in a kiss that continued after cheers from the other yacht were no longer to be heard.

"Well done!" declared Mladen, and Radko resumed playing.

They drank raki and ate, while Mladen proposed toasts, and the sea was wrapped in the transparent, starry blanket of a southern night.

Viktor's mobile played its ring tone.

"*Gold!*" cried Lyosha. "*Gold!* Andrey Pavlovich is over the moon!"

"Good lads! Very well done!"

"What's that music?"

"A wedding."

"On the yacht?"

"On the yacht."

"Whose?"

"Mine, ours."

"Pull the other one!"

"No, really."

"True love?"

"Better than that – fate! Only, don't tell Sonya and Nina yet."

"I won't. Oh, Isayev's out trying to find you. We leave tomorrow. What do I tell him?"

"Tell him I'm defecting and hope to be forgiven."

"Best of luck to you both," said Lyosha warmly.

★

"To Ukraine!" proposed Mladen, told the news.

Viktor drank, though feeling that Ukraine had very little to do with the present festivities. Excusing himself, he went below, and returning, stood and proposed a toast.

"To my parents, now dead, and to you, Vesna's father!" A clinking of glasses. "And in recognition of the wonderful woman you've made of her, a small present . . ." He handed Mladen his gold brick.

At a loss for words but smiling broadly, Mladen took it.

"Not just for me, but for the family," he said. "You don't know yet, but we have a house large enough for all of us. My brothers have bought us a restaurant, and this" – he touched the gold – "shall be your future. We'll live in amity together. I'll teach you my father's trade. Baking. We all need bread. With this we'll buy a bakery, and ensure you and Vesna and my grandchildren a good life."

"Good money in baking, and I'm used to heat," Seva had said, and Viktor looked across at Misha as if to ask, "Remember Chechnya?"

"And Misha – can he be dropped off in the Antarctic?" Viktor asked.

"Not in the Antarctic, but where we pass islands with penguins, yes, I give my word."

481

EPILOGUE

A month later they anchored off a large island where any number of inquisitive penguins gathered on the cliff to watch them.

It was blowing hard, and before releasing Misha to chilly freedom, Viktor dialled his flat and to his amazement got straight through.

"Sonya, can you hear me?"

"No need to shout. Where are you? The Antarctic?"

"Very near. Misha's about to leave us."

"Give him a big kiss from me. Oh, they've been ringing you from work. Auntie Nina says I'm going to have a little brother or sister. And Uncle Lyosha's got a car. He's a champion now. Got his gold medal hanging up. He's off to a tournament in Bulgaria."

"Good. Love to everyone. I'll ring in a week or so."

Pocketing his mobile and squatting, he kissed the top of Misha's head.

"That's from Sonya who loves you very much."

Misha nodded, looking Viktor squarely in the eye, then turned to watch the other penguins diving cleanly into the sea. And after one last look at the four of them, he too dived cleanly in without so much as a splash.

BERLIN – PARIS – KIEV – LAZAREVKA 2002

ANDREY KURKOV

A Matter of
Death and Life

'Kurkov's eye for the absurdities of Ukrainian life is as sharp
as ever'
Sunday Telegraph

Marital troubles?

Sick of life?

Suicide the answer?

Why not get yourself a contract killer?

Nothing easier, provided you communicate only by phone and
box number. You give him your photograph, specify when and
where to find you, then sit back and prepare to die. Murdered,
you will be of greater interest than ever you were in life. A
mysterious killing lives long in the popular memory

Our hero meticulously plans his own demise, except for one
detail: what if he suddenly decides he wants to live? This darkly
funny tale is Kurkov on top form.

'A perfectly balanced read'
Scotland on Sunday

VINTAGE BOOKS
London

BY ANDREY KURKOV
ALSO AVAILABLE FROM VINTAGE

☐ **The Case of the General's Thumb**	0099455250	£6.99
☐ **A Matter of Death and Life**	0099461587	£6.99

FREE POST AND PACKING
Overseas customers allow £2.00 per paperback

BY PHONE: 01624 677237

BY POST: Random House Books
C/o Bookpost, PO Box 29, Douglas
Isle of Man, IM99 1BQ

BY FAX: 01624 670923

BY EMAIL: bookshop@enterprise.net

Cheques (payable to Bookpost) and credit cards accepted

Prices and availability subject to change without notice.
Allow 28 days for delivery.
When placing your order, please mention if you do not wish to receive
any additional information.

www.randomhouse.co.uk/vintage